FURY OF
DESTRUCTION

COREENE
CALLAHAN

OLIVER
HEBER
BOOKS

PUBLISHER'S NOTE: This is a work of fiction. Names, characters,
places, and incidents either are the product of the author's
imagination or are used fictitiously. Any resemblance to actual
persons, living or dead, business establishments, events, or locales is
entirely coincidental.

0 9 8 7 6 5 4 3 2 1

For Alain – my Rocketman

1

Mid-morning. The witching hour. At least, for him.

Lying in bed, ears open, eyes closed, nothing but quiet around him, Gage inhaled deep and exhaled slow. He needed the release. Required all the patience he could muster to keep the restlessness at bay. His mind urged him to move. Tense muscles seconded the motion, making his hands twitch, heart thump, and brain burn.

He forced a couple more long, deep breaths.

Shoving the sheet aside and getting up for the day wouldn't solve the problem. Neither would heading to the weight room in the underground lair. Hitting the heavy bag in Black Diamond's gym might relieve the edginess, but he knew it wouldn't satisfy.

Nothing did lately.

His near miss in Prague had twisted his shit the wrong way.

Now, he was off-kilter, swimming in a sea of nothing good. Each time he closed his eyes, the memory came—the kill room, the torture and brutality, his inability to stop it. A total mindfuck for a male who was nothing but strong.

The memory sent him swimming inside his own mind.

Trying to stop the mental whirl, he cracked an eye open. Blacked-out room. Quiet space. Nothing but hours of agony ahead of him. He glanced at the bedside table. Dimmed down, the digital clock glowed in the dark and... yup. 10:47 AM. Right in the zone. Smack dab in the middle of prime time, when he should be sleeping, getting the required hours of ZZ's to keep him healthy and strong.

Emotional storm clouds didn't care. The smoky wisp of recall churned, billowing inside his head, dragging ghosts to the surface every time he closed his eyes.

Stacking his hands behind his head, Gage stared up at the ceiling. Shadowed Douglas fir paneling stared back. Nothing but straight seams and glossy varnish. He traced the lines with his gaze, looking for imperfections, finding some in the rich, knotted wood. He loved those whirls. Enjoyed the way the grain moved, sliding through each plank, single pieces meshing to create a beautiful whole.

A quirk of character.

Something he never tried to curb.

Curiosity was part of his makeup. His mathematical mind never stopped observing and analyzing. He enjoyed taking things apart and putting them back together. Trained as a mechanical engineer, he loved physics and equations almost as much as his brothers-in-arms. His pack—the males he lived with inside Black Diamond—made him feel normal, whole, like a puzzle piece clicked into the place it belonged. A lovely trick, given he'd never belonged anywhere. Never felt accepted—or valued—by anyone, until Haider.

Gage shifted against the sheets.

Strange thing—acceptance. The power of being welcomed, embraced by those around him, changed a male. Most of the time, in good ways. Sometimes, though, affirmation led to complacency... to laziness and the belief in infallibility. Fat cat syndrome. King of the hill disease. Call it whatever the hell you wanted. The label didn't matter. What did, however, was the fact he'd fallen into it in Prague.

Far too arrogant.

Way too relaxed.

Not enough edge.

A deadly combination for a dragon warrior on the hunt.

The realization struck home like a barbed fist. His muscles twitched. Gage scowled at the ceiling. He needed to have his head examined. Or bashed in. One or the other. Whatever. He didn't have a preference. Given the mental turmoil, either option would work right now.

Taking another deep breath, he reached for calm. His chest expanded. Slow inhale followed by a measured exhale, he searched for steady in a sea of topsy-turvy. He needed to settle down. An even emotional grid was the goal. The return to his normal self sounded good too, but...

He wouldn't be getting that inside the lair today.

Or any time soon.

The changes inside Black Diamond should've eased his troubled mind. Made him happy. Love, after all, was in the air. In every corner of the lair, treating him to a face full of lovey-dovey every time he turned around. He didn't blame the warriors he called brothers. Taking a mate was serious business, one no male could resist when he found his match, but... shit. The

PDAs—all the closeness, heated looks, and whispered innuendos—set him on edge, making him realize what he didn't have, and never would.

Pessimistic much?

Yeah, sure. Abso-fucking-lutely. But that didn't mean it wasn't true.

He wasn't built for connection. Proof positive rested in the fact he trusted few, and allowed even fewer close. Proximity felt dangerous, like life and death to him. Shoving the sheet off his bare chest, Gage piled another pillow behind his head. Egyptian cotton rustled, settling at his waist as he marveled at his luck. Finding a home inside the Nightfury pack had been a long shot. A real Hail Mary on all fronts. The fact Haider had convinced Bastian of their worthiness still surprised him.

Why?

No clue.

Haider could charm the pants off a sociopath.

His mouth curved up. Yeah. His best friend was just that good. A master negotiator who used words as weapons and took no prisoners. Forget arguing with the male. He'd given up a century ago, deciding to go with the flow, protecting Haider's back as he moved through Dragonkind circles. Why Haider choose him was anyone's guess. He'd never asked for the male to lay out his reasons. Didn't intend to, either. All he felt was thankful. Grateful to be pulled out of hell and given a second chance with a warrior who loved him like a brother and relied on his abilities and intellect.

Something to celebrate.

And protect.

He frowned. Maybe that was why Prague bothered him so much. Failing to detect the ambush pushed all his protective buttons. He'd dropped the ball, allowing momentary distraction—a female in distress—to blur his focus. A mistake that landed him and Haider in a world of hurt. Had he done his duty, none of it would have happened. Neither of them would've been tortured inside a kill room designed to break males.

"Fuck," he muttered, running his hands through his hair.

He had one job—protect Haider's back. Normally, a task at which he excelled.

As a bronze dragon with strong leanings toward brutality, limits didn't apply to him. The more critical the situation, the better he liked it. Haider wasn't stupid. The male knew he was a touch left of center and still, after years of brotherhood, his friend's unshakable belief in his worth startled Gage. Surprised and humbled him, which meant...

He needed to be honest.

Be first to start the conversation. Come clean and tell Haider he was messed up. Wasn't sleeping well. Kept jolting awake, dreaming of the kill room as residual pain interrupted his rest and sapped his strength.

Chest so tight it hurt, Gage clenched his teeth, fighting to stay even, to contain the frustration and find his usual baseline. He shouldn't feel this way. Combat, and the violence that accompanied it, never bothered him. But as silence drifted and morning stretched toward afternoon, remembered anguish licked through him. He couldn't douse the flames. Like wildfire, cerebral burn scorched earth inside his mind.

He fisted his hands.

Prickles of pain scored his scalp.

He needed to get up. Right now. Before his dragon half took over and trashed his room. A bad idea, given

Osgard—his adopted son—slept less than ten feet away.

Flicking the sheet away, Gage rolled to, then sat on the side of his king-size bed. Feet on the floor, hands curled over the edge of the mattress, he bowed his head. Taut muscles squawked, protesting the stretch and—

Static swirled against his temples.

Prickles streamed down his spine. Aggression surfaced as adrenaline gathered in his veins. Dragon senses sharp, he mined the signal. Vicious. Unyielding. Focused. Brutal vibration combined with bad attitude expanded the scope, fine-tuning his sonar.

His mouth curved. Thank the Goddess. Just what he needed to turn the tide—a male on a mission, and the balls to back it up, headed in his direction.

The monster inside him seethed, begging to be set free.

Tracking the male across the garage, Gage remained unmoving, and head tilted, listened to boot soles thud on the concrete floor. His visitor skirted the workbench. Heavy footfalls approached the stairs leading up to his loft. Magic rolled as his sonar pinged, picking up the threads, setting up grids, giving him the lay of the land.

Not far now.

Just two flights and the heavy frame of his front door away.

Eagerness playing him like a piano, he pushed to his feet.

He wanted a fight. Craved the knuckle-grind of combat, so the warrior about to bang on his door better be ready. He loved a good brawl. His nature demanded it. His dragon half needed lots of exercise. Thrived on playing skull-thumping games of keep away. Enjoyed chaos and the life-affirming smell of blood in the morning.

Dominate or be dominated.

Kill or be killed.

A simple enough ethos, and yet, he held his position and waited for the male to make himself known.

Probably not the best idea, but—

Boots hit the first step and started to climb. The sound banged around inside his head. Like the threat of an oncoming storm, the air inside his home thickened.

Breathing deep, he sucked the energy in through his pores, breathing in the faint hum like his lungs did oxygen. Anticipation, peppered with a dash of rage, twisted the molecules around him, tumbling into a kaleidoscope of emotional color.

Longing made his fingers twitch.

Gage pushed to his feet.

His bare foot nudged a pillow abandoned on the floor. Frowning at it, he kicked the annoying thing aside. Soft fabric slid against his skin. He tried to ignore the silky feel. Didn't work. It never did. No matter how many times he turned a blind eye.

Lips twisted, he shook his head.

Frickin' Daimler. The Numbai—the Nightfury pack's go-to guy—was a complete menace. No need to label him anything else. The male tossed luxury around the same way Gage threw punches, assaulting the loft he lived in above the garage with fluffy towels, plush area rugs, and expensive throw cushions.

A whole army of the feather-filled fuckers.

He scowled at the one sitting lopsided against the headboard. The thing had ruffles on it. Blue and white *ruffles*, for Silfer's sake. Dismay ran downhill into disgust. Gage rolled his shoulders. Someone, please, shoot him now. He didn't need pretty pillows. Didn't want anything fancy or soft, but well, hell... try explaining that to Daimler.

Suppressing a sigh, he stepped around the end of his bed. Naked, bare feet whispering over the Turkish rug, he monitored the male's proximity. Halfway up the stairs. Moving steadily. Trying to be quiet. Maybe twenty seconds away from his front door.

He glanced to his left.

The night-light he didn't need, but always kept plugged in, glowed against pale walls, light bleeding onto the edge of the second bed shoved into the back corner of the room. His own sat between it and the door, providing a bulwark against the outside world. An odd set up for a Dragonkind male. Necessary all the same, a concession made for his teenage son.

Fast asleep, face turned toward the light, hands open and relaxed instead of fisted, Osgard lay sprawled across the mattress. His chest rose and fell in a predictable pattern. Nice and easy. Breathe in, breathe out. No sign of stress or the nightmares that often plagued his sleep.

Gage's chest tightened. He took a moment to send the Sun Goddess a word of thanks. *Progress*. Finally. At last.

After months of worrying Osgard would never recover from the abuse he suffered at Zidane's hands (and the Archguard pricks protecting the sick bastard), the kid was making strides, inching forward, healing a little at a time. Hope—Forge's mate, a psychologist and trauma specialist—said it would happen, that the youngling's fear would eventually fade.

He hadn't believed her.

Not at first. And no wonder.

After watching Osgard struggle day after day,

doubt seemed like a smart response to her steady guidance. Her advice had always rung hollow, the words without merit or meaning, but as he watched his son sleep like a male who knew he was safe, the truth hit him. She'd been right... about everything.

Including her advice about him. Hope kept telling him to relax and be himself.

Be himself.

Seemed like a terrible suggestion.

His destructive nature didn't make him an ideal candidate for fatherhood. Not by a long shot. And yet, her words tolled through his mind, then belled inside his heart. Gage flexed his fingers. Open. Closed. Make a fist, then release it. Thank God for Forge's female. Without her, he would have made so many mistakes with Osgard. Rushed the youngling. Been less patient with his progress. Worried more than he did already while making things worse for Osgard instead of better.

All right, so it wasn't perfect.

The kid was still afraid of the dark. Couldn't close his eyes, never mind go to sleep, without Gage watching his back. On the upside, though, he'd stopped tossing and turning. Wasn't screaming himself awake anymore. He was sleeping through the day now, getting the rest he needed to stay healthy and strong. And eat? Gage's lips twitched. Holy shit, could Osgard eat, putting away so much food, Daimler's inner chef danced with delight every time he laid eyes on the kid.

Which no doubt explained the growth spurt.

Six inches taller and twenty pounds heavier... all in just a few months. Osgard was going to be warrior-sized, a big male with a sharp mind and iron will when he finished growing. Something to be proud of, someone for Gage to guide and protect.

Satisfaction grabbed hold, making him choke up for a second. Lucky. He was so goddamn *lucky* to be a father. Four months ago, he would've scoffed at the idea. Told any male stupid enough to suggest it to shove his opinion somewhere uncomfortable. His upbringing, after all, hadn't been normal, or anywhere near stable.

Chief executioner for the Archguard, his sire had lived by the sword, driving Gage so hard he wondered sometimes how he survived. The brutality had been bad enough, but the emotional distance had been worse.

Something he would never do to Osgard.

He might not know how to be a good sire, but he knew what a bad one acted like, so... mark one down in the win column for him. He was already ahead of the curve.

Dragging his attention from his son, Gage refocused.

The male invading his den paused on the landing outside his front door, no doubt contemplating the odds of entering unscathed. About a billion-to-none, given his mood and the fact—

"Gage."

The rough growl burst through mind-speak, scoring his temples.

Gage cursed under his breath. Shit. Bastian. His commander stood on the threshold, about to enter his loft. A space all the Nightfuries knew was off limits. Call him paranoid. Call him antisocial. Call him whatever the fuck you wanted, but he didn't like others in his home. He lived outside the main lair for a reason. But B? Tangling with the warrior would get him zapped with enough electricity to short-circuit his brain and send his cerebral cells scrambling.

"What?" Black mood leading the way, Gage crossed to his bedroom door.

"You awake?"

"Yeah—why?"

"I'm coming in. You hit me, and I'll rip your brain out through your nostrils."

Gage bit down on a grin. *"I could use a fight."*

"So could I, but..." Bastian paused, sounding tired, so unlike his usual kick-ass self that Gage tensed. *"Not right now."*

Intuition flickered.

Gage frowned. Something was wrong. Off in a way he couldn't put a finger on, but knew existed all the same.

"Come in, but be quiet," he murmured, giving B what he needed—a clear invitation into his private space without the usual fallout. *"Osgard's still asleep."*

B grunted, acknowledging the warning.

Gage let his magic roll. The handle of his bedroom door turned without making a sound. A second later, the heavy wood panel swung open on well-oiled hinges. Quick feet took him toward the exit. He stepped off the rug onto the hardwood floor. Osgard grumbled in his sleep. Gage paused, waited for the kid to resettle, then crossed the threshold. A mental command closed the door behind him as he conjured a pair of his favorite jeans. Worn by time and use, faded denim settled on his skin. Night vision sparking in the dark, he walked down the hallway and into the kitchen-slash-great room.

Timber-beam ceilings greeted him. He scanned the open space as the floor lamp sitting next to the long sectional in the living room activated. Illumination spilled into the kitchen, reflecting off black marble countertops and light grey cabinetry. Skirting the island, Gage stopped in front of the coffee maker. Opening and closing doors, he set up the fancy-ass machine Daimler bought him and flipped the ON switch.

The machine gurgled.

The front door closed with a soft hiss.

The sound of footsteps echoed off the vaulted ceiling.

Glancing over his shoulder, he tipped his chin in greeting. "Can't sleep?"

Bastian shook his head.

"Myst?"

"Asleep. Finally," B said, looking troubled.

Gage frowned. Pregnant female. Trouble sleeping. Not a good combo. "What's up with her?"

"She's uncomfortable... all the time. The baby's growing fast. Almost too fast, and—"

"You're worried."

"She's suffering, and I have no reference point. I have no idea what's normal for a female carrying a Dragonkind infant." Dark brows cranked down, B raised his hand and scowled at his knuckles, and Gage knew what he was thinking. His commander wanted to hit something, outsource his frustration to his fists.

Understandable.

A healthy impulse for any Dragonkind male.

Gage should know. Most nights, ripping shit apart was the only thing that kept him even.

"My mate is strong, but she isn't a big female," Bastian murmured, flexing his fingers. "Shit, Gage. She's got six weeks to go, and my son isn't slowing down. He's taking all the available space inside her. How's she going to go another month?"

"Can you take the baby early?"

B shrugged. "Not ideal, but might have to. She's hurting, and I'm—"

"Fucked up about it."

"Unable to relax," Bastian said at the same time.

Gage huffed. "Join the club."

"The entire reason I'm here, brother."

His brows collided. What the hell? Bastian couldn't know. He'd locked it down, making sure none of his brothers-in-arms clocked his inner turmoil. No way should his commander be able to sense—

"I know it's bothering you, Gage." Striding past the dining table, Bastian plugged him with a don't-lie-to-me look.

"Shit," he muttered, liberating two mugs from an open stretch of shelves. Setting the pair beside the machine, Gage turned to face his commander. Intense green eyes met his. He gritted his teeth. Frickin' Bastian. He should've known he couldn't hide from him. Nothing escaped the male. "How did you know?"

"I've always been able to read you."

"Not that well."

"Well enough to know Prague's fucking with your head."

Leaning back against the counter, Gage frowned at his bare feet. No sense lying about it. He planned to tell Haider anyway, so...

He blew out a long breath. "Fuck, B. I'm spiraling. I can't shut it down."

"You told Haider yet?"

Gage shook his head.

"You should."

"I know." No way he should be shielding his best friend from the truth. As his wingmate, Haider needed to know he wasn't on solid ground. He wa suffering from what amounted to a messed-up mental screen. Sleep-deprived and unfocused. So hungry he drifted toward energy-greed, moving toward nothing good, far too fast. Which left him wondering what he was doing flying out of the lair each night. His condition would lead to problems in the field. Something no one needed, given the Razorbacks' propensity to pop out of dark corners. "I just—"

"But not for the reasons you think."

His attention snapped back to his commander. "What do you mean?"

"You're safe in the sky." Hooking a low-back chair with his foot, Bastian pulled it away from the island. Steel feet slid across the limestone floor. The scraping noise stopped as he unloaded, parking himself on the upholstery. "I'm not worried about you in battle, but... you think, maybe, if you're struggling, Haider is too?"

Shock jolted through him.

Gage opened his mouth, then closed it again. Talk about self-absorbed. He'd been so caught up in his own situation, it hadn't occurred to him Haider might be suffering. The male was unflappable, so smart Gage often wondered if his best friend had any weaknesses at all.

"You're stronger than most, Gage." Green gaze intent, B leveled him with a look. "Mentally, you're the toughest around, so stands to reason—"

"I'm not the only one messed up about it." Crossing his arms over his chest, Gage listened to the coffee machine gurgle behind him. The smell of dark roast swelled in the kitchen as something else occurred to him. He didn't want to ask. Really, *really* didn't want to know, but... "And Nian?"

"Not doing well either."

"Hell."

"Yeah," B said, planting his forearms on the countertop. "Look, I know you like to let Haider take the lead, but he's disappeared so far inside his own head, he's practically nonverbal. You need to be the one to step up—to lead Haider and Nian into healthier headspaces."

"I'm not like Haider, B. I'm not good with words."

"Not asking you to be. What I need for you to do is knock some sense into them. Someone needs to start the conversation, Gage, and given Haider and Nian are both Metallics, it's gotta be you."

Uncrossing his arms, Gage gripped the edge of the countertop. Polished granite grounded him, making him feel more solid inside his own skin. His mind did the rest, allowing realization to rise. He could fight it, pretend he wasn't capable, but... B was right. As a bronze dragon, he could push Haider and Nian in ways other males couldn't.

Gage sighed. "Now I really want to hit you."

B's mouth twitched. "Another time."

"Sooner rather than—"

"Later. Yeah, I got you," Bastian said, a feral light in his eyes. Rapping his knuckles against counter, he pushed away from the island. "Hope's on standby if you need her."

Gage nodded. He might. One thing he'd learned with Osgard, trauma manifested itself in all kinds of different ways and—

The rapid bang of boots on the stairs outside his loft hammered the quiet.

Bastian turned toward the foyer.

Gage frowned.

His front door slammed open.

Wrath in his dark eyes, Sloan strode over the threshold.

Straightening away from the counter, Gage flexed his hands. "You wake my son, I slit your throat. Sound like a fair exchange to you?"

"Fuck you," Sloan said, voice hushed, tone full of snarl. "I'm going to cut your balls off."

The threat raked over him.

Gage's eyes narrowed. Any other day, he would've welcomed the attitude. Today, running on too little sleep and a messed-up emotional grid, Sloan was barking up the wrong tree.

With a murmur, he conjured a hunting knife. The well-worn hilt settled against his palm. A quick rotation in his hand, an even quicker flick of his wrist, sent the dagger hurtling, end over end, toward his friend.

Moving like an inbound missile, Sloan leaned sideways.

The knife whistled past him.

A loud thunk echoed as steel slammed into the doorjamb behind him. The blade quivered a moment before his friend countered, unleashing a load of earth magic. The smell of fresh-cut grass blew into the room. Baring his teeth, Sloan used his mind to yank the knife from the wooden frame and hurled it back in Gage's direction.

Bastian laughed.

Gage dodged.

The dagger streaked past his ear and slammed into a cupboard door. Focused on the blade quivering inches away from his head, he admired Sloan's handiwork, then grinned. "Nice shot."

"Don't," Sloan said, eyes shimmering with anger. "I'm not in the mood for your shit today."

"So I see," he murmured, watching Sloan set up shop next to Bastian. Dark skin glowing in the soft light, the male slammed his laptop down on the countertop. Gage blinked. Oh, man. Shit really had gone critical if Sloan was upset enough to mistreat his hardware. The Nightfury IT genius loved computers more than people. "What the hell, Sloan? Why aren't you sleeping?"

"I would be... if you weren't such a dumbass."

His brows popped toward his forehead. "What did I do?"

Sloan glared at him. "Where's your computer?"

"On the coffee table."

"I'm taking it away."

"What—why?" Excellent question, the perfect one to ask, given his friend's level of fury. Not that he got to voice it before Sloan turned and walked away, leaving him standing in front of his coffee maker. "You touch my shit, I'll crack your skull."

Already in the living room, Sloan snorted. "Try it and I'll strangle you with your computer cable."

Unease drifted down his spine.

Not good. Sloan wasn't playing. Which amounted to a problem. A huge one.

Quiet and even-tempered, not much raised Sloan's blood pressure. Not that he spent a ton of time with the male. Sloan kept to himself most nights, never venturing beyond the computer lab beneath Black Diamond.

A circumstance in need of change.

The male spent too much time alone.

He needed to get out more.

Everyone inside the lair thought so, but that didn't mean he wanted the cyber sleuth digging around in his private business. The fact Sloan didn't care—had invaded his space with enough attitude to launch a nuclear attack—signaled trouble. *Big trouble*. Bad mojo. At least, for him, 'cause... yeah. Only one thing raised Sloan's ire enough to keep him out of bed: cybersecurity and the safety of the Nightfury pack.

"Give me your password." Ass planted on the sectional, Sloan cracked Gage's laptop open. "I need to see what the hell you've been doing."

Instinct warned him to say nothing.

Gage rattled off his password instead.

No sense pissing Sloan off by trying to lock him out. The male would simply hack in, and he'd be in the same place—standing in his kitchen with Bastian eyeballing him and Sloan gearing up to rip his balls off. Something a smart male knew to avoid. Earth dragons were a breed apart, and Sloan was a prime example.

His friend despised liars.

A quirk of character, Goddess knew, but one Gage wasn't willing to risk. And given his friend's body language—annoyed, determined, zero patience for anything but straight talk? No doubt about it. A complete no-brainer. His computer would go bye-bye if he refused to cooperate.

Gage scowled.

Fucking hell. He was just getting the hang of using the laptop.

Last week, he actually managed to order automotive parts online for the Vette he and Osgard were rebuilding. A big step forward for him. He didn't understand computers. Most days, he didn't want to, but, well... sometimes the internet came in handy. Now, though, was hardly the time to point out that momentous fact. Or reveal his budding tech savvy. Not with an angry earth dragon sitting in his loft.

2

Planted on the couch, algorithm up and running, Sloan opened another window into cyberspace. Hunting for the problem, his fingers flew over the keyboard. He frowned at the fifteen-inch screen. Annoyance made him type faster. The rapid click of keys should've soothed him. Deep forays into the internet usually did, but...

Not today.

Gage, and whatever his brother had been up to in recent weeks, threatened his calm. He could feel it rising, the raw, elemental twist, the incendiary curl as his dragon half drifted toward rage.

Taking a breath, he locked his beast down, doing his best to stay even.

A difficult thing to do.

His better half always teetered on the edge of rampage. Ready and willing to shred the facade and step into wrath. He'd worked for decades to curb the seething rush of his temper. To find center and peace —the Zen he needed to operate at optimal capacity.

Most days, he managed.

Sometimes, he cracked.

Here, now, inside his friend's loft, didn't need to be

one of those times. He could control the destructive nature of his earth dragon. Lock it down and stay present, instead of backtracking into the past, unearthing things best left buried.

Mining Gage's data, Sloan concentrated on the problem in front of him.

Sometimes having friends sucked.

Computers were much easier to be around. More cooperative with a helluva lot less attitude, and the mess that accompanied it. Switching screens, he dug deeper, tracking his brother-in-arms' activity across the web.

A chat room window popped open.

Gaze narrowed on the prompt, Sloan bit down on a curse. Freaking Gage. The male was a walking, talking pain in his ass.

Shifting the laptop on the coffee table, Sloan opened his own super computer. Dual screens running, his attention bounced between the two. Full of wormhole viruses, Gage's machine chugged along, slowing him down, impeding his ability to find the breach.

He flicked his fingers across the trackpad. The antivirus software he'd designed went to work, ferreting out one problem after another. He examined each one, filed it away, clearing the crap out of his path until—

"Pain in my ass," he muttered, resisting the urge to slap Gage upside the head as he located the source. Another private chat room, much like the first, but so far off the grid, he wondered how his friend had found it. Scowling at the computer, he scanned the text, reading his packmate's conversation with an unknown human. No one else involved in the chat, but...

An image appeared on-screen.

His brows collided.

He drew in a breath, inhaling deep, exhaling slow, to maintain his cool. What the hell did Gage think he was doing? No way he should be revealing that kind of information online. The beautiful, but little-known Nightfury crest was off limits to outsiders. Every warrior knew it, but, well... shit. Proof of his friend's carelessness sat on-screen, staring him in the face.

The need to hammer his friend made his knuckles itch.

A natural reaction. Gage deserved every bit of his wrath. The male had done the unthinkable. Gone outside the pack and shared the image that symbolized the Nightfury pack with a stranger.

A goddamn stranger.

The other occupant in the chat room might not know what the crest meant—or to whom it belonged —but the Razorbacks did. Which equaled big trouble for Gage and the human now in possession of the information. Flexing his hands, Sloan shook his head. Freaking Gage. Without knowing it, he'd unleashed a monster, landing the Nightfuries in clusterfuck territory.

Footfalls sounded to his left.

Skirting the end of the sectional, Bastian set up shop across from him. Seat cushions hissed as his commander sat in a low-slung, deep-seated armchair. Green eyes leveled on Sloan, B tipped his chin. "What are you looking for?"

"Hang on." Returning his attention to the laptop, Sloan wrote code to patch over the breach. "Give me a minute."

Nodding, B settled deeper in the chair and, raising his legs, crossed his combat boots on the glass-topped coffee table. "Do your thing."

"Shit." Perched on the back of the couch, Gage swung his bare feet over the low back. He swiveled and dropped into the middle of the sectional. The steel frame shuddered with the shift. Focused on his work, Sloan ignored the male as he settled beside him. "I really fucked up, didn't I?"

"We'll get to that in a second," he murmured, concentrating on his firewall.

Repairing the tear would be easier from the Hub —his computer lab seven stories beneath Black Diamond's aboveground lair, but he couldn't wait. Didn't want to risk it. Every second counted.

A simple search, and Gage's interaction would be flagged by Razorbacks. Wouldn't be difficult to do. The bastards were tech savvy. Almost as capable as him at hiding their trail online. Whoever ran the enemy's system was good, and a male like that always set up automated searches, picking over cyberspace, looking for anything of interest, searching for things to use against the Nightfury pack.

Something he worked hard to prevent every day.

His IT skills—the algorithms he ran—obliterated all trace of his pack's activities. Well, most of the time. The AI (Artificial Intelligence) unit he'd created, and was still perfecting, kept his system tight. Strong and impenetrable. Just the way he liked it, but Gage's foray into the internet had messed with his system.

Jumping screens, he returned to the chat. His gaze caught on the human's call sign. Hands poised above the keyboard, he glanced sideways at Gage. "Who's S.R.?"

His friend's brow furrowed. "A contact."

"What kind?"

Gage looked over his shoulder. Scanning the

mouth of the hallway leading to his bedroom, he drew a breath, then cursed low and quiet.

Sloan growled at him. "Gage."

Shifting to the edge of the couch, his friend rested his forearms on the tops of his thighs. Big hands laced between the spread of his legs, he bowed his head. "No one's supposed to know. I wanted it to be a surprise."

"You shared the Nightfury crest online, set a meet with S.R., a... shit, I don't know what the hell he is, but that swings our asses out there. The Razorbacks pick up that thread and—"

"We'll fly into an ambush," B growled. "What the fuck, Gage?"

Heavy muscles flanking Gage's spine rippled as he shifted. One second ticked into another before he gave up the goods. "He's a designer. A goldsmith."

Sloan blinked. "Goldsmith?"

"Yeah."

"Why do you need one of those?" Bastian asked, brows raised in surprise.

"Because, I..." Looking as though he was being skinned alive, Gage grimaced. Rolling his shoulders, he raised his head and plugged Sloan with an intense look. "Osgard picked a date."

"A date?" B took his feet off the coffee table. Sliding forward in his seat, he mimicked his warrior's pose, encouraging him to talk. "For what?"

"His birthday."

Shock spread at the pronouncement.

Silence descended like acid, devouring logic as Sloan struggled to understand. He stared at Gage. The male looked back, holding steady, refusing to explain.

Enlightenment struck like lightning.

He sucked in a sharp breath.

Holy hell. His friend was bringing Osgard into the fold. For real. No fooling around. The youngling might be new to the Nightfury pack, wasn't even blood kin, but his friend didn't care. Not surprising. Gage only knew one way to do things—*his way*. He'd never been one to stand on ceremony. Toss in his protective nature, the kid's vulnerability and... bingo. His pack-mate's adoption of Osgard was nothing but a formal-ity. One he planned to make official. Which meant...

The deal was done.

Gage loved the youngling. Fiercely. Without reser-vation. Full acceptance on display, making it clear to him and Bastian he expected the rest of the pack to fall in line.

The realization hit him like a hammer to the heart.

Sloan closed his eyes. Goddess. Gage was lucky. So very lucky to be a father. Sloan would've given any-thing to say the same. To be granted a second chance. To have his son by his side, instead of buried six feet under Texas soil alongside his mother.

The memory burned through him.

Grief opened into a well of emptiness, leaving him hollow inside. Nothing new. The anguish never went away. The loss was always there, the wound ever-present, like a thorn just under his surface. Heartache, the soul-deep laceration, showed no mercy, persisting after a decade of mourning. The pain so stark, Sloan wondered some nights how he kept on breathing.

Chest tight, heart hurting, Sloan hit the enter key. His AI went to work, writing over the breach.

Clearing his throat, he turned toward his friend. "You're having a medallion made for him."

"He's my son. Part of our pack now." Gage flexed his fingers, then fisted his hands. "He needs to know he's accepted. All the way. No reservations. The chain and pendant we wear during ceremonies will communicate that better than anything else. I don't want him doubting his worth, Sloan. He deserves that kind of security from us. From me."

"Agreed," Bastian murmured, nodding. "It's a good idea, brother, but—"

Gage growled. "I fucked up when I put our shit out there."

"Why didn't you come to me, Gage?" Hurt that he hadn't, Sloan frowned at his computer. Code crawled across the screen, the firewall back up and running with its usual efficiency. Battling the need to punch his friend, he closed the laptop with a gentle snap. "You know I'll help. You know I'll always—"

"I know. Brother, believe me, *I know*, but I wanted to do it on my own. Probably selfish, but... Oz needs that from me. I want him to know, no matter how fucked up his beginning, he's loved."

"Actions speak louder than words," B said, sitting back, making the chair squeak.

"Yeah." Reversing course, Gage pushed away from his knees and relaxed into the back of the couch. Bronze gaze rooted to timber-beam ceiling, he shook his head, then glanced at Sloan. "How bad is it?"

"We're good," he said, unable to hammer his friend for screwing up. Not now. Knowing why Gage messed with his system changed everything. *Everything.* Given the opportunity, he would've done the same thing. "I patched the firewall and cleared the viruses, but we're still on the hook with the goldsmith."

"You sure the Razorbacks will pick up the—"

Sloan huffed. "One hundred percent."

"So the human's screwed."

"Pretty much."

"Fucking hell." Gage scrubbed his hands over his head. "I want that medallion for Oz."

"And you'll get it." The armchair groaned as B pushed to his feet. "When're you supposed to meet with S.R.?"

"Tonight. Midnight. At a twenty-four-hour diner on Bainbridge Island."

Bastian nodded. "Sloan, we need intel."

"Addresses."

"Yeah. The human's home, office, and where Gage set the meet."

Gage perked up. "We going hunting?"

"You wanted a fight?" Striding past the end of the couch, B headed for the door. "You're going to get one."

"Outstanding." A feral glint in his bronze-metallic eyes, Gage cracked his knuckles. "Turn the tables. Use the goldsmith as bait. Set an ambush and wait for the Razorbacks to investigate."

"That's the idea," B said over his shoulder. "Get some shut-eye. Both of you. We fly out the second the sun sets."

The front door opened, then closed.

Heavy footfalls echoed as his commander made his way down the stairs.

Sloan smiled at his brother-in-arms. "Might turn out to be fun."

Gage grinned back. "Fucking A."

And just like that, the last of his anger fell away.

He couldn't stay pissed off at Gage for gumming up the works. Not with the promise of a scale-splitting fight on the horizon. The male's heart had been in the right place. And as Sloan packed up his equipment and followed his commander out of the loft, he couldn't help but be grateful. For the opportunity to witness Gage's love and acceptance of Osgard, sure. But mostly, for the chance to meet the enemy in open air. Nothing, after all, exorcised his demons and soothed his wrath-filled soul more than ripping apart Razorbacks.

wouldn't help but be grateful for the opportunity to…

3

Grabbing his protein shake off the counter, Gage took a slug of blended mixed berries. The taste of cherries slid over the back of his tongue. Enjoying the hit of sweetness, his dragon half purred. The burst of magic unleashed a feel-good vibe as he rounded the kitchen island and swept the scene.

A sea of designer cabinetry.

Grey veins cutting through an ocean of Carrara marble countertops.

Daimler standing by the toaster, talking a mile a minute. Osgard listening, ass planted on a low-backed stool, eyes on the Numbai, lips twitching as he shoveled more porridge in his mouth.

Relief tightened his throat.

A month ago, he wouldn't have believed it possible. The kid kept proving him wrong. Becoming more comfortable inside the aboveground lair. Standing his ground instead of retreating when he encountered one of the other warriors inside the lair. Playing with Exshaw (Mac's wren, and newest addition to the Nightfury pack), wrestling with the miniature dragon when Tania and Mac needed a break.

All good signs.

The best, though, stared him in the face. The spark of humor in his son's eyes as he listened to Daimler rattle on about—

Gage frowned.

Fuck. He didn't know... the ideal filling for chocolate cupcakes or some shit.

Not that the subject mattered. Only one thing did. His son was recovering from the abuse he suffered in Prague. Not in leaps and bounds, but little by little. Talking it out with Hope. Sharing details with him. Dealing with the trauma. Inching forward, coming back to himself, doing what younglings did—discovering who he was and the male he'd grow into being.

Striding past the first couple of stools, Gage paused beside his son. Raising his hand, he gripped Osgard's nape. He tugged, making Osgard rock in his seat. The kid accepted his affection. No flinch. No hesitation. A miracle, given what he'd been through.

He flexed his hand.

Osgard glanced up at him.

Gage tipped his chin. "You good?"

"Yeah," the kid said, spoon halfway to his mouth. "You on mission tonight?"

"Whole pack's flying out."

"Mac taking Exshaw?"

"Probably," he murmured, watching his son's face fall. His mouth curved. Crazy kid. Only someone half bent wanted to *play* with Exshaw. Vicious little fucker never said quit, although... surprise, surprise... outside a few scratches, the wren never hurt Osgard. "He'll be back later. You'll get your wrestling match in then."

Osgard nodded. "I'll take Millie for a walk instead."

"Good thinking. J.J. will appreciate it," he said, giving his kid another jostle, wondering why Wick allowed his mate to name an American bulldog Milli-cent. The breed demanded something more, a better name than the pansy-ass one J.J. chose. "Later."

"Later. Kick some ass."

Gage nodded, intending to before he left the lair. Bastian had given him a mission. One that couldn't wait. Not if he wanted to get back on track. Getting into it with Haider would suck, but the grab-the-sil-ver-dragon-by-the-horns approach always worked best. And honestly? He needed the relief. So did his best friend. Meeting the challenge head-on, talking about Prague and what bothered him, would do that faster than pussyfooting around the problem, so...

No stalling.

Finding Haider and kicking his ass needed to happen now. Before the pack flew out for the night. Otherwise he'd back off, shy away, and let the status quo lie.

Never a good strategy when dealing with Haider.

The male liked to talk—needed the outlet and re-lease. Gage could've shrugged it off, blamed the lapse on circumstance, but he refused to cede the responsi-bility. Distraction—being caught up in his own shit and Osgard's situation—wasn't an excuse. He should've realized without being told Haider was hurting. Should've paid closer attention. Figured it out sooner. The fact he hadn't pained him.

Giving his son another playful shove, Gage headed for the exit. He sucked back more of his shake, and en-tering the main corridor, called on his magic.

His dragon half uncoiled deep inside him.

Magic streamed through his veins.

The superconductor inside his mind came online. Metal alloy spiked in his blood, powering up magnetic force. Power bled through his skin. Doors along the hallway shuddered, hinges and brass knobs clattering in reaction to his proximity. Asserting control, he caught the shock wave by the tail. The rattle 'n' shake downgraded, settling into low electrical hum as he fired up his sonar.

He released an ultrasonic pulse, propelling it like a heat-seeking missile.

His radar pinged.

The magical web expanded, rambling down the corridor, over white walls and chunky chair rails, then dove deep, sinking through wooden floorboards. A blip appeared on his mental screen and... bingo. Silver dragon at one o'clock. Not in his bedroom or the aboveground lair.

Gage pursed his lips.

Figured.

Since returning from Europe, Haider spent the majority of his time in one of two places: the well-equipped weight room, or the wine cellar Forge built —and continued to improve—in the underground lair.

Boots thumping against glossy wooden floorboards, he turned into another corridor. He murmured a command. Steel quivered. Twin elevators activated. Gears ground into motion, dragging stainless steel cages up from below. Seven stories down, the subterranean complex boasted the best of the best. Plenty of space. Lots of toys, state-of-the-art equipment, and the LZ—the launchpad where every Nightfury mission started and ended.

Well, at least *most* of the time.

Landing outside the garage and his loft after a night of hunting had been known to happen, but he preferred the LZ. He liked splashing through the waterfall at the end of each night. The cold, wet, and chilly, along with the routine, served two purposes. The first realigned his emotion barometer, moving him from vicious predator back to fair-minded male, getting him ready to reenter the lair. And the second washed enemy blood off his scales.

One of the elevators dinged.

A set of double doors slid wide.

Mind on the first mission of the day, Gage stepped inside and, with a mental command, set the machine in motion. Huge magnets went to work. The cage descended on a fast glide. Less than a minute later, the elevator opened into a diamond-shaped foyer. The smell of heavy-duty floor cleaner assaulted him, making his dragon senses flex in displeasure. His nose twitched. Shaking off the olfactory onslaught, he stepped out and hung a right. Twelve-foot ceilings and chiseled white-washed walls greeted him. Rough. Rugged. Seething with attitude and energy. The perfect framework for his fast-deteriorating mood.

Frickin' Haider.

His best friend needed his face rearranged.

He should be the one initiating the play. The one talking. The one getting the ball rolling and the conversation started, instead of forcing Gage do it. The fact he hadn't taken the initiative cranked Gage the wrong way. Haider must be really messed up. The male never missed an opportunity to—

A shriek blasted up the corridor.

The sound wave hit him like a baseball bat. Pressure expanded inside his head. Agony tore at his temples. In mental meltdown, his body jerked. The shake flew out of his hand. Pink slush splattered across the wall. Glass shattered against concrete as his shoulder slammed into the side wall and magic blew up the corridor.

Wings flapped.

The wren screamed again.

Debilitated by the shriek, Gage folded forward, then went down on one knee.

A growl rumbled up the corridor. "Goddamn it, Mac."

"Shut up, Ven," Mac snapped, sounding like he wanted to rip the male's head off. A good possibility. Venom always brought out the best in others. "Exshaw —settle down."

A nasty snarl echoed.

Venom cursed. "I'm going to kill the little—"

Shock waves exploded out of the gym, knocking Gage on his ass.

A raging wall of water followed, roaring through the open double doors. The white-capped curl slammed into the wall. Water washed up the corridor. Holding his head in both hands, sitting in a puddle, fighting nausea, Gage struggled to regain his equilibrium, but...

Goddess, it hurt.

Every time the wren screamed, Nightfury warriors dropped like flies. Daimler and Tania put a stop to it fast, teaching Exshaw some manners inside the lair, but every once in a while, Exshaw let loose and males hit the deck.

Ears still ringing, he planted his hand on wet concrete and jackknifed to his feet. Drenched denim sticking to his skin, he shook his head. The buzz between his temple downgraded. Pain leveled out, dissipating as he put himself in gear. He came abreast of the doors and looked into the gymnasium.

Huge space. Cinder block walls. A fantastic playground beneath industrial lights. Right now, though, it looked like a war zone.

Athletic equipment strewn everywhere. Broken lightbulbs and glass on the floor. And Mac, standing at center court with a pissed-off look on his puss and Venom pinned to the floor... by a motherfucking water snake.

Gage's brows collided.

Holy hell. He didn't know a lot about water dragons, but... *that* couldn't be normal. He'd never seen anything like the magic Mac wielded, making him glad he stood on the outside looking in.

"Let go, Mac." Ruby gaze aglow, water flew as Venom grappled with the serpent.

Controlling the magic-fueled viper, Mac kept him pinned to the floor. "You gonna do that again?"

Venom bared his teeth. "Jesus, man. I didn't hurt him."

"Exshaw doesn't need that shit, and neither do I."

"How am I supposed to know what he's capable of if I don't test him?"

The byplay made him search the gym.

His gaze landed on Exshaw.

Smooth blue-grey scales ruffled, the miniature dragon sat near the back wall, on an apparatus used to sharpen dragon claws. Bladed spine ramrod straight. The ring of spikes encircling his throat standing on end. No mistaking the meaning behind his bared fangs. An unhappy miniature dragon stared down from his perch, watching the scene unfold from a safe distance away.

Gage huffed in amusement.

Brilliant yellow eyes with vertical pupils shifted in his direction.

He tipped his chin, greeting Exshaw. The wren hissed at him. Gage smiled, enjoying his pissy attitude, and returned his attention to the wrestling match.

Venom threatened to tear Mac in half.

Gage shook his head. Not smart. Given his level of pissed off, goading Mac equated to a bad idea. The warrior was protective of everyone and everything, but mess with his mate or his wren and shit got serious... in a hurry. Feet planted between the jambs, he glanced at the male holding up the wall next to the door.

Intense golden eyes met his.

Gage raised a brow.

A male of few words, Wick shrugged.

Fair enough. No need to intervene. If Wick, Venom's wingmate and best friend, wasn't worried, he shouldn't be either. Venom and Mac would work it out. The Nightfury warriors always did. Sometimes with words. Sometimes with fists. And sometimes with magical snakes wielded by a water-loving maniac.

Tipping his chin, he left Wick to supervise and returned to the hunt. Round lights embedded in the polished concrete floor lead the way up the main corridor, dumping him into another. His net expanded. Perception narrowed, allowing him to sense Haider. A hundred yards away. Behind the ornate, cast-iron door with wooden inlay at the end of the hall. Vibrating like a tuning fork, so deep inside his own head he hadn't sensed Gage's approach yet.

Weird.

Worrisome.

Not Haider's usual MO.

The male epitomized alert. He paid attention, to everything, at all times. The lapse signaled real trouble. The kind Gage knew a friendly chat wouldn't break through.

Locked on his prey, Gage cracked his knuckles. Time to get serious. Time to step outside his comfort zone and help Haider help himself. The thought struck him as bizarre. An odd sense of irony hit him. He shoved it aside. The time for thinking had come and gone. Action was required, so instead of going in soft, he ramped into a run and, letting lethal lead the way, went in hard.

Magnetic force frothed out of him into the corridor.

The nasty blast of energy rammed the steel door.

The heavy frame shook.

Metal groaned. The lock popped. Hinges whined. A courtesy call. A love tap. A warning to the warrior standing inside a wine cellar designed for one purpose—to soothe a male's wounded soul.

A clang echoed through the underground lair.

The door to the cellar flew open.

Hands cranked into fists, Gage roared over the threshold, prepared to give his friend an attitude adjustment the only way he knew how—with brutality and a ball-busting fight.

THE SECOND THE door slammed open, Haider tossed the packet of cigars. The high-end, banana leaf wrapped Cubans slid across the Burlwood table, bumping into his new humidor. Exotic wood casing. Top-notch instrumentation. The best money could buy.

Not that it mattered.

Tonight wasn't about good cigars.

The moment belonged to pain. To rage and a safe space in which to express it.

Flexing his hands, he turned to face his best friend. The male he loved like a brother and couldn't live without, stalked toward him. Down the aisle, between stacked whiskey barrels. Beneath the arched, brick ceiling. Past wine fridges and expensive racks housing bottles of fine Scotch.

Bronze gaze aglow, Gage snarled at him.

Shifting into a fighting stance, Haider moved out from behind the table, giving Gage a clear lane and a better shot at him. Desperation cranked him tight. The need to fight did the rest, preparing him for the face full of flack he was about to receive. Gratitude streamed through him. Haider drew in a deep breath, struggling to control pent-up emotion, but...

Thank fuck.

Finally.

Thank fuck.

The showdown he craved.

He needed the fight. Longed for the pain. For the chance to untangle the mess inside his head and expel the hurt.

Usually, he used words to express himself. Too bad the usual tactics no longer worked. Since Prague, he hadn't been able to find any words. He'd searched and searched... and searched... but the gift of knowing what to say, when to say it, never came, leaving him stranded behind mental barricades.

Nights tore him apart.

Days ruined his concentration, becoming nightmarish instead of restful. The quiet inside the lair cranked him tight, stealing his peace of mind, gifting him with a bad case of insomnia.

Forget about bad dreams.

He longed for the day he had them again. At least then, he'd be sleeping. Hour after hour. Minute by minute. He tossed and turned, finding no comfort in his bed.

The internal pressure never let up.

Writing it in his journal didn't help. Time spent in the weight room didn't exorcise the demons. Neither did ignoring the problem and trying to forget. Flashbacks plagued his nights. Exhaustion blurred his days. Words failed him. Nothing made sense anymore. He was upside down and backwards inside his own head, with no avenue of escape.

"You idiot." Bristling with hostility, Gage kicked a chair out of his way. The Louis IX flew sideways, slamming against the stone wall. Wood splintered. His friend didn't stop. Moving like a freight train, Gage stomped past the sitting area. "Why didn't you say som—"

Haider didn't let him finish.

Desperate for the fight, he swiped a tumbler off the table. Amber liquid splashed over the rim. Fifty-year-old Scotch splattered across the limestone floor. The scent of hard alcohol rose. Clenching his teeth, he pitched the glass sidearm. Light refracted off cut crystal as it hurtled toward his friend's head.

Magic powered up, Gage opened his hand, palm pressed out. Fine crystal stopped a foot away, hovering in midair. His friend flicked his fingers. The glass flew out of his path. A smash sounded as it exploded against the stone wall.

"No talking," he said, low tone, lethal intent. "Fight, asshole."

Gage's eyes narrowed. "Have it your way."

He always did.

Now was no exception and... thank the Goddess for Gage. His friend dropped the desire to yak and attacked. Technique perfect. Strength on display. Giving Haider what he wanted—an outlet for the pain he needed gone but couldn't let go.

Gage's fist jabbed through his guard.

Knuckles cracked against his temple.

His head snapped sideways.

Not waiting for him to recover, Gage unleashed a combination. Jab. Right hook. Uppercut. Furniture went flying. Violent sound ricocheted inside the cellar, beating against hand-carved woodwork. Relishing the burn, Haider blocked punch after punch, countering with vicious intensity, giving as good as his friend gave, feeling alive for the first time in weeks. More like himself, less like a wounded male with no idea how to stop the bleeding.

Fists leading the way, he roared and launched himself at Gage.

His fist connected.

Gage grunted and stumbled sideways.

Satisfaction scored through him. Without mercy, Haider kept at him—block, spin, parry. Knuckles bleeding and body bruised. Footwork perfect. Take a punch. Deliver one of his own. A beautiful dance fueled by agony and the inability to express it with words. Each blow widened the bottleneck inside him. Excess emotion poured out, making his chest heave and his throat hurt.

Fucking Archguard.

Asshole Zidane.

The sadistic bastard had torn him wide open, shoving humiliation deep, unleashing waves of self-recrimination. All the *if-onlys* surfaced to taunt him. If only he'd paid closer attention. If only his intel had been better. If only he'd listened to instinct and gotten them out of Prague sooner—the second he knew staying was too dangerous—he would've saved Gage hours of being tortured in a kill room designed to strip warriors of dignity.

Failure.

A bitter pill to swallow.

Now, guilt ate him alive, shaking his foundation, making him question the male he believed himself to be. Was he truly a male who protected others? Or did he like covert missions too much? Had he over-stepped his bounds and sacrificed Gage to get his fix? His brow cranked low, Haider circled his friend. Fists raised, he shook his head, trying to puzzle it out.

Maybe he'd become that kind of male. A warrior more interested in the winning than doing the right thing. One addicted to the game. A game he'd never lost before, but... there was always a first time for everything. The mistakes he made in Prague spelled out the truth. Arrogance pushed him into foolishness and the belief he controlled all the variables.

The realization jackhammered through him.

Flinching, Haider dropped his guard. Bad decision. The hesitation was all Gage needed to launch the next attack. His friend's fist connected. Knuckles cracked against bone. Pain detonated inside his head. A cut opened under his eye. Blood spilling down his face, Haider stumbled backwards, then sideways. Gage took advantage and grabbed hold. Big hands wrenched him forward, then twisted him around, locking him in a half nelson.

With a roar, he bucked to break out of the lockdown.

Muscles working, Gage held on tight, then kicked his feet out from under him. His knees slammed into the floor. Agony rocketed up his legs. Anguish furled inside his chest. He howled as emotion boiled over.

"I'll kill you. I'll fucking end you," he snarled at Gage.

"Let it go, brother," Gage said, calm voice, soothing cadence. "Let it out, Haider."

Bleeding pain, he fought his friend's hold. "Fuck off."

"Good. Tell me how it is."

Heat bloomed behind his eyes. "I can't. I can't."

Gage shook him, rattled his bones. "Why?"

Air abrading the back of his throat, he fought to contain the emotion. Gage tightened his grip on him. The dam broke. Truth poured out. "I'm sorry. I'm sorry. I'm so fucking sorry."

"What for?"

"It's my fault. I should've known. I should've pulled us out sooner. I had intel. All the signs were there. I was having too much fun, playing a game I was too arrogant to see I couldn't win. I should've—"

"Bullshit."

"Known. I should've *known*."

"Jesus-fuck, Haider. You're powerful, but you're not all-knowing." Gage increased the pressure, holding him down. "You need to let go of what happened in Prague."

"Have you?"

Gage paused. "No. I've been beating myself up, too. I'm having trouble sleeping. I close my eyes, drop off, and the nightmares come, but I just realized something. The world we live in isn't *knowable*. We can prepare. We can plan for all possibilities, but some things are uncontrollable. Shit goes sideways, brother. Always has. Always will. That isn't your fault. It isn't mine either. But, Haider... we're alive. We made it out in one piece, and that's a fucking miracle."

The harshness of Gage's voice jolted him. "I just—"

"I know." With a sigh, his friend loosened his grip,

releasing him from the chokehold. Hunched over, Haider lifted his head and glanced at his friend. Dark brows cranked low, Gage planted his ass on the floor. Knees bent, forearms resting on his knees, he met his gaze, the regret easy to read. "I feel it too. The guilt, the mind-fuck, but not talking about it isn't working. You're suffering. So am I. And Nian? Shit, he's—"

"Screwed up too." Moving with care, elbow pressed to his sore ribs, Haider set up shop next to his friend on the floor. Propped against a row of barrels, he wiped the blood off his cheek with the tail of his ripped T-shirt. "I see his pain. It echoes mine."

"Yeah."

Studying his beat-to-shit knuckles, Haider frowned. "You think we need Hope?"

"Maybe," Gage said, expression pensive. "Or maybe we should try working it out together first—as a trio. As Metallics."

"You and Nian... oil and water, man," Haider said, throwing his friend a sidelong look. "You think that's wise?"

"I don't dislike him."

"Since when?"

Gage shrugged. "The namby-pamby's grown on me—like a wart."

Haider snorted. "We'll have to corner him."

"I got no problem with that," Gage said, flexing his hand. "Beating some sense into the male will make my night."

Relief streamed through him. His mood lightened another notch. "So we have a plan."

"We have a plan," Gage said, echoing his statement. "As long as you use your words and stop crawling back inside your head. Hell, man—you're the talker, not me. This communication shit is hard."

Haider laughed, feeling better by the moment. Crazy, but knowing he wasn't alone, and that Gage still had his back despite his messy mindset, made all the difference.

"Got something else on the go you should know about."

"What?"

"A way to get Zidane, and by extension, the Archguard."

Interest flared in Gage's gaze. "Whatever it is, I'm in."

"Figured." Haider's mouth curved. Made sense. A no-brainer, really. Which made him wonder why he'd kept his pet project a secret so long. Hiding things from his best friend wasn't smart, given Gage's level of lethal and the fact he wanted Zidane dead as much as he did. "I need your help with recon and sourcing contacts. Warning, though."

Waiting for the punch line, his friend raised a brow.

"Nian's gotta be in the loop."

"I can live with that."

"We do the legwork first. When the intel's solid and we're ready to execute, we'll take it to Bastian."

"The others are already gathering." Bronze eyes shimmering, Gage popped upright. Big boots landed with a thump on stone. With a grimace, he rolled his shoulder and headed for the door. "Lay it out on the way."

Ignoring the aches and pains from the fight, Haider rolled to his feet. "You wanna tell me what we're into tonight?"

"Fixing my fuck-up. B'll explain before we fly out."

He nodded. Fair enough. All things in good time. Patience, after all, was his forte.

Gage threw him a sidelong glance. "Tell me about your plan for Zidane. Can't wait to sink my claws into the fucker."

Haider grinned and started talking.

He needed a second opinion. A brilliant tactician capable of lethal precision. Someone he trusted to bounce ideas off of without them boomeranging.

Gage ticked off every one of the boxes on his gotta-have list. Messed up in the mental arena, he'd forgotten how much he needed his best friend. To keep him steady. To tell it to him straight. To be there, like he'd always been, no matter how tough the situation. Which meant... time to open his mouth and get his idea—no matter how strange—into the open. The sooner he shared, the sooner he'd know whether his plan to take out Zidane and the Archguard landed north of brilliant or south of suicidal.

4

Boots planted on cracked tarmac under a starry sky, Ivar unboxed more electrical cable. Humid air whispered over the nape of his neck. His dragon half stirred. Magic uncoiled. His skin tingled as pink fire licked over his shoulders, the inferno inside him burning brighter in the wake of a warm spring breeze.

Extinguishing the flames, he unsheathed his hunting knife. Lethal edge glinting in the moonlight, he sliced through another box top. Steel decimated the cardboard. The zing echoed across the blacktop, carving through wisps of fog to reach the forest's edge. Crickets stopped chirping. Bullfrogs ceased calling. Quiet reigned as he flipped the box open and grabbed the industrial-sized spool. With a yank, he liberated the coil of heavy-duty cable from its confines and picked up the one sitting beside his feet.

The crickets started up again.

As insect song rose above the treetops, he tucked both spools under his arms and turned toward the dilapidated hangar sitting a hundred feet away. Footfalls rapping against pitted concrete, he approached the building and a pair of beat-up doors. More dented than smooth, rust ate through metal, making faded blue paint curl away the surface.

Satisfaction clawed through him.

Hamersveld had been right.

The abandoned army base ticked every box on his list. Miles from city streets. Buried deep in the Cascade mountain range. Overgrown with vines and thick woodland. Long forgotten by humans and US government.

A total waste of Department of Defense resources, but perfect for his purposes.

With just ten days until the Meridian realigned, Ivar needed everything in place. Set and ready to go. A secure facility deep underground in which to lock himself down. The fallout shelter sitting three stories beneath the old hangar fit the bill. Thank fuck. He didn't know what he would've done had the abandoned human complex not been available. Toughed it out, most likely, but now, he didn't have to—not while locked inside an impenetrable vault designed to withstand nuclear war.

Thick concrete walls were part of it.

The bitch of a steel door he couldn't break through, even in dragon form, added to the tally, downgrading the situation from fubar to doable.

Upgrades needed to be made. Comfort, after all, had always been one of his priorities. The entire reason he stood on a beat-to-shit runway, miles from 28 Walton Street—the lair he shared with the five warriors who made up his personal guard—surrounded by construction supplies. But with all the details sorted and two weeks of nonstop work, the finish line lay within sight.

A few repairs left to make.

Some testing to complete, but...

He couldn't afford any delays or mistakes. A shift in the timeline would equal disaster. For him, sure. But mostly, for Sasha.

Halfway to the door, Ivar paused mid-stride. The soles of his boots scraped over crumbling asphalt. He kicked at a raw patch, making pebbles roll, and bowed his head. Knotted muscles pulled. Closing his eyes, he held the posture, relishing in the discomfort. He needed the distraction. Wanted the pain. Maybe then he'd stop thinking about her. Forget about doing the right thing and fall heart-first into the wrong one.

He wanted to do it. Say to hell with the consequences and go to her. Stay in her bed, in her arms, feed the addiction, lose himself in the odd effect she had on him.

Being with Sasha was a revelation. Stunning. Strange. Satisfying in ways he couldn't explain and wasn't sure he wanted to understand.

She soothed him... without trying.

No matter how difficult his night, she made his days better, smoothing out his rough edges, helping quiet his mind, encouraging him to relax. Crazy as it seemed, she stabilized his volatility, giving him time to think, feel, and wonder about things he never had before.

Odd things.

Disconcerting things.

Dangerous things.

Given a choice, he would've turned away. Taken a hard pass and left her to her own devices. He should've gone that route. Killing his fascination would be safer. Sensible. The smartest path to take. Too bad he hadn't embraced the mindset. No matter how hard he resisted, he always circled back, buckling beneath the weight of his obsession.

Now he was stuck. In so deep, his interest in her approached compulsion.

A stronger male would seize what he wanted—what the continued health of his race demanded. Always the best decision. One problem with the usual direction. His dragon half was entrenched. Certain. Insistent. Intractable. The stubborn SOB refused to risk her. Ivar couldn't blame him. Each time he thought about Sasha dying, every cell in his body rebelled. Which left one option...

Protect her at all costs.

Even if that meant shielding her from himself.

The whole reason behind upgrading the fallout shelter.

If he couldn't get into open air when the Meridian realigned, he couldn't return to her, never mind knock her up. No pregnancy meant zero possibility of her dying while giving birth to his child.

Raising his head, Ivar leveled his chin and stared at the solution. Stoic in neglect, the hangar had stood the test of time. As he moved toward the structure, his gaze drifted over the roof. Mounded over with dirt, long grass grew on the curved top and down the sloped sides, hiding it from the air. An ideal hidey-hole. Camouflage at its best. Those who didn't know it was there would never find it, ensuring privacy during *the hungering* and—

Jesus, he was messed up.

So turned around inside his own head, he'd abandoned his principles.

Sasha presented him with unequaled opportunity. Was an untapped resource. The scientist in him should be rejoicing. He should *want* to impregnate her. Planting his baby in her belly was mission critical, the entire reason he developed the serum and the breeding program in the first place.

He needed strong females with high energy to unlock the Goddess of All Things' curse and free his species. He'd spent decades learning about genetics and fertility. Years of study and experimentation. Hours bent over his worktable, looking through microscopes, sequencing human and dragon DNA. All of which had produced results. Excellent data points. A clear path forward. Optimal timelines. Now was the time to test his hypothesis and tweak the serum, but... was he doing any of that?

Nyet. He was not.

Like an idiot, he was doing the opposite, standing in the middle of nowhere, rebuilding a fallout shelter designed to keep him from doing his duty.

Worse, he hadn't even injected Sasha with the serum.

He could've—at any time.

She afforded him ample opportunity on a regular basis. Sleeping in his arms. Trusting him to hold her. Infecting him with such deep satisfaction, he'd left the battlefield. Or rather, his laboratory.

Scientific experiments took a backseat when it came to her. His drive to crack the magical code blocking Dragonkind males from siring females disappeared when pitted against Sasha. What he believed was required to save his race no longer mattered. Not when faced with the possibility of losing her.

The second he'd laid eyes—and hands—on Sasha, locking himself down during the realignment became necessary. *The hungering* wasn't to be taken lightly. The biannual event plagued his kind. Twelve hours of carnal excess coupled with intense, soul-twisting bliss.

The affliction didn't discriminate. Young. Old. Weak. Strong. *The hungering* struck with equal viciousness, causing Dragonkind males to lose their minds when breeding instinct overrode common sense.

Most warriors locked themselves down.

He never had, preferring tranquilizers to being imprisoned. This time, though, drugs wouldn't be enough. Nothing short of a nuclear bunker possessed enough strength to hold him. His need for Sasha was simply too strong.

Blinded by need, focused on her, his dragon half would take control the moment the electrostatic bands ringing the planet realigned, propelling him toward her. And she'd be doomed. Doomed to accept him. Doomed to satisfy him. Doomed to die when his child arrived months later.

With a growl, Ivar compelled one of the doors open.

Magic whiplashed in front of him.

Rusty hinges squawked as the panel swung inward.

Jacking the spools of cable higher, he sidestepped through the open door and strode into the hangar. Dragon senses firing, he took in the space. Musty smell. Corrugated steel walls. A heap of broken furniture sitting in the middle of the stained concrete floor. No one around. Tilting his head, he listened for a moment. Voices welled in the silence, spiraling up the staircase, coming from down below.

Quick strides moved him across the open space.

Quicker feet took him into the belly of the beast.

Boots banging against well-worn treads, he descended farther into the gloom. His night vision sparked. Infrared switched on, allowing him to see in the dark. Halfway down, a glimmer of light ate through the darkness. The spiral staircase went from pitch-black into lightening shadows.

Pain pricked his temples.

Narrowing his gaze to protect his light-sensitive eyes, he rounded the last landing and, thumping down the remaining treads, entered a tight corridor. Two doors on his left. Three to his right. One at the end. He ignored each one and, with a murmur, spoke into the silence. The energy shield he set in place to protect the bunker reacted, scanning his DNA.

The wall tucked beneath the staircase went from solid steel to indistinct wave.

A second later, an archway appeared.

Skirting the banister, he dipped his head beneath the lintel and stepped into a large foyer. Conditions improved. Concrete transitioned from rough to smooth. Rusted-out steel walls met recently painted plaster. A fresh smell replaced damp, musty air. Ivar breathed deep, enjoying the changes as he glanced at the light globes bobbing against the high ceiling, then shifted his attention to the warrior beside the vault door.

Raising a brow, Midion scowled at him. "About time. Needed that fifteen minutes ago."

Ivar frowned back. "You looking for a fight?"

A vicious gleam entered the male's blue eyes. The corner of his mouth curved up. "Absolutely."

"Later," he murmured, liking the idea of kicking his warrior's ass. After weeks of being cooped up, he needed a scale-rattling brawl, and Midion always delivered. Setting the twin spools on the floor, Ivar tipped his chin. "How's it going?"

"Getting there." On his haunches beside the control panel, Midion tugged at wires sticking out at odd angles. "Should be ready to test the vault door in an hour or so."

"Good," he said, stepping over a bunch of tools scattered on the floor. "You need anything else?"

"A cappuccino."

Ivar huffed. Trust Midion to ask for the impractical... and fancy-ass coffee. Especially while in the middle of nowhere. Then again, he should've expected the request. The male was a caffeine addict. A coffee snob who drank so much of the stuff, it was a wonder he got any sleep during the day. "Gonna have to gut it out a while longer."

"We need a descent machine here." Twisting wires together, Midion threw him a look of disgust. "Not that thing pretending to be a coffee maker in the mess hall."

"Your responsibility. You want one, get one."

"Next trip."

The comment made him pause mid-stride. "You locking down with us?"

"Syndor and Rampart too," he said, picking up a screwdriver. "None of us are ready for infants of our own."

Understandable. Most warriors weren't. Fatherhood didn't come naturally to many Dragonkind.

"Though..." Turning a screw, Midion glanced at him. "I'm surprised you want to."

Ivar frowned. "What—lock down?"

"Yeah."

"Why?"

"You've got a female."

Surprise made him tense. "Hamersveld tell you that?"

Midion shook his head. "Been watching you cross

the street to visit her. Figured you'd breed her when the time came."

Hell. Talk about ineffective.

He'd snuck around for months, keeping his visits on the down-low, determined to protect Sasha, and shield himself. All for nothing. He'd done a piss-poor job of it. Hamersveld knew all along. His friend had confronted him weeks ago, tossing Ivar's covert activities in his face while flouting pack protocol by allowing a valuable high energy female to escape.

Freaking Hamersveld. Total pain in his ass.

Though why he gave into frustration was anyone's guess.

Hamersveld was who he *was*—a water dragon with strong opinions.

His new first-in-command disliked the breeding program. Not for the reason most males would either. He didn't object to the serum or the end goal. He wanted what Ivar wanted—to be free and clear of humankind once and for all. What he didn't like was imprisoning females. Hamersveld believed there was a better way. And honestly? His objections to the project made a whole lot of sense.

Rolling his shoulders to break the tension, Ivar reached for calm. "Does everyone inside the lair know about her?"

His warrior shrugged.

Which meant *yes*.

Fucking hell. He'd lost his edge.

"Not planning on breeding her, Midion," Ivar said, although he wanted to—in the worst way. The dichotomy, the emotional push-pull, confused the hell out of him. He kept ping-ponging between what he wanted and knew he couldn't have—sons and daughters with her laugh, her smile and gorgeous brown eyes. "Families are for other males, not me."

Midion nodded. "I hear you."

Ivar hoped so. He'd rather yank out his fingernails than talk about it again.

Leaving his warrior to his work, Ivar stepped over the lip of the vault door and entered the huge space. Designed to house human elite in times of trouble, the bunker boasted the best of the best. Polished marble floors with colorful inlay. Fluted columns with fancy scrollwork top and bottom. A soaring ceiling more suited to a cathedral than a fallout shelter.

All in place before his inspection.

The décor, though, was all him.

Half the room was a lounge area. Neutral colors. Colorful rugs on the floor. Deep-seated couches and comfortable armchairs placed for maximum effect. Enormous throw pillows lined the back of the huge sectional, providing a kick-back-and-stay-awhile vibe in front of the entertainment center. The kitchen with its center island and granite countertops had been a bitch to install, but he and Hamersveld completed it with time to spare. The only thing left to finish was—

"Ivar, you bring it?" Deep voice. German accent. Pissy attitude.

Ivar sighed. "You ever gonna let it go?"

"He broke my fucking nose." Expression as black as his eyes, Denzeil prowled around one of the fluted columns. Size thirteens planted beside the cherry-wood dining table, he aired his grievance. "Put me in the infirmary. Was laid up for days. He didn't have to—"

"You touched his female."

"She was trying to escape."

"You should've let her," he said, going another

round with his friend. Same argument, different night. Understandable. Bruised egos healed slower than broken bones. "Had she managed to get out of the lair, Sveld would've retrieved her."

Denzeil grunted.

He raised a brow, waiting for him to back down.

"I don't like him."

"I don't care," he said, tone hard, authority absolute. "Sveld's my XO. I appointed him to the position of first-in-command for a reason. You will respect my decision."

"*Ja*," Denzeil murmured, reverting to his native tongue.

"D, I mean it."

"I know. I just thought..."

"I know what you thought," he said, struggling to be patient. Losing his temper wouldn't help his cause. Neither would coddling the male. "I need you on IT, D. Had I named you XO, you couldn't do what you do. You wanna be outside the lair every night dealing with my warriors, settling disputes, setting up combat training, scheduling patrols?"

Denzeil frowned as realization dawned. "You didn't pass me over."

"*Nyet*." He shouldn't have to explain. Really, he shouldn't, but... Ivar flexed his hand to keep from hammering the male. A difficult impulse to quell. The exchange made him want to punch the idiot so badly, the urge approached desperation. "No one else can do what you do with computers. And Hamersveld excels at keeping others in line. Win-win for me. Win-win for you. Not being XO doesn't make you any less important to me. All right?"

"*Ja*," he said softly, relaxing into the reassurance. "All right."

Done with the love-in, Ivar yanked the new circuit board out of his back pocket. The plastic protecting complex circuitry crinkled. He tossed the entire mess toward Denzeil. "That what you're looking for?"

Snagging the package out of midair, he turned it over in his hand. "Perfect."

"Need more cable?"

"No. Finished rewiring while you were gone." Doing an about-face, Denzeil headed back in the direction from which he came. "Come see. Won't take long for me to fire up the new system."

Already on the move, Ivar followed his friend around the column. Tucked into the back corner, the com-center sat inside a large nook. Away from the TV and kitchen. Easy to access. Hardly noticeable. The best of both worlds. Useful when needed, ignorable when not.

Shoving the heavy pocket door further into the wall, he crossed the threshold. High ceiling. White-washed walls. Six flat screens mounted above the wall-to-wall countertop doubling as a desk. Computer nerve center racked inside sturdy steel housing, fronted by glass doors and bolted to the concrete floor.

Fiddling with one of the sections, Denzeil inserted the new circuit board. Ivar watched the male work, flipping switches, typing in commands, booting up the system. The souped-up computer whirled. Green lights flickered across the equipment. The monitors powered up. Code crawled across the middle screen and—

"Shit."

Ivar glanced at his friend. "What?"

"Getting an alert." Gaze on the monitor, Denzeil closed the glass door and moved toward the desk. Fingers flying over the keyboard, he began a search. Seconds ticked into more, stringing him tight. A chat room popped up on-screen. Denzeil sucked in a quick breath. "Holy hell—Nightfuries."

"Where?"

"Looks like..." Attention bouncing between screens, Denzeil pieced the intel together. "Bainbridge Island. Midnight. One of the assholes is meeting someone at a diner."

Ivar glanced at his watch. Well, well, well... would you look at that? 10:47 PM. Little more than an hour away. Time and plenty to call the Razorback pack to order. Once in the city, Bainbridge Island was nothing but a hop, skip, and jump from Seattle.

Tons of time.

Few miles to travel.

Multiple avenues of attack.

The perfect opportunity to set an ambush for Bastian. A male he'd once loved and respected, but considered his nemesis now.

Excitement skittered through him. His mouth curved.

Denzeil smiled back. "Time to go hunting."

"Yippee-ki-yay," he murmured, leaving the com-center.

Pace steady, he skirted a column, jogged passed the kitchen and between two chairs. Reaching the vault door, he ducked the curved top, collected Midion and fired up mind-speak. Reaching Hamersveld had just become priority number one. The sooner his pack mobilized, the better. He didn't have a second to lose. Not if he wanted to maintain the element of surprise and blow Nightfury warriors out of the sky.

5

Bainbridge Island – Edge of Tomorrow

Mop in hand, Samantha Redhook pushed the rolling pail backward with her foot. Rubber wheels moved without making a sound across tile floor. Sudsy water sloshed in the grey bucket. She paid the swirling bubbles no mind. Same old, same old. Different night, identical outcome. A sad state of affairs, but the universe had spoken and...

Her situation was what it *was*—recent and soul-bruising.

A real confidence killer.

No sense dressing it up with ribbons and bows. Putting polish on the problem—tidying up the truth —never changed it. And denying what stared down the barrel at her? Samantha pursed her lips. Well...

There were names for that kind of behavior.

And *stupid* topped the list.

The thought made her sigh.

She needed to lighten up. Give hope a chance, stick to the plan, and start working the problem. The financial crunch wouldn't defeat her. She refused to allow it, no matter how many past-due notices landed in her mailbox. Or how often the bank called.

The most recent email-slash-threat played inside her mind.

Her throat tightened.

A death grip on the mop handle, she shook her head. At some point, the universe would shift in her favor, lighten up and back down. It was simply a question of odds. Only so much bad happened to a person before fate changed direction, eyed some other poor schmuck, and throttled *them* with its displeasure.

A lovely bit of logic.

Samantha prayed it proved accurate.

She needed a break. From the turmoil. From the uncertainty. From the constant worry that dogged her by day and interrupted her nights. Like a virus, trouble hung in the air around her, making it hard to breathe, taking its toll, making her wonder what the hell she was doing. And why she clung to tenacious belief when all signs pointed in the opposite direction. Toward her downfall and the eventual loss of her home. The only one she'd ever known.

Anger burned through her.

Taking it out on marble tile, she scrubbed until her arms hurt. Tired muscles complained. Her head told her to stop. Emotional upheaval willed her to keep going. Wielding the mop like a world champion, Samantha kicked the pail behind her and backed toward the door. In moments, she stood between the jambs.

She stepped back onto plush carpet.

The shift from hard tile to soft pile barely registered.

Eyes narrowed on the floor she was murdering, she attacked an imaginary smudge. The spot disappeared beneath a furious swipe of the mop. Practice gave way to perfection as her gaze swept the private bathroom off the head honcho's office. Searching for missed spots, she surveyed her handiwork in a corporate world gone quiet for the night.

Five weeks in, and she always got the same assignment.

Third floor.

Fancy offices.

Fine by her.

She might not enjoy working the night shift, but at least her boss liked her. Evidence of it rested in the fact he trusted her to clean the upscale headquarters of corporate raiders—otherwise known as lawyers—who expected nothing less than spick-and-span clean when they came into work each day.

She should've taken pride in her work. Basked in the sense of accomplishment. Seen the value of her efforts and given herself a pat on the back.

Most people would've.

Not her.

Accepting praise as a member of the cleaning crew felt like self-sabotage. Like waving a white flag in surrender. Insidious decline. Subtle shift in mentality. A sure sign she was headed in the wrong direction. Pretending everything was all right, when it wasn't, would only bring her more grief. More pain. More insecurity. Not what she really wanted—success in her chosen field and financial independence.

All great on paper.

Not so easy to implement in real life.

No matter how many pep talks she gave herself, uncertainty plagued her. Like a pack of piranhas, it nibbled around the edges, infusing her with doubt, insisting she should be farther along by now.

Reason insisted it wasn't true.

Everyone, after all, worked at their own pace.

Too bad pride disagreed, labeling her a failure, opening wounds best left undisturbed.

Setting the mop in the pail, Samantha shook her head. Grand would be so disappointed. She could almost see him. Salt-and-pepper eyebrows raised as he treated her to *the look*. One he'd mastered. One meant to convey a strong message—she was wasting time, allowing fear to rule and belief to flounder. And despite the obstacles standing in her way, she knew he was right.

She ought to be home in her workshop. Hard at work on the next project. Designing new configurations. Out pounding the pavement in search of new clientele. Details deep in her real profession, the one passed down from him to her, not slinging a mop for *swanky folk*.

His words, not hers.

Samantha's mouth curved as memories of him surfaced. So gruff. A terrible grouch on the outside, her loving grandfather on the inside. Ever ready with an encouraging word. Always game to teach her something new... and set her straight. The guiding force in her life, until seven weeks ago.

Flexing her hands on the wooden handle, she closed eyes. So many hours spent at his side. So much time paying attention to the little things, watching his hands move, mimicking his technique, absorbing the knowledge he wanted to impart and needed her to learn.

Grief tightened her throat. *I miss you so much, Grand.*

The words drifted inside her head. Opening her eyes, she stared at the dirty water in her bucket. Despair spiraled through her. Mental anguish became physical pain. It always did when she thought of Grand. Trying to wipe it away, she stripped off her rubber gloves and turned toward the corner office.

Neat and tidy.

Everything squared away.

Just as it should be, and still, negative self-talk surfaced, telling her she'd never make it and failure lurked around the next corner.

Knocking the ever-ready argument aside, Samantha grounded herself in Grand's belief in her. She must remember all the lessons he taught her. Keep each and every one close, just a mental touch away. What other people thought didn't matter.

She was strong.

She was smart.

She was good enough. Worthy of the best life had to offer.

More than capable of getting her online business off the ground. Her grandfather had been adamant, pushing her hard, pouring all his knowledge into her, but...

His sudden passing had knocked her off balance.

His heart attack had broken hers, spinning order into chaos, making her question the plan along with her own abilities. Could she do what he expected of her? Step out of the shadows into the light of the real world? Was she accomplished enough to achieve the goals he established for her? The bar was set high. His plan played to her strong suit and yet, worry gnawed on her, pushing into her uncertainty. Now she didn't know if she'd survive in a society—and a profession— that labeled her inferior. Handicapped. Less than capable and—

Movement flashed in her peripheral vision.

Her attention snapped towards the interior glass wall.

Mr. Choi opened one of the double doors. Leaning into the office, body half in, half out, he said something.

Her gaze tracked to his mouth.

His lips moved again.

Unable to hear his words, she read his lips. *Almost midnight. Time to pack up.*

Angling her wrist, Samantha glanced at her smartwatch. The dark face lit up. The second hand pushed time toward the top of the hour. She blinked in surprise. Wow. He was right. Time flew when you weren't having fun. If she didn't leave in the next few minutes, she'd be late for her appointment. The entire reason she'd asked permission to knock off early tonight.

Using ASL (American Sign Language), she signed, "Give me five minutes."

Accustomed to her deafness, her boss picked up the hand-delivered message and nodded.

Rolling her pail across marks left by the vacuum, Samantha inspected the desk and credenza. Dusted and wiped down. All the lawyerly knick-knacks resting in their proper place. Her focus jumped to the sitting area. Plump throw pillows lined up like soldiers along the back of the couch and sitting in comfortable armchairs. Expensive artwork housed in black frames hanging on the long wall opposite her.

Precise, level lines. Angry strokes of color behind spotless glass.

Par for her course.

Her detail-oriented brain refused to leave a corner untucked.

She enjoyed neat. Liked tidy. Needed order as much as oxygen to feel in control of her environment.

With one last look, she pushed her equipment through the open door. Wheeling the mop and pail down the wide hall, past more abstract art, she turned right into the utility room. She made quick work of dumping the water. Everything back in its proper place, she shrugged out of her Choi's Cleaning Service smock and grabbed her army-inspired jacket and bike helmet off the hook by the door. Soft cotton settled on her shoulders. The brain bucket went on her head. Finished clipping the clasp, she unzipped her backpack.

Gaze roaming over the interior, she rechecked its contents.

Sketchbook tucked in its compartment.

Invoice and authentication papers right where she left them—inside a brown envelope with a metal clasp. And sitting snug inside an ornate gold and leather case set inside a pretty box at the bottom of her bag? Her latest design. A work of art. A gorgeous piece commissioned by G, a guy she'd never met and didn't want to.

She'd had a plan.

A good one.

G blew it out of the water two days ago, refusing to pay the balance on the invoice until he inspected her work. She'd balked, insisting he do business her way. He'd held firm, listing his conditions. One—an in-person meeting. Two—to see the medallion with his own eyes before sending the last money transfer and completing the transaction.

The idea made her nervous.

She wasn't good with strangers. And in-person meet-and-greets? Acid churned in the pit of her stomach. Talk about uncomfortable. *The* nightmare scenario for her. People reacted badly when meeting her the first time. No one knew what to do when faced with a deaf girl. Awkwardness always ensued. So yeah, meeting G face-to-face didn't appeal, but beggars couldn't be choosers.

She needed the money to keep the bank at bay.

And the IRS wolves from her door.

Pace quick, Samantha resettled the medallion case in the bottom of her bag. She wanted to blame her client for being intractable. A couple messages in— that's all it took—for her to realize G was stubborn, exacting, difficult to deal with, but well... hell. Her work might be exceptional, but for what she was charging him—a cool nine grand—disagreeing with the guy didn't seem smart.

G wanted to pick up the medallion himself, so forget about using a private courier service. Time to buck up, step into the light, and do what Grand expected. It didn't matter that he was gone, never to return. She knew he was watching. She felt him all around her—in the air she breathed, everywhere she looked, down deep in her bones. Nothing left to do now but to make him proud. Which necessitated making her own way in the world... and collecting her first commission without him.

She checked her watch again.

11:51 PM.

Time to get a move on.

Myrt's Diner sat a brisk five-minute bike ride away. She didn't want to be late. Not her first time out of the gate. Perfect might be impossible, but punctual was a definite must.

A quick tug, she re-zipped her backpack.

A faster sling tossed it over her shoulder.

Leaving the utility room, Samantha made her way out of the swanky office and into the stairwell. Soles tapping against concrete treads, she descended three floors and, swinging into the posh lobby, headed for the exit. She pushed through the revolving door. Vibrations hummed against her palms as gears went to work, releasing her out onto the sidewalk. Damp March air greeted her. Breathing deep, she drew the crispness into her lungs. Gorgeous night. Not too cold. Not too warm. Just right as winter released its grip, making room for the coming spring.

Head on a swivel, attention on the wide, tree-lined avenue, Samantha crossed the sidewalk toward the bicycle stand. Practice and quick hands unlocked her bike. Unease made the hair on the nape of her neck stand on end. Something was off. Not by much. Hardly at all. Just enough for her to feel the quick shift of air. The sudden prickle of molecules against her skin. The drift from normal night to unsafe environment.

Pinpricks danced across her senses.

Her eyes narrowed on the end of the street.

Nothing and nobody.

Samantha shook her head. The creeping sensation dissipated, releasing her one talon at a time. Gripping the rubberized handles, she rolled her bike out of the looping metal. Probably nothing. Most likely nerves getting the better of her. A reaction to her unwanted, upcoming meeting with a strange guy in the middle of night, and yet...

And yet...

Might be something more.

More sensitive than most, she sensed things others couldn't. An odd whisper on the wind. Vibrations in the air. The subtle shift in a person's mood. Small things most people never noticed, but to which she was uniquely attuned. Grand believed her deafness gave her an advantage—made her more intuitive, more observant, more perceptive and aware. Useful skills in a world gone quiet, in environments that might prove dangerous to her if she didn't pay attention.

On high alert, she looked around one more time, then positioned the pedals and hopped aboard. Knees pumping, she rolled away from the building, and thankful for the glow of streetlights lighting her way, swung onto the bike path.

Toward her future.

Toward better days and productive nights.

A place where creditors and overdue bills didn't exist, and guys with more money than sense paid her to do what she loved. Hopes and dreams. Purpose and ambition. The kind that left only one thing for her to do—pray G showed up and paid what he owed... and that the strange current electrifying the air stayed static until she completed the transaction and made it safely home.

6

Streetlights eating through the darkness, Samantha jumped the curb, thrilling at the feel of going airborne a second before her tires landed on the newly laid sidewalk. Her bike jolted beneath her. A quick adjustment in trajectory. A fast rotation of her feet on the pedals. She changed gears, sprinting toward Myrt's, trying to outrun the feeling that someone watched her.

Stupid.

Probably nothing.

Just her overactive imagination playing tricks. Still...

Samantha couldn't shake the feeling. A nasty zip hung in the air, rubbing up against her skin, raising the fine hair on her nape. Something she'd experienced once before, while working late in her workshop. Same prickling sensation. Same intense vibration. She felt now like she had then—nervous, uncomfortable in her own skin, plagued by paranoia. As though someone stood outside her window... watching, waiting, debating whether or not to pounce.

Same bad feeling.

Different night.

No help for it right now.

An overdue mortgage payment dictated the play, so instead of heading for home, she brushed aside her disquiet and leaned into the pedals. Her hands flexed on the bike grips as she engaged the brakes. Rubber locked, sliding over concrete. The handlebars dipped, threatening to throw her over the front tire as she shuddered to a stop in front of Myrt's. One foot on the sidewalk, the other on a pedal, she peered through the wide front window.

Mostly quiet.

Nothing remarkable going on.

Just two old-timers, butts planted on stools in front of the long counter, ratty baseball caps tilted back, nursing cups of the best coffee on the island.

Her gaze tracked to the booths along the opposite wall. Empty. Cleared and wiped down. Sugar and condiments lined up next to the wall on each table. No G in sight. At least, not yet.

Tilting her wrist, she glanced at her watch. Two minutes to midnight. Well, good. She'd beaten him to the diner. Now, she could set up. Tuck herself into a back booth. Watch the front door. And steel herself for his reaction when she showed him the medallion in person.

Samantha drew a fortifying breath, and clinging to courage, hopped off her bike. Rolling it forward, she propped it against the front of Myrt's, but didn't bother with the lock. No need. Not here. Myrt didn't pull punches—on his turf, outside his diner or... well, anywhere, really. And only idiots messed with ex-Army Rangers.

Adjusting her backpack, she headed for the front door. A nod to a different era, Myrt's was a fixture on

Bainbridge Island. Around for decades, passed from one generation to the next, the diner boasted good coffee, the best breakfasts around, and décor straight out of the 1950s.

Hot pink walls with framed pinup girls and cartoons from WWII. Black-and-white checkerboard floors. Deep-seated booths with faded turquoise vinyl that stuck to skin in summer and was always cool to the touch in winter. A long counter down one side, round stools with bright pink upholstery that swiveled, but never moved. And more chrome accents than any one place should ever have attempted.

A throwback with apple pie charm.

A grand old dame well past her prime.

One of her favorite places in the world.

Grabbing the tarnished door handle, Samantha hauled it open. An old-school bell moved above her head. She didn't hear it, but took a moment to remember the sound. Ten years without her hearing might be a long time, but some things a girl never forgot. Like the sound of birdsong in early morning. The rustle of leaves and the rumble of waterfalls. The click of utensils against ceramic plates and the tinkling of bells above shop doors.

All right.

So the memories had faded. None were as sharp as they'd once been, but she clung to each one anyway. Remembering how things sounded made her feel normal, as though she participated in what others perceived instead of being shut out. Forever on the outside after fifteen years of being on the inside. Normal. The same. A hearing person. Not the deaf girl everyone saw when they looked at her now.

Hooking her thumbs in her backpack straps, she crossed the threshold. The smell of coffee and sweet syrup hit her as she watched Myrt look toward the door from the kitchen. Black eyes collided with hers through the pass-through. She tipped her chin. Myrt grinned back, pearl-white teeth flashing against his umber skin, eyes crinkling as he spotted her. Trim hips and flat belly leading the way, he strode out of the kitchen and back behind the counter.

The dish cloth in his hand flicked. His mouth moved.

Veering toward him, she read his lips.

"Java?" Reaching for a white mug on a tray next to the industrial coffee maker, he raised a brow.

"Fresh pot?" she asked, using her hands to sign, but also her voice. A necessity. A skill she practiced as much as possible. She might not know how she sounded when she spoke—probably a garbled mess, lacking in both pronunciation and inflection—but she didn't want to lose the ability to communicate out loud. No matter how self-conscious it made her. "Or has it been sitting a while?"

"Just brewed."

She made a gimme gesture.

"You got it," he said, grabbing the handle of the stainless-steel pot.

The scent of coffee greeted her as she stopped to pick up the huge mug he set on the worn countertop. He handed her a spoon. Samantha doctored her cup of joe, dumping four sugars into the mug.

Myrt watched her. A furrow between his brows, he shook his head.

"What?"

"Not keen on watching you poison yourself."

"Please," she said, scoffing at him, tapping the spoon against the ceramic rim, picking up the familiar argument where it always left off. "Sugar is life."

Myrt's lips twitched. "Sweet tooth. Gonna get you one day."

She shrugged. "Something's gonna get me in the end. Might as well make it something I enjoy."

"Get yourself a man, sweetheart. He'll give you something sweet every night, if you let 'im."

Her lips twitched. "Forever a romantic."

"Better that than a sugar addict."

In answer, she took a giant sip of her sweetened coffee.

He laughed, swiping the rag across the counter, finding her amusing when no one else did. A bone of contention with her grandfather. Then again, anyone as jovial as Myrt fell under immediate suspicion with Grand. Opposite in temperament, two sides of the same coin—one man gruff to the point of antisocial, the other always full of good humor.

"Don't foist your health-nut, organic-loving nature on me, man."

Myrt blinked. "Foist?"

"Yeah, *foist*."

"Big vocabulary for a little girl."

"Hell," she muttered, enjoying the banter, taking another sip of hot, sugary goodness, resisting the urge to throw the spoon at him. "You're a throwback. Spending too much time in here. You've gone 1950s on me."

Dark eyes sparkling, he grinned. "Wanna donut?"

"Is it made of wheatgrass?"

"No—quinoa."

She made a face.

He laughed again, then asked, "Why're you here so late?"

"Meeting someone."

His brows popped up. "At this hour?"

"Necessity."

"Good call, meeting here. You need me, I got a shotgun tucked away in the back."

"Good to know," she said, deadpanning, trying not to laugh. "I'll holler."

"See that you do, imp," he said, moving down the counter to deliver coffee refills to men who looked more like living skeletons than living, breathing customers.

She watched him go, thankful for his friendship. Seemed strange a twenty-five-year-old girl would make friends with a guy pushing seventy, but she had. She appreciated his honesty. Liked the way her treated her. Felt almost normal every time she stepped inside Myrt's. And no wonder.

An army vet with more mileage on his face than most roads, Myrt had seen his fair share of hardship. He understood people. Took life—and anyone who crossed his path—at face value. No judgement. Unfailing kindness. Zero pity.

A gift in many ways.

More ways in which Myrt sailed from awesome right into fantastic.

Corralling the spoon against the ceramic lip, she pivoted toward her favorite booth. She spent hours inside it each week. All hours of the night or day. Whenever she struggled with a project, she made her way to the diner. Something about the place sparked her creativity, allowing her to sink into the kind of flow that often escaped her in the workshop.

She could execute there. Mold gold. Manipulate silver. Work with bronze. Unleash her skill in tangible ways to create beautiful pieces. Design, however, was a different animal. Anytime she wrestled with concepts

—with sketching something completely new—she needed to get out.

Out into open air.

Out of the shop and home office.

Out of her own head, into mental spaces full of possibilities. Where nothing was off limits and imagination took flight.

Almost to the booth, a burst of heat swirled across her nape. Gorgeous sensation. Beautiful starburst. A nip of pleasure that cut through the lingering unease. The tight knot behind her breastbone loosened. She drew in a deep breath, enjoying the reprieve. Movement in her peripheral vision made her look toward the entrance and—

Mug halfway to her mouth, Samantha stopped short.

Her mouth fell open as she spotted the guy now standing just inside the door.

Her first thought—it was a criminal. A crime against nature for a man to be that beautiful. Tall, at least six-and-a-half feet of broad-shouldered, long-limbed perfection in flawless proportion. High cheekbones in an arresting face with a square jaw and well-defined brows. Brown eyes that glinted orange in the soft glow of overhead lights. Bronze-brown hair shorn short on the sides, but left long on top, giving him an aggressive look that both shocked and tantalized.

Striking.

A devastating stroke of masculinity.

He was sculpture come to life.

A shiver chased pleasure down her spine. Samantha drew in a calming breath as she watched him scan the space.

His gaze skipped over her.

His focus snapped right back, landing on her with

weight, pressing into her skin, making her twitch beneath his regard. Interest, already intense, sharpened in his eyes. His lips parted. Something close to awe crossed his face, sparking an equal reaction in her.

The tip of his tongue touched his bottom lip.

He took a step toward her.

Samantha battled the urge to follow suit. The sudden need to get closer overwhelmed her. Strange, but... there was something about him. A quality. A vibrance. An intensity that held her attention to the exclusion of all else. Forget the diner. Never mind Myrt looking on with amusement. Ignore the eerie vibration of foreboding still hanging in the air. She wanted to know about him.

Curiosity compelled her.

But also killed the cat.

A fact she needed to remember. Her reaction to him wasn't normal, never mind smart. Not with her nerves jangling and alarm bells going off inside her—

"You the goldsmith?"

As his mouth moved, Samantha fielded another unexpected urge. Just as strong. More compelling. She wanted to hear his voice. Ached to become intimately acquainted with his range and intonation. Was he a rough baritone or smooth bass? Her stomach dipped in longing. Her chest tightened with regret. She'd never know. Never have the pleasure of listening to him.

Her hearing was gone.

Stolen by meningitis at fifteen.

Stripped away by an illness her mother hadn't recognized in time. The delay had sealed her fate, leaving her with bilateral auditory nerve damage, but as he repeated the question, the yearning to know the way he sounded came again.

An impossible wish.

Completely bent.

But standing there looking at him, overwhelmed by his male beauty, she'd never wanted anything as much in her life. His voice would no doubt be as spectacular as the rest of him. Devastating. Deep. Delicious in ways no red-blooded woman wanted to miss.

Pace measured, eyes glued to her, he approached cautiously. As if he expected her to bolt. "Please tell me you're S.R."

"I am," she said out loud, white-knuckling her mug so her hands didn't move. Stupid, but she refused to sign. She didn't want him to know she was deaf. Not yet. She wanted to see if she could fake it. If she could fool him. If he'd notice she didn't sound normal while she prolonged the fantasy that a man as beautiful as him might be attracted to a woman like her. "G?"

"Gage." His expression said neutral. His eyes screamed interested.

A flurry of excitement rippled through her. Cupping her mug in both hands, she took a sip of coffee to cover her reaction. Sweet and bitter hit her tongue, steadying her, allowing her to complete the introduction. "Samantha. Sam, for short."

"You bring the medallion, Samantha?" he asked, ignoring her nickname.

She nodded.

"Is it in your pack?"

Strange question. One that caught her attention, then moved on to suspicion. "Yeah—why?"

His mouth curved. "Smart."

"What?"

"You're smart, but also wary. Mistrustful. Good combination in a female."

Her brows snapped together. "What're you talking about?"

"Feisty too. Full of attitude," he said, tilting his head, gaze growing sharper. "I like you better and better."

"Well, I don't like you. You're starting to piss me off."

He grinned. "Definitely mine."

Two words.

Cryptic message.

An inside joke. Or something. Samantha didn't think she wanted to know. Nor did she feel the urge to guess.

Moving toward the nearest booth, she set her mug on the tabletop. Keeping him in her sights, she shrugged the pack off her shoulders. "I've got the papers and—"

He shook his head, making her pause.

She frowned. "You don't want to see it?"

"I do," he said. "But not here."

"Not here?"

"Sorry to say, Samantha, but plans just changed."

"How?"

"Can't stay here. It's no longer safe, *volamaia*."

First Myrt with *little girl*.

And *imp*.

Now *volamaia*, from a stranger. No doubt another pet name of some kind.

Her eyes narrowed on Gage. Seriously? Had all the men in her vicinity been thrown back to the 1950s tonight?

Temper moving from brisk simmer to hard boil, Samantha clung to composure. By her fingernails. Walking out on him wouldn't get her what she wanted. Winding up and clocking him with her bag might be satisfying in the moment, but wouldn't aid her cause either. So instead, she leveled her chin and stared at him, conveying her displeasure with a look. And a serious amount of attitude.

"I'm good here. Totally safe."

"Not anymore."

She took a step back.

His lips twitched. "I'll explain later. For now, I need you to come with me."

Go with him?

Not frigging likely.

Gage might be beautiful, but he didn't look trustworthy. He looked aggressive. Strong. Tough. Uncompromising. A loaded amount of lethal wrapped in a warped sense of humor.

All in all, too much for her to handle.

But as he positioned himself between her and the door and moved in her direction, Samantha knew he was done talking. Discussion over. Commence operation *Leave the Diner*. She read the intention in his set expression. Recognized the unyielding light in his eyes. Knew by the way he held his body and flexed his hands, he wasn't joking.

He expected her to leave with him.

Really.

Seriously.

This instant.

The guy must be on crack. Or smoking something just as potent.

Shrugging her pack back on, Samantha sidestepped. Pace mirroring his, she kept him at a distance and retreated toward the back hallway. Bathrooms lay in that direction. Along with an exit into the alley. The perfect pathway to freedom, and away from Gage—customer turned crazy person.

Herding her backwards, he shook his head. "Sorry, *volamaia*. Wish I could do things differently."

Samantha didn't respond.

She was too busy figuring out how to outrun him. Fifty steps to the back door. A quick sprint around the building to her bike. Seconds, and she'd be gone, racing down the forest path to her house. All she needed to do was make it outside... before he laid hands on her and foiled her escape.

7

S talking his mate across the diner, Gage banished a pang of remorse. He hadn't lied to her. He was sorry. For his intensity. For coming on too strong. For frightening the hell out of her, sure. But mostly for what was about to happen. Might suck for him, but the situation was about to become a whole lot worse for her.

Releasing a breath, he locked down the frustration.

So much for best-laid plans, 'cause... yeah. No question about it. Samantha might not like the idea, but she was coming with him.

A shame his first encounter with her panned out this way. Given half a chance, he would've approached her in a more respectful way. Spent time. Taken her out on a date. Seduced her with purpose. Made her his in ways females enjoyed, deserved, and should expect from a male.

Nice. Neat. And normal.

Nothing about the situation, however, came close to *normal*.

He'd walked into the diner expecting to meet a human male.

He'd come face-to-face with his mate instead. A female so vibrant she took him by storm, bashing him against mental rocks, smashing through his usual calm, making his dragon half rise so hard he still suffered from cerebral whiplash.

Blindsided.

Taken off guard.

Call it whatever the hell you wanted. The sight of her—watching her move, seeing her face, realizing who she was—kicked his ass and... shit. How he'd managed to keep his hands off her qualified as a mystery.

A giant one, given his nature and the need running rampant inside him.

His restraint amazed him.

The desire to touch her had become *everything*. The air in his lungs. The blood in his veins. The magic driving his DNA.

Pace steady, eyes glued to her, he followed her retreat. He wanted her in the back hall. The closer she was to the emergency exit when he got ahold of her, the better. A few quick strides, and he'd be out the door, into the alley, and on his way.

Lots of space back there.

More than enough to shift into dragon form, get airborne... and the hell out of Dodge before any Razorbacks showed up.

"Samantha," he murmured, trying to calm her.

"Stay back," she hissed, pointing her finger at him.

He bit down on a chuckle.

Fuck, she was cute. So full of piss and vinegar, she made his blood run hot. The way she looked didn't help matters. On the petite side, but curvy. Straight, long blond hair. Brilliant blue eyes. Golden freckles on her pale skin, making him think of sugar sprinkles.

Beautiful sunbursts of bioenergy raging around her. Intense. Surging. So potent he struggled to contain his reaction.

Flexing his hands, he locked down the urge to lunge at her. Took a breath. Took a beat. Took what he needed to recalibrate, allowing the gap to widen between them.

Didn't work.

Unsurprising.

Fixated on her, his dragon half refused to power down. The longer he looked at her, the worse it became, moving him beyond need into compulsion. Fierce yearning opened inside him. Now all he could think about was her skin against his. What her hands would feel like in his hair. And her taste. Goddess preserve him. He wanted to know what she tasted like... *everywhere*. Her mouth. Her pulse point. Each tiny freckle. The sensitive spot behind each knee. The slick heat between her thighs.

His imagination fired, supplying details.

Bet she tasted incredible.

Bet she'd be an experience. A gorgeous trip into the unknown as he connected to the Meridian through her and fed his vicious side. He'd reward her, of course. Push her beyond pleasure. Make her come over and over. Again and again. Satisfy her so well, make her scream so hard, her throat would go from husky to hoarse and—

Inching backward, Samantha swiped a sugar jar off the countertop. Glass. Heavy. Vintage. The style matched the diner. Not his thing, but somehow, the hot pink and turquoise decor went together, giving the place a cool, retro vibe.

She raised the jar.

He shook his head. "Don't throw it."

"Leave me alone. This doesn't have to become a thing."

His mouth curved.

Become a thing.

Seriously fucking cute.

Especially since, it was already *a thing*. At least, for him.

"Put it down, *volamaia*," he murmured, calling her "wildcat" in Dragonese.

Her gaze dropped to his mouth. "What?"

Her confusion raised his instincts. Primal need twisted toward logic, forcing him to think.

He repeated the instruction.

Her gaze stayed on his mouth, making him realize she did that... a lot. Too much. More than normal, or the right reasons—like physical attraction, and the desire to be kissed.

Trying to puzzle it out, Gage opened his senses wide and... there it was. A spark of *otherness*. A whisper that suggested *different*. Something about her was off. Underdeveloped or damaged. Unfed by the powerful energy she owned. Hunting for an explanation, he unleashed his magic. The air heated. Magnetic threads spun into invisible bands, frothing out in front of him, moving to surround her. He pulled the threads, searching, unearthing, reading her energy.

No answer came back. Just a semblance of *something*.

He couldn't put his finger on it. Didn't know what he sensed, but it was in her voice. In the rounding of consonants and flattening of vowels. Her accent wasn't one he recognized, and having been raised in Europe, he knew many of—

"*Gage.*"

The growl exploded inside his head, lashing through mind-speak. *"Give me a second, Haider."*

"No time, man. We've got inbound."

"How many?"

"Multiples. More than one pack," Bastian said, the zip of electricity cracking through the link. *"Too many males from too many directions. I can't get an accurate count."*

Shadowing Samantha's retreat, Gage adjusted his trajectory. Every time she shifted, he followed. Slow movements. Steady increments. Trying his best not to scare her as he herded her toward the rear of the diner and turned B's comment over in his mind. Multiple dragons inbound. No headcount. Information B couldn't break down.

Unusual, given his commander's unique talent at dissecting enemy males' strengths and weaknesses from a distance.

"Razorbacks?"

"Not all of 'em. Some I don't recognize."

He bared his teeth. *"Zidane. His death squad has landed."*

Reacting to his fury, Samantha flinched.

Regret cranked him tight. He raised his arms, hands out, palms up, the gesture reassuring. "Easy, Samantha. It's all good. Just straightening a few things out."

She made a face. One that communicated plainly she thought he was crazy.

He smiled, enjoying her attitude.

"Maybe," Haider said, sounding eager for the fight. Gage understood. His best friend wanted to kill Zidane, as much as he did. *"Intel's still sparse, but—"*

"It's a good guess." Scales clicked. The sound of wings flapping sounded as Bastian took flight. *"Haider*

and Nian—hunker down, watch Gage's six. Rikar, Sloan —with me. Mac, Forge, and Ven—fly north. Wick—you're rover, under radar. Let's beat the bushes, boys. See who flies out."

"B—"

"Don't fuck around, Gage," B said, tone soft, almost melodic. A sure sign the Nightfury commander meant what he said. Expected orders to be followed and Gage to toe the line. *"Grab the medallion and get out."*

In theory, a great suggestion.

In practice, impossible to follow given his mate sat in the kill zone.

Goddamn it. What a clusterfuck.

Trust a female to blow up a good plan.

His strategy had been simple. Use the goldsmith as bait. Put a giant X on his back by flying in solo. Grab Osgard's birthday present and get out before fireballs started flying. But with Samantha in the mix, the original bait and switch went from great idea to upside down and backwards.

"Slight problem," he said, stepping right as Samantha veered left.

"Figures," Mac said, pissy attitude joining the party. *"Using you as bait was bound to backfire. Motherfucking maniac."*

Forge snorted.

Gage killed the urge to roll his eyes.

Frost crackled through the link as Rikar chimed in. *"Do you have him or not?"*

"Her," he said, putting the Nightfury pack on alert.

Jar raised like a weapon, the female in question snarled at him.

Attention half on her, half on the conversation, Gage took a second to admire her spirit, along with her form. She knew what she was doing. Arm cocked at the perfect angle. Hand positioned just right and... hell. She presented a puzzle he wanted to solve. Strong stance. Quiet voice. Loads of attitude. Soft heart. How he knew that about her amounted to another mystery. His female was full of contradictions. Her expression and squared shoulders screamed *don't mess with me*. The slight tremble of her fingers and uncertainty in her eyes conveyed something else. A vulnerability he recognized and, despite his aggressive nature, wanted to protect.

The pregnant pause lengthened as his brothers-in-arms absorbed the information.

Venom broke the stalemate. *"Her?"*

"Yeah, man... her. An HE. My mate."

"Shit. You sure?" Rikar asked, surprise in his voice. *"You touch her yet?"*

"No," he said, knowing what the Nightfury first-in-command meant. *"Don't need to touch her. My dragon half's already locked on."*

"Fuck," Haider muttered. *"Get her out of there, man."*

"Plan to, but she's..." Gage paused, wondering how best to describe the look on her face. Perturbed? Yep. Obstinate? Absolutely. Intent on cracking his skull open with a jar of sugar? Without a doubt.

Haider cursed. *"Let me guess—uncooperative."*

"Bordering on homicidal."

Nian huffed. *"Your favorite kind of female."*

"Shut it, namby-pamby," he said, slinging his favorite insult at the male. As a former member of the Archguard—once celebrated, now reviled—Nian made for an excellent target. *"Like you're any different. What was her name again?"*

Taking the bait, Nian growled. *"I'm going to rip your tail off and shove it down your throat."*

Gage chuckled. Fuck, he loved teasing the male.

The pansy-ass prince never disappointed. Though, he was getting better. Despite his cushy upbringing, Nian was learning, growing into his warrior skin, allowing nature to win out.

About time.

After months of standing on the sidelines, Nian was finally engaging, throwing his weight around, making his presence known. A good thing. Excellent progress. Fun to watch, 'cause... yeah. Lethal was always welcome inside the Nightfury pack. And despite the blue blood running through his veins, Nian wielded the kind of brutality Gage couldn't help but appreciate.

"*Lads—focus,*" Forge murmured, thick Scottish brogue out in full force. "*Squabble later. Move yer arses now.*"

Gage nodded, even though no one could see him. "*Give me a minute.*"

"*You got two,*" B said. "*Rogues approaching the three-mile marker. Fifteen males. Five fighting triangles.*"

"*Might need more than that, B. I don't want to—*"

"*Buddy,*" Venom said with a wealth of understanding. "*You're gonna scare her, no matter what. Just get it done.*"

Sound advice.

Terrible outcome.

Samantha wouldn't react well to him locking her down and...

Shit.

He hated to do it, but his hands were tied. Hauling Samantha out of the diner was the safest bet. The most responsible move. Knowing it, however, didn't mean he liked the idea. Not without her consent. A female's choice mattered. Was paramount, but as heavy static morphed into intense sensation, clawing down his spine, Gage knew every second counted. Stalling wasn't smart. Neither was nursing the urge to coddle her. Shield her. Protect her from what was about to land outside the door.

Becoming more aggressive, he walked forward. "Listen to me, Samantha. I—"

"Back off."

"Can't do that."

"I'm not going with you," she said, a warning in every word.

"You are, wildcat," he said, hoping she heard the apology in his voice.

Aura flaring like a supernova, she scuttled sideways.

He pressed his advantage, watching the show, loving the intensity of her bioenergy. Gorgeous bursts of bright orange energy. Scorching in intensity. Potent in its power. So beautiful she stunned him with the majestic complexity, by embodying the Meridian, the most powerful force on Earth.

Each surging strobe of energy heightened his hunger, making his blood rush and his dragon half yearn to hunt. To chase. To capture and conquer. Not the best urge, given the situation, but well...

She unearthed, then dragged primal instincts to the fore as he tapped into her frequency, taking what she owned and had yet to share. Without compunction, he connected without touching, tunneling into her emotional grid. She blinked as his bioenergy collided with hers. He pushed the boundaries, linking in, burrowing until she gave ground, accepting the wave of soothing energy.

Her throwing arm started to drop. She swayed, absorbing the magical current, breathing with him as her biorhythms aligned with his.

"Good. That's good, Samantha. Take my hand."
Reaching out, he brushed his fingers against hers.

Energy arched from her into him.

Samantha jolted. Her eyes widened and—

She jerked backward, defying his magic, breaking his hold. The thin threads tethering her to him stretched, then snapped. The cosmic link detonated. Gage flinched. His female hissed and, swinging the jar, aimed for his head. He raised his arm to protect his face. Her hand collided with his shoulder. The top flew off the sugar jar. White grains exploded out, then rained down as he rotated his hand and grabbed her wrist.

Pulse point snug against his palm, he pulled her toward him. The Meridian reacted, zapping him with a white-hot current, invading his chest, stealing his air. Choking on shock, knocked senseless by his mate's potency, he sucked in a breath. Then lost it again when Samantha elbowed him in the ribs. A second later, her heel slammed into the top of his foot.

Pain streaked up his leg.

He grunted. "Fucking hell."

Being as gentle as he could, he wrapped her up, back pressed to his front. He lifted. Her feet left the floor. She reared, attempting to reverse head-butt him. He countered, locking his frame, using his strength, pinning her folded arms against her chest.

Teeth bared, she tried to bite him.

"*Volamaia*—stop."

"Asshole—let go! You're out of your mind!"

"Samantha, baby, listen to—"

Click-click.

The sound stopped Gage short. His gut went cold. A shotgun. The motherfucker behind the counter pointed a *shotgun* at his back.

"Take your hands off her," a deep voice touched by a hint of New Orleans rolled through the quiet. "And back away—slowly."

Struggling to control the female-turned-hellcat in his arms, Gage kept his back to the human. If the gun went off, he didn't want his mate getting hit. So instead of doing as instructed, he widened his stance, tucked Samantha closer, making himself a bigger target, and let his magic roll. Magnetic force supercharged the air around him. His sonar pinged, laying out a grid inside the diner. Intel boomeranged, returning to him, allowing him to see without looking. The picture formed in his mind as he assessed the level of threat.

One male.

A lone human standing behind the counter. Single barrel shotgun leveled on him. Hands steady. Resolve firm. Not a lightweight like the others curled up on the floor, taking shelter between pansy-ass, pink-topped stools.

Well, shit. So much for situational awareness.

Normally, he paid closer attention. Did his duty first. Resisted fucking around. Taking precious minutes to soothe Samantha had not been time well spent. No matter his aversion to forcing her out of the diner, he should've grabbed her and made tracks off Bainbridge Island.

His bad.

Something to kick himself for later.

But honestly? In his defense? From the moment he laid eyes on Samantha, he hadn't been able to see anything else. Forget the humans inside Myrt's Diner. Brush aside the weird color scheme and crazy decor. Ignore the threat of Razorbacks about to land outside the door. His mate held his attention to the exclusion of all others, making him feel like a dumbass. Like a youngling. A green, inexperienced warrior with skewed priorities, dulled senses, and every bit of his attention behind his zipper.

Gage sighed.

Smooth. *Real smooth.*

He'd mucked up the entire situation. Made it worse by trying to do the right thing, instead of kidnapping her right out of the gate. Now, instead of one problem, he had two to solve. In rapid succession. Question was: did he kill the human on the way out the door? Or play nice and just maim the idiot holding him at gunpoint?

8

Temper slanting toward savage, Samantha bucked to break Gage's hold. Huge hands kept her wrists pinned to her chest. Locked muscles created a cage around her. No give. Zero leeway. Complete lockdown. And yet he hadn't hurt her.

His grip on her wrists wasn't bruising.

The cage he made with his body didn't contract around her.

He held her gently, containing her without deploying viselike pressure.

Gage wasn't even breathing hard. Frigging hell. Totally crazy. The nutjob needed to be taken down a notch. Or seven, but... no chance of that happening. Not right now. No matter how hard she fought, he held firm, making her face facts. She was screwed. Caught, contained, and furious with no way out.

The realization made her want to commit murder.

Uncaring, he wielded his superior strength, lifting her like she weighed nothing, containing her with little effort, unfazed by her efforts to maim him.

She hissed at him.

His mouth moved against her temple.

He was saying something, talking to her, trying to

calm her. His gentleness pissed her off. The least a kidnapper could do was act like an asshole. Rough. Uncaring. Brutal and beyond redemption. But as Gage walked backward with her in his arms, defying her will, blasting through her boundaries, brushing aside her resistance, he treated her with care.

Precision in motion.

Gentle lockdown deployed.

Patient in the face of her freak-out.

Heart thumping, fear rising hard, she fought harder, threatening him with every horrible thing she could think of. Nothing. No reaction to her warnings. No forward progress for her at all, which showcased her weakness in blinding color. Bright blues. Brilliant reds. Stunning yellows. Every hue flashed through her mind, swirling, mixing, burning helplessness into her brain. His strength terrified her. His control, the restraint he showed, floored her. No matter what she did, he countered. A little shift to the right. A minor adjustment to find better balance as she raged against him.

Diabolical.

Almost admirable.

Frustrating as all frigging hell.

Particularly since she couldn't yank her hands free. Couldn't unleash her fists and hit him the way she wanted. He'd taken the possibility of her landing a punch away, bending her elbows, folding her arms inward, containing her so effortlessly, she screamed in exasperation and... unleashed her feet.

Kicking backward, she aimed for his shin.

He widened his stance.

The heel of her boot sailed wide of its target. She redoubled her efforts and reared. He turned his head to the side. The back of her skull rammed into his collarbone. Pain radiated, slamming into her temples. She jerked. He tightened his hold, tucked in closer, nestling his mouth against her ear, keeping her from head-butting him.

His mouth moved again.

She didn't bother to turn her head. Didn't try to see his mouth or decipher the movement of his lips against her skin.

Gage planned to take her against her will.

He had no right.

She hadn't given him permission and—

Gage stilled against her. He stopped backing toward the door.

Samantha registered the change, but didn't react at first. Busy fighting, she continued to struggle, determined to throw him off balance.

His lips ceased moving as he raised his head. The underside of his chin brushed the top of her head. His hands contracted around her wrists. The flex and release told a story. Conveyed a message, one she read in her bones, alerting her to a new kind of tension coming from him.

A warning.

A precursor to something.

And not something good.

An odd vibration sizzled into the air. Fine hair on the nape of her neck stood on end. Samantha shuddered as the ominous ripple rumbled through the diner, over her already frayed nerve endings. Blistering heat rose, making heat bloom on her skin and awareness rise.

Strange.

Unnatural.

Completely crazy, but...

She felt everything. Perceived Gage in ways that

weren't possible. Beyond the physical. Beyond the feel and scent of him surrounding her. Perception tore wide open. The inky tendrils tunneled deep, connecting with intuition, only to magnified. Her blood rushed. Her body became hypersensitive as the odd vibration sank deep.

Through her skin.

Into her muscles and bones.

Down into the heart of her.

Shivering, Samantha turned inward. A link to something opened inside her. Something strange. Something otherworldly. Something that felt *inhuman*. Every breath she took strengthened the sensation, heightening her senses, connecting to her an emotional grid not her own. Focused on the connection, she examined the bridge from her to... somewhere else.

She drew in a shaky breath. "Is that you?"

Gage nipped the edge of her ear. *"You feel me?"*

"I hear you," she whispered, disbelief giving her shell shock.

"Inside your head?"

Chocking on the idea, unable to speak, Samantha nodded.

"Fuck, that was fast," he murmured. *"I haven't even fed yet."*

Her brows collided. "What?"

"Later, volamaia. Company's coming. Time to go."

Samantha didn't react to his decree. His words barely registered. She was too busy freaking out as shock spun her around the lip of insanity. Panic sailed into her mental harbor. Her chest compressed. Her gut went cold. What the hell was going on? What was happening? Who was he? Every question she wanted answered collided inside her head. The noise coalesced as fear stole her ability to think straight.

It wasn't possible.

She hadn't heard a sound in ten years. And yet...

And yet...

She heard him. Clearly.

Deep voice. Soothing tone. Enthralling sensation dancing across her skin, making it difficult to breathe as thoughts not her own sounded inside her head. The blurry outline of a plan assaulted her. The distinct impression of limited time entered her mental space. Words like *egress, flight path* and *packmates* bounced around her brain. Samantha blinked as brilliant images swamped her. All clear. Strict attention to detail. None of which made sense.

More words winged into her mind.

His words? Or hers?

She couldn't tell. The lines had blurred inside the weird connection, dragging her in, even as she tried to claw her way out. The link solidified, clicking into place, sinking inside her.

Samantha jolted against him. "Holy crap."

"Quiet."

A solitary word.

Immeasurable joy.

Samantha started deep-breathing. "What's going on?"

"Later," he muttered, his deep voice coming through loud and clear.

Battling tears, she gripped his forearm. "Gage."

"Shh."

"Say something else. More than one word."

She wanted to hear his voice for more than a split second. A couple of words weren't enough. She needed whole sentences. An entire book's worth in order to wrap her brain around the fact she was hearing him. Really *hearing* him—a voice, for the first time in ten years.

He sounded real—his baritone concrete, solid, tangible.

She knew her own voice.

Sort of.

She felt her throat vibrate every time she practiced. She'd worked for years to remember how to form the words. Practiced speaking every day to keep up the skill. Asking Grand about her enunciation, forcing him to sit and listen while she read aloud, ensuring she held onto the only thing that truly belonged to her—her voice. Didn't matter that she couldn't hear it. Who cared that she didn't sound normal, like a hearing person, anymore? All that mattered was holding onto the ability to communicate with the wider world.

Holding onto that piece of herself.

The connection amplified. Static washed into her head.

"Get ready, Samantha. When I move, it'll be fast."

"Who's coming?"

"I'm dealing with it. Just be ready—yeah?"

Drawing a breath, she shook her head. She needed to know what—

Gage growled.

Sound waves crested, then crashed, rippling into a symphony inside her head. Devastating. Beautiful. Freaking painful. She wasn't used to the sensory input. Couldn't hold all the noise. The concussive blast spilled over, unleashing a stream of agony behind her eyes.

Gaze locked on something behind him, Gage tucked her closer. The symphony stopped. Pain downgraded. Sound disappeared, leaving her with the usual silence as the temperature changed. Heat poured out of Gage. He adjusted his grip. Both of her wrists captured in one of his hands, he wrapped his arm over her chest as the air thickened, taking on a strange bronze hue.

The haze intensified, expanding to envelop the back booths.

Danger.

This is what *danger* felt like. Clawing. Cloying. Searching for a way to break free.

Crazy, maybe, but Samantha recognized the tension. Connected to it in a way she couldn't explain, but knew existed. Rational arguments held no sway. Intuition ruled, spoon-feeding her information. Sips and swallows. A little at a time. The shift in atmosphere spoke volumes. The tightening of Gage's muscles completed the picture, telling the story louder than words. The change in him signaled trouble. The kind that came with screaming, dying and... explosions.

Focused on the man vibrating against her, Samantha tensed as Gage pivoted. Slow rotation. Precise and controlled movements. Her gaze jumped over the pass-through beyond the long counter, over the stools sitting like soldiers in front of it and—

Her gaze landed on Myrt.

She sucked in a quick breath as she grasped the *why* behind Gage's reaction. Dark eyes flat, expression set, Myrt stood behind the counter. Hands steady, finger curled around the trigger, he leveled a single barrel shotgun at the man holding her against his chest.

Samantha swallowed around the lump in her throat. "Myrt, put it down."

"Not until he puts you down."

The right outcome.

One that wasn't going to happen.

Not like this.

Gage didn't seem like a guy who enjoyed ultimatums. He seemed like one who excelled at taking out targets. He was too focused—too aggressive, too entrenched—to do anything other than get his way. Which placed a bull's-eye on Myrt. And honestly? Samantha didn't like her friend's odds. Not after what she sensed coming from Gage. He was out of Myrt's league, ex-Army Ranger or not. Which meant if her friend didn't back off, he'd end up hurt. Or worse... dead.

Not something she wanted on her conscience.

What happened next would be her fault, if she didn't contain it.

"Gage—you can't hurt him," she said, going for calm and quiet, hoping her voice conveyed the right message.

Volume control had always been difficult, but under stress? Her ability to modulate worsened. With Gage's hands on her and Myrt holding a gun, it went from bad to worse. Had she said that out loud, or inside her head? Had Gage heard her? Was the spooky mind-meld-voodoo working? She didn't know. Couldn't tell. Was turned around and upside down inside her own senses.

The buzz scratched at her temples.

His deep voice rolled inside her head. *"I may have to, wildcat. We need to leave. I don't have time to talk him down."*

"I don't know what's going on, but..." she paused to take a shaky breath. "If you want me to walk out of here without a fight, Myrt doesn't get hurt. That's my condition."

He huffed. His breath caressed her cheek. *"You're coming with me either way, but—"*

She growled at him.

His lips twitched. *"I'll see what I can do."*

"Yeah, you do that," she muttered, feeling the growl in the throat.

"Behave, wildcat. Be just a second." Nipping her earlobe, he released his grip on her wrists.

His hand slid from around her wrists.

His gaze met hers. She saw the shimmer. A weird glow. A harbinger of strange things to come. Or awful ones. She couldn't be sure, but... *shit*. She had a bad feeling. A terrible one about Gage and his methods. Something told her his approach wouldn't involve gentleness. Not when it came to Myrt. Or anyone other than her.

Samantha opened her mouth to remind him his promise.

She didn't get the chance.

Baring his teeth, he snarled at Myrt. The haze inside the diner thickened. A strong metallic smell rolled into the air, assaulting her senses. More than sulfur. Less than dirty gasoline. The smell combined the two, mixing into toxic swill, delivering a warning a second before Gage flicked his fingers.

The shotgun barrel jerked, slamming into the coffee maker.

Knocked sideways, Myrt reeled backward.

The lights flickered.

Utensils flew out of drawers. Forks, knives and spoons streaked into silver blurs, whipping across the diner. Samantha ducked and, arms curved over her head, watched the massacre as culinary tools joined the parade. Heavy appliances levitated in the kitchen. Pots, pans, and an alarming number of butcher knives slammed through the pass-through. Moving at warp speed, the mess smashed into the wall behind her.

Sharp knives sank into the plaster. Dust puffed out, raining down as steel spatulas dropped like stones, hitting tabletops before bouncing off booth seats and falling to the floor.

Her mouth fell open.

With a curse, Myrt fell, disappearing behind the countertop.

Gage made a fist.

Stuck to the steel side of the coffee maker, the shotgun whirled in his direction. He caught it with one hand as pots and pans rolled across the checkerboard floor. Dented on one side, a saucepan stopped a foot away, then rocked in place as though trying to soothe itself.

"He's alive." Expression fierce, Gage glanced at her. Eyes glowing with orange fire, he raised a brow. *"Satisfied?"*

Well.

Not really, but...

Talk about wild—and weird—and maybe, even a little bit wonderful. He hadn't hurt her friend. Not really. He'd stayed true to his word, knocking him on his ass instead of killing him. Much appreciated, although the mess inside the diner gave testament to Gage's level of unhappiness. Trashing the place hadn't been necessary, but done to make a point.

One she noted.

He didn't appreciate having a gun leveled at him.

Good to know. Onward and upward. Time to tackle the next problem. Namely...

How to avoid going with him.

She glanced toward her bicycle. Still propped up against the outside wall. Undisturbed. Right where she left it. Mind churning, Samantha performed the necessary calculations. Fifteen steps to the front door. Seven more across the sidewalk. Twenty seconds tops and she'd be on her bike, racing across the road, away from Gage, and onto the forest trail.

She shifted to the balls of her feet, getting ready to run.

"I wouldn't advise it." Transferring the shotgun from one hand to the other, he stretched his hand out, palm up, inviting her to take it. *"A deal's a deal, and you've pissed me off enough for one night,* volamaia."

"Right," she whispered, heart hammering so hard she felt it in her temples and wrists. Shifting toward the front door, she tried to decide. Renege on the deal or not? Running seemed like the best option. The more sensible choice, but as she met his gaze and he held hers, fascination battled with prudence, throwing the practical approach off track.

Her hesitation was the opening he needed.

Lunging toward her, he reached for her.

He didn't make it.

A second before he made contact, the diner shook. Gage cursed. Samantha's attention snapped toward the front of the diner. The question on the tip of her tongue died. Horror replaced it, stealing her air as a monster appeared out of thin air, rooting her feet to the floor.

Grabbing her on the run, Gage hauled her into his arms. Struck stupid, she didn't fight him. She kept her eyes glued to the window as he threw her over his shoulder and, without looking back, sprinted toward the rear exit. Unable to look away, Samantha stared at the beast.

Her mind rebelled as her brain took a snapshot.

Dear God in heaven. She wasn't seeing things.

A dragon stood on the blacktop outside the diner. Dark brown scales shimmering under the streetlights. Huge hooked claws gouging faded asphalt. Pointed fangs bared, saliva glinting off a nasty set of razor-sharp teeth. Black eyes aglow with citrine light, spike tail swishing back and forth, the beast hissed at her through the glass an instant before it exhaled and a fireball shot from its throat.

9

G rabbing his mate on the fly, Gage hauled her off her feet and glanced over his shoulder. Her breath caught as she landed hard, bumping up against him. He didn't pause to gauge her response. Didn't stop to make sure she was all right. Didn't look down to see the look on her face. He kept going, preparing for the onslaught, counting off the seconds, too busy lulling Zidane into a false sense of security to worry about what his mate thought about him manhandling her—or the fact she wasn't screaming.

A reaction that would've been justifiable.

More than valid, given who stood outside. It wasn't every day, after all, that a human got to witness Drag-onkind in action. And Zidane wasn't hiding.

Not bothering with a cloaking spell, the prick stood out in the open. Less than ten feet from the din-er's front door, giving Samantha an eyeful of dark brown scales, bared fangs, and black eyes glowing yellow with fury.

The Archguard prince in all his glory.

Zidane was right on time. Playing the game just as Gage expected, letting arrogance rule, leaving himself open to attack. Though, sad to say, the male didn't have a death wish, making sure his kill squad set up within striking distance, hoping to catch Gage in the open and off guard.

An unlikely scenario.

He'd clocked the enemy pack's approach minutes ago. Sensed the kill squad's progress, tracking the idiots as Zidane flew in low, slithering across Bainbridge Island, trying to slip under his radar. Other than hitting Haider up, he'd let the scenario unfold without giving up the game.

Stupid, maybe, but...

Fuck it.

Already behind the eight ball, he decided to play along. To use his mate's stubbornness (Samantha might be gorgeous, but her feistiness threw up obstacles) to his advantage. Instead of fighting with her, he made an executive decision and changed the plan. One Haider and Nian both objected to, but... whatever. He was the one on the inside. The one with the clearest view.

His packmates would adjust while he reeled Zidane in. Playing fox to the kill squad's hound wasn't his usual MO, but some situations called for unconventional methods. So far, the strategy was working. Zidane, the dumbass, took the bait, landing on the street, putting a bull's-eye on his scales.

Fireball notwithstanding.

The coming inferno should've concerned him. It didn't. Probably said something about him. A whole lot of nothing good, but then, he'd always been a grab-a-dragon-by-the-tail kind of male. Long odds suited him. So did violence, the bloodier the encounter, the better his dragon half liked it. But as the fireball sizzled in the back of Zidane's throat, orange glow reflecting in wide windows, making the humans inside the diner scramble into the kitchen, Gage didn't stick around.

He made tracks.

Boots thumping across checkered linoleum, he shifted Samantha. Slinging her over his shoulder, he ran around the end of the long counter. Flames flashed in the corner of his eye. Magic warped the interior of the diner. Hot pink walls and turquoise booths disappeared behind a wash of yellow film. His senses throbbed as a rank odor filtered in—sulfur and jet fuel mixing into toxic swill.

He knew the scent.

Recognized the stench.

Had breathed it in, along with the pain, inside a kill room. A room that now sat five thousand miles away, unlike the male crouched outside.

Arrogant prick.

Begging to be set free, his dragon half flexed deep inside him. His beast wanted out into open air. Needed the fight. Longed for payback. The need for vengeance rode him hard, threatening to derail him.

Gage locked it down.

Moving too fast, giving up his advantage, wasn't a smart play. He wanted Zidane to remain overconfident. In the kill zone. Otherwise, the slippery bastard would buck the constraints and escape into the thick fog rolling over Bainbridge Island.

A circumstance Gage refused to contemplate.

He'd waited months to get his claws on Zidane. No way would he mess up the best chance he was likely to get. A clear shot. A straight arrow from goal to mission accomplished. The satisfaction of ripping Zidane apart—of hearing the screams and reveling in the scent of dragon blood tainted by the filth of Dragonkind aristocracy—drove him. He wanted it more than he remembered wanting anything.

A sizzle burned through the air.

Reacting to the warning, Gage reached for his magic.

His dragon half uncoiled, and he got ready. He must time it just right. No matter how much he wanted to kill Zidane, Samantha came first. He needed to get her out of the line of fire. Tuck her somewhere safe, then go back for her. Not optimal. Or advisable with a female as strong-willed as his mate, but outnumbered by the enemy, Gage knew the fighting would be fierce. And like it or not, he couldn't fight with her curled up in his paw and hope to get her out unscathed.

Accustomed to hunting other Dragonkind, Zidane's warriors were well trained. More deadly than most of the Razorbacks. So, yeah. The next few minutes mattered. For him, no question. For Haider and Nian too. But he worried more for his mate.

The idea of her being hurt cranked him tight.

His dragon half reacted to the unpleasant thought, propelling him forward. He hauled ass into the corridor at the back of the diner. His senses throbbed, giving him a timeframe. Counting down the seconds, he glanced over his shoulder. Five. Four. Three. Two...

Blastoff!

The fireball erupted from Zidane's throat.

He yelled at Haider. *"Shield up!"*

"Done," his best friend growled. *"Move your ass."*

"Nian—"

"I got your six. Get out the back door and airborne."

Gage didn't answer.

Snarling at the door, he unleashed a wave of magic. Magnetic force tore through metal. Hinges twisted. Steel screamed. The door blew outward, cart-wheeling into the alleyway. Blasting over the thresh-old, Gage cleared the frame. He shifted mid-stride, transforming from human to dragon form. Tucking Samantha into one of his talons, he leapt toward the wall opposite him. Sharpened for battle, his claws struck brick. Chunks of stone crumbled, slamming into dumpster tops as he climbed the side of the building.

The instant he reached the top, he unfolded his wings and launched skyward.

Caught in an updraft, he spiraled up and scanned the sky. Wings extended, he banked hard as the fire-ball slammed into Haider's force field.

Flames splashed out, then up, licking over the in-visible barrier.

Buildings along Main Street shuddered. Street-lamps rattled. Car alarms went off, shrieking as trees caught fire and orange flames reached the top of the shield. The curved lip acted like a slingshot, whipping the fireball back in Zidane's direction. The male jumped sideways to avoid the fiery backsplash.

Too little, too late.

Zidane roared in pain as the blaze engulfed him.

The smell of scorched scales blew into the wind.

Gage grinned, baring fang. Excellent. Perfect de-ployment. He loved his friend's ability to conjure force fields. Invisible. Strong. Undetectable. All of it worked in his favor, luring the leader of the kill squad in. The inferno might not kill the bastard, but it would take him down a notch. Weaken his magic. Make him vul-nerable in the coming battle, easy pickings for him and his brothers-in-arms.

"Holy hell," Samantha wheezed, sliding around in the center of his palm.

Glancing down, he checked on her. Wide-eyed. Pale-faced. One hundred percent freaked out. Completely normal under the circumstances.

He should probably say something, attempt to reassure her, but as he swung into another turn, flying hard to join his wingmates, looking for a place to hide his mate, he knew nothing he said would help. She needed time—to process and come to terms with who and what he was—the Dragonkind male who planned to keep her.

So...

No sense talking.

Little reason to waste his breath. Explanation would come, but not right now.

He must find a safe spot to secure her. He needed his talons free and her out of danger as fast as possible. Before Zidane and his squad launched another attack.

Scanning the sky, Gage pinged his best friend.

"Hold on," he said, pushing the instruction into her head.

She jolted as his voice penetrated.

Her eyes teared.

Gage frowned, distracted by—

A black dragon uncloaked, broadsiding him at full speed.

His head whiplashed. His lungs spasmed. His muscles contracted. Shock bled into agony an instant before he whirled into a body-torquing spin. Wings bent at odd angles, spiked tail lashing empty air, he lost altitude, plummeting into another mind-bending rotation. He heard Samantha scream. Gage tried to hold on, but he got hit again, and Samantha flew out of his talon, rocketing into open air.

S houlder aching from the collision, Azrad bared his fangs. Goddess help him. Talk about a stupid move. Ambushing Gage didn't qualify as a good idea. Under normal circumstances, he would've gone through proper channels or—

He snorted.

Toxic mist rose from his nostrils as he contemplated the truth. *Proper channels*, his ass. Nothing about him veered toward the straight and narrow. Out-of-the-box thinking suited him more. Summed up his attitude. Was the strategy he employed most nights.

Banking wide right, he cranked his head around. Night vision pinpoint sharp, his gaze caught on the Nightfury warrior. Metallic orange-bronze scales flashed. Magnetic field warping the air around him, Gage spun across the night sky, losing altitude.

Yeah. No doubt about it. A completely stupid move.

A pissed-off Nightfury was a dangerous animal, but...

Beggars couldn't be choosers.

He needed Gage. Everything hinged on the male agreeing to his plan, and with the Razorbacks watching closely, it wasn't as though he could hit Gage up in the usual way. The second he opened a line of communication, he'd blow his cover, out his friends, and get them all killed.

Gritting his teeth, Azrad marveled at his bad luck. He liked to think of himself as a skilled strategist. As a male who always had a solid plan. One who saw all the variables, made split-second decisions, and executed with precision. Tonight kept proving him wrong.

The plan started out simple enough. His play wasn't that complicated—lie in wait, time it right, get the Nightfury's attention. But with the Archguard kill squad taking up valuable real estate, slamming into Gage, spending him spinning mid-flight, became the best he could come up with on the fly. Which made him question his sanity.

Along with his commitment to the cause.

Wanting to rescue the high energy females imprisoned by Ivar was one thing. Putting himself in Gage's line of sight was quite another. He'd gone over it, then over it again. No other option existed. They needed the brutal SOB. Without Gage, he couldn't see a viable way forward.

Kilmar and Terranon wanted him to go to Bastian, but...

Azrad shook his head. Contacting his older brother—commander of the Nightfury pack—amounted to a bad idea. As much as he longed to be a part of Bastian's life, his new-found sibling couldn't help. Not with this. Not in the way that would work long term.

A shame.

Total mind-fuck territory, given he yearned for the kind of relationship only true blood kin could provide

—the camaraderie and closeness most males never experienced. Not in his world. As a species, Drag-onkind was too competitive. Familial connections were hard to come by. Par for the course when most warriors weren't born of the same female, never mind inside the same household. The divide bred mistrust. The separation ruined families, making it difficult to create kinship, beyond the association of individual packs.

A world divided.

One he'd felt isolated inside until he discovered the truth.

The second Prosper—the Numbai who once served his sire—gave him his father's journals, he learned about Bastian. The realization he had a blood brother, that he wasn't alone, sent him hunting for the Nightfury commander. The trail of information brought him to Seattle. Luck did the rest, providing him with an opening—a way into his older brother's good graces and the Nightfury inner sanctum.

Positive outcome.

Forward momentum in the right direction. Until he hit a snag. A big one that threatened everything he worked toward. Which made Gage's involvement un-avoidable. Paramount in every way that mattered. Bat-shit crazy too, given the Nightfury warrior's level of lethal, but...

Complicated circumstances called for unorthodox solutions. Hence his rash decision to blindside a Nightfury most considered unstable. Add in violent. Throw on merciless. Top it off with destructive to the point of scary. Label the warrior whatever you wanted, but after watching and waiting for weeks to find the right Nightfury to approach, Azrad understood the truth. Gage might be volatile, but he wasn't stupid. If he played his cards right, led the male far enough from the fighting, created a safe space, the Nightfury would listen.

Before he tore his head off.

For something he hadn't counted on and couldn't control.

Eyes on the sky, Azrad blew out a breath of frustration. Talk about bad luck. He'd timed the ambush perfectly. Had accounted for every variable, expect one—the female Gage protected. He hadn't counted on *her*.

A bad turn.

Awful timing.

The pinnacle of unlucky.

But then, unexpected things showed up in the middle of missions. A smart male knew when to pivot. Adjust. Make a new plan. Like right now.

Wheeling into a hard turn, Azrad kept his eye on the female. Ejected from Gage's talon by too much g-force, her body arched as she launched skyward. Opening his wings, he tucked into a tight spiral and sliced beneath her. He waited for her upward motion to stall. Her momentum stopped. She hung in midair, beneath a blanket of clouds, above pinpricks of street-lights below, almost floating. A second before gravity grabbed hold, he made his move.

He flicked his talon.

Tiny holes opened in the ends of his overlong, jet-black claws.

Strong as steel, gossamer threads shot from the hooked tips, spinning across the sky, spanning the space between her and him. The sticky strings surrounded her, then caught hold, enclosing her in a ball of spider-spun webbing. With a murmur, he knit the edges together, weaving a rope of unbreakable threads. Winding the tether around his paw, he opened his wings and flipped upright.

Encased inside the web, she swung wide like a wrecking ball.

The rope pulled tight.

The webbing flexed around her. A damp updraft caught her gasp as she whipped full circle below him.

Gage roared behind him.

Azrad took off, blasting away from town with the female in tow.

Not his original plan. Not even his second, third, or fourth choice. Using a female as bait never amounted to a good idea when dealing with the Nightfury pack. Bastian's warriors were picky that way, but—

Metallic orange-bronze scales flashed in his peripheral vision.

Powerful magnetic force clawed at the tip of his quadruple-bladed tail. Sensation sizzled over his scales. Discomfort edged by pain sank deep. His muscles twitched. The spikes along his spine rattled.

Azrad gritted his teeth. Shit. He'd known the Nightfury was powerful, but... shit. The magnetic field Gage wielded was fierce. Body-torquing brutal. Mind-bending in intensity. More than uncomfortable—deadly, if he let the warrior get too close before he was ready.

Quick and quiet.

He had it all planned—the location scouted, the timing set and his speech prepared. Now all he needed was for Gage to rein in his attitude long enough to listen.

A long shot, but... hell. Long odds were better than certain death.

Keeping an eye on the female swinging in his net, and the other on Gage flying like a male possessed in his wake, Azrad increased his wing speed. Not too fast. Not too slow. He didn't want to lose the Nightfury, just keep him chasing while avoiding the lash of lethal magnetic force trying to drill holes through his scales.

Flying fast, Azrad opened a link through mind-speak. Static hissed into his head as he pinged his friends. *"Mission accomplished."*

"He's in the pipe?" Terranon asked, deep voice rolling on an Australian accent.

"Bearing down on me like a pissed-off viper."

Kilmar snorted. *"What'd yah do?"*

"I broadsided him, then..."

"Then?"

"Stole a female."

A pause. Nothing but radio silence coming through the connection.

Seconds ticked past. One after the other, while his friends absorbed the information. The silence spoke volumes. None of it good.

Dropping his affable Aussie demeanor, Terranon growled. *"Random chick or—"*

"His?" Kilmar said, finishing T's thought. A usual occurrence when the two males got going. *"Goddamn it, Azrad. Don't tell me you're messing with another Night-fury female."*

"Don't know. Don't care. He's on my tail, giving chase, so—"

"You're fucked." Kilmar sighed, sounding aggrieved. *"I'm turning around. I'll be there in—"*

"Stick to the plan," Azrad said, rocketing toward the north end of the island. Deserted area. Far from prying eyes. Innumerable clearings to set down in and set up fast. *"I can handle him."*

Terranon snorted. *"Buddy—this is Gage we're talking about. He doesn't have an off switch."*

Kilmar seconded the opinion. *"He's going to gouge your eyes out and piss in your dead skull."*

Lovely visual.

Not what he wanted to hear with the warrior in question on his tail.

"Trust me," he said, knowing he asked a lot. His warriors might love him, but after what Kilmar and Terranon had endured, trust came hard. The risk, though, was worth the reward. He needed Gage invested. On his side. Able to help when he requested backup. No way he wanted to go into Razorback lockdown without having a solid line open to the Nightfury pack. *"Keep it tight. Cover my absence. Ivar and Sveld can't know I'm AWOL. If either gets wind I'm gone—"*

"I know," Terranon grumbled, resignation in his tone. *"Get it done, Azrad. But if you can't, get the hell out. We can only play keep-away with the Nightfuries for so long."*

Didn't he know it.

Being undercover with the Razorbacks meant fighting against his brother's pack. Or at least, looking like they were. Playing pretend, however, came at a cost. One he kept weighing, and Bastian didn't like. Given a choice, his big brother would've pulled the plug on the operation months ago. Azrad understood. Really, he did. Might make him a jerk, but he enjoyed the idea Bastian worried about him.

He was eyeballs-deep in nothing good.

Risked everything inside the Razorback pack.

Anything could go wrong.

He navigated the dangers every day. Weighed the risks every night... and discovered something interesting about himself.

He was good at this shit. Excelled at subterfuge.

Evaded with ease. Lied and deceived, using every weapon in his arsenal to trick and divert. Kind of surprising given his shaky beginning in life. But prison had taught him innumerable lessons. Things no male ever forgot. Experience had molded him into something more—a skilled operative with excellent instincts. So...

Like it or not, he needed to trust his gut.

Now, with Gage dogging his ass, was a prime example.

Locating the break in the trees, Azrad reeled the female in and went wings vertical. He sliced between two giant oaks, then set down fast. His talons raked over the ground. His claws caught. Green moss and dirt exploded into the air, raining down around him as he flicked the rope. Trapped in the sticky webbing, the female revolved in a circle above his horned head. She cursed. He slowed the rotation and, with a murmur, looped the cable over a high branch.

She swung like a pendulum ten feet off the ground.

Sliding sideways, Azrad rocked to a stop halfway across the clearing. Tree branches creaked. Quiet fell. He counted off the seconds, waiting for Gage to reach him and, drawing a deep breath, prepared for the showdown.

An orange glow broke through barren tree branches.

Ancient oaks lashed the night sky, thrashing under pressure.

A spine-curling magnetic pulse blasted through thick forest. Bark blew off massive tree trunks. Debris kicked up, blowing old leaves across the large clearing. Crouched like a cat, heart racing, adrenaline pumping, he planted himself between Gage and the female... and got ready to fight.

SPEED SET TO APOPLECTIC, Gage rocketed out of heavy cloud cover. His night vision tightened the screw, allowing him to see everything in stark detail. New buds unfurled on treetops, dancing across the forest canopy. The texture of the tree bark and brittle leaves lying like dead soldiers on bent root structures. The ripple of water rolling onto the end of the island. He saw it all as he scanned the ground, dragon senses honed to a fine point, searching for signs of Samantha.

Nothing yet.

Little to go on but a thin hunch.

One that cranked him tighter by the moment.

Worry took up the cause, picking him apart, making his scales click and his horns tighten. His sonar pinged, hunting for a threat, but... fucking hell. Talk about a bonehead move. He never should have left the diner without a taste. Without opening a link and tapping into Samantha's bioenergy. A sip of her essence. A single point of connection, and he would've been able to track the unique signal she left in her wake—from anywhere. Across rough terrain. Over mountain tops. From as far as five hundred miles away.

Which drove home a simple fact—having scruples sucked.

If he'd forgone the usual niceties, he wouldn't be flying blind now. Or stuck looking for a needle in a haystack. For the brilliant flash of his female's aura across a dark stretch of forest in the middle of the night.

Tweaking his night vision, he switched to infrared, looking for telltale signs of female energy and body heat. A faint glow snapped his head to the left. Wings spread wide, he veered toward it, following the faint streak—the fading light—across the forest floor. Dialed in, he fine-tuned his sonar. Magic crawled through his veins. A sharp ping echoed inside his head and—

There.

Just up ahead.

A mile from the water's edge. Breaking through the tangle of twisted tree limbs.

His focus narrowed on a clearing. The glow intensified. His dragon half snarled, zeroing in, sensing Samantha from five hundred yards away. Tucking his wings, Gage rotated into a spine-bending spiral. His velocity increased. Wind kicked off the end of his jagged horns. White contrails hissed, blazing behind him as aggression turned the screw, honing instinct to an even sharper point.

Another flash of orange.

More blurred traces of body heat.

Rage rolled through him, upping his level of volatility. He wanted to kill the male. Hurt the warrior who'd taken his female. Make him flail, scream, and beg for mercy. Over and over. Again and again. He couldn't wait to sink his claws into the idiot. Prove his worth and protect his mate while he took the male apart for daring to touch a female who belonged to him. Primal instinct cemented the desire, shoving prudence aside, making Gage twitch with impatience.

He could almost feel the splash of dragon blood on his scales. Knew the scent of death and wanted to smell it again. Needed the satisfaction of supremacy.

Of absolute dominance as he watched the asshole squirm while fear sparked in his eyes.

Flying in fast, he aimed for the clearing. X marked the spot. In the narrow space between thrashing branches and massive tree trunks. Gage tucked his wings. Blowback slammed through the parkland. Wood moaned. Bark blew off the trees as his paws slammed down.

Forward momentum propelled him across the open space.

His gaze went from shimmer to brilliant glow as he slid, battle-sharpened claws ripping grooves in the ground. Debris kicked up. Piles of leaves blew in all directions, dusting his scales, whirling between thrashing trees. Looking for any sign of Samantha, he searched high and low, every inch of open terrain.

Fucking hell.

Still nothing. Weird as hell. Worrisome too, given he sensed her. All around. The throb of her bioenergy so powerful his dragon was tuned in, but unable to pinpoint her exact location. And yet, he knew she was here. Somewhere. Cloaked in heavy magic. Hidden away by—

His gaze struck the male standing across the clearing.

Rage injected savagery into his veins. Gage inhaled hard, preparing to unleash hell. Liquid metal and poison combined, pooling at the back of his throat. Rocking to an abrupt stop, he bared his fangs.

Liquid metal splashed over his tongue.

A noxious smell spilled into the air.

"Shit—wait!" Already in human form, the warrior dove sideways, taking cover behind a tree, scrambling to avoid his lethal exhale. Good plan. The nastiness of his liquid metal couldn't be measured. A combination of heavy metal and corrosive elements, the lethal cocktail turned anything biological into living statuary, enclosing males in an inescapable shell. A slow death. Singularly unpleasant. Warriors went mad as hours turned into days, then weeks, inside their own bodies. "It's Azrad! Jesus, Gage, it's me. Your female's all right. Swear to Silfer, man—she's okay."

The yell made him pause.

Hot swill bubbling in the back of his throat, Gage debated.

Kill the little prick or not?

Bastian wouldn't be happy. His commander encouraged his warriors to have impulse control. Add that to the fact B would prefer his baby brother remain in once piece and... hell. He couldn't do what he wanted—unleash hell and give the idiot what he deserved for the crap he'd pulled tonight.

A slow, agonizing death.

Tip of his spiked tail twitching, Gage snapped his jaw closed. His razor-sharp teeth slammed together. The loud click of enamel echoed through the quiet. Frustration took hold as he swallowed. Liquid metal scorched his insides, making his throat hurt and stomach burn.

Fucking Azrad.

The prick was a pain in the ass, crossing boundaries most warriors knew better than to approach. B's brother had a knack for pushing the envelope, taking risks and using his relationship with the Nightfury commander as cover in whatever fucked-up game he decided to play next.

Annoying.

Frustrating.

Batshit crazy.

And even though Gage wanted to nail the male for

being irresponsible, he knew better than to act before he listened. He'd learned that from Haider. His best friend knew how to play the game, and given the risk Azrad took tonight in reaching out, Gage understood the stakes.

Azrad might be reckless, but he wasn't stupid.

Which meant... something was wrong. Very, very wrong.

Firing up mind-speak, he pinged his best friend. *"H—got a development. I'm off-grid. You good?"*

"Never better." The sound of wind whipped through the connection. Claws shrieked against scales. Bones snapped. A male screamed. Haider laughed. *"Been a while since rogues came out to play. Fuck, man... this is fun."*

Gage huffed. *"Glad you're enjoying yourself."*

"Whatcha got?"

"Azrad. Forced meeting... the little prick."

A pause, then...

"You need backup? Nian and I can break—"

"No. Hold the line." Tilting his horned head, Gage eyed B's brother. *"I'll keep you posted."*

"Your mate?"

"Unhappy. In one piece." Probably. He hoped. Prayed. Gage clenched his teeth. At least, she'd better be, or Azrad would end up a statue in the middle of nowhere. *"I'll let you know when I'm airborne."*

More screaming.

Haider laughed again. *"Later."*

"Yup," Gage said, severing the connection, annoyed he wasn't in the fight. Sounded like a good one. The kind of claw-cracking battle a warrior hated to miss, but... he clenched his teeth. Seemed as though he was destined to fight a different battle tonight.

Shifting from dragon to human form, he returned

his attention to Azrad. Eyes riveted to the tree Azrad hid behind, he conjured his clothes. Faded jeans and a long-sleeved Henley settled on his skin. Stomping his feet into his motorcycle boots, he growled, "Get out here."

Leaves rustled.

Azrad popped out from around an old oak. Shimmering indigo eyes met his.

Gage bared his teeth. "Where is she?"

Dressed in jeans and a beat-up army jacket over his bare chest, Azrad stepped over a fallen log into full view. The red spider inked into the side of his throat gleamed in the moonlight. The metal stud piercing his eyebrow winked as he glanced toward the branches overhead. "Up there."

He looked up, but saw nothing. His brows collided. "Where?"

Murmuring in Dragonese, Azrad flicked his fingers. The cloaking spell he controlled expanded. Pushed out and up. A cone of silence dropped over the clearing. Air stilled. Mist hovering above the turf froze as the walls became opaque, blocking out their surroundings, freezing the moment in time.

Cool trick.

Powerful magic.

Gage didn't care. He was too busy staring at Samantha.

Caught inside a net, she dangled from a high branch—attitude in full flame, angry energy making her aura glow bright orange. His lips twitched as relief hit him. Thank the angels. Give the Sun Goddess her due. Azrad hadn't lied. His mate looked healthy and whole. No bruises on her skin. No scrapes that he could see as she struggled inside the netting. More web than rope, the filaments were odd. White.

Gossamer thin. Strong as hell, thin threads cable-like as though Azrad commanded elements of metal, but...

If that were true, Gage should be able to sense it.

Metallics—the subset of Dragonkind that manipulated metal—always recognized each other. Gold, silver, copper or bronze, warriors of his subset gravitated toward one another. Fast friendships formed. Brotherhood usually followed, but Azrad wasn't easy to read. No matter how deep Gage mined for information, incomplete intel came back. Magical lines blurred, scrambling the results, twisting the usual acceptance into mistrust.

His eyes narrowed. "I sense the steel. What kind of dragon are you?"

Azrad shrugged, acting as though the question didn't bother him.

Gage knew differently. He might not be able to read the male's magic, but he saw his face. Recognized the unease in his eyes and the tension in his body for what it was—uncertainty.

He raised a brow. "What kind, man?"

Holding his gaze, Azrad stared him down, refusing to answer.

"I'm here for a reason, Azrad. You want my help—tell me."

A muscle flexed in the male's jaw. "I don't know what I am. No one's been able to tell me."

"No one?"

"I seem to be an amalgamation. A mix of magical abilities."

"Have you—"

"Hey, assholes!" Samantha yelled, a load of pissed off drifting down from on high. "You mind?"

Azrad blinked.

Glancing up, Gage grinned. "How you doing up there, wildcat?"

"You're dead when I get down."

"Not much incentive for me to—"

"Gage," she gritted, vowels rounded, speech less clear. Intuition flickered again, warning him. His magic contracted, hunting for the reason. Samantha distracted him, turning his attention, yanking at the netting. "Stop being a jerk."

She sounded tough.

Gage knew better. He read the fear in her bioenergy and hated he was to blame. She'd been through hell tonight. Her reality had been torn wide open by the realization Dragonkind existed. Her tidy world wasn't so tidy anymore. His fault, not hers. Even so, he refused to regret it. If he hadn't messed up and asked her to make the medallion, he never would've met her. Wouldn't be staring at his mate. Or have the chance to woo and win her... to make her his for life.

Determination pushed playfulness aside.

He must start as he meant to go on. She was scared. He reacted to her distress. The undeniable need to protect and soothe—to wipe away her fear— overwhelmed him.

Immediate impulse.

No need to learn the behavior.

His dragon understood what to do and how to act.

"Okay, *volamaia*," he said, meeting her gaze. "Give me a second. Azrad..."

"Yeah, man. Got it," the male said, unleashing his magic.

The tree limb she was tied to creaked and swayed. The cable started to uncoil, lowering her toward the ground.

She drew a shaky breath.

Attuned to her, Gage breathed with her. In. Out. Catch and release. Synching his biorhythm with hers, he allowed her to tap in and borrow his calm. Her chest hitched. Holding her gaze, allowing silence to rule, he sent a wave of magic to surround her. Soothing ripples. Calming vibrations. The chaotic thump of her heart downgraded to more normal ranges. Not perfect. Not even close to settled yet, but...

It was a start.

Her acceptance pacified his dragon half. Gage exhaled long and slow, willing her to follow his lead as she approached the ground. Azrad opened his mouth. Gage shook his head, warning the male to stay quiet. He didn't need the male in the mix. And Samantha didn't need the reminder they weren't alone.

She was freaked out enough.

The magic-fueled cable continued to unwind.

Samantha dropped another foot. And another, coming within range. Five feet above his head. Now four. Then three. The instant she came within touching distance, he sliced through the webbing with a mental swipe, cutting through steel filaments wrapped in gossamer thread. The pocket encasing Samantha tore open. She spilled out. He caught her mid-tumble, pulling her into his chest.

Side pressed to his front, she took a swipe at him.

Her elbow came around.

With a huff, Gage blocked the blow.

Samantha growled. Frustration spiraled into the energy field and... Gage grinned. Goddess, she was adorable. Scared half to death, and still she remained wild and fierce. Her indomitable spirit impressed him. Her gorgeous scent caught his attention. Her lithe body—small, strong, curvy—aroused his, making him react in predictable, but wholly inappropriate ways.

Grappling with him, she kneed him in the thigh.

With a grunt, Gage shut her down. Gently. Using his superior strength against her, he pulled her into his embrace, trapping her against him. It wasn't fair. It wasn't right, but even as he told himself to let her go, his arms tightened around her. Chest pressed to her back, he wrapped one hand around her wrists, set his mouth to her temple, then cupped her throat.

She shivered.

Gage murmured in reassurance. He refused to make the same mistake twice. The nature of his kind dictated the play. He needed a taste of her. A small one. A couple of swallows. Just a little of her bioenergy to ensure he never lost track of her again.

With her snug against him, he burrowed beneath her surface. The Meridian rose to greet him, tying him to her... and her to him.

She made a low noise. "What are you doing?"

"It's all right. Settle, Samantha. I'm not going to hurt you."

"You—"

"Easy, wildcat."

Hands warm on her skin, he set his mouth to her temple and opened the connection. The Meridian surged. Powerful energy rushed through the link. Ravenous hunger hit him. Gage groaned as he got his first taste of his mate. Glorious power. Delicious and life-affirming. Beyond all experience. Unlike anything he'd ever felt.

Samantha quivered in reaction.

Locking down his greed, he drank in gentle sips, keeping the flow light, soothing her while he took what he needed to keep her safe. Battling the need to take more, to drink deeper, he kissed the shell of her ear and pulled away. *"All done, baby."*

She swayed in his arms.

Her eyelashes fluttered.

A second later, he got what he wanted—the sight of her pretty blue eyes. Holding her gently, he turned her in his arms. Undone by the feeding, she blinked a slow up and down. Stroking her back, he mined her energy field. Life force humming. Gaze unfocused. Body relaxed. Brain foggy. All good. No need for worry.

He asked anyway, needing a verbal response. *"All right?"*

"No, I feel weird," she said, slurring her words a little.

He smiled. *"You'll get used to it, volamaia."*

Unable to keep her eyes open, she leaned into his embrace.

With a murmur, Gage pulled her close, loving the feel of her, enjoying her trust, grateful to have her in his arms.

A shuffling sound came from behind him. "Does it come naturally?"

"What?" Gage asked, having forgotten about Azrad.

Brow furrowed, Azrad stared at Samantha, then glanced at him. "The gentleness? The patience?"

Seeing his confusion, Gage raised a brow. "You ever been with a female?"

"Yeah, but..." The male paused, then gestured to him and Samantha. "Never like that."

"Comes naturally to a male with his mate."

Azrad opened his mouth, then closed it again. "Jesus, man. No wonder you nearly killed me."

"Still might," Gage muttered, patience waning. The comment soured his mood, reminding him he owed Azrad for stealing Samantha. Bruises, for sure. Maybe even a couple of broken bones. No one touched his mate. Not even by accident. "You gonna start talking— or do I need to beat you with an ugly stick?"

Head tipped back, gaze on his mouth, Samantha whispered, "I vote for the stick thing."

Gage snorted.

Azrad rolled his eyes. "I need a lifeline."

"Why?"

"I'm in, Gage. Right inside the inner circle. I've been given first pick," Azrad said, excitement sharpening his features.

"Of what?"

"The HE females Ivar's got imprisoned inside his lair."

Rage sparked, fizzing inside his veins. "You gotta be kidding me."

Azrad shook his head, confirming his worst fears. "It's fucked up, I know, but I won the dragon combat competition, so I choose first."

"When's this happening?"

"No clue," Azrad said, rolling his shoulders as though the conversation made him uncomfortable. "No parameters. No location. It's hush-hush. Need-to-know, secret ghost-spy shit."

Secret ghost-spy shit?

Sounded like a bad movie.

Gage frowned. "And you want me... why? To pull your fat out of the fryer when it goes bad? 'Cause man, I gotta warn you—Ivar's far from stupid. It's gonna go bad."

"Not if I play it right. Not if I have the right backup." Flexing his hands, Azrad put himself in gear, pacing away from him, then pivoted and walked back. Plugging him with an intense look, the crazy SOB continued, "I might not know the setup—where

I'll meet the females, or how many days I'll get with the one I choose before the Meridian realigns, but..."

"Let me guess," he said, scowling at the male. "You've got a plan."

Flexing his hands, Azrad nodded. "Yeah. A good one."

"Might as well re-label it a death wish now, and be done with it."

"I have to do it. I promised Bastian. I—"

"B'll understand, Azrad."

Stubborn, clearly set on impressing big brother, little brother dug in. "I'm going to get them out. Every single one of those HE females—I'm gonna make sure they're safe. Best case scenario, I'll be let inside the main lair, the one Ivar shares with his personal guard, but—"

"Fuck, I get it," Gage said, understanding Azrad's dilemma. "He could set you up anywhere. Safe house. Warehouse. On a ship in the middle of the ocean."

"Yeah. No clue what he's got planned. Ivar doesn't share widely. Not even sure the warriors who live with him know what he's up to. But the Razorbacks in the rank and file? Those males have no idea what's really going on. None know the plan ahead of time."

"Smart," Gage muttered, tucking Samantha closer. Caressing her in slow sweeps, he slid his hands down her back. Up and down. Feeding her energy. Keeping her relaxed. "You know who'll be joining you inside Ivar's little shop of horrors?"

"Two of the five."

"Who?"

"Kilmar and Terranon."

Azrad's best buddies. The male might not be batting a thousand, but he was close. At least, he wasn't headed into the enemy's inner sanctum alone. "Lucky."

"Not really. KK and T are strong fighters. We placed one, two, and three in the competition." Kicking through a pile of dead leaves, Azrad sent debris flying. The smell of decay and damp dirt whirled into the air. "As for the two other males involved—I can guess, but there's no way for me to know until Ivar calls the meet."

And Azrad wanted to hedge his bets before that happened. The male was setting up an escape hatch, one only he and the Nightfury pack could guarantee.

Gage grunted as the truth hit him. "The theatrics tonight—you attacking me—subterfuge and misdirection. You want one of us to link in, create a cosmic connection with you."

"Not just any Nightfury—you."

Cupping Samantha's nape, he set his chin on top of her head. "Why me?"

"Magnetic force."

One corner of Gage's mouth curved up. Of course. Elementary. He should've guessed. Azrad wasn't just smart. The male might be a genius. The superconductor in Gage's mind produced enough magnetic force to disguise any connection he made with Azrad. Strong link. One hundred percent undetectable by other Dragonkind warriors. A huge plus, given what little brother planned to walk into... all to take down a tyrant and save a handful of human females.

Commendable.

Honorable.

A move worthy of his and Bastian's ancestral line.

Eyes narrowed, he assessed B's brother. Azrad stared back. Solid. Confident. Powerful with the smarts to back up his play.

Between one moment and the next, Gage made his decision.

Adjusting his hold on Samantha, he picked her up. She inhaled deep and exhaled slow. Some of her tension returned as he walked around Azrad and set her down on a fallen log. Hitting his haunches in front of her, he brushed thick, blond strands out of her eyes. Soft tendrils tempted him to do more.

He shut down the inclination and, fingers curled around her jaw, leveled her chin. Her gaze met his, then dropped to his mouth. "Sit tight. I'll be back in a second, and then we'll go. Get you home—yeah?"

Her throat worked as she swallowed. "Sure."

With a nod, he pushed to his feet and turned toward Azrad. He moved into the center of the clearing, going toe-to-toe with the male. His gaze began to glow. A shimmer of bronze washed into the air, painting the inside of the cone of silence orange. "Get ready."

Azrad nodded.

Gage didn't hesitate. He sent out the signal. Sharp, stunning, spear-like, his magic spiraled through space. Powerful barbs struck. Azrad stumbled backward, cursing as Gage entered his mind. The male's dark lashes flickered. His body jerked. Gage showed no mercy, using experience and his strength to deploy the mental hooks, digging through cerebral space.

Powerful magic exploded around him.

The barbs sank deep.

Mental strings formed, braiding into connection, allowing him to feel Azrad. Holy fuck. He'd been right. The male was powerful and also... a bit of a mutt. A curious blend of magical origins. No clear dragon subspecies embedded in his DNA. Azrad's dragon half was mixed race—half spider, some earth, fused with equal parts venom and metallic.

Magic flexed.

Azrad flinched. "Fuck."

More information came through the threads.

"*B know any of this about you?*" he muttered, opening mind-speak, forging a stronger bond, burying the link deep. So deep no one but him would ever find it.

"*No,*" Azrad rasped, the low sound full of pain. "*I've only ever linked in with Kilmar and Terranon.*"

"*No Razorbacks?*"

"*Fuck, no. Don't want any of those idiots inside my head.*"

Gage snorted in amusement.

The cosmic connection solidified, becoming tangible, alive in a way only magic could manage. A deep sense of brotherhood bled through the bond, infecting him, hammering Azrad.

Gage held the link a moment more, then let it go, allowing it to forge its own pathway. "*Link's solid. You reach out—anywhere, anytime—I'll hear you.*"

Azrad opened his eyes. He blinked. Once. Twice. A third time as the glow in his eyes moved from shine to shimmer. Inhaling deep, he exhaled smooth. "*Thanks, man.*"

Gage tipped his chin, feeling the male's gratitude like a punch to the throat. "*Go. Before you're missed.*"

His new brother-in-arms nodded.

One last look, and he dismissed Azrad. Time to grab his mate and go. Boot soles churning in exposed soil, he turned toward his female. Only to find the log empty and Samantha gone.

11

In a fight to end all dragon fights, Sloan split the difference. Revolving out of a tuck, he went wings vertical, slicing between two enemy males. The pair adjusted, flipping in midair, staying on his tail as more rogues joined the fight. A smart move. More than he expected from the Razorback pack.

The idiots were better trained than he remembered.

All that time away.

Over a month off-grid, tucked away, nowhere near Seattle and the city center. Now Sloan knew the why behind the disappearing act. Ivar had been busy training the more inexperienced members of his pack. Good plan. One that was paying off, as enemy warriors grouped together, their mission clear—swarm him, then down him.

Why?

Good question.

Most of the time, the Razorbacks tried to slice his and his packmates' throats. Not tonight. At least, not with him. Instead of trying to kill him, the bastards kept trying to corner and catch him.

Gritting his teeth, Sloan dove toward the ground.

Jagged stone teeth rose from the cliffside, snarling at the night sky, standing tall as ocean swells rolled in, crashing against the rock base. Salty spray splashed over and around boulders buried in the surf. The smell of brine blew into the air.

His sonar pinged.

Night vision razor-sharp, Sloan checked his six.

Four males had become five.

Flying in formation, the pack split in two. Three dogged his tail, searching for ways to hem him in as the others banked right. Instinct told him the duo was more dangerous. More experienced fighters. More powerful magic. More intense vibe.

Sparking mind-speak, he pinged his wingmates. *"Boys—got a problem."*

"Where the hell are you?" The snap of fangs echoed inside his head. B's voice. Soft, almost melodic, dangerous as all freaking hell. *"Power down the earth dragon shit. I can't track you when you're throwing off that much energy. Muffles the signal."*

His mouth curled. Good to know. Even better to exploit. *"Thought I'd take a walk on the wild side."*

"Sloan—don't be a dumbass," Rikar said, frost dragon raging as arctic chill blew through the connection. *"Get back—"*

"Gonna play a little longer. Something's not right with these assholes."

Rikar snorted. *"What was your first clue? We got a mix of nothing good."*

"What're you sensing?" B asked, ignoring his first-in-command's comment.

"Odd mix. Got five on my tail," Sloan said. *"Three are serious about bringing me to ground. The other two—the more powerful males—are playing. Making it look good, but they don't seem serious."*

Rikar grunted.

Bastian growled. *"Scale color?"*

Wind rattling his spikes, Sloan blasted around a rocky outcropping. A quick twist. A faster dive. A string of evasive maneuvers, and the trio dogging him lagged behind, losing sight of him in the rocky terrain. Rocketing over the treetops, his horns tingled. Sensation raked his scales. Glancing over his shoulder, Sloan adjusted his trajectory and...

Yeah.

Right there.

The pair looked aggressive. Were flying hard, keeping up, chasing him, but Sloan knew better. The warriors were dancing the dance, with no plans to take it past touch and go. Zero contact. No intimacy. Just two-stepping, making it look good so they could say they tried.

His eyes narrowed.

"Sloan," B said, the snarl in his tone conveying a message. His commander was losing patience.

Which meant...

He better start talking—fast.

"Rogue one—lime green scales with black accents. Acid dragon, maybe," Sloan said, guessing, providing what intel he could while in flight. *"Rogue two—huge male. As big as me, but tri-eyed."*

"Tri-eyed?"

"Warrior's got six eyes, B—three on each side of his head. One's damaged and... Jesus. Never seen that before."

"Are his scales bright copper?" B asked. *"Corroded green edges?"*

"Yeah."

Rikar huffed. *"A Metallic?"*

"Looks like it. Powerful SOB. Both males are fast in flight, but... give me a sec."

He broke off to gauge the threat level.

Slicing between two rock faces, he slowed his velocity to reel the duo in. A risk. One he shouldn't be taking, but he couldn't shake the feeling something was wrong. For Razorbacks, the pair was off-script, making him wonder what the hell was going on... and what the males would do when he tested them.

Radar up and running, he tracked the pair. One went low, rocketing after him into the ravine. The other flew high, maintaining a dragon's-eye view. Both slowed and sped up when he did, maintaining a precise distance.

"Neither are engaging." Sloan frowned. *"It's freaking weird."*

"Not really," B said, sounding resigned. *"You got a black dragon hiding in the weeds?"*

Widening his net, Sloan sent his magic rolling. *"Just the two. No lone male anywhere on my grid."*

Rikar sighed. *"Azrad."*

Bastian grunted. *"Probably."*

"Terranon and Kilmar?" Sloan asked, the idea taking hold.

The theory made a lot of sense.

He didn't know Azrad and the warriors who shadowed him well—had never seen either in dragon form—but given the game Azrad and his friends played, that wasn't surprising. Horns-deep in Razorback territory, the trio was so far undercover, all of the Nightfuries worried they'd never get out. Bastian wanted to pull his little brother out. Azrad refused to let him. The male was on a mission, one honor made him cling to like a drowning man to a sinking log.

"Drop the shield, Sloan, and engage," Bastian said, calling the play. *"Give Azrad's boys cover and—"*

"*A few bruises too,*" Rikar muttered, claws shrieking against enemy scales.

Sloan hummed. "*Plausible deniability.*"

"*Exactly,*" Bastian said, wind whistling through the connection. His commander snarled. An enemy dragon screamed as the sound of snapping bone echoed inside his head. "*They go back beat-up, no one can say they didn't fight. Go gently, Sloan, but make it look good. Give 'em something to complain about. We'll finish up here and meet you around the tip of the island.*"

Coming up over a sharp outcropping, Sloan banked hard. Shaped like a scorpion's, the tri-pronged stingers on the end of his tail swung as he whipped around. Lethal barbs spun on the tip, revolving like bombs, ready to be thrown. Fangs bared, he snarled at Kilmar, warning the male.

Lime green scales flashed as the male put on the brakes, but—

Too late.

He was already in the kill zone, flying down the pipe.

Lining him up, Sloan twisted into a sideways flip, giving the male time to react. One second stretched into two before he flicked the end of his tail. Full of flammable scorpion venom, round stingers with spiked exteriors spun off the tip. The instant the bombs left his tail, three identical ones grew back, restocking his arsenal as the bombs he launched whistled through the air.

Seeing the load of lethal, Kilmar ducked, then dodged.

Bright green webbing stretched.

Timing the flight, Sloan propelled each stinger, directing the lethal cocktail. Two bombs curled away, flying wide. The third he allowed to hit Kilmar's shoulder. Venomous liquid splashed up and out, coating lime green scales. The acrid smell of acid blew into the air. He saw the male's eyes widen as the poison clawed through his scales. Fire licked over his interlocking dragon skin as the particular brand of poison caught magical fire.

Hissing in pain, Kilmar wing-flapped, losing altitude.

Torquing up and over, Sloan grabbed the male's tail. With a snap, he flipped the male upside down. Kilmar went topsy-turvy. Damp air slammed into him as the big male wing-flapped. Watching white fire rage over Kilmar's shoulder, he counted off the seconds.

Three.

Two.

One.

Reaching out with his mind, Sloan snuffed the flames. He could've let it burn. Could've left more than a mark on Kilmar, but that wasn't the objective. Not tonight. Not while playing keep-away with Azrad's buddy.

He wanted to scorch Kilmar, not leave him with permanent damage.

Playing his part, he went after the male. Kilmar played along, grappling with him as Terranon blasted into view. Green eyes aglow—damaged one closed, five others narrowed on him—he swiped at his tail. Rotating into a somersault, Sloan swung around. Flexing his talon, he raked his claws across Terranon's scales. Copper flecks burst like confetti over his snow-white paws as he left bloody tracks along the male's side.

"Fuck," Terranon growled, deep voice cutting through humid air.

Sloan grinned. "Something to remember me by."

Kilmar inhaled, drawing air over his fangs. The smell of acid infused the air. Bilious yellow-green foam shot from his throat.

The stream lit up the dark, sucking all the oxygen from the sky.

Wheezing, Sloan folded his wings. Gravity took hold, yanking him toward the forest canopy. The deadly spray hissed above him. The tips of his horns tingled, sizzling as droplets of acid blew over his head.

Done playing, Sloan called on his magic. The earth below him rumbled. Wind gusts shrieked over land. Treetops rocked. Boulders burst like asteroids from the cliff top. Huge. Jagged. Deadly. A revolving field of spinning debris full of deadly gas. Tail whipping behind him, Sloan dove inside the raging wall of flying rock. Controlling the flow, he spun the collection of dirt, rock and shale into faster rotation as he plucked a paw-sized chunk out of the whirlwind. Spotting Kilmar and Terranon flying around the edges, he pitched the huge stone like a baseball, hurling it out of the debris field.

He heard the pair curse.

Sloan laughed and—

"Master Sloan."

Clipped, full of worry, a crisp English accent rolled through mind-speak.

Keeping Kilmar and Terranon busy dodging, Sloan linked in. *"What is it, Daimler?"*

"What's your password?"

Eyes on his playmates, he hurled more stones. More cursing. Sloan smiled as he growled at the Numbai trying to mess with his fun. *"Stay away from my computer."*

"I would like to, but I can't," Daimler said, polished

English accent strained. *"Lady Angela isn't inside the lair. One of the Denalis is gone. I need to activate the GPS system and—"*

"Christ." What was it with females tonight? First, Gage's mate gumming up the works inside the diner. Now, Angela, traipsing around the city on her own. In the fucking dark. Prime hunting time for Dragonkind warriors.

Rikar was going to lose his mind.

Understandable reaction, if a little over the top.

Something he told the Nightfury first-in-command on a regular basis. With good reason. An investigator of unparalleled skill, Angela knew how to hunt. She was smart. She was tough. She owned guns and knew how to use them. Toss in her ability to ferret out facts and get males—both human and Dragonkind—to talk and... yeah. She rocked in a variety of ways.

He'd gotten close with her over the past few months.

She'd become his friend, hanging out in his computer lab, dragging him down whatever twisted snake hole she'd uncovered to get at the truth. Sometimes, it turned out to be nothing. Most of the time, whatever she had caught in her teeth materialized into another piece of her puzzle. No matter how tiny, every bit of information counted, which, like it or not, made him Angela's partner in crime.

And also...

A bit of a cheerleader.

Tossing more rocks at the males circling the debris field, Sloan cursed under his breath. Rikar was going to do more than lose his shit. He was going to kill him for encouraging her.

"Does Rikar know?" Tumbling like an acrobat, Sloan sliced between whirling rocks, heading away from

Kilmar and Terranon. Playtime was over. With Angela AWOL, the mission had just changed. *"Have you told him?"*

"Not yet," Daimler said, annoyance in his tone. *"I plan to re-acquire her before her mate notices she's gone."*

Sloan blinked.

Re-acquire her? What the hell did Daimler think Angela was—a lost artifact? Not that it mattered. The night officially qualified as fucked up, with Zidane's kill squad mixed up with the Razorback pack and B's little brother in the mix.

"Find her, Daimler," he said, rattling off his pass-word for his system. *"Keep me up to date. I'm going to—"*

Muffled by magic, a female voice came through the link.

Daimler reacted. Magic flamed through the link. The connection whiplashed, knifing the inside of his skull. Pain clawed over his temples as static hissed inside his head.

Sloan jerked sideways.

Jagged rocks scored his wing-tip. Shale rattled against his scales as he struggled to stay airborne and stabilize mind-speak. Alarmed by the volatility, he listened to the cosmic link flicker. Expand and contract. Dial in, then fade out. Daimler's voice broke through the chaos. Raised voices. Broken words. Warping sound, obliterating his ability to understand.

Cranking his magic to maximum, Sloan dove beneath flying debris and fine-tuned his sonar. *"Daimler—say that again."*

"Myst."

Concern tightened his chest. *"What about her?"*

"Contractions. She thinks... Braxton Hicks. But..."

The connection died.

Then sparked back to life.

Staccato words machine-gunned through the hissing connection. *"Okay, but need... Bastian. Home."*

The link snapped.

"Shit," Sloan growled, wondering how to break the news to Bastian.

Bastian's mate wasn't in trouble. Braxton Hicks contractions happened sometimes. A reality B didn't like and couldn't get behind. If Myst struggled, her mate took it seriously... false alarms and all.

Wings spread wide, Sloan banked into a tight turn. Covering his retreat, he unleashed a blast of magic. The debris field exploded. Rock shrapnel flew. Boulders blew sky-high, then rained down, hammering the cliffs, falling into the ocean, blasting Kilmar and Terranon.

The pair cursed as the shock wave hit.

Sloan didn't care. Nor did he turn around.

Already raising Bastian on mind-speak, he tracked his commander across the night sky, rocketing over towering treetops toward the center of town, knowing every second counted. Myst and her unborn infant might not be in any real danger, but the second B found out, retreat would be called.

Just as well.

With the sky full of enemy dragons, the original plan shot to shit, the Nightfury pack needed to re-group, shift focus and re-strategize. Before Ivar got the upper hand and one of his brothers-in-arms ended up injured or worse.

12

F oolish or not, sometimes a girl had to go with her gut. Even if it meant catching hell when she got home.

Angela Keen knew that better than anyone. She'd taken her fair share of risks as an SPD homicide detective. Knew her way around a gun. Scienced the heck out of crime scenes while on the job, earning her membership in the bad-ass club along the way, and yet...

Stealing an SUV from the Nightfury pack qualified as more than risky. Although... she pursed her lips... *stolen* was perhaps too strong a word. Borrowed without permission seemed a better fit, but *c'est la vie.* A hunch was a *hunch.*

Slowing the Denali to a crawl on the deserted street, Angela took in her surroundings, knowing her break from pack protocol couldn't be helped. A good investigator followed leads where each one led. Period. No negotiating the angles. Or ignoring details. Clues, no matter how tiny, must be followed, so... really. While others considered it stealing, she called it something else—a necessary evil to further her cause.

A lovely label.

Perfect rationalization.

One that didn't change the facts.

She was going to be lectured to death at the end of the night. When she turned up the drive and slid the blacked-out SUV back into its parking spot inside Black Diamond's garage, pissy attitude would come from all sides. The girls, Daimler (the Nightfury's go-to-for-everything guy), certainly. But it wasn't her friends, the Numbai, or Bastian, commander of the Nightfury warriors, who worried her most. Her concern landed closer to home, smack dab in personal territory—her mate's reaction to her sojourn outside the lair. At night. By herself.

Rikar wouldn't be happy.

He didn't have a lot of rules. Didn't make her feel like her choices inside Dragonkind's world were limited. Awesome guy that he was, Rikar gave her a lot of leeway, and a ton of latitude while she chased down leads. Leaving the lair at night to drive around a Seattle neighborhood, however, didn't fit inside the box he'd drawn.

Particularly since it put a target on her back. Easy pickings for enemy warriors with no conscience and even less mercy.

She shouldn't have done it. Shouldn't have taken an SUV without letting Daimler in on the plan. She'd given her word, after all. Promised her mate more than once, but...

"Hell," she muttered, flexing her hands on the steering wheel.

Rikar was going to tan her hide. And not in fun ways.

With a sigh, she wrestled with the guilt, then let it go. Her mate might not like it, but she needed to be here. Needed to follow her instincts, even as dread sparked, warning her to run. Shifting in the leather seat, Angela tried to ignore the unease. It didn't work. The sense of foreboding arrived right on time, circling like a shark, taking chunks out of her certainty. All the *what-ifs* plagued her mind. Every *never-should've* preyed on her fears, making her relive her time imprisoned inside the Razorback lair.

Night after night, the questions circled.

Day after day, the nightmares came.

She'd yet to uncover the mystery. Questions were plentiful and answers scarce, which only made her want to solve the puzzle all the more. She needed to know what had been done to her. What did the serum Ivar injected her with do? What was its purpose? How was the magical compound affecting her? Would there be long-term repercussions?

So far, no one could say.

Her blood tests always came back clean. The CT scans showed nothing unusual. Nice. Neat. Normal. She kept being given a clean bill of health. Time and time again. Month after month. A prognosis to feel good about, but... big problem with the forecast. Medical tests might show a steady baseline, but Angela could *feel* the difference. Like a bloodhound on the trail of a fox, she sensed the shift. The creeping insistence. The uncoiling unease. The deep, dark, and unexplainable slithering through her veins.

She was changed.

Nowhere near *normal*.

She wanted to bury her head in the sand. Ignoring what she sensed—and what the investigator inside her insisted was real—would be safer. Advisable on all fronts. Too bad she couldn't do it. She valued the truth too much. Finding answers to questions that made most people cringe, lit her lamp, so... yeah. She was diving deep, instead of turning away. Solving the puzzle. Finding some closure. Making peace with her past. Nice idea, if somewhat of a lofty goal.

Angela snorted and, grabbing a roll of Life Savers from the center console, peeled away the wrapper. Hard candy gleamed beneath streetlights. Her mouth curved. Cherry red. About time her favorite flavor made its way to the top of the rotation. Popping the Life Saver into her mouth, she cracked it in two, enjoying the hit of sweet as she ran through what she knew. Information streamed into her head, taking center stage inside her mind.

Six women missing. All high-energy, judging by the individual profiles she'd built using social media accounts, medical and school records, and talking to every family member and friend she could find. Each one gone for months. Police reports filed, but none of the girls found. The cases had gone cold. All six sat collecting dust on detectives' desks. Angela knew why. Missing person cases were difficult to close, but that wasn't why her former colleagues hadn't turned up any actionable leads.

In truth, there wasn't anything to be found.

The Razorbacks had been careful. Snatching their targets. Covering their tracks. Imprisoning each woman in a Razorback stronghold surrounded by powerful magic. Location unknown. Place undetectable. By now, all had been treated with the same serum as her, while being held by a rogue pack for reasons Angela didn't want to acknowledge.

She clenched her teeth.

For real. In all seriousness. Sometimes ignorance was bliss.

Ignoring her wishes, recall tightened its grip. Her hands twitched on the wheel. The Denali rumbled as she circled onto another block. Faded pavement. No sidewalks. Narrow gravel shoulders butted up against tiny front yards as green grass met crumbling edges of asphalt. She scanned the street again, searching for what bothered her about the neighborhood. Looked normal. Seemed neat, but as she moved into the heart of the suburb, her stomach sloshed, throwing a bad taste into her mouth.

Sucking on the Life Saver, Angela mainlined the sugar like an addict, looking for a little relief. None arrived. Something about the neighborhood north of Seattle bothered her. What, exactly? Good question. Every time she came close to putting her finger on it, the reason escaped her.

Disquiet churned up mental debris.

All her *maybes* circled.

Maybe she'd been held in the neighborhood—before the Razorbacks transferred her to the underground facility she'd escaped from. Maybe she'd seen something important. Maybe she held a vital detail inside her head. One that would help crack the case, allowing her to rescue the other women. Frowning, Angela reached for the unknown memory and...

Nada. A big goose egg on the information front.

Each time she tried to remember her time inside Ivar's lab, the blurry images floating around in her brain sank like stones, tumbling back into the mental abyss.

Deep pit.

Darkness personified.

Dangerous to her mental health. A bottomless hole full of questions, making anxiety bubble as she hunted for the truth.

Rikar didn't know the half of it. She hadn't shared her concerns. Or about the bad dreams that jarred her awake each afternoon. Selfish, maybe, but he had enough on his plate. She refused to worry him, which honestly? Made her feel like a terrible mate. The worst, given how much he loved her.

But it was more than that.

She hated hiding things from him almost as much as she despised herself for doing it. She liked the open communication and understanding he gave her. And yet, here she was—being dishonest, sneaking around, breaking every rule in the book.

Angela sighed. "This is so messed up."

The words bounced around inside of the SUV, giving credence to the claim. Taking a breath, Angela cranked the wheel, moving at a snail's pace in front of homes gone dark for the night. Not the best neighborhood. Not the worst. A section of greater Seattle she'd never visited before.

Surprising, really.

As a former SPD detective, she'd traveled the city, going wherever murdering slimeballs drew her. Which, sad to report, was all over Seattle. Retired now, she...

With a snort, Angela cranked the wheel, making another turn.

Retired.

Right. Way to put a nice spin on it.

She hadn't retired. She'd disappeared. Big difference. But despite the upheaval, she didn't regret the shift in her life's trajectory. She loved Rikar. Loved the life she was building with him, along with the other dragon warriors. She'd gained brothers. And now had a flock of new sisters. A solid unit of sisterhood. The best girls in the world, ones who accepted her without hesitation, providing the kind of camaraderie Angela had never experienced before meeting the women mated to the other Nightfuries.

The thought kicked up more guilt.

The girls would kill her if they knew she wasn't inside the lair.

She'd begged off meeting around the kitchen island for a slice of Daimler's triple-decker chocolate cake. Practically a crime. Daimler could bake—and by that she meant, *BAKE*. The Numbai made the best desserts. Devoted to the Nightfury pack, he kept everyone fed and watered, delivering good eats each day.

Heaven for a girl who despised cooking in all forms.

Hitting the brakes, Angela banished the thought of chocolate cake, and idling at a stop sign, looked both ways. An odd vibration prickled over her skin. Fines hairs on her nape stood on end as small shock waves followed, ebbing, flowing, buzzing in the air. Investigative instincts kicked up, narrowing her focus.

Her gaze roamed over the small houses bracketing both sides of the street. Tidy A-frames sat beside aging bungalows, recently mowed grass gleaming black in the moonglow. Crooked fences contained some yards, open lawns with groomed flowerbeds dominated others. Nice. Neat. Cozy arrangement that could've been found in small towns the world over.

The hum in the air told another story.

Attuned to the odd vibration, Angela scanned the street again, then went with her gut, and turned left. Spiked tires rolled over cracked pavement. The quiet rumble joined the growl of the Denali's engine as she crept down the street, moving at a snail's pace.

Her gaze caught on the old firehouse at the end of the block.

Strange, yet normal.

A throwback. A piece of nostalgia with its brick façade and arched, stone window lintels. Three bays across, the garage doors looked beat-up, as though none had been opened in decades. Cracked and chipped with holes in some spots, the glass panes didn't look much better. The rest of the building wasn't in any better shape—pitted brickwork, yard overtaken by weeds, crumbling concrete in the drive, though...

Her gaze ghosted over the structure again.

Rolling to a stop six houses down, Angela shifted into park. Engine running, focused on the fire station, she frowned. Something about the place raised her antennae. She didn't know what. Couldn't say why, but—

Headlights flashed up ahead.

A beat-to-crap Jeep with a faded black top pulled into a driveway two houses away. Angela watched a blond hop out. Without looking around, the woman slammed the driver's door and cranked the back one open. Hiking books planted in the gravel driveway, she reemerged with—

"Holy hell."

Angela blinked. *Bats.* The woman had a cage full of *bats.*

Very weird. Kind of funny, given the level of the woman's enthusiasm as she talked to the furry little freaks. The blond slammed the door. Chunks of mud under the Jeep's frame hit the ground as she pivoted toward the house, and Angela made a split-second decision.

Might be a bad idea.

Rikar would probably throttle her, but...

She needed to appease her curiosity. Collect a

little intel. About the old fire station, sure, but mostly about the neighborhood. Maybe if she knew more, she'd figure out what drew her here. Maybe it was nothing. Maybe she was just being paranoid. Maybe the constant unease was getting to her.

Whatever the case, she needed to know.

Maybe the woman with a cage full of bats had an answer. Something to add, so instead of analyzing her next move, she went with her instincts. Grabbing the handle, she popped the latch, swung the Denali door wide, and stepped out.

Her boot soles landed on gravel.

She flipped the door closed.

The slam echoed down the street.

The blond stopped talking to her bats and looked her way.

Angela waved, nailing down a persona on the fly. Friendly. Non-threatening. Bubbly with a hint of ditzy. The last nearly killed her, but... whatever. Adopting a personality when undercover was necessary, if not always pleasant.

"Hey!" she chirped, buttoning her jacket, tucking the Glock strapped in the holster under her arm out of view. Approaching with a measured pace, she stopped at the end of the blond's driveway. "Sorry to bother you. I know it's late, but... do you have a sec?"

Keeping the cage between her and Angela, the woman's eyebrows popped up.

Witnessing the reaction, Angela toned down the friendly, reading the blond, adjusting the persona. Walking forward, she paused beside the Jeep's back bumper and hitched her thumb over her shoulder. "Saw the house down the street for sale online. I work a lot, just getting off shift and—"

"Shift?"

"Working nights. Looking to get out of my studio apartment downtown. Thought I'd swing by while I was out. You know, scout the place before I commit to a visit."

"You looking to buy?"

"Yeah. I'd like more space. Someplace quieter. A deck to barbeque on," Angela said, shrugging, hoping her made-up story put the woman at ease. Maybe she lived on Walton Street for similar reasons. "You like this neighborhood? Is it safe? Friendly?"

"Safe enough."

Odd answer. Cop intuition pinged like radar. "What do you mean?"

"Nothing, really. Just a weird feeling I get sometimes. Probably just me. Can't say for sure, but..." Her brows collided. "Never mind. Don't let me scare you away. The Coulter's house is nice. Totally worth a visit. I'm just having a..."

As she trailed off, Angela's instincts twanged. "A what?"

The woman huffed. "Weird week. Or maybe, month. I don't know. I've lost track."

Angela laughed.

The woman's mouth curved. "I'm Sasha."

"Angela. Good to meet you," she said, completing the introduction. "Well, thanks. I should be getting—"

"You wanna come in? I'm gonna be up for a while and—"

"Night owl?"

"Guilty," Sasha said, swiping long bangs out of her eyes.

"Me too."

"Great. Good." Sasha nodded, coming to a decision, extending friendship. "I'll crack open some wine

—or put on a pot of tea... whatever—and dish about the neighborhood. Give you a sense of the people."

"That'd be great." Unable to believe her luck, Angela followed her new friend up the drive. Gravel crunched beneath her boot soles. Unease kicked in her stomach. Again. Like always. Warning her to be careful as she trotted up shallow treads and stepped onto a poorly lit front porch.

Not that she thought Sasha was dangerous.

On the contrary.

The woman was likeable. Seemed genuine enough, but as Sasha unlocked the door and carried her furry friends over the threshold, Angela checked over her shoulder. Just to be sure. Another wave of disquiet hit as she scanned the street. Something was off. Not by much. Hardly at all, just enough for her to clock it.

The nothing-special neighborhood—and its collection of small houses—struck her as ominous. Like a bad seed just planted, as though the section of suburbs protected secrets long buried, never to be unearthed. Which made her one of two things—on the right track or...

Completely paranoid.

Rechecking her Glock, Angela shook her head.

No doubt about it. She'd crossed into uncharted territory. Had stepped way, way over the line. But even as she crossed the threshold, entering a stranger's house, she couldn't make herself back down. Or head for home. Rikar might lose his mind, but some things were worth the price of admission. The odd vibration in the air—the mystery surrounding Walton Street— was one of those *things*. Angela could all but smell it.

13

Breathing hard, Samantha scrambled up the embankment. Steep climb. Heavy brush. Huge trees throwing scary shadows as the moon peeked through angry storm clouds. Legs pumping like pistons, her boot soles ground into the loose dirt. Debris tumbled, falling in her wake as she zigzagged between huge trunks. Focused on the top of the rise, she gauged the distance to freedom. To the trail she knew sat over the ridge.

Not far now.

Just a few more—

Her feet slipped as she reached the top. Thrown off balance, she pitched forward. Her hands clawed through damp dirt. She hit the turf chest first. Air left her lungs as she backslid, momentum threatening to undo all her hard work—her run, the climb, her perfectly timed escape from Gage... and all the freaky dragon stuff.

God help her.

Dragons.

What the hell? It didn't seem real. *Couldn't be real.* But even as she tried to rationalize what she'd seen, Samantha knew Gage couldn't be explained away.

Nothing would erase what she'd seen. Or keep her safe now. She understood the truth with a clarity that scared the crap out of her.

Gage wouldn't let her go. Not now. Not after what she'd witnessed.

Pure supposition? Maybe, but she didn't think so. There were reasons no one knew dragons existed. Good reasons. Important reasons—like, oh say— hiding the fact a secret race of *dragons* occupied the skies over Seattle... and who knew where else. Was it a worldwide sort of thing? Were there dragons *everywhere*? Flying around preying on people? Pulling the wool over billions of humans' eyes while they went about doing whatever the hell they wanted?

Seemed like a good guess.

And the makings of a massive cover-up.

The idea freaked her out, prompting her to run from Gage when he turned his back. Even though she really didn't want to go, which was *weird*. Outside her experience. Borderline insane, but she'd never felt that kind of connection with another person. He'd done something to her in the clearing. Taken something and given something different back. The intensity of her reaction frightened her. The unreal quality of his effect on her still hummed in her veins, making her vibrate from the inside out.

Tuning in, she mined the sensation. Her senses narrowed and... yeah. Definitely there, the ghosting heat, the buzzing inside her head, triggering a response, demanding answers, which was...

Unadvisable.

Dangerous.

Stupidity on a whole new level.

Samantha didn't want to know. She wanted to escape. Run from it. Hard and fast. And never look back.

Chest heaving, she sucked in another lungful of air, but kept moving, clawing her way up the hillside. Her feet hit a blanket of wet leaves. She slipped again.

Desperation took hold.

Thinking fast, she flipped over and dug her heels into the ground. Her heels caught against raised roots, halting her tumble. With no time to lose, she climbed backwards, crab-crawling the rest of the way. Slick turf turned to compact dirt. Scrambling onto the trail, she crouched next to a tree, and looking both ways, determined the next course of action. She knew the island well. Rode the trails on her bike every day. The stretch she stood on fed into a small marina.

She frowned.

Well, not a marina so much as a dock. One wooden pier. Multiple small crafts. Boats more suited to day-fishing, than a pleasure cruise around the island.

Trying to slow her heart, she pressed her hand to her chest. She forced her breathing to slow. In. Out. Catch and release. *Think, don't panic. Think, don't panic.* She repeated the words as she plotted out the most direct path to the dock. Strong muscles—all the hours she spent on her bike—propelled her across the trail.

Samantha stayed low, praying her luck held as she entered the thinning bush on the other side of the pathway. She might not be able to hear Gage, but intuition told her she would feel him. The odd hum in her veins insisted she wasn't crazy. Might seem insane, but being deaf had fine-tuned her other senses. Sight. Smell. Touch. Atmospheric pressure. All played a part. She used each to move through the world, often sensing things others didn't, so... no discounting her theory about Gage, no matter how bizarre.

The smell of brine hit her.

She upped the pace, running flat out. Dodging brambles, jumping over a fallen log, she dipped beneath a low branch and burst onto the beach. Half sand, half shale, loose pebbles rolled beneath her feet. Focused on her target, she veered left toward the finger dock. Anchored to concrete blocks on the sand, the wooden pier jutted into the water. Her eyes narrowed. Two canoes overturned on top of wooden planks. Three steel, open-topped skiffs with outboard motors bobbing in the surf, ropes tied to metal cleats.

Launching herself onto the dock, Samantha sprinted down the pier. She skidded to a stop beside the last boat and hopped inside it. Her feet slammed against the steel bottom. The skiff rocked. She didn't bother to steady it. Checking the outboard, she fiddled with the controls, then yanked the red gas tank out from beneath the lip at the stern. She read the gauges. Half a tank. Just enough juice to get around the tip of the island.

Once past the outer breakers, she'd motor past the harbor that housed the main marina and head for home. Her house sat on the east side of Bainbridge Island, facing Seattle across the expanse of Puget Sound. After beaching the boat, a quick climb up the narrow cliffside path would dump her in her backyard. Pack a bag. Disappear for a while. Wait for the coast to be clear, then return home.

As good a plan as any.

Tugging the ropes, she unmoored the skiff. Wind pushed her off the dock. As she drifted past the end of the pier, Samantha grabbed the outboard's engine cord. She yanked. The motor sputtered. She pumped the bulb on the gas tank and tried again. The small outboard roared to life.

She grabbed the handle, cranked the throttle, and

opened up the engine. The motor whined. The boat shot forward. Paranoid, she glanced at the sky. Nothing yet. No strange vibration in the air. So tense her muscles hurt, Samantha gunned it, pointing the bow toward the bright lights of Seattle.

Waves kicked up.

Water splashed over the steel hull.

The air went wired. Intense prickles raced down her spine. Her skin chilled. Clenching her teeth, Samantha leaned forward in her seat, urging the boat to go faster.

"Crap." Looking skyward, she glared at the storm clouds. "Don't you dare! Don't—"

Metal whined.

The bolts holding the motor against the stern snapped.

The outboard flew off the back of the skiff.

Frozen in shock, she watched the engine sink as jagged blue lines spiked around the boat. The fine hair on her nape rose, standing on end. Fear slammed through her. Fury rammed it aside, pumping adrenaline through her veins. Baring her teeth, Samantha inhaled hard, filling her lungs, planning to yell at the dragon-jerk messing with her—

The boat shot upward, leaving the surface of the water.

Levitating in midair, Samantha tried to dive overboard. The boat changed, morphing into liquid metal around her. Steel transformed into a bronze ball, trapping her inside, leaving her staring through uneven holes as the orb rocketed into the night sky.

~

IN FULL FLIGHT, dragon senses locked onto his wayward mate's signal, Gage blasted over the tip of Bainbridge Island. Magic up and running, he laid down a grid, interconnected points blanketing the landscape in all directions. Hunting. Seeking. Following her escape route from rough to smoother terrain, he scanned the causeway, then banked right toward the beachhead.

Nightfury chatter broke into his concentration. The conversation expanded inside his head. Eyes on the ground, he listened in. Choppy surf blew across the bay below. Choppier comments came through mind-speak.

Turning the dial, he fine-tuned his sonar. Static evened out as the link strengthened. He assessed the situation from outside the three-mile marker, locating each fighting triangle, identifying each of his brothers-in-arms' voices.

Lots of fast flying. Lots of complex strategy being employed. Lots of claws ripping into scales combined with grunts of pain. Not good by any measure.

His pack was under heavy attack.

From multiple directions.

By two different packs.

Any minute now, Bastian would call the play. End the game and exit the field by ordering Nightfuries to haul ass. Retreat. Find cover. Hole up. Whatever it took, just as long as his warriors bugged out and ended the night breathing.

Spiraling into a spine-bending flip, Gage clenched his teeth. The spikes along his spine rumbled in the damp air as his tail lashed the night sky. Searching the ground, he debated—stay on Samantha's trail or let her go. For the time being. He didn't like the last option, but...

He'd fed.

Drank deep enough that if push came to shove, he could find her again. Anywhere. Anytime. Without any trouble at all.

The idea cranked him in dangerous directions. Went against the grain. Letting her run felt wrong. He needed her with him. Wanted his hands on her. His mate in his arms, not running in the opposite direction. And yet, he waffled. Protect his pack's flank? Shield his female from harm?

His dragon half voted to re-acquire her.

Immediately.

Gage felt the tug. Knew on which side he would land. His brothers-in-arms were warriors, vicious and self-sufficient, well able to fend for themselves. Samantha was vulnerable. A female staring down the barrel of a new world order, so...

Really.

Easy decision.

Toss in a pack of rogues on the hunt, combine the Razorbacks with the Archguard kill squad, and the path became crystal clear. His mate was a target Zidane wouldn't hesitate to exploit. A simple computer search, and his enemies would know everything—her name and address, where she worked, any credit card receipts and favorite haunts. Which meant, letting her go wasn't an option. Would qualify as the height of stupidity, given the gong show playing out over Bainbridge Island.

Gage sighed.

Talk about a clusterfuck. The entire plan was shot to hell. And now, he was flying solo, two warriors shy of a fighting triangle. No wingmates within range. Zero backup if things went south. On his own in open skies teeming with enemy warriors.

Not good.

Haider was going to kick his ass when he caught up to him. The confrontation wouldn't be pretty, but—

A flash of orange glow caught his attention.

His gaze snapped toward the middle of the bay.

He spotted her within seconds. Inside a small boat. Blond hair—half in a ponytail, half out—being whipped around her head by the wind. Body angled toward the front of the skiff. Shoulders squared, gaze forward. Determination on display as she pointed the skiff toward open water and opened up the throttle on the small outboard motor.

The engine whined.

Wings spread wide, he drifted into position above her, debating. Swoop in and grab her? Or deploy his magic and point the boat toward the shore? He could land and meet her there. Pick her up, hold her in his arms, calm her down before—

Sensation ghosted over his horns, making his sonar vibrate.

Wheeling into a tight turn above her, he sent out an exploratory ping. Two males. Breaking through the three-mile marker. Flying in hot. Less than a minute to intercept.

He could feel the pair, knifing through heavy cloud cover and soupy fog, tracking his position around the tip of the island. Probably not a bad thing. He'd have to face the Pied Piper at some point. Better now, than later. Even if it meant scaring the shit out of Samantha.

Again.

For the...

Hell. Gage didn't know. He'd lost track of the number of times he'd frightened her tonight. Clenching his teeth, he shook his head. Not the most auspicious start to the relationship he planned to build with her, but with the battle over Bainbridge Island deteriorating, he needed to move. No second-guessing. Or picking over the options. Quick and clean was the way to go. The best way forward if he wanted to get his mate out of harm's way and home in one piece.

Focused on his mate, Gage flipped into an updraft. His speed went from spine-bending to smooth glide. White contrails scoring the sky behind him, he leveled out above the boat. Night vision pinpoint sharp, he tracked Samantha's trajectory, timing his approach, needing the snatch-and-grab to be smooth, not jarring.

The skiff bounced over a whitecap.

Bow dipped toward the bottom of the next swell.

She powered into the next wave, and he called on his magic. The Metallic inside him answered. Magnetic force gathered power and speed, throbbing through his veins. He held the pulse a moment, letting it build. Heat lightning crackled through his muscles, tunneled into his bones, then whiplashed, rising through the surface of his skin.

The boat started to shake.

A moment later, it left the surface of the water, levitating above the swells. The steel hull liquified, turning to fluid bronze, streaming into tentacles, closing around Samantha. Holding her in the center of the magnetic storm, he mined her bioenergy. Her vitals landed on his mental screen, giving him a baseline. He felt her surprise, heard her gasp, sensed her heart as it picked up a beat, then another, slamming against the inside of her breastbone.

Remorse hit him.

He hated to do it. The last thing he wanted to do

was frighten her, but he couldn't wait. So instead of stopping, he murmured to her, pushing his voice past her psychological barriers. She flinched, turning her head to one side as he linked in and slipped behind her defenses. As he talked to her, pushing his voice into her mind, he manipulated the metal. Bronze whirled into a loose structure, then solidified, forming a sphere around her.

He made it pretty. Polishing the bronze to a high shine. Sculpting different-sized leaf-shaped holes in the surface. Solid. Protective. Form and function combining to create beauty—more work of art than ugly cage.

Trapped inside his creation, she cursed.

Amused by her colorful vocabulary, he issued a mental command.

The sphere obeyed, jetting away from the water, rocketing skyward, moving like a flying saucer toward him in the dark as he gained altitude.

Pretty and functional.

The complete package. Utter perfection formed in the blink of an eye.

Not that Samantha appreciated the effort.

His best guess based on all the yelling? She didn't share his opinion. Or consider the sphere beautiful at all.

His lips twitched as she glared up at him, eyes narrowed, expression set, fists raised, threating him with violence. The kind most males never wanted to hear from their beloved—stabbing him in the heart while he slept, drowning him in a puddle, castration with scissors and... poisoning him with soup.

With fucking soup.

Gage clenched his teeth to keep from laughing.

Jesus. She was a bloodthirsty little thing. Smart,

strong, fierce and... inventive on the promises-of-violence front. Lovely traits. Things he appreciated about her as he burrowed deeper, solidifying their connection, talking to her through the link, trying to calm—

"Dickhead!"

"Samantha, baby."

"Pea-brained asshat!"

"You're all right. Completely safe. I've got—"

"Dickless jack-off!"

He huffed in amusement. *"Not sure that's possible."*

"What?" she snapped.

"Can't be dickless and a jack-off. That's what's called a physical impossibility."

More threats.

Another round of creative name-calling.

Despite the clusterfuck going down on the island, Gage chuckled, enjoying her temper. And the fact she'd lost her fear. Now, all he sensed coming from her was a shitload of pissed off. *"Hold on, wildcat."*

"You hold on," she said, snarling at him. "Or better yet, shove it right up your—"

"Asshole." The deep growl clawed through mindspeak, thumping on his temples, muffling Samantha's threat, even as it finished the sentiment behind it.

Gage blinked.

Uncanny. Per usual, his best friend had perfect timing.

"Haider—"

"Shut it," Haider growled, wind blasting through the link. *"I don't wanna hear it. You shut down communication again, I'll rip your horns off."*

"And what—fuck up my sonar?"

Haider cursed under his breath.

He relented, knowing he'd worried his friend. Not something he liked to do. Not to Haider. They'd been through too much. Survived some serious shit and come out stronger. Or, at least, relatively intact. *"Sorry, man. I had my hands full. Needed to concentrate. My mate—"*

"You got her?" Nian asked, voice low, his angry vibe infecting mind-speak.

"Yeah," Gage murmured, glancing behind him. His eyes landed on the sphere. Controlled by him, the globe rocketed in his wake, following his flight path beneath the deepening storm. Lightning forked, stroking the underbelly of thick clouds. Bronze gleamed in the glow as he watched Samantha punch the inside of the curved wall. She yelled at him again. Something about gutting him with a dull penknife. *"I've got her."*

Picking up on his tone, Haider snorted. *"How pissed off is she?"*

"Who cares?" Nian snarled, what little patience he owned long gone. *"We need to get the hell out of here."*

"B's called it," Haider said, explaining the mass exodus Gage sensed over the island. Nightfuries were bugging out in pairs and trios. In multiple directions. Splitting the sky and enemy attention, giving Ivar and Zidane more than one tail to chase. *"Full retreat."*

Gage grunted, not liking the play, but understanding it. With Razorbacks and the Archguard's kill squad occupying open skies, outnumbered became problematic for the first time in years. Usually, he and his brothers loved fighting multiple males at the same time. Tonight pushed the envelope, dealing a strange hand, which necessitated a more complex battle plan. *"Regroup where—at home?"*

"Or the safe house." Silver scales flashing, Haider flew into view. *"Whatever works best."*

"Safe house is closer," Nian said, pointing out the ob-

vious. Rolling in hot, he spiraled out of dark clouds, gold scales winking as he knifed through rising fog to set up shop on Haider's wingtip. *"I vote—"*

"No fucking way," he said, knowing which location Nian would pick. The namby-pamby was all about expediency. The path of least resistance. In Nian's view, the most direct route always equaled the best plan. But with Samantha in tow and Osgard waiting (no doubt worried) at Black Diamond, Gage didn't want to hold up at the safe house all day. Not if he could avoid it. *"Home."*

Nian sighed. *"You're always so difficult."*

"Fly closer... I'll show you difficult."

Haider chuckled.

Nian rolled his eyes.

Not that Gage saw it. Nian wasn't close enough yet, but... he felt the prick's reaction from a mile away.

Along with the warriors tracking his fellow Metallics.

Twelve strong, the Razorback-slash-kill squad wasn't messing around. Four to one ratio. Not great odds for him and the warriors with him. Any other night? Maybe. But with his mate in the hand, Gage refused to allow pride to rule. Not tonight. He'd never fought against four males at once. Three, sure. No big deal. But with the Ivar-Zidane combo, being too aggressive this early in the game wasn't the best strategy. Not until he and the other Nightfuries knew exactly what rubbing up against a trained kill squad meant in open skies.

Locked on, he tracked the enemy pack across the island. Just inside the three-mile marker. *"How you wanna play it? Make a break for it or—"*

Haider snorted. *"We're gonna fly right past the bastards."*

Gage's mouth curved. Of course, they were. A master illusionist, Nian could fool anyone. Inexperienced male. Skilled warrior. Didn't matter. Once the namby-pamby got going, no one broke through his illusions or matched his magic. *"Nian, you good to go?"*

"Powering up."

"All right. Give me a grid. Start the countdown," he said, reeling in the sphere. He wanted his mate closer, sitting in the palm of his paw before any rogues reached him... and the force of Nian's magic hit.

Propelling the globe, he slowed its velocity. Polished bronze flashed as it came abreast of him. Cold metal brushed his scales. His talon closed around the globe. Sharpened to brutal points, the tips of his claws clinked against hard surface. Bright blue eyes met his through one of the cut-outs. Mouth moving a mile a minute, she beat the sides of her fists against the inside of the sphere.

"Stop, volamaia," he murmured, gravel in his tone, concerned she might hurt herself. Exhaust herself... or both. It took a lot of energy to pound on something that hard.

She punched the bronze surface again.

"Samantha. Know you're pissed, but hurting yourself's not gonna help."

Unwilling (or unable) to listen, her fists rained down.

The scent of blood suffused the air.

Gage growled as he realized she'd broken skin. He moved to intercede, turning the valve, opening the connection wide. The Meridian surged. Pleasure prickled down his spine as energy flowed from him into her, flooding her senses, drawing on her tension, surrounding her in warm comfort.

Bloody knuckles raised, she resisted his attempt

to usurp her will. Gently, carefully, he upped the bandwidth. His magic slid beneath the surface of her skin, then sank deep, invading her muscles as he entered her mental field. Tone soft, he talked to her, pushing words into the head, tipping the outcome in his favor.

Unfair.

Completely unethical.

Gage didn't care.

He disliked her distress. Hated the idea she was hurt, so instead of allowing her to continue, he shut her down, aligning her bioenergy with his, forcing the fusion, strengthening the connection. Her heartbeat slowed. She took a ragged breath. One after another, until choppy became smooth. Anger and adrenaline drained from her system, allowing her to take measured breaths.

In.

Out.

Calming down. Heartbeat settling. Finally.

She blinked as her fists unclenched. On her knees, she sagged a little. He hit her with another round, pushing more calming energy through her veins. She shifted from knees to ass, sitting in the middle of the sphere, hands cupped in her lap.

"What's that?" A furrow between her brows, she frowned up at him. "What are you doing?"

"Helping you relax."

"I don't want—"

"I know. I'm sorry, wildcat. I know it isn't fair, but this is the way it's gotta go right now, yeah?"

"No."

Unable to help himself, he smiled at her, baring huge amounts of fang. Probably not the best strategy. He wanted her to relax, not freak out again.

"How is this possible?" Swaying inside the sphere, she shook her head. "How is any of this possible?"

"A question for later," he whispered, leaning into energy-fuse, allowing it to tighten its grip, becoming hers as he made her his. A moment in time. What started as a nothing-special night had become immensely important. His mate. Energy-fuse. Rare connection. Something most Dragonkind warriors never got to experience, never mind taste. And his female? Fuck. She was sweet. Feisty with a hint of vicious, sure. Stubborn. Smart. Opinionated. But oh, so fucking *sweet.*

"You're a big jerk, you know that? A big dragon jerk. *Huge.*"

"Settle, wildcat," he murmured, amused again as he watched her resistance fade. With a grumble, she settled on her side. Knees to chest. Eyes closed. Body relaxed. Curled in a ball, supported by the bottom of the sphere.

"You done babying her?" Nian asked, blasting over his back, making the spikes along his spine clatter.

The comment should've pissed him off. Made him react and go after the namby-pamby for the show of disrespect. Gage couldn't bring himself to care. Not with his mate in the palm of his paw. *"You find your female, you'll understand."*

Nian grunted something unintelligible.

Flipping up and over, Haider settled on his wingtip. *"She asleep?"*

"Almost."

"Good." Gaze on the sphere, Haider glanced at Samantha, then at him. *"We've got incoming."*

Gage checked his sonar. *"Two miles out."*

"You guys ready?" Circling back around, Nian flew in on his other wing, completing the fighting triangle.

Mercury gaze aglow, Haider tipped his chin.

Getting ready for the energy burn, Gage grunted. *"Let it fly, man."*

Nian nodded. *"Going vertical first. Any fireballs fly, I'll rotate the axis to horizontal. Be ready for the shift. Formation tight. Fast in flight."*

He and Haider agreed.

Nian wound it up, then let it go.

Bright light strobed across the sky. Static electricity crackled into the void as a boom exploded beneath storm clouds, joining the rumble of thunder, amplifying the charge in the air. Rain splattered across his scales, then evaporated in a wave of cataclysmic heat that cut through the cold. Mist disappeared. Dry, acrid air descended, eating through the humidity.

A thin, vertical seam split the night.

Gold slivers of lightning erupted from the center of the splice, widening the seam. The illusion strengthened, gathering force and speed, unstitching the sky, bending time and space, creating a narrow gap no one but those inside Nian's inner circle could see.

Tucking Samantha close, Gage flew straight toward it. He counted down the seconds to entry. Ten. Nine. Eight. At seven, he went wings vertical, preparing to thread the needle and—

A black hole opened in front of him.

Spinning, churning, sucking at the atmosphere, the whirlpool expanded, then contracted as a red dragon spiraled from its depths. And on the tip of his tail—males one and two of a fighting triangle. One yellow, the other bright green.

"Fuck—a vortex."

"Hellfire," Nian growled as energy exploded and the illusion shook, destabilizing the seam.

Adjusting mid-flight, Gage tucked his wings. The rogue snarled at him. Enemy talons swiped at him. He torqued into a tight flip. Claws raked his scales, glancing off hard interlocking dragon skin. Opening his wings, he faked one direction, then banked hard in the other. Lashing out on the fly-by, he punched the green dragon. The rogue's head snapped sideways. As the bastard reeled, Gage grabbed one of his horns. He whirled into a spin, dragging the male across the sky. One rotation turned into another. And another. At the height of the third go around, he took aim and hurled the warrior toward his buddy.

The two Razorbacks collided. Green and yellow scales clashed. Wings tangled. Tails flailed. Talons whirled as the pair scrambled, losing altitude.

"Nice," Haider said, hammering the red dragon on the fly-by. Dragon blood arched, painting the sky and silver scales red. *"Go, Gage. Get your mate to safety."*

"On my six," he hissed, not trusting his friend to retreat when he slipped into the seam and the illusion closed around him. *"Don't fuck around."*

"Right behind you, man."

Not believing him for a second, Gage scowled. *"Haider, I mean it. The rest of the rogue pack isn't far behind."*

"Trust me."

Trust him? Was he insane?

No way he could trust Haider to keep his word. His best friend liked a good kill almost as much as he did. The stubborn SOB wouldn't abandon the field without inflicting maximum damage—and serious amounts of pain—first.

Somersaulting between the two idiots who'd managed to untangle, Haider nailed one, then turned his attention to the other. *"Gage—go."*

"Don't worry." Growling, Nian stabbed the red

dragon with his tail, then grinned at him over the bastard's head. *"I'll get him there."*

Shit.

He hoped so.

Retreating didn't feel right, but as Samantha shivered inside the sphere, Gage knew he had no choice. Haider was right. He couldn't risk her. His mate came first. Losing her wasn't an option. His connection to her might be new, but the attachment was already strong. Brutal in intensity. Powerful and compelling. As necessary to him as oxygen.

So instead of doing what he wanted, he listened to his friend. Flying fast, he sliced into the seam, disappearing behind the illusion, leaving Nian to do a job that had always been Gage's—protect Haider's back... in all situations.

Crazy.

Unprecedented.

Wholly uncomfortable.

A mind-fuck of masterful proportions. One he didn't like as he blasted along the narrow corridor created by Nian. Multicolored swirls whirled across the sidewalls as he held his mate secure in his palm and followed the mirage slicing through space, hoping, praying, bargaining with the Goddess of All Things.

Not much else to do but hope.

Hope Nian was equal to the challenge. Hope the Archguard prince wasn't the namby-pamby Gage liked to call him, and he pulled Haider away. Before things went sideways. Before his packmates ended up hemmed in, with no way to escape the rogue pack nipping at their heels.

14

T wisting into a flip, Haider vaulted up and over the Razorback. His silver scales blurred in the tilt-a-whirl. The rogue tried to adjust, keep up, bright yellow scales contorting in unnatural ways. Locked on to his target, he timed his strike, waiting for the male to spin in pursuit.

Yellow spikes shivered down the bastard's spine.

Haider rotated into a backflip and lashed out with his tail. The tip slammed into the male's neck. Silver spikes sliced into yellow scales. Poisonous spurns buried in his tail punched through hard dragon skin. He yanked his tail away. The small spikes released from the tip, embedding in the enemy's scales.

The rogue grunted in pain.

More spurs grew along the length of his tail. An instantaneous reloading as he spun the other way and swiped at the male. His claws caught, cutting into the male's underbelly. Blood splashed up his forearm. He curled his talons, digging deeper and, wings flapping, dragged the Razorback sideways, waiting for the spikes he'd left deep in the rogue's scales to go to work.

Any second now, the spurs would whirl into motion. He heard the grind and tear. Listened to the ass-hole scream. Watched as the spurs burrowed into the rogue's hide, tunneling beneath interlocked scales, reaching muscles, carving pathways through bone.

Razor-edged teeth bared, he counted off the seconds. Three. Two. One. Time to move. Dropping the male like a hot potato, Haider whirled and flew in the opposite direction. Any moment now. Less than—

The spurs stopped digging.

A click sounded as the mini-bombs detonated. Pop. Pop. Boom! Shredded from the inside out, the rogue exploded. Unable to resist, Haider glanced over his shoulder. Red haze misted the air. Yellow scales-turned-shrapnel blew outward, then rained down as the Razorback disintegrated, ashing out midair.

His mouth curved.

Fantastic.

An excellent bit of fun.

One that inexperienced males never saw coming. Most Dragonkind recognized his subset of dragon, and thereby, his specialized skill set. As a silver dragon, he boasted a hefty arsenal. More than his fair share of surprises, but if forced to choose, the mini-mines along the sides of his tail topped off his list. His exhale was a close second, but if push came to shove, he preferred claw-to-claw... or tail-to-explosion... fighting.

Swinging around, he banked into a tight turn. Flakes of dragon ash flew into his face. He circled around again, improving his line of sight, and searched for Nian. Lightning forked overhead. Thunder boomed, rattling his scales. Ignoring the sound and light show, Haider kept looking. He scanned the skyscape. His wingmate couldn't be far. A master illusionist, Nian always muffled his signature, making him difficult to track.

A point of pride for the male. One Haider always cut straight through.

Much as it bothered the Archguard prince, Haider never got fooled by spacial delusion. Another of his gifts. The ability to see with clarity was a talent of his Dragonkind subset. What most males missed, he picked up right away. A prickly subject with Nian, given Haider outed him every time. No place to hide. Nowhere to run. A circumstance to which the newest member of the Nightfuries had yet to adjust.

Haider didn't care.

Life was hard. Nothing came easy. Respect must be earned, and the bonds of brotherhood grown in time-honored ways.

Raised inside the Dragonkind aristocracy, Nian hadn't understood how a strong pack operated. Not really. Not at first. He'd taken too much for granted, expecting to be given what he hadn't yet earned. He wasn't entitled. Not exactly, but he'd been handed too much, too fast. The political system in Prague shielded him. Powerful males—like his sire and Rodin, leader of the Archguard—had coddled, spoiled, and catered to him. Whatever he wanted, he got. The rest he'd taken. Which left his education in the real world lacking.

Being welcomed into the Nightfury pack—having to scrape, claw, and earn his place—had shaken Nian's foundation. He'd been dropped into a Dragonkind microcosm. One where a single mistake could get a male killed. Used to power plays, not life-and-death battles, the idea qualified as a revelation for Nian, but he was learning. Slowly. Surely. Becoming more warrior, less pampered aristocrat, but that didn't mean there weren't hiccups. Or that he didn't backslide into arrogance every once in a while.

Gage kept him on track.

Might seem cruel, but his best friend knew what he was doing. Keeping Nian humble. Reminding him of his place. Sharpening his fighting skills in dragon combat training, leaving cuts and scrapes on his golden scales, bruising his ego, teaching him an all-important lesson. Brotherhood trumped all. The bond the Nightfury warriors shared was unbreakable. Unshakable. Incorruptible. Far more valuable than the prestige to be found in the power corridors of Prague.

A fact he knew Nian had taken to heart, even as he struggled to put it into practice.

Scanning left to right, Haider frowned when he didn't spot his target. He fired up mind-speak. *"Nian."*

A wave of static washed into his head.

The connection solidified.

"What?"

The snap in Nian's voice made him smile. There it was—pissy Nightfury attitude up front and center. Proof positive Gage was rubbing off on the male. *"You busy?"*

Nian snarled. The sound of claws raking scales spiraled through the link. Bone snapped. A dragon shrieked. *"Take a wild guess."*

Haider laughed. *"Want help?"*

"Fuck off. These two are mine."

More attitude.

Vulgar language.

Excellent. The male was definitely learning.

"Hate to rain on your parade, but party time's over," Haider said, monitoring the buzz in the air. He adjusted his sonar. Nine unique dragon signatures flashed across his mental radar. He tracked each one's

location. Three separate fighting triangles. Tight for-
mations. Flying fast. Setting up the approach, coming
from different directions—north, south and east,
trying to push him and Nian further west... toward
open water and the ocean. *"More rogues on the horizon.
Time to go."*

"I'm almost done."

"Buddy—"

"Give me a second. I just need—"

KABOOM!

An orange mushroom cloud bloomed, blowing
sky-high less than a mile away.

"Shit," Nian rasped, sounding in pain.

"What the hell?" Spinning around, Haider rocketed
in the direction of the detonation.

"Another vortex." Wind whistled through the connection. Labored breathing followed as golden scales
flashed, and Nian tried to adjust. *"Three males just uncloaked. Not nine, twelve males and... Haider, I'm hit.
I'm—"*

"How bad?"

"Bad."

"Ten seconds out. Power up—open another seam," he
growled, watching Nian flip and whirl, trying to avoid
the claws of four warriors at once. Another hit him. A
second nailed him with his tail. His wingmate grunted
as he lost altitude, falling toward the choppy surf below. *"I'll grab you on the fly."*

"I'm not sure... I don't think..."

"Yes, you can. Gut-check time, Nian. Power. Up."

He snarled the last two words, then saved his
breath. The male knew what he needed to do. So did
Haider.

Muscles straining, moving like an inbound missile,
he blasted into the fighting circle. The colorful collec-

tion of rogues scattered, but not fast enough. Fangs bared, claws deployed, he body-slammed the closest dragon. The warrior tumbled end over end. His bladed tail came around. Haider ducked beneath the backlash. As he came up on the other side, he took aim at the three other converging on him.

He flicked his tail.

Spurs flew, hunting, seeking, using body heat to paint a target on each rogue. Normally, he would've watched the panic. Enjoyed the scramble. Reveled in the carnage. Not tonight. Not right now.

Nian was in trouble. One wing torn. Blood spilling from a deep slash along his side. Wing flapping. Struggling to stay airborne and out of the water.

Listening to rogues curse and dodge mini-bombs now exploding in open air, Haider tucked his wings and dove toward his friend. Humid air blasted over his horns. The smell of brine kicked up. His focus narrowed as Nian tumbled into an uncontrollable spin. He adjusted his angle and, rocketed beneath his friend's spine, reached out.

Golden scales shimmering, Nian's tail came around.

Silver met gold as he grabbed hold with both talons. Taut muscles pulled along his sides, threatening to tear. Haider held on, bearing Nian's weight as he opened his wings. Metallic grey webbing stretched, hyperextending his shoulders. With a grunt, he ignored the agony and, swinging full circle, slowed his descent.

Nian groaned.

Haider snarled at his friend.

Hanging upside down from his talon, Nian cursed, but powered through the pain. Heat mushroomed around him. Magic blew up and out, filling the air with golden shimmer.

A seam opened above rolling whitecaps.

Enemy males roared overhead. Two dove, arrowing toward him.

Watching the duo approach, Haider clenched his teeth, grip slipping, trying to fly and hold on to his friend at the same time, but...

Shit.

Nian was too heavy. No way he'd be able to drag him through the seam into the illusion in dragon form.

Wings working overtime, lungs pumping like billows, he glanced down at Nian. *"Shift, man. You gotta—"*

Quick on the uptake, Nian transformed, moving from dragon to human form.

Load lightened, Haider reestablished his grip.

Talon curled around Nian's naked body, he flew toward the seam. Blood welled on Nian's abdomen. Haider gritted his teeth as it coated his scales, dripping down his forearm. Worry kicked up. He shoved it aside and, angling his wings, sliced into the seam, disappearing behind Nian's illusion.

"Close the entrance."

Dangling from his talon, feet swinging in midair, Nian frowned. *"Huh."*

"The seam, Nian. Close—"

A loud clap sounded behind him.

"Done," his friend whispered, struggling to remain conscious.

"Stay awake. Don't fall asleep."

"The cut's too deep. I'm not healing right. I need—"

"I know," he growled, knowing his friend needed an infusion of healing energy. He needed quality time

with a human female. Direct access to the Meridian—source of all living things. The sooner, the better. *"I'll get it for you."*

Nian blinked, fighting to remain awake. *"Shit, it hurts. If I don't... if you can't—"*

"Shut it. You're gonna be fine." Not a lie, but not honest either. Nian was in bad shape, in need of an emergency energy infusion. Otherwise, he'd fall asleep and never wake up. Opening a second connection, Haider cut into Black Diamond's feed, pinging the Numbai who ran the Nightfury lair. *"Daimler."*

"Here, Master Haider."

"Call the service. Two females to the safe house... now."

"Who's hurt?"

"Nian. He took a bad hit."

Daimler sucked in a quick breath. *"Come home."*

"No time."

"I'm on it," Daimler said, tapping on something. A touch screen, maybe. Doing what he always did—acting with expediency, getting the Nightfury warriors whatever they needed, whenever they needed it.

"How long?"

"Twenty minutes."

"Nothing sooner?"

"There's a nightclub five blocks from the safe house."

"Address."

Daimler rattled off the location.

On mission, Haider plugged the pin into his mental map.

"Do you still want the girls?"

"Yeah," he said, grimacing. He didn't enjoy connecting with working girls. The thrill of the chase and heat of the hunt suited him more, but after abstaining for over a month, he needed to feed.

Much to Gage's disapproval, he'd been putting it

off, not wanting the closeness. Shying away from the intimacy. Refusing to be touched by anyone. Females included. Totally fucked up, given how much he loved spending time with the fairer sex, but... hell. No use denying the truth, or that what happened in Prague continued to mess with his head. Now he flirted with edges of energy-greed. A dangerous condition for his kind. Ravenous hunger equaled big trouble—and dead females—if a male tapped into her core energy and took too much.

"Haider?"

Knowing avoidance was no longer the answer, he drew a fortifying breath. *"Get them to the safe house."*

"You'll keep me—"

"I'll let you know," he said, unable to keep the concern out of his voice.

He glanced down at Nian.

So much blood.

Way too much.

Worry thumping on him, he watched Nian blink, a slow up and down. Haider increased his wing speed, slicing through the void on a direct route to the safe house and the nightclub beyond. Bright multihued colors swirled along the sidewalls, rushing ahead of him as he pushed himself hard. He needed to get his friend into the arms of a female. Faster than fast. Before Nian lost consciousness and slipped away, one slow, ragged breath at a time.

T all pines rising jagged below him, Sloan set a fast course toward Black Diamond. On point, leading the pack, he leveled out over the woodlands, then pushed the pace. His brothers-in-arms fanned out behind him, flying in tight formation, on the lookout for more trouble as damp winds turned cold. Condensation beaded, then slid into streams across his scales. Huge treetops reacted to the wing rush of multiple males in full glide, swaying as in the blowback.

Branches creaked below him.

Ghostly illumination spilled across hills, reaching into valleys.

Shadows thickened.

White cliff faces came into view.

The sight should've made him feel better. Relieved some of his tension, helping him unwind. On any other night, the familiar landmark would've set off a chain reaction. A welcome one, as his dragon accepted the cue, allowing the beauty of Mother Earth to embrace and soothe him—mind, body, and soul, but...

Not tonight.

Not after what went down over Bainbridge Island.

Sloan blew out a breath in frustration. Curls of toxic mist rose from his nostrils as he rocketed past the twenty-mile marker. His sonar pinged. His dragon laid out the timeframe. Not long now. Just minutes from home. From cutting through the waterfall and landing on the LZ. From walking inside the underground lair he shared with the other Nightfury warriors. One moment stitched into the next. Hardly any time at all, and he'd be in his computer lab, a breath away from getting what he needed—a little peace, a lot of quiet. A chance to think, work the problem, and put the pieces together.

His mind drifted in that direction.

His body followed, swerving off course.

Angling his wings, Sloan corrected his trajectory. The forest thinned. Tall pines stepped into shorter aspens, then rolled into foothills and rocky terrain. He took the cliffs head-on, rocketing up the sheer face. At the ridgeline, he flipped up and over. His wingtip scraped across the jagged top. Loose boulders lost their perch, exploded off the bluff. Large pieces of shale blew skyward.

Wings tucked, he somersaulted over the other side.

Sharp stones pinged off dragon scales.

Mid-flip, Sloan glanced over his shoulder. His mind took a quick snapshot, laying out a detailed picture.

On his six, Rikar banked hard, white scales flashing as he avoided flying shrapnel.

"*Fuck.*" A blur of midnight blue, Bastian dodged left, then came back right.

Ducking behind an airborne boulder, Venom bared his fangs. "*Goddamn it.*"

True to form, Wick said nothing. Tucking his

wings, he dove deep, then rose hard, rocketing around the towering cliffs without comment.

"Jesus, laddie." Flight path disrupted by barrage, Forge flipped sideways and... grunted as he slammed into Mac. *"Watch the family jewels. My female needs those."*

Shoving the Scot off his wingtip, Mac laughed.

Exshaw squawked at Forge. The sharp burst of sound shook the airwaves. Sloan's horns vibrated. Pain raked the insides of his temples. Coming out of the spiral, he jolted, struggling to control the spin as the wren shrieked again.

His brothers-in-arms groaned, wavering in flight, losing altitude as Exshaw reprimanded the Scot for banging into Mac.

"Quiet, Exshaw," Mac murmured, calming the miniature dragon. *"Sloan?"*

"Yeah."

"What the fuck?"

Sloan tensed. He didn't want to share. Not surprising. He rarely told the others what was on his mind. *"Just keeping you on your toes."*

"Bullshit," Rikar murmured, detecting the deflection, reading him with an eerie precision Sloan didn't appreciate. Not that the Nightfury first-in-command cared what he thought. Or that he wanted to be left alone. Rikar pushed when he needed to, intervening before volatile tempers boiled over and Nightfuries clashed. His ability to understand the warriors under his command—to intuit when and where to apply pressure—qualified as scary.

Banking around a rocky outcropping, Rikar flew in close. Ice-blue eyes aglow, he bumped Sloan with the side of his tail. White scales met dark brown ones dusted with green and gold. *"Spill, Sloan. What's both-ering you?"*

He wanted to say, "Forget about it."

Meeting his friend's gaze, Sloan swallowed the lie. Normally, he wouldn't hesitate. He'd deflect. He'd distract. Fall into comfortable patterns and do what he always did—shrug it off, change the subject, or his favorite option... keep his mouth shut. He was the poster boy for standoffish. Being a loner came easy. After the loss of his son, emotional retreat hadn't been an option. It had become a necessity. A matter of survival as he grieved and fought to stay sane. The concern in his XO's eyes, however, dug deep, unearthing an unusual reaction from him.

For the first time in a long time, honesty bubbled up, choking him with everything he never said. He was tired of the bullshit. Of staying on the fringes of his pack. Of being on the outside looking in, like a youngling with his nose pressed against the glass, waiting for Bastian or one of the others to voice their concerns and call the play.

Always safe.

Rarely vocal.

Committed to avoiding connection. A kind of self-imposed isolation that kept him in a cage. One of his own making. Problem was...

He didn't know to break out or through it. The only thing he knew for sure was, it couldn't continue. Descending another one hundred feet, he flew over the river. Dark water flowed. He followed its snaking line toward Black Diamond, replaying his earlier conversation with Gage. The whole thing was whacked. The male had gotten into trouble. Made a mess online, put the Nightfury pack at risk, instead of asking for his help. The realization floored him, forcing him to reevaluate how he interacted with his brothers.

Brotherhood was about service. About family. About support, sharing problems, and listening to others. He'd been doing a piss-poor job of both for... well... *ever*.

"Sloan," Bastian murmured, flying in on his other side.

Flanked by his packmates, Sloan sighed. *"You were there, B. You saw what I saw."*

"Yeah," he said, voice soft, green eyes focused and fierce. *"And?"*

"The entire fight was fucked up. From start to finish," he said, mind flipping through the facts. *"No Razorbacks around for months. For months, man, then suddenly —they're every-fucking-where. Sky's full of the assholes."*

"Zidane—"

"Yeah, he was there." Raising his brow, he eyeballed his commander. *"To be expected, B. With all the Archguard bullshit, we knew he'd show sooner than later, but he had—what? Six warriors? Not enough to fuck up our strike plan. Not enough to force a retreat, even with the Razorbacks in play."*

Unease crawling along his spine, Sloan took suspicion out for a spin. *"Lotta Razorbacks in the mix, but... the rest? No scent of Ivar on any of 'em. Where the hell did they come from?"*

"Mercenaries," Bastian said, like he knew and wasn't surprised. *"Out for the purse."*

"You got intel," he said, more statement of fact than question.

B nodded.

Sloan frowned. *"From whom? Didn't come through my system."*

"Numbai network. Underground channels. Kept on the

DL from Dragonkind packs," Bastian said, eyeballing him, watching his reaction. *"Daimler's been talking to his counterparts in Prague."*

Forge huffed. *"Clever. How much has the Archguard put on our heads?"*

"Five million—each," Rikar said, filling in the blanks, clearly in the know.

Forge whistled long and low.

"Motherfuck," Mac muttered.

"You didn't say anything." Eyes narrowed on Bastian, Sloan flexed his talons. Make a fist. Release the knuckle-cracking tension. Open. Close. His razor-sharp claws clicked as anger streamed through him. A death grip on his temper, he glared at his commander. *"Thinking that's information we all need to know, B."*

Seeing his struggle, Bastian's lip twitched. *"Would knowing it have changed tonight's battle plan?"*

His brows slammed together. He hated to admit it, but...

Good point.

Annoying as all freaking hell, but Bastian wasn't wrong. Nothing would've changed how things played out over the island. The Nightfury pack would've flown out—no matter what. Which meant Bastian had a plan. Still had one. His commander didn't do random. He calculated odds. He strategized and prepared for all outcomes. He manipulated perception, keeping the enemy guessing.

"Needed you in the sky tonight, Sloan," Bastian said, revealing he'd been part of the equation. A variable B weighed in making the decision. *"Not behind a computer screen."*

He sucked in a sharp breath. *"I would've—"*

"Buddy," Rikar said, voice soft, but firm. *"Given that*

information, would you have been able to resist disappearing into the dark net to find out more?"

An accusation.

A gentle one, but a fact Sloan couldn't refute. As the realization took root, he shook his head and whispered, *"I've become that bad, haven't I?"*

"You're you," B said, letting him off the hook. *"And, man, we like the way you are, but we need you for more than your computer skills. You've got other sides to you, Sloan. Lethal ones. Tonight was about reminding you of that fact."*

"Pushed me out of the nest."

"Like a baby bird."

Sloan rolled his eyes.

B grinned. *"You have fun?"*

His lips twitched. *"Wicked amounts."*

"Then it begins." Giving him another tap with his tail, Rikar took the lead. Frost crackling in his wake, white wings glowing in the moonlight, he banked around the last curve in the river, setting up his approach to the waterfall. *"No more hiding behind computer screens. We fly out at night, you're part of the pack. I'll be riding your ass to make sure."*

"Terrific," he muttered.

Quiet in the exchange—a miracle, given how much the male liked to talk—Venom chimed in. *"Can I be part of the riding-his-ass team? Never tried it before, but beating the snot out of Sloan sounds like fun."*

Mac snorted in amusement.

"Careful, lad." Purple eyes gleaming with laughter, Forge flipped over his wingtip. *"Earth dragon mojo is nasty mojo. You might end up with sand in uncomfortable places."*

His brothers-in-arms laughed.

Sloan smiled, enjoying the taunt and tease. Surprising. A real eye-opener, given he'd never been razzed before. He witnessed the others take verbal shots at each other on a regular basis, but had never put himself in the line of fire. Until now. Which felt... he frowned... good. Life-affirming. As though he'd denied himself something important. A *something* the other Nightfuries wanted to provide.

Being included in the banter clued him in.

His brothers-in-arms had been watching. Waiting for the go-ahead. Bastian pressing him, Sloan welcoming the guidance, cleared the field. Cracked the door open. Now it stood wide, allowing acceptance to rush in, solidifying his place while reassuring him he had one.

The heaviness he carried around like a lodestone lightened.

The knot in the center of his chest unraveled.

Breathing out, Sloan let it go. It wasn't perfect. The grief, the longing for a life lost, persisted, but as he rounded the bend, saw the waterfall tumble and mist rise, he finally understood. He wasn't alone unless he chose to be. With help, he could heal. All he needed to do was be honest. Take his dark thoughts to his brothers. Allow the pack to help him heal the wound that refused to close on its own.

Pain was part of life. He knew that better than most, but it wasn't always filled with misery. Bright moments existed. Ones filled with love, laughter, and light. He saw it every day inside the lair—at meals when the entire pack gathered, in the way his brothers treated their chosen females, and good-natured ribbing around whatever sporting event happened to be on TV. All he needed to do was take off the blinders, open his eyes, and look. But more than that —really *see*.

Increasing his speed, Sloan fell into line. The river below. The waterfall ahead. Rikar and Bastian on point, the rest of the Nightfuries falling in behind him. His XO and commander sliced through the wall of water. Sloan went wings vertical and followed suit. Wet hit his scales, then washed away as he blasted into the hidden tunnel.

Swallowed by darkness, the light of the moon disappeared.

His night vision sparked, allowing him to see in the black. Details came into sharp focus. Smooth stone gave way to jagged rock. The smell of must kicked up as the tunnel narrowed. Avoiding serrated outcroppings, Sloan angled into the next turn. He took it fast, the roar of the waterfall fading as he shot into a straightaway. Light perforated the dark. The glow grew in size and strength, drawing him toward the huge cavern.

Bigger than a footfall field, the cave was a thing of beauty. Smooth walls. Soaring dome ceiling. Two-thirds open area, one-third landing zone. Wide enough to launch or land four dragons at once.

Eyes on the LZ, Sloan exited the mouth of the tunnel. He opened his wings. Water wicked off his scales as he put on the brakes. The powerful thrust whipped dust across the cave. Stalagmites at the rear of the landing zone shivered as light globes reacted, bobbing like jellyfish against the curved ceiling.

Sloan barely noticed.

He was too busy watching B and Rikar land.

White scales rippling, his XO set down first.

Bastian didn't bother to land. Folding his wings, he dropped the last fifty feet. His back paws slammed into stone. Shock waves rippled, making the decapitated Honda sitting in the middle of the LZ quiver.

Rust flew off the side of the hatchback, joining pieces already littering the ground around the car. Bastian kept threatening to get rid of the thing. No one wanted him to give the hunk of junk the heave-ho.

Good memories were wrapped up in the beat-to-shit Honda.

The first time Myst entered the lair and changed their lives forever. Mac's maiden voyage in dragon form and disastrous first landing on the LZ—and the Honda's decapitation. Venom kicking the crap out of it after a frustrating night of patrol.

So many great memories. Not enough time to go over them all.

At opposite ends of the platform, B and Rikar shifted from dragon to human form, conjuring clothes, getting out of the way, giving the warriors bringing up the rear more room to land. Hanging like a ghoul over Myst's old car, Sloan dropped into a smooth landing. His claws scraped over granite, scoring marks across the stone. Between one breath and the next, he transformed, and with a murmur, conjured his favorite pair of jeans. Throwing a long-sleeved crewneck on his back and Air Jordan 1's on his feet, he skirted the Honda and headed for the—

A wave of energy pulsed across the landing.

The car spun sideways, sliding toward the edge. Metal shrieked. The pressure increased. Another blast hit. Powerful energy slammed into his chest. His lungs seized. Pain spiked through his ribcage. Unable to breathe, he hit one knee, wheezing, reeling, struggling to draw a breath.

Palms pressed to his temples, Rikar stumbled backward. "What the fuck?"

"Shit," Bastian whispered, more expulsion of air than curse. "Myst. My mate. She's—"

Another round of powerful energy rocked the cavern.

Blown off their bases, stalagmites fell over. Bits of rock billowed from the back of the cave. Dust rained down. Air hissed as light globes deflated, drifting from seventy-five feet up.

Forcing his lungs to expand, Sloan struggled to his feet. "Move! Bastian—move! Open the portal. Get into the lair and find her."

Venom landed behind him. "What's happening?"

Sloan didn't answer.

Already on the move, he sprinted toward the portal. Bastian pushed past him. Reaching out with his mind, he added his magic to his commander's, thumping on the energy shield protecting Black Diamond, requesting entry. The monster guarding the lair didn't argue. As though it somehow knew what was wrong, it opened without the usual fight.

Stone moved from solid to wavy.

An archway opened in the cave wall.

Bastian raced over the threshold.

Sloan stayed on his heels. His feet left rough stone, slamming down on polished concrete as he ran up the ramp toward the clinic. He murmured. The motion detector activated, pulling the sliding glass door sideways. Rivulets of energy poured out, painting the air with a blue glow, building into a steady stream, splashing into the wall in the corridor.

Bastian disappeared over the threshold. "Bellmia!"

A step behind him, Sloan heard the roar, felt the agony, but blocked by Bastian's body, he didn't understand. Couldn't assess the situation until he came around the end of the stainless-steel examination table.

His eyes landed on Myst. "Goddess."

Gaze riveted to Bastian, she sat on the floor, arms hugging her very round belly... a pool of blood spreading beneath her. Shock hammered him. Fear for her picked up the thread, slamming his heart against his ribcage, turning the inside of his breastbone into a punching bag.

"Holy shit," Rikar said from right behind him.

The XO's voice jolted through him.

His medical training kicked in.

Glancing over his shoulder, Sloan plugged the Nightfury first-in-command with an intense look. "I need a second pair of hands. Can't be you or any of the other warriors. Bastian won't permit any of you to touch her. Not in his current state. I don't care who, just get someone here. Get them here *now*."

Rikar nodded.

Ignoring the build up in the corridor outside the clinic (and the other Nightfuries' concern), he waded into the fray, forcing Bastian to pick his mate up and move. Green eyes glowing, beast raging, aggression rising, his commander snarled at him. Sloan didn't care. Knowing he had no time to waste, he bullied his friend into compliance. He barked orders, keeping the male moving and Myst calm as he tore through cabinets, pulling out what he needed to save her life, praying the baby was all right, and B didn't lose his unborn child.

16

Cocooned in warm comfort, Samantha drifted in and out of mental fog. Thoughts came. Awareness went, ebbing in, flowing out as she lay curled on her side, head resting on her outstretched arm, waiting for the voice to come again. She knew it would. The quiet murmur always did. Deep. Intense. Drawing soft circles on the sides of her temples. Making her senses buzz and excitement swirl as the rumble rolled beneath her layers, telling her to relax, encouraging her to sleep, drawing her deeper into relaxation.

Sound waves.

The beauty of another's voice. A reality long kept from her. Both beautiful and brutal. A haunting reminder of what she'd lost, but now, by some stroke of luck, had returned to her.

Eyes closed, thoughts mired in mental drift, Samantha waited for him to say something else. She wanted to hear him again. Feel the vibration. Count out the syllables. Revel in the rumble of his baritone and never let the promise of it go. Which seemed... unhealthy somehow. Wrong in ways she couldn't explain, and wasn't sure she wanted to while he whispered in her ear, invading her mind, tempting her to trust when it had yet to be earned.

Not entirely.

Which meant...

She shouldn't be waiting. She shouldn't be wondering. She needed to clear her head, get up and get moving. Acting in her own best interest amounted to self-preservation. The kind every woman ought to own.

The voice came again. Low. Intense. Gorgeous in its intensity.

Samantha shook her head, trying to get her bearings as urgency poked and prodded, shoving her closer to awareness. She didn't know why, but fighting her way out of the drift needed to happen, and happen now.

Shifting on the warm, smooth surface, she shuffled around, moving her arms and legs, flexing her fingers and toes, making her body obey. As her muscles fired, her mind turned over. The drift eased. She clawed through mental fog, reaching for clarity, but got nothing but blur. Lots of confusion. Too many questions. No answers, though she knew a couple of things for sure.

Things like: her throat hurt from yelling. Her arms and hands ached from punching. And that, she was in some kind of ball. Or cage. Or...

Her brow furrowed.

Was it a carriage?

A picture of Cinderella drifted through her mind. She batted it away, unwilling to go that far. No sense searching for pumpkins. Girls like her didn't get the fairy tale. Girls like her fought and scraped and looked out for themselves. Girls like her didn't get to indulge in or wish for easier ways. She'd learned that early in life, just after her seventh birthday, the first time she watched her mother spiral out of control.

Down.

Down.

Down in an ever-steady descent of drugs and alcohol.

From then on out, the lessons hadn't stopped. She took hit after hit. Watching her mother battle and lose to addiction—while others took advantage—over and over. Again and again. Waking up in the hospital to find both her hearing and mom gone, nothing but thin reasons from the nursing staff explaining why. Flying halfway across the country to meet her grandfather. Just out of the hospital—deaf, scared, and alone. At the mercy of a man she'd never met and didn't know.

Grand (bless him) had turned it all around, stopping the trajectory of her life, lifting her up instead of dragging her down. Getting her the help she needed. Learning ASL right alongside her, making her laugh as he fumbled, helping her heal, becoming her touchstone in a world gone suddenly silent.

Her godsend.

Now gone.

Lost to her forever.

Anguish turned the screws. Her chest compressed as memories surfaced. Contracting into a tighter ball, Samantha battled the grief, forcing herself to remember the good instead of the bad. The laughter over homemade meals. The pale blue of her bedroom walls as she sat cross-legged on her bed, tucked safely inside Grand's home. The long hours spent beside him in the workshop, standing side by side, hands working on new and old designs.

She took a deep breath.

As her lungs expanded, a grounding sensation rolled in. Her fingertips started to tingle. She felt her chest move. Breath in. Breath out. Nice and easy as she swayed, the rhythm so smooth it threatened to drag her back under. Fighting the pull, she sank back into her body bit by bit, forcing her brain to work. Images flashed across her mind. The diner. The medallion. Running through the woods. The shimmering bronze of Gage's eyes.

The memory jolted her.

Rolling forward, she pressed her palm flat against the floor and pushed up. Sore muscles squawked. Her knuckles started to burn. Pain ghosted up her arm. Gritting her teeth, she kept going, moving with care, curling her legs under her, assessing the damage. All good. No cause for alarm. She might be a little banged up, but nothing said *okay* like realizing all your limbs were still attached.

Lifting her head, she opened her eyes.

And blinked.

Crap. Nothing but blur.

She rubbed her eyes with her fingertips, mashing her lashes together. The grit disappeared. She tried again. Her vision went from wavy to clear. Tipping her head back, she looked up and around. Definitely a ball. Bronze structure. Smooth curved walls with leaf-shaped cut-outs. Bursts of multicolored light across a black sky beyond the dome. Almost like the aurora borealis, but brighter. Flashier. A whirling, swirling, flying collection of color everywhere—side to side, top to bottom—and...

Yup.

Definitely not a dream. Absolutely, one hundred percent undeniable. She sat inside a globe, which rested inside an enormous dragon paw tipped by lethal-looking claws, with fireworks going off.

Samantha scowled at the dragon ignoring her. In full flight, bronze scales gleaming, he blasted across the sky. The color array reacted. Explosions of blue turned into green, red and gold. Lovely. Truly excellent. She was worse than screwed. She was toast. About to lose her temper and go postal on a dragon-slash-man-slash-whatever the hell he called himself.

Probably not the best strategy given the size of him. Factor in the fangs, claws, and scales and vicious inclinations and... yeah. Definitely something to think about, but as she glared up at him, Samantha couldn't reel in the urge. She wanted to yell at him. She wanted to hit him with something harder than her fists. But mostly, she wanted to know what the hell was going on.

Her eyes narrowed on her target. "Gage."

The snap in her voice tipped his head down. The orange glow in his eyes hit her, making the bronze ball shine as he met her gaze. Surprise popped his brows up. *"You're awake."*

"And homicidal," she said, hating the fact she loved the sound of him. That voice. His *voice*. She shivered. God, it was beautiful. Hearing it shouldn't surprise her. Not anymore. Not after the night she'd had, but that didn't change the fact every time his voice sounded inside her head, relief hit her so hard, she wanted to cry. Swallowing the lump in her throat, she narrowed her eyes, putting on a show, pretending something she didn't feel. *"Just in case you're wondering."*

Baring huge fangs, he grinned at her. *"You want a shot at me?"*

"I want to stab you with a butcher knife."

His grin turned into a smile.

Charmed, but not wanting to be, she glared at him. "You don't seem very concerned."

"Wildcat—you put your hands on me, I'm not gonna get your claws. You're gonna give me your heat... all the need you've got bottled up inside you."

Her brows collided.

Now, wait just a minute. She might not be the most experienced woman in the world, but... Samantha pursed her lips. Hell. Better to be honest. Lying to herself had stopped the instant she lost her hearing. She became a realist—fast—so... all right. She wasn't experienced. At all. She hadn't had the time or opportunity. Most guys shied away from girls like her. Still...

Gage didn't need to be so blunt about it. Outing her like that was just plain uncool.

"You don't know shit," she said, challenging him, trying to make herself feel better.

"I'm inside your head, Samantha. I know your thoughts. I feel you with every breath I take. My heart now beats for yours," he said soft, sweet, raising goosebumps on her skin. *"You don't understand yet, but you're mine. The female made and meant for me. I put my hands on you, you're gonna react, and not with violence. You wanna taste of me as badly as I do you. It's gonna be hot. It's gonna be wild. It's gonna finish with me deep inside you."*

Words.

Just words.

None of them should matter, but somehow each one did. The idea he desired her dove deep beneath her surface, leaving curls of pleasure in its wake. As it streamed through her, carving pathways into unseen places, she wondered and imagined... and burned with so much want a chain reaction started inside her.

Her core tightened. Her breasts swelled. Her skin grew sensitive in preparation of his touch. Now, she *needed* to know. Craved the closeness, every ounce of pleasure instinct promised he'd deliver.

Unnerved, she fisted her hands. "I'm... that's..."

"What, baby?"

She cleared her throat. "Not going to happen."

"How much you wanna bet?"

Nothing.

Zero dollars.

Absolutely no poker chips were hitting her lust-cluttered table.

She wanted him. Had been attracted to Gage on sight, enthralled by the way he moved and looked. Tall, dark, and dangerous. A lethal cocktail. Powerful temptation for a woman who played it safe and never walked on the wild side. A ride Gage promised without even opening his mouth. The second he entered the diner, catastrophe struck. Her world tilted, stripping away all sense of equilibrium. Sure, she'd run scared, was still doing it, but that didn't make Gage wrong.

Attraction was a powerful thing. And curiosity? Well, that witch always rode shotgun. Turning the wheel. Twisting the path. Leading her along dangerous avenues.

His insistence she belonged to him should've garnered a sharper response. Immediate refusal. Harsh denial, and, yet, it didn't. His certainty captured her attention, making her pause and evaluate. Despite wanting to tell him to go to hell, she couldn't. It wouldn't be honest, given everything he said rang true.

It wasn't rational.

It was longing and gut-wrenching need.

Her mind reeled with the knowledge. Palm pressed to her chest, she tried to slow the throbbing beat of her heart. She inhaled deep and exhaled smooth. It didn't help. She was tumbling down a rabbit hole. Out of control. In serious trouble. Struggling to make sense of something that never would. How in God's name had it happened? What made him so appealing? Samantha frowned. Or was it that she was just weak?

"Want my advice?"

Trying to not hyperventilate, she shook her head. "Not really."

"Don't fight it, wildcat. Accept what you can't control. I have."

"Easy for you to say," she said, waving her hand in front of her, gesturing to him. "You're all... dragon-y."

He snorted. Bronze flecks sparked from his nostrils. Metallic flakes swirled a moment, then drifted back, rushing over the jagged horns on his head. *"Dragon-y?"*

"You know what I mean." Swallowing, she worked moisture back into her mouth. "And anyway, I don't need your advice, 'cause I'm—"

"Don't worry, volamaia. I'll be gentle... the first time."

Her eyes widened in alarm. "I haven't agreed to anything."

"You will."

"Arrogant much?"

"Just the right amount." Adjusting his grip on the ball, he rotated her in his palm. *"You'll see the benefits when you're tangled up with me in bed."*

"Holy hell," she muttered, unsure whether to laugh or be appalled.

Gage wasn't similarly afflicted. He laughed outright.

Her eyes narrowed. "I don't think I like you."

"Lie to yourself all you want, wildcat, but you already do."

A circumstance to lament.

And ponder.

And kill. Dead. As quickly as possible.

She couldn't afford to lose whatever game Gage played. Self-preservation was more important than the pleasure he promised. She needed to keep reminding herself of that all-important fact. She might want to know what being *tangled up* with Gage felt like, but that didn't mean she'd give in. Disaster lay in that direction. She wasn't a normal girl. He was far from a normal guy. Put them together, and bad things were bound to happen.

Terrible things.

Awful things.

Things no sane person wanted or welcomed.

But as she met Gage's gaze, certainty slipped, and she lost sight of the goal. No matter how hard she tried, she couldn't deny the connection. She felt it growing, expanding, taking shape inside her. Tangible. Touchable. Tethers tying her to him, and him to her. Not a figment of her imagination, but *real*. Curiosity pressed in, prying questions loose.

In that moment, Samantha realized something important. Something shocking. Something more than a little left of center. She wanted to know everything about him. Interests and hobbies. What made him laugh. The things that made him sad. The way he tasted, the texture of his skin, the way he looked when he woke hard-bodied, messy-haired, and sleepy-eyed in the morning. It was madness. Pure, unadulterated *madness*, yet somehow, made perfect sense. Everything he promised, along with her unfettered reaction to it, felt good. Right in ways that both scared and excited her. And as longing speared through her, Samantha allowed her mind to wander. Thoughts of Gage between her thighs pushed in, his mouth hot against her—

"Hmm, I like the way you think."

Heat hit her cheeks. "Stop reading my mind."

"No way. It's like a wonderland in there. Full of promise and—"

"Gage!"

"All right, I'll let it go." Lips twitching, he winked at her. *"Time to get serious anyway."*

"What?" she whispered, knowing 'serious' to a dragon meant *'SERIOUS'!* to her.

The temperature dropped.

Each breath became a white puff in front of her face.

Samantha moved from her butt onto her knees. "Gage—what's that mean?"

"Hold on." Looking ahead, he shifted mid-flight. His wings went from horizontal stretch to vertical line. A second later, he banked, angling into a sharp turn. *"It's about to get rough."*

Shit.

Again?

Seriously?

Her stomach dropped. She'd had enough rough, thank you very much. A little smooth wouldn't go unappreciated. But as air buffed Gage, shaking his massive, scaled frame, battering him like an airplane in turbulence, Samantha swallowed her request. Raising her arms, she pressed her hands flat against the side walls, stabilizing her seat inside the ball.

Swirling color outside faded.

Total darkness descended.

Gage's eyes started to glow. Orange luminescence ate through the blackness like twin spotlights as the space around them contracted, making her realize Gage wasn't flying through the sky. He jetted through a narrow tunnel, walls moving like fabric, undulating into shimmering waves.

A blast of wind hit.

A twister formed in the void.

Gage jolted, then flipped, seesawing around a tornado. Banking fast, he rocketed around another, playing chicken in violent windstorms. He flipped. Her breath caught as gravity let go and she went weightless. Upside down, hair flying around her head, she stopped going up and started to come down. Arms pinwheeling, Samantha flailed, trying to turn in midair. She needed to get her feet under her. She needed to—

Gage somersaulted the other way.

The ball around her disintegrated.

Ribbons of bronze roped the space around her, then wrapped over and around Gage, becoming one with his scales. In free fall, Samantha opened her mouth to scream. She landed with a thump in the center of Gage's palm. Air rushed from her lungs as a warm dragon paw closed around her. Sitting in his palm, she watched his talons contract, holding her secure as the flight grew rougher.

Time stretched.

The wind raged.

The texture of the walls thinned.

Pinpricks of light bled through the seams. Watching the violent barrage, Samantha wrapped her arms around one of Gage's talons. Holding on hard, horror spinning her mind in terrible directions, she watched the fabric tear. The tunnel exploded out-

ward. City lights flashed in a blinding surge of
brilliance.

"Son of a—"

"Bitch!" Samantha yelled, finishing Gage's thought
as he rocketed out of the tunnel, straight into the side
of a building.

~

FACED with a wall of steel and concrete at close range,
Gage considered smashing through it. For a split second. Before a different thought arrived hard on its
heels. Demolition derby might be fun on an ordinary
night, but no way, no how. A quick snapshot provided
details—blinds on windows, lamps on side tables, the
flash of white cabinetry through new windows. People
lived inside the pockmarked brick building. Which
made putting a dragon-sized hole in the side of an office tower-turned-condominium-complex a bad idea.

Humans talked.

Journalists reported.

A bunch of people KO'd while asleep amounted to
bad publicity. Not that he cared, but with Samantha
huddled inside his paw, he didn't want to make life
any more difficult. Not for her. Definitely not for him.
Killing humans wouldn't put him on her good side...
or him closer to getting her into bed.

Torn wide open, the tunnel rumbled around him.

Glass rattled in heavy steel frames.

Gage gritted his teeth, about to face-plant, at full
speed, into the side of a building. With no time to hit
the brakes, he sped up instead of slowing down.
Counterintuitive to most. Perfectly reasonable to him.
More speed equaled greater maneuverability. And as
his reflection flashed across arched windows, Gage

used momentum to his advantage. Tucking one wing, angling the other, he threw his head back. Wind whistled off his horns, carving through humid air. His bulk torqued into a spine-bending flip.

Hurricane-force winds struck the building, ripping chunks of brick from its carcass. The complex shuddered. Spinning upward, he tried to avoid making contact. A no go. The spikes along his spine raked over fire escapes. Sparks flew as his sharp edges sliced through solid steel. His tail whiplashed... a second strike.

The structure bolted to the side of the building groaned.

Split down the middle, the section of stairs listed to one side, then gave up and let go. Steel shrieked against brick as it fell off the side of the building. Nine stories of stairs landed in the parking lot, crushing cars, setting off alarms, cutting through power lines at the back of the lot.

Lights behind windows started to come on.

Gage murmured.

Magic sparked in his veins, then came online. A cloaking spell closed around him. As he disappeared into thin air, his senses contracted. Hearing sharper than any beings' on Earth, he picked up human chatter. Sheets rustled. Feet hit the floor. Fingers doing the walking, the residents inside the upscale condos began dialing 911.

Lying belly-down in the center of his palm, Samantha whipped around, her eyes huge as she watched sparks fly and headlights flash.

Deploying another evasive maneuver, Gage shot toward the roofline. His claws caught concrete. More sparks flew as the lethal tips scored the side of the complex.

"Holy crap," Samantha breathed, her mouth hanging open.

Finding her amusing, he flashed fang and opened his wings, and using the brick facade as a launchpad, pushed off. He rocketed skyward on a sideways spin. The foundation shook. Humans yelled in alarm. Balconies on the top floor groaned, industrial-sized bolts buckled beneath the pressure, sending platforms full of patio furniture into free fall.

One collided with the next, collecting more on the way down.

The tangled mess hit the ground with a crash.

Wheeling into a fast turn, Gage surveyed the destruction. He clenched his teeth. Fucking hell. So much for quick and quiet. Forget about making a silent getaway. Any rogues patrolling the area (a distinct possibility, given the clusterfuck on Bainbridge Island) would already be on high alert, and he'd just banged a gong. Announced his arrival at... he scowled at the condo complex.

Where the fuck had he landed?

Looking around, Gage scanned his surroundings. Night vision turned night to day, allowing him to see everything. Landmarks leaped into focus. He cursed as he got his bearings. Once an industrial park, now a residential area full of refurbished warehouses and renovated brick buildings. Condo central, miles outside the city center. Nowhere near Black Diamond.

Goddamn it. Nian needed his head ripped off.

The male never listened. Tonight appeared to be no exception. Instead of ensuring he exited the illusion close to the Nightfury lair, the namby-pamby set him down north of Seattle, along the shoreline, a five-minute flight from the safe house.

"Little prick," Gage growled under his breath, not liking his options.

Two existed.

One—take the risk, bank hard, and head for home —while hoping the Razorbacks didn't catch on, and he made it out of Seattle without drawing attention.

Two—play it safe and land at the safe house Rikar set up for his mate. He wanted to go with the first option. Fly fast for Black Diamond. Settle Samantha into his loft. Sleep curled around her in his own bed. Be present so his son had what he needed. Osgard might be healing, but he wasn't the epitome of mental health yet. He held onto fear. Became jumpy as hell— wouldn't sleep—without Gage to shield him during the day.

Totally whacked.

Completely alarming, but...

His son needed him. Would for a while, so spending the day at the safe house wasn't optimal. Wings swaying in an updraft, Gage debated. Risk his mate. Protect his son. An untenable position. One he couldn't—

"Hey. You all right?"

He glanced down.

Blue eyes full of concern met his.

"No," he muttered, refusing to lie to her.

"What else is wrong?"

Amusement spiraled deep, relieving some of his tension. *"What else?"*

"Well, given we nearly crashed into a building, I'd say things are all kinds of wrong," she said, sass out in full force, hands moving in smooth patterns. "But I've decided to let that go, 'cause—"

"Good of you," he said, interrupting, biting down on the urge to laugh.

Ignoring the interruption, she sailed on. More hand signals. Beautiful. Smooth. Symmetry in motion as her palms turned and fingers moved. "You looked worried."

"Not worried, wildcat... frustrated."

"Why?"

"I wanna go home. I want you in my arms. In my own fucking bed, not one in town."

Shock winged across her face.

"Get used to the idea, Samantha. It's gonna happen," he said, shifting in flight, drifting down the coast toward Magnolia Street. Well, guess that answered that. His dragon half knew where he wanted his mate—inside the safe house, and... hell. Who was he kidding? The beast was right. Osgard would recover. Samantha was more important than a missed night of sleep. Moving from slow drift to fast glide, he held her gaze and opened a link into mind-speak. *"Haider—how close are you?"*

And hope sprang eternal.

Even knowing the right way to go, he wanted to exhaust all avenues. Maybe with backup, he could make it to Black Diamond. Maybe with wingmates, he wouldn't have to choose between—

A snarl rippled through mind-speak, raising his hackles. His scales tingled. The spikes along his spine rippled. Loud music rolled through the cosmic link. Thumping bass. The hard vocal edges of a rap song. Human voices shouting along.

Muffled by the music, Haider's voice cut through. *"Damn it, Nian... let go. Let go of her."*

Gage blinked. *Her?*

What the fuck?

A female moaned.

The sound of a scuffle bled through the connection.

"No... don't," Nian rasped. *"I need her. I need—"*

"Let go," Haider said, tone tight. *"Right now."*

Gage growled. *"What's happening?"*

"Nian's lost his mind." Haider sighed, sounding resigned and pissed off at the same time. *"Took a bad hit. I got him what he needs, but... fucking hell."*

"Where are you?"

"Hang on, man. I gotta—"

More snarling.

Lots of cursing.

The sound of a fist cracking against bone, and Nian grunting in pain. The female whimpered, then whined, begging for more pleasure. Talking in a firm tone, his best friend backed her off while struggling to control Nian at the same time.

Upping his wing speed, Gage sent out an exploratory ping.

Magic laid down a grid, rushing over houses and apartment complexes, hunting for the signal Haider emitted like a beacon. A blip appeared on his mental screen. His eyes narrowed. Close to the safe house. A few streets over, in the commercial district running through the neighborhood full of restaurants and bars.

"I'm on my way."

"No," Haider said, voice guttural and strained. *"Almost done. Won't be here much longer. Got company coming to the safe house that'll finish him off. Meet us there."*

Got company coming.

Code for the high-price call girls Daimler kept on speed dial.

Gage huffed. Terrific. Just great. Another minefield

to navigate. A reality he didn't want to share with his mate just yet. Not that he'd be availing himself of call-girl services anymore. His days of fucking strangers was over.

Long gone. Good riddance.

Finding Samantha changed everything. In the best possible way. With her in his life, the struggle for him ceased. Her bioenergy matched his down to the decimal point. Perfect pitch. Precise frequency. Now, when he fed, he'd get what he needed. A steady stream of nourishment calibrated to the exact specifications his magical makeup required to stay healthy and strong.

So yeah, no more hookers.

And absolutely no lying.

He didn't want to freak her out, but would have to come clean at some point. Sooner or later, reality would come knocking, and she'd bear witness. See those girls called in to service the un-mated Nightfuries.

It didn't happen often, but wasn't rare.

When shit went sideways, a Dragonkind warrior didn't have time to charm a female. Up close and personal took time to achieve in the wilds of society. A male didn't have that luxury when he needed an immediate infusion of energy. Under normal circumstances, warriors healed fast. Minor injuries didn't require skin-to-skin contact. But when disaster struck, feeding by plugging into the Meridian—through a human female—became a matter of life or death.

A reality his kind lived with every day.

One ensured by a vengeful Sun Goddess.

By fault or design, she'd hamstrung his race. Fracturing all ties to the Meridian with a few angry words. Cutting his kind off from the electrostatic bands ringing the planet, forever blocking Dragonkind's ability to enter the stream. Without the ability to draw from the source, a male would starve to death. Slowly. Painfully. Brutally. Wasting away. Becoming a shell of his former self. Suffering until his heart stopped beating, and he disintegrated into a pile of ash.

Which put human females on the hook.

A male required three points of contact to feed—nape, temple, and base of spine. Simple. Clean. Effective. Though, most warriors took it farther, giving females what most demanded. Hot, sweaty sex and multiple orgasms. Gage hummed. The sound vibrated in the back of his throat, turning into a purr. An image of Samantha wrapped around him winged into his head. Bodies connecting. Pleasure erupting. Heat and powerful energy flowing, sustaining him, pleasing her.

Fuck.

He could hardly wait for it to happen. Couldn't wait to strip her down and put his hands on her. Skin to skin. Heart to heart. Her taste in his mouth. Her hands in his hair. Her curves pressed hard against him. His scent on her, and hers all over him.

With a low growl, Gage searched the shoreline. He spotted the house up on the rise. Windows glowing with soft light, the house was a thing of beauty. Modern lines. Slanted roof. Huge yard landscaped in an elegant design. Cleverly placed outdoor lights acted like a runaway, leading him in over the water. Swinging wide, he leveled his wings and lined up his approach. Craggy beachfront gave way to rolling lawn. He picked his spot, and rolling in on a fast glide, folded his wings.

Gravity yanked him out of the air.

His back paws thumped down, causing a chain reaction. Different-sized pots with colorful plants jumped along the walkway. Terracotta clanked as he settled his wings. A gust of wind blew onto the wide stone patio. Garden lights hanging from the trellis swayed. Gage hardly noticed. Desire riding him hard, focused on his mate, he shifted from dragon to human form. Talons turned to hands, then slid down her back.

She startled.

Her head tipped back as he wrapped her tight against him. Breasts to chest. No space between her and him. Setting her flat palms against his bare chest, she took a deep breath. No doubt preparing to tell him off, back him up and... set a boatload of bullshit boundaries. She started to talk. Eyes glued to her mouth, unable to wait an instant longer, Gage dipped his head and invaded her mouth, cutting off her attempt to scold him.

17

Tangled up with Gage, Samantha lost her mind. Completely. Totally. No other way to explain it. Deep in his embrace, his taste in her mouth and her hands on his skin, desperation scrambled her molecules. The consequence? Her brain malfunctioned, sending the wrong signals, telling her to pull him closer, hold on harder, and pray she got every bit of him.

All he promised her.

A bad idea, but...

She needed more. Deeper contact. Lots of skin on skin. For him to lay her down and strip her bare.

With a growl, he slid his hands beneath the hem of her shirt. Callous palms rasped over her back, around her waist, up her ribcage. Pleasure burned through her. The touch-kiss combo sent her spinning. Desire burned through thoughts of her pulling away. Incendiary need. Unstoppable pleasure. A blast of desire so devastating, thoughts of retreating slipped away.

Fisting her hands in his hair, she deepened the kiss. Thick, soft strands in her grip. More of his taste in her mouth. More of his intensity wrapped around her. She shivered in delight as a tremor rumbled through her. Intellect ended up buried beneath the rubble. And yet, good sense refused to let her go. Remnants of it called through the debris, turning her attention, trying to dig her out.

Mind reeling, body heating, she grappled with the eternal question.

Should she? Or shouldn't she?

Sleeping with Gage would be a mistake. Samantha knew it deep down. The more entangled she became with him, the harder it would be to leave. But as the avalanche he unleashed inside her continued, Samantha struggled to find balance. Prudence urged her to push him away. Logic insisted she shouldn't be kissing him back. And self-preservation screamed, predicting dire consequences if she slipped beneath his spell. Problem was...

She didn't want to stop.

The more he gave her, the more she wanted. She longed for one night. Just one night. A safe place to express everything she kept bottled up inside. All the heat. All the yearning. A way to exorcise her demons and shake the loneliness, if only for a little while. And Gage? God, he was beautiful. He might be intense, but instinct told her he'd be an amazing lover. Dominant. Skilled. Strong, yet gentle. Coaxing a response from her she'd never been able to admit, never mind felt free enough to unleash.

Sex had never been easy for her.

From the second she started noticing boys, her deafness had always been a barrier. A mountain to climb. A river to cross. An ocean to swim. No one wanted to date the girl who couldn't hear. Well, no one but jerks. Those guys wanted to feel her up in the backs of cars and brag about it to their buddies the next day. But good guys—the ones who stuck around after sex, wanting to talk, liking the closeness—always went for the normal girls. Ones they could actually *talk* to without needing a notepad. Or a crash course in ALS.

But Gage didn't know yet.

He hadn't guessed, which made her feel both bold... and crappy.

Dishonesty never went unpunished. She should come clean. Tell him before they went any further, but as he nipped her bottom lip, Samantha let the truth go. She wanted one experience. Just one without judgement. Without feeling the need to explain. So, she went for it. Went after him and, one hand tunneling through his hair, sent the other searching.

Fingers spread wide for maximum contact, she stroked over his shoulder, across his chest, under his arm, down his back, learning the texture of his skin. Heavy muscle contracted. His body reacted, becoming harder against her belly. Emboldened, she dove beneath the waistband of his jeans.

His groan vibrated down her throat.

Reveling in his reaction, she licked over his bottom lip. Her mouth brushing his, she demanded, "More."

Breathing hard, he tipped his chin down and opened his eyes. Orange flecks glowed in his bronze gaze. Fierce. Intense. Conveying the strength of his need. His hands flat against her back, he pressed in, making her arch into him. He bared his teeth. "Be sure, *volamaia*."

Her throat vibrated. The sound came from deep inside her. Could've been a growl. Could've been a rough whimper. Samantha didn't know. She couldn't hear it, but she saw Gage's reaction.

His expression grew fiercer. The shimmer in his gaze intensified.

On her toes, she dropped her head forward, pressing her forehead beneath his jaw. Day old whiskers grazed her. Pleasure spiraled through her. Brutal. Beautiful. So crazy good. The best kind of rush as her mouth trailed over his pulse point. A gentle suck. A quick flick of her tongue. Easy-to-read communication. No need for words. She used some anyway, rounding him with her arms, talking against his skin. "More, Gage. Everything. Hot. Hard. Heavy. I want it all."

His grip on her firmed. Tingles erupted, sparking inside her as his hands slid down. Slow glide. Steady pressure. Beautiful, devastating sensation as he cupped her behind.

He lifted.

She received the silent message and hopped up, wrapping her legs around his hips. Needing more of him, she dipped her head. Her lips hit his. Head tipped back, he opened his mouth. She slid inside, getting a contact high as she tangled her tongue with his and drank deep.

Addiction.

This was how it started.

With burning need and unquenchable thirst. Gage was like that—tempting her with the promise of oblivion, making the world fade away. And as he started walking with her wrapped around him, she got her fix. Mainlined him. Memorized him. Filing the feel of him away to draw from later. Taking what she wanted, getting what she needed, knowing that when passion and pleasure faded and the truth came out, the recriminations would start, and the way he looked at her would change.

～

WILD NEED SPIRALED FROM HER, hitting him like a
body shot, rocking him off his foundations. Blind to
everything but her, Gage fisted his hand in her hair.
Thick strands clung to his skin, caressing him as he
deepened the kiss. She mewed in welcome, kissing
him back with a hunger so stark she undid him. Stitch
by stitch. Thread by thread. Fiery passion pulling him
apart. Aroused female stoking his passion higher.
Beautiful bliss calling his name.

Consumed by her heat, he lost his equilibrium...
along with his mind. So good. Unbelievably sweet.
Unabashed in her desire to get closer.

His mate. So fucking *wild*.

One hand gripping her ass, the other tangled in
her hair, he held her hard against him, legs wrapped
around his waist, breasts pressed to his chest, tongue
dueling with his, and stepped onto the pathway. The
soles of his boots thumped across stone as he headed
for the raised patio. He needed to get her into the
house. Needed to get into a bedroom and strip her
down. Needed her naked beneath him... and his
mouth between her thighs.

Gage groaned. Fuck, a taste. He wanted a taste of
her right now. Didn't think he could wait. Didn't
think—

Small hands fisted in his hair, Samantha rolled her
hips.

Her core stroked the ridge of his erection. Gorgeous heat burned through his button fly. Pleasure hit
him like a closed fist.

His pace slowed.

Halfway across the patio, he stopped walking,
struggling to stick to his plan. One that involved a bed,
a soft and sweet loving, not a hard fuck. He'd
promised her gentle the first time, but... Goddess. She

was too good. He wanted her so badly, and as her hands roamed, one down his back, the other over his shoulder, nails scraping his skin, kissing him like he'd never been kissed before, Gage knew he wasn't going to make it. Her acceptance obliterated his control.

Fucking hell.

All around him.

She was *all around him*. Hands on his skin. Fingers in his hair. Tongue in his mouth. Soft curves undulating against his hard angles. The heat between her thighs scorching him. Every bit of her fantastic.

All of it a revelation.

He'd had a lot of women. Been greedy all his life and fucked more than his fair share. In many countries, on several different continents. None of them came close to the beauty of Samantha. She met and matched his desire. Fired his imagination. Overwhelmed his senses, making him want in ways he never had before. Not once since his *first shift* almost two hundred years ago had he desired a female the way he wanted her.

A long time to live without meaningful connection.

A lifetime spent waiting for the one meant to be his.

A gift. She was a *gift*. Precious. Wild. Natural and unabashed in his arms, taking what she wanted, refusing to hide her need, cracking him wide open. And as the Meridian surged, streaming through her, nourishing him, Gage finally understood. He hadn't realized how much he needed his mate until now. He'd thought he was fine. A self-contained male. No serious hang-ups. Content with life. A completed package, no missing pieces.

Samantha proved him wrong, making it clear he

needed more than a quick exchange with a strange female at the back of a club.

Fine on its face.

Nowhere near good enough.

He should've realized sooner. Fuck, he saw it everywhere he looked. Inside the lair. All over the mated Nightfury warriors' faces. In the way each one revered his chosen female, placing her well-being above all else. The right female brought a male contentment. Samantha didn't know it yet, but what she gave him couldn't be quantified. Deep connection. Soul-stealing acceptance. Life-affirming desire, meeting each of his caresses with one of her own. Ramping him higher. Shoving him past the limits of his control. Binding him to her so tight, desperation came knocking. Off-balanced, breathing hard, trying to remain gentle, he turned his head and tore his mouth from hers.

Her grip on him tightened. "No. No. No."

"*Volamaia*, wait. I... we—"

"No." Gaze on his mouth, she rolled her hips again and... fuck. She was fighting dirty. Fanning his flames. Pushing him in the direction she wanted him to go. "No waiting. Now, Gage... now."

"Sam—"

"Please. Please. I need it. I want it. *Please*."

The desperation in her voice wrenched control out of his hands.

Unable to withstand the onslaught, Gage gave in. With a snarl, he stripped the pack off her back and tossed it aside. Her jacket followed. Both landed with a thud on the stone patio. He pivoted toward an outdoor lounger. Round. Huge. Able to accommodate multiple males, the daybed sat in front of a wall of windows. Low light glinted from behind the pulled shades, bathing the bed in shadows, making the thick cushions look more black than red.

Three quick strides took him to it.

A faster descent took him down.

Samantha's back landed on the daybed. Thick cushions sighed as he settled against her. She moaned. He reared, and hands working fast, yanked her shirt up. Her arms jerked up as he tore it off her. Blond hair tumbled around her shoulders. Smooth skin bathed in soft light. Racy black bra with a red bow between her breasts. Gorgeous fucking female.

His.

All his.

Needing his mouth on her, he tugged at the lace, tucking the cups beneath her breasts. Nipples furled tight, she made a sound at the back of her throat. Part purr, mostly needy. Dipping his head, he went at her. No warm-up. Zero concern for her delicacy. His mouth closed around a pink bud and sucked... hard.

"Ohmigod." Her head flew back, pressing into the cushions. He sucked harder, then backed off and nipped the tip, grazing her with his teeth, unable to be gentle, giving her rough. Her back arched, hips bucking as she got what she wanted—hard and fast. "Yes."

He switched to the other breast. Paid homage. Gave her the same treatment, a mixture of rough and gentle as he suckled one nipple and rolled the other between his fingertips.

"Fuck," she moaned.

Keeping at her, he stroked down her skin with his free hand. His hand slid over her ribcage and across her belly, learning the feel of her, memorizing each curve and every hollow. A quick snap, and he opened her jeans. A fast yank and the zipper gave, sliding down halfway. He didn't wait. Using his knees, he spread her wide. Without mercy or warning, his hand slid down and in, beneath satin and lace, straight to the heart of her.

He closed his eyes, ecstasy whipping through him as his fingers slipped through her wet. Hot. Tight. So fucking slick she was drenched. Holding her nipple between his teeth, he licked over the sensitive tip and played in her heat. Thrust two fingers in, stroked over the tight bud at the top of her sex. Circle hard. Advance. Retreat. Setting a fast pace. Forcing her to ride to his rhythm as he worked at her breasts. One, then the other, refusing to let her up for air.

Hands fisted in his hair, she rode the wave, hips bucking, whimpers coming from her throat, so deep in need she begged for the pleasure.

He upped the pace, feeling her writhe beneath him.

She lost her breath. A tremor raked her. "God. Please, Gage. I'm close... so *close*."

Releasing her breast, Gage pushed onto his knees, breaking her hold on him as he yanked her jeans and boots off. More black lace. He tore the panties down her legs, settled in between, and put his mouth on her. The majesty of her hit his tongue. Groaning, Gage threw her legs over his shoulders and, licking deep, worshiped her.

Unapologetically.

Giving no quarter.

Glorying in the scent and taste of her.

She arched like the wildcat she was, raking her nails over his skin as he took what he wanted and gave what she demanded.

Setting a fast pace, he pushed her toward the brink. Little heels digging into his shoulders, she tilted her hips, pressed up, begging for more. He pushed her back down, holding her still, making her take him the way he wanted to give it.

"God," she rasped, straining against him, tittering on the edge.

Gaze riveted to her face, he circled her clit with the tip of his tongue. Her bottom lip trembled. Her mouth moved. No sound came out as she reached for the pleasure. Watching her, he bit down gently, holding her bud between his teeth. Her breath hitched. She froze, mouth open, eyes closed, back arched, quivering beneath him. He made her wait a moment, then flicked her. A strong, rough stroke right over top of her clitoris.

Her body jerked.

Head tipped back, Samantha screamed in pleasure.

Gage laughed as she shook and, ripping open his button fly, surged between her thighs. He found her on the first stroke, thrusting deep, filling her full. Blistering heat closed around him. Hot. Wet. So fucking tight he groaned as he sank into heaven and she contracted around him. Locking her arms and legs around him, she gasped his name. He rode her through her orgasm, pushing her into a second as he reached for his own.

Pressure built at the base of his spine.

Planting his forearm into the cushion, Gage unhooked her leg from around the back of his thigh. He pushed her knee high and wide, riding her harder, pounding deeper, watching her take him as he sank inside her.

His focus moved from their connection to her face. "Eyes."

"Gage."

"Eyes, Samantha. Give' em to me," he murmured, gripping her chin to get her attention.

Her lashes fluttered. Gorgeous blue eyes met his. Unfocused. A little shocked. Hazy with pleasure. "Please."

Chest brushing over her breasts, he cupped her thigh, held her wide, powering in, sliding out, working her as he held her gaze. "Go again, wildcat."

She shook her head, defying him.

He thrust in, paused, grinding against her. "Again."

"Gage," she whispered, breath hitching.

"You're going to give it to me again, *volamaia*. Not gonna stop until you do," he growled, lifting up, reaching in, hitting the spot.

Her core contracted around him.

Hot.

Tight.

Fraying his control.

She shuddered in his arms.

The second he felt her start, Gage dipped his head. His mouth met hers. She opened, tangling their tongues, moaning down his throat, taking him to heights previously unknown as she came apart around him. Again. Finally. For the third time. Her climax shoved him over the edge. Unable to hold on, Gage let go, body bucking, heart racing, soul rejoicing as delight brutalized him and his mate brought him to paradise, welcoming him home.

18

Flat on her back on thick cushions, half canopy of the outdoor daybed rising above her, Samantha lay pinned beneath Gage. He hadn't moved. Neither had she. She liked where she was—bare skin pressed to his, his arms snug around her and hips beneath her thighs. His lips ghosted over her pulse point, moving against her throat.

Heaven.

The absolute best.

More than she ever expected from a man in bed.

The affectionate touch messed with her head, even as her heart sighed, loving his heat and weight and the scent of musk and man. Nestled in for the long haul, she cradled him with her body, pressed her cheek to his temple and breathed. Her eyes slid closed, blocking out the night as emotion swelled, threatening to spill over. This right here. *THIS* was spectacular. Stupendous. Everything she wanted. All she dreamed about, which meant one of two things.

Either she was crazy, or altogether brilliant.

Samantha weighed the options, but couldn't decide. All she knew was... letting him make love to her, being held by him in the aftermath, qualified as one of those *never-have-I-ever* moments. Never had she ever slept with a man she'd just met. Never had she ever had sex outside, beneath the stars in open air, where anyone might walk by and see. Never had she ever been given multiple orgasms by a man-dragon who knew how to use his mouth and fingers and tongue.

Her core tightened, rippling around him.

Still inside her, Gage rumbled in reaction. As the vibration moved from his chest into hers, his teeth grazed the side of her throat. She drew in a long breath. Holy. God. So good. So freaking *good*... but also very, very bad. Samantha knew it. Could sense emotional ruin lurking just around the corner. Plotting. Waiting. About to drop a bomb she wanted to avoid.

Hands moving on his back, she opened her eyes and stared at the curving canopy. Beige canvas above her head. Bright red cushions beneath her back. Gage all over her. She'd gone insane. Completely lost her mind along with her self-respect. She wanted to ask what the hell she'd been thinking, but with her body still tingling, she didn't bother.

She knew what she'd been thinking.

Nothing. Absolutely *nothing* at all.

Somewhere along the way, passion snuck in, stole her brain, then dragged common sense into the depths of a mental alley and shot it. With a double-barrel shotgun. Chewing on the inside of her cheek, Samantha teetered off the edge of worry. As she fell, the truth—the pesky one that scared her—came calling.

She didn't want to face it. Didn't want to acknowledge anything but the beauty of the man in her arms, but as her emotional train crashed, she refused to look away. Her decision to sleep with Gage bordered on irresponsible. Toss ill-advised and wrong-headed into the slice-and-dice of her mental salad, and all of a sudden, brilliant wasn't looking quite so smart anymore.

No matter how much she wanted Gage, having him wasn't a good idea. Making love to Gage ranked as...

Samantha pursed her lips.

Well.

She wanted to label it "a mistake."

Her heart got there first, inserting "fantastic," "eye-opening," and "absolutely worth it" into the already confusing mix. And well... okay. Lying in his arms with his body warm and heavy against hers, refuting the assertion became difficult. Near impossible.

He'd been amazing. Full stop. A combination of gentle and rough, the kind of lover she fantasized about on a regular basis. Alone in her bed. Late at night when loneliness snuck in and she had nothing to do but imagine. She'd dreamed of a man like him. Dominant. Focused. Sexual wizard in bed.

Unable to help herself, savoring the feel, she ran her hands over him. Soft caresses. A gentle exploration—fingers drifting over his back, thighs tucked to his sides, jaw pressed against his hair. Enthralled, she breathed him in again. Spicy scent. Decadent and addictive. One hundred percent him. No aftershave. No fancy colognes. All Gage, a soothing mix of masculine musk, heat, and hard body.

Errant thoughts floated away, taking self-recrimination with it.

She should enjoy him while it lasted. Soak in the experience. Commit him to memory. Revel in his ready affection. Go with the flow, instead of doing what she always did—worry about the bumpy road ahead—'cause God, he was beautiful. Powerful. Attentive. Honest as all frigging hell.

Her mouth curved as she admitted he hadn't been wrong. Arrogant in his prediction, sure, but not off the mark. The second he kissed her, she ignited, flaring bright, becoming the wildcat he liked to call her. Thinking about it, she wondered what came over her. She'd never been comfortable with sex. Being different threw up barriers, making intimacy difficult, but that wasn't it. Or at least, not all of it.

She'd just assumed she wasn't one of those women. The kind who took what they wanted without hesitation or apology. Business. Relationships. Sex. Didn't matter the domain or the people involved, women with confidence went after things. Expected things. Worked to create the life they wanted, instead of accepting the scraps society threw at them.

Her brows furrowed.

Something to ponder. Something to strive for and—

Gage shifted. His hips pressed deeper, making pleasure ripple through her as his mouth moved against her throat.

Words.

He was talking to her. Saying something. Praise, maybe. An inquiry, perhaps, making sure she was okay. None of which she could hear. Or understand without being able to read his lips.

Tension flickered through her.

Her muscles locked, causing her hands to still on his back. Denial along with a healthy dose of God-not-yet, made her curl into him. Deeper. Tighter. With a shiver of dread. The need to keep him close rolled through her. Swinging her legs in, she curled one around the back of his thigh. The other settled across his lower back as she panicked, trying to figure out what to do, how to act... the best way forward.

His chest vibrated against hers. More words, heralding disaster as he expected a reply she couldn't give.

Throat gone tight, Samantha swallowed past the fear, knowing playtime was over. She couldn't continue to hide. Sooner or later, he'd notice she couldn't hear. Figure it out and confront her, so no help for it. She couldn't go back, could only go forward, which left nothing for her to do but rip open the wound. Come clean, step out from beneath the barrier she used as protection and... watch him retreat.

Big hand drifting over the back of her thigh, he repeated himself. She felt the vibration. Felt his lips move against her throat.

"Gage."

With a hum, he kissed her pulse point.

She shivered, reacting to the gentle touch, then took a fortifying breath. Like a Band-Aid. She needed to rip it off just like a Band-Aid. Quick and brutal, no matter how painful.

"I can't hear you, handsome," she whispered, bracing for his reaction. "You've gotta raise your head. I need to see your lips if you want me to understand."

He stilled. The lazy, highly pleasant caress along the back of her thigh ceased. Face still pressed to her throat, his fingers flexed, tightening around the side of her knee. A second later, he moved. Heavy muscle contracted. His chest brushed over the tips of her breasts as he shifted his hips and pulled out, leaving her empty. Hollowness hit her as he planted his forearm in the cushion by her shoulder. Thick strands of his dark hair messy, he raised his head. Bronze eyes with oranges flecks met hers. Expression set, brows furrowed, he stared at her.

Her stomach clenched.

His gaze bore into hers. "Say again?"

She read his lips, and then, heart racing and hurting rising, looked him in the eye. "I can't hear you. I'm deaf."

His eyes narrowed.

Panic made her blurt, "Happened when I was fifteen. Meningitis. Bad fever. Touch and go, I almost didn't make it."

"What the fuck?"

And she kept blathering, "My mom... my mom... she was on another bender. Never home. Off with... shit, I don't know who. But I managed to make it onto the walkway outside our apartment. Bad neighborhood, but good neighbors. One of them got me to the hospital."

He scowled at her.

She held the line, refusing to look away, waiting for the explosion. For his temper to spike, then rumble into view. One moment slid into the next without him saying anything. Her heart picked up the pace, slamming inside her chest as he studied her.

Time stretched.

Wretched delay. Felt like forever—hours, days, a year—as she waited for him to react. For him to push away and treat her the way most people did after finding out she couldn't hear. Become uncomfortable, make their excuses and back away, rejecting her out of hand.

STARING DOWN AT HIS MATE, Gage struggled to control his anger. Left alone in an apartment in a bad neighborhood. Young. Scared. So sick she burned with fever. A fifteen-year-old girl trying to fend for herself as she waited for her mother to come home.

The idea sent him sideways inside his head.

His dragon half reacted.

Anger turned to fury.

The fucking bitch. How dare she leave Samantha to suffer like that? Clenching his teeth, Gage suppressed a growl. What kind of woman did that to her child? What kind of mother failed so completely? An abusive one. A drug-addled one. A selfish one with zero control and even less sense.

Way of the world.

Parents dropped the ball all the time. Children suffered the consequences, looking after themselves, growing up too fast, or worse, getting dropped into the system. But his mate? Shit. She'd suffered more than most, getting dealt a raw deal—becoming sick, losing her hearing, being struck by bad luck and a worse mother.

Brushing the hair away from her face, Gage grappled with the truth. She'd been hurt by someone who should've loved and cared for her. She'd been wronged, then discarded, and as he watched pain gather in her eyes, he knew he needed to lock himself down. Samantha didn't need him to be angry on her behalf. She needed soothing, his understanding along with a conversation. Which meant...

He needed to bank his rage and find his voice.

Silence wasn't helping her. He saw it in her face. Felt it in the raging beat of her heart. And yet as her words came to him again, echoing inside his head, Gage struggled to move in that direction. Her admission sent his vicious half rambling. The pain in her eyes did the rest, making him imagine what he'd do if he ever came face-to-face with her mother.

Wouldn't be pretty.

His mate would no doubt object.

His way of righting wrongs was not hers. Not human at all. He wouldn't be turning the other cheek. Dragonkind operated under a different set of principles. His kind was comfortable with violence... and using it to protect their own.

"Gage—get off me," she whispered, sounding so broken his heart lurched. "You need to—"

"No," he growled, battling to bring his reaction to the wrong done to her under control. One moment slid into another before he managed to lock it down. His anger receded, leaving him with a clear mind and a clearer way forward. "I don't, *volamaia*."

"You can't—"

"Wanna bet?"

She blinked. Surprise sparked in her eyes, making bright blue even bluer.

He settled back in, trapping her beneath him, making sure she stayed put as he plotted the best way forward. He'd missed so much. Hadn't done his duty as her mate and paid close enough attention. Had he listened to his intuition, he would've realized sooner. Understood faster that something other than her high-energy status set her apart. Made her different and unique. Had he clued in, he would've put her at ease the moment he met her, and she wouldn't be looking at him with fear in her eyes now.

Gage released a pent-up breath.

Deaf.

Jesus. His mate was *deaf*.

Now he understood everything. The little things that hadn't made sense before made perfect sense now. The odd accent. The sight rounding of consonants and flattening of vowels. Her focus on his mouth when he spoke to her. She couldn't hear the sound of his voice without power of mind-meld.

Empathy rose hard on the heels of the realization.

Holding her gaze, heart aching for her, Gage murmured her name. No doubt reading compassion as scorn, she flinched, then tried to escape by sliding out from underneath him. His hand flexed around her knee, keeping her leg curled around his hip. Setting his other hand under her ear, he slid his fingers into the hair at the nape of her neck. Palm resting against her jaw, he swept the pad of his thumb over the apple of her cheek. She tried to turn her face away. He held firm, delivering a message of his own.

No hiding.

Zero retreat.

He needed her with him. One hundred percent focused on him when he explained. The uncertainty in her eyes provided details, filling in the blanks. The picture of her life became clear in an instant. Now, he knew what she faced day in and day out—how others treated her when they found out, the way she moved through the world, and what she expected of him now that he knew.

He clenched his teeth.

She expected him to reject her.

The idea shoved compassion out of the way. Disbelief galloped in to replace it. His brows snapped together. Was she out of her fucking mind? She must be, if she thought he'd ever let her go. After what they just shared? After all the heat and pleasure and... fucking hell. She was beauty personified. Generous in her passion. Gorgeous in her acceptance. So hot she drove him wild—made him lose control—without even trying.

Sassy. Smart. Beautiful.

His mate was the whole package. He liked everything about her. Enjoyed the way her mind worked. Appreciated the fact she wasn't afraid of him. Loved the way she met and matched him in and out of bed. She interested him. She challenged him. She excited him. One look at her and his body reacted, becoming hard, preparing to fuck... like say, the way it was doing right now with her blue eyes on him and the pink tips of her breasts on display.

Hmmm. His mate. Gorgeous pain in his ass. At least, right now, given he couldn't make love to her again. Not with her head fucked up. Round two would need to wait until after he made a few things clear and eased her fears.

Sweeping his thumb along her bottom lip, he held her gaze and deployed his magic. The Meridian hummed. Energy surged. Prickles shivered down his spine as the link opened, connecting him to her. Cradling the power in the seat of his mind, he expanded the scope and slipped inside her mental frame.

Samantha's eyes widened as he entered her mind. She jerked in reaction, lips parting on a sharp, indrawn breath and...

Resistance was futile.

He dipped his head and kissed her. He made it wet. He made it deep and long, taking his time, needing her to understand. She was his. *His*. Every fucking inch of her. No going back. No using her deafness as a way to push him away. He refused to allow the deflection, and her, to hold him back. He wanted it all. Every little piece of her. Didn't matter if she didn't like those pieces of herself. He did, which left her playing catch up, but... whatever.

"*Volamaia*," he murmured, lips brushing hers.

Her hands flexed in his hair. She shifted beneath him, restless and wanting, but managed a breathy, "Yeah?"

"Are you out of your fucking mind?"

She flinched at the fierceness in his voice. "What?"

"You haven't been listening, Samantha."

"Of course not," she said, tone tart, meeting his anger with attitude. "I can't hear you."

"Bullshit. You hear me just fine."

Wet hit her eyes. She blinked, trying to stave off the emotion. "Gage."

"You think I care?"

"You should," she whispered, a catch in her voice. "Nothing about me is easy. Nothing about being deaf is—"

"You haven't," he said, interrupting her, repeating himself. *"You've been listening, just not paying attention. You're my mate. My fucking mate. Doesn't matter how you come to me, I want all of you. Every piece. Light. Dark. Whole or broken. All my life... almost two hundred years... I've been waiting, wanting you, with no hope of ever finding you. If you think after living without you for so long, after finally meeting the female meant for me, I'd let you go, you are..."* he said, pressing the pads of his fingers into the side of her head. *"You're out of your fucking mind."*

"How can that be?"

"Dragonkind, wildcat. We live by a different set of rules. Ones you're gonna learn. Ones I'm gonna teach you. But it starts now. You and me—we start now." She lost the battle with her tears. One slid from the corner of her eye, rolling over her temple into her hair. Stroking over the wet trail, Gage wiped it away. *"No more running, Samantha."*

"I don't know what I'm getting into."

"You don't need to."

"What if we don't work?"

"We work."

"You can't be sure."

"I am," he said with firm conviction. *"No shaking a foundation that's already well set."*

Apprehension stole into her expression. "You're freaking me out."

"Not surprised. That's gonna happen. Until you learn our ways, I'm gonna freak you out, but stick with me. Take my hand, and I promise to guide you through the nightmare. Turn your bad dreams to good. Love you. Shield you. Give you what you need and everything you want."

"Big promises."

"Nothing but the truth."

"Love?"

"It's already happening. Energy-fuse, Samantha... the cosmic bond between mates has already taken hold. The connection's strong. So fucking strong, baby. Feel you with every breath I take. Want you with everything I am. Can't get enough, so I'm gonna take more. And you're gonna give it to me."

Another tear fell.

He wiped it away, soothing her with his touch. *"Gonna have it all, wildcat. Every little piece. Burrow in, dig down until I reach the heart of you."*

"You think I'm gonna give you that too?"

"Yeah."

She rolled her eyes. "Arrogant."

"Yeah."

"Annoying."

He grinned, encouraged by the fact she hadn't shut him down. His mate might be unsure, but she wasn't a coward. She was leaning in, allowing him to guide her

into the unknown, trusting him to keep his word—
and her safe—along the way.

Holding her gaze, he nipped her lower lip. *"Time
for round two, volamaia... slow and gentle this time."*

Interest sparked in her eyes. Her head tilted on the
cushion. She pursed her lips, playing at contempla-
tion, trying to act like she was thinking about it. The
wiggle gave her away, telling him she wanted him as
much as he did her. Seeing it, feeling it, Gage wasted
no time. He deepened the kiss and dragged her back
into desire, giving what she wanted, getting what he
needed, a slow, steady loving in the arms of a female
he'd waited a lifetime to claim.

19

S torm clouds rumbling in the distance, Ivar flew over the human neighborhood on a fast glide. Southeast end of Bainbridge Island, a small community facing off with Seattle across Puget Sound. Raindrops spattered over his scales. Water rolled off the tips of his horns as he tilted his head and scanned the ground, getting the lay of the land.

Set at equal intervals, streetlights glowed in the haze.

His night vision flickered, reacting to bright light from three hundred feet up. He curled his lip, baring the points of his fangs. Stupid LEDs. The fuckers always messed with his light-sensitive eyes. Gaze narrowed, protecting his retinas from the glare, he switched to infrared. The scene evened out, allowing him to pick up details.

Wooded area. Rambling suburb. Old houses situated on big lots with mature trees and old-growth hedges. Slowing his speed by half, he searched for his target, gliding over the winding gravel road in front of human homes perched on cliffs overlooking the water.

Sharp drop-off.

No beachfront.

Boulders, some jagged, others smooth, tucked against the base of the cliffs.

Ivar scanned the terrain again. His eyes narrowed on a low-slung rooftop. Small bungalow shaded by huge oaks. No car in the driveway. No lights on inside the house or any of the others along the street. Quiet. Calm. Everyone tucked in for the night, humans dreaming dreams that would never come true. *Guess X marked the spot.* Not that he wanted anything to do with the female's house. He hadn't picked the location. Didn't want to take the meeting, or need the aggravation, but...

Some things couldn't be avoided.

Lightning flashed across dark water, throwing out a warning. Ivar took the hint, even though he didn't need it. He knew what he was flying into—a bad situation. A clash of titans, the first of many rounds with a sadistic warrior with a superiority complex.

And daddy issues.

Ivar should know. He knew the male well. Had spent more time than he wanted to admit becoming acquainted with Zidane. He growled long and low. Archguard asshole. Spoiled brat. Rodin's firstborn son merited both titles. He'd earned them, clashing with Ivar in Prague, bad-mouthing him to Daddy Dearest, trying to score cheap points in an effort to put Ivar down and make himself look better. Butting up against Zidane had happened far too often. More than necessary before Ivar jumped the Atlantic, making the move to Seattle.

Not his favorite memories. More like lessons in extreme frustration populated by bursts of monumental unpleasantness. And now here Zidane was again—a world away from Prague, encroaching where he didn't belong.

He sighed in resignation.

His cross to bear. Along with a battle Ivar didn't want to fight, but like anything in life, sometimes random events collided to produce disagreeable results. Like, oh say, Zidane setting up house in his territory.

His fault in many ways.

He'd set the ball rolling months ago. Accepting blood money from Rodin. Sharing information about the breeding program and his ongoing feud with the Nightfuries. Telling Rodin things the male didn't need to know. His decision to play nice with Dragonkind elite, make friends instead of enemies, sounded like a good idea at the time. Now Ivar knew he'd made a mistake. He should've dug deeper, looked harder, considered more than just his immediate needs.

Normally, not a problem.

He excelled at calculating odds and weighing risks. This time, however, he'd been wrong. Inviting Rodin in, accepting the devious male's help, counted as more than just a misstep. Mistakes, after all, could be fixed. Sidestepped. Manipulated. Turned around. Call a patch-up job whatever you wanted, but this... Zidane in Seattle couldn't be fixed, or ignored.

Shaking his head, Ivar made another pass above the house, wondering what possessed him to get in bed with Rodin.

The answer came immediately to mind—money.

Lots of it.

Millions and millions and... fucking millions.

The massive cash infusion helped with setup. Without it, his new lair—the spectacular complex sitting beneath 28 Walton Street—wouldn't exist. And the state-of-the-art laboratory inside it? Ivar clenched his teeth. Forget about it. The facility would be nothing but plans in the back of his head. A pipe dream that would've taken years, not months, to build.

Hindsight being what it was, he realized now he should've gone another way. A better one. Found alternative sources of income. Taken longer to build his dream and left the politics and power plays to males with more patience. If he had, he'd have nothing but the Nightfury pack to worry about, instead of the entire Archguard breathing down his neck.

The price of doing business.

Unfortunate, but true.

Still... he never should've kept Rodin in the loop about Lothair. Or informed him his best friend (and former XO) had been killed by the Nightfury pack. The wrong play. Again. No question about it now, but back then, the news of Lothair's death sent him into emotional free fall. Cracked wide open, he'd bled sorrow. Intellect had floated downstream with it, causing him to ignore the risks and act with uncharacteristic rashness.

Months later, he still hurt. Still mourned and missed the male. He thought of Lothair all the time, which forced him to face all the things he could've done better on a daily basis. Time should've dulled the pain. Everyone said so, but it hadn't. Nothing did. But worse, now he was stuck with the consequences. The biggest one—the Archguard kill squad currently camped on his doorstep.

His temper erupted at the thought.

Pink flames flared between the spikes riding his spine. As inferno-like heat flickered across his scales, Ivar struggled to shut it down. Going off half-cocked wouldn't help. He needed to stay calm. Be cold and deliberate in order to deal with Zidane. He must walk the line, execute with precision, deploy a certain amount of diplomacy. Otherwise, the Archguard asshole would smell a rat and Daddy Dearest in Prague would be informed.

Breathing deep, Ivar exhaled slow.

Resolve set, he circled into a holding pattern above the house and reached out to the warriors flying in his wake. Magic sparked inside his mind, opening a cosmic link to his personal guard. *"Sveld's with me. We take the meet, the rest of you patrol the area. Denzeil, inside the three-mile marker. I want the asshole to sense you. Rampart, Midion, and Syndor, set up outside it. Azrad—where are you?"*

Fine-tuning his sonar, Ivar waited for the newest member of his pack to answer. Static crackled through the connection.

Mind-speak twisted.

Heat burned across his temples as the powerful male linked in. *"North end. Heading for the center of town. Got Terranon and Kilmar with me."*

Ivar's mouth curved. Made sense. The trio never went anywhere without each other. *"Any intel to share?"*

"Yeah. Nightfuries are fucking pansies," Azrad said, disgust in his voice. *"Bugged out fast. Hardly got any blood on my claws."*

Ivar grinned.

Flying in his wake, Hamersveld snorted. *"Not to worry, whelp. You'll get another shot at Bastian."*

"Hope so. No fun otherwise." Scales rattled. The cacophony shuddered through the mind-speak as he heard Azrad shift in flight. *"Where do you want us?"*

"East side, across the Sound. Find a spot in the port, hunker down. Be ready to move on my say-so," Ivar said, setting up a parameter. Denzeil playing rover. One fighting triangle to the west, another on the east, both

outside the three-mile marker. The distance would ensure his warriors stayed off Zidane's radar, until Ivar
wanted him to know they were there. *Settle in, boys.
Stay sharp. No one comes in, no one goes out.*

"Ten four," D said, all about the trucker talk... per
usual.

Completely annoying, but what could he do? He'd
been trying to break the male of the habit for years.
Nothing worked. Denzeil never listened. He kept on
keeping on, so instead of killing the idiot, Ivar put up
with it. A necessary evil, given D's wicked ability to set
up computers and infiltrate the systems of others.

Glancing over his shoulder, Ivar pinged his new
XO. *"How many you sense in the area?"*

"The whole squad," Hamersveld said, Norwegian
accent rippling beneath a rumble of thunder. Water
dragon out in full force, his smooth shark-grey scales
flashed as he flipped up and over, dragging raindrops
in his wake. Loving the waterworks, Fen (a miniature
dragon, Hamersveld's wren) played in the blowback,
twirling through the spray, snapping at droplets with
his tiny teeth, staying on Hamersveld's jagged, saw-
tooth tail. *"Three males in the house. Three in the weeds
two miles away."*

Water splattered across Ivar's scales.

As he shook off the splash, Hamersveld rolled in
on his left wingtip.

"Six warriors. Not a lot," Ivar murmured, mind shuffling through the facts like cards in a deck. Zidane's
sudden arrival in Seattle. No warning. No coordination between Rodin's allies already in the area. No request for a meeting before tonight. A kill squad with
only six Dragonkind males. Ivar shook his head.
"Doesn't add up. What am I missing?"

"Won't know until we talk to the bastard." Tucking his

wings, Hamersveld vaulted up and over, switching sides, making mini-cyclones funnel in midair. Fen chased the deluge, splashing through one wall of water, only to dive horns-first into another. *"One and one never makes two with Zidane."*

Claws snicking against metal, Rampart chimed in. *"Small kill squad. Different country. Strange city. He's either got a death wish or a really good plan."*

Midion huffed. *"Or at least, thinks he does."*

Never one for words, Syndor grunted, agreeing with his wingmates.

Ivar sighed. Again. For what seemed like the tenth time tonight.

Fucking Zidane.

The male was unhinged if he believed six warriors would do the trick. Going after Bastian took skill. Hell. He'd been trying to sink his claws into the male for years. *For years,* without any success. So yeah... six warriors against the Nightfury pack wasn't enough. Which made him think Zidane wasn't in Seattle to just kill Nightfuries. His mission included something else.

A secondary task given by the Archguard, maybe?

One that involved the Razorback pack. *His* pack. *His* warriors. All *his* fucking hard work. Ivar snarled low in his throat. *"Rodin."*

"No doubt," Hamersveld said, picking his train of thought out of thin air.

"New game, Sveld."

"Fucking right."

"Zidane first."

Black eyes rimmed by pale blue cut in his direction. *"Agreed."*

"Good." Already dissecting the problem, Ivar changed tact—mental, strategic and physical. Zigzag-

ging across the sky, he broke down the components, formatting a new action plan on the fly.

Much as it pained him to admit it, Zidane wasn't stupid. Unstable? Absolutely. Vicious? One hundred percent. Dumb? Not even close.

A thrill-seeker, the male thrived on the unexpected. The more uncertain the situation, the more chaos caused, the more Zidane liked it. Impatience made him volatile. Arrogance made him foolish. Excellent traits for a sadist who enjoyed torturing others, not the best *modus operandi* after being made commander of a kill squad whose mission was hunting and killing Nightfuries.

Not that Ivar was complaining.

Zidane's faults worked in his favor. Were things Ivar planned to use to his advantage. He needed to fly under the radar. Appear to be cooperating with the kill squad, while he kept the Razorbacks on the periphery of the fight. A delicate balance to strike. A difficult plan to execute. One he needed to pull off, 'cause... no doubt in his mind. The further Zidane stayed from his pack, the safer his warriors, his laboratory, and the breeding program would be from Archguard interference.

Hamersveld thumped him with his tail to regain his attention.

Ivar threw him a sidelong glance.

Angling his head, his friend tipped his chin. *"Swing wide, Ivar. Make another pass."*

The warning in his XO's voice made him tense. Trusting his friend's instincts, he reacted without question and, increasing his wing speed, banked right. As he veered away from the bungalow, Ivar searched the ground. Nothing moved. No enemy warriors on radar. Zero danger to be found within immediate proximity.

Ivar circled into a holding pattern. *"What did you see?"*

"Nothing."

His brows collided. *"What the hell, Sveld?"*

Hamersveld didn't answer. At first. Ivar clued in a second later when his XO shut down mind-speak, only to open a new link.

The connection flared.

Not an open line. Two-way communication—him and Hamersveld only.

He threw his friend an incredulous look.

"Need a word before we go in. Don't want the others hearing."

Wheeling into another turn, Ivar skirted the edge of the neighborhood. *"Talk."*

"You notice anything different about the Nightfuries tonight?"

"No—why?"

"During the fighting tonight, you didn't see it?"

"See what?" All he'd witnessed was carnage. The brutal onslaught of Bastian and his bastards followed by a hasty retreat. A new strategy for the Nightfury pack. Effective as hell. Annoying as fuck. He had multiple males headed to the infirmary thanks to the Nightfury hit-and-run.

"The mating mark." A fierce glint in his eyes, Hamersveld raised his paw. Making a fist, he drew a hooked tip of a dark blue claw across the back of his knuckles.

Ivar frowned. *"Mating mark?"*

"Stuff of legends. The magical mark denoting a mated male. More myth than fact," Hamersveld said, tone soft, a hint of awe in his voice. *"Tales made up by lonely males*

with too much time on their hands, but... Hristos, Ivar. I think... I think—"

"What?"

"It might be real."

A band of pressure snaked around his chest. His throat went tight as his heart went into overdrive, pumping blood through his veins, making his scales tingle and his temples throb. His mind shifted, landing on Sasha. Pesky neighbor. Beautiful female. Sex kitten extraordinaire, spectacular in and out of bed. The woman he fought, but failed to ignore and... Jesus. *Mating mark. Might be real.* The words echoed inside his head. Was Hamersveld really saying what he thought he was saying—that claiming a female, that keeping her safe from the curse of Dragonkind, was possible?

The question lit off like fireworks inside him. Hope and desire exploded into the fray, spinning him off his mental moorings.

Battling to stay even, Ivar growled, *"Explain."*

"Shit, I don't know where to start."

"The beginning. I want to know everything," he said, impatience riding him hard.

"Heard about it growing up. The old guard never stopped talking about it. They dreamed of meeting their mates. About energy-fuse and the intense bond forged between a male and his chosen female." Flexing his talons, Hamersveld shook his head. *"Never seen it. Not once. None of them had either, so I always figured energy-fuse and existence of mating marks was nothing but bullshit. Been alive a long time, over three hundred years, and never seen one. Until tonight. On the Nightfury water rat. The Scot was marked too."*

Ivar drew in a sharp breath. *"Forge?"*

"Yeah." Hamersveld rolled into another turn, flying

further afield. *"Thought I caught sight of another, but the black-scaled bastard was too fast. Couldn't get a good look at the back of his talon."*

"Energy-fuse," Ivar whispered, staying on Hamersveld's wingtip, staring at him as though he'd grown another head. *"How's that even possible?"*

"Don't know, but the Nightfuries do. Bastian's figure it out, Ivar. He knows how energy-fuse works. If his warriors have taken mates, he's got it all. Every piece of information —the words, the ritual, what's required during the mating ceremony to tie a male's life force to a female's. The only way to ensure she survives childbirth."

"A family," he rasped, having difficulty taking it in. *"A male could have a family and keep his female. He wouldn't be forced to choose between his youngling and mate."*

"Exactly," Hamersveld said, bumping him with his wingtip. *"A mated female would be safe. Protected by her male's magic through the bond. His for a lifetime."*

A well of yearning opened inside him. *"Sasha."*

Ignoring him, Hamersveld kept talking. *"Total game changer. You'll be able to claim your female without hurting her. And I can—"*

"Go after Natalie."

"I miss her," he murmured, sounding equal parts angry and broken. Understandable. Warriors didn't tolerate weakness of any kind. And missing a female, longing for her without ceasing, counted as a big one for a Dragonkind male. *"I want her back."*

"I know."

No joke.

Nothing but the truth.

Ivar understood. He really did. After fighting his need for Sasha, Ivar knew exactly where his XO sat. In the middle of an emotional shitstorm—needing a female so badly it hurt, while at the same time, refusing to put her at risk. In truth, Hamersveld hadn't been the same since allowing Natalie to escape the breeding program. His friend had done the unthinkable. Gone against the grain, defied pack rules, risked everything to give the female safe passage to places unknown.

Something that still pissed him off.

Even though he understood the reason behind his XO's actions, losing a valuable HE so close to the realignment didn't sit well with him. He'd wanted ten high-energy females to start, but had settled for six. After Hamersveld's stunt, he was down to five. Not optimal. More test subjects ensured better results. As a scientist, he appreciated precision, planned each experiment with exactitude, choosing the variables, optimizing the procedures while respecting scientific standards.

Standards Hamersveld skewed the night he took Natalie from the lair.

"Know you want Zidane dead, Ivar, but we need to pivot. Tweak that plan."

"Da," he said, reverting to Russian, his mother tongue.

A bad habit.

His fail-safe when he needed to focus.

Even after years spent living abroad, speaking English took extra effort. The kind he didn't need as he sorted through the new information, looking for a different angle. Better ones that would turn the tide in his favor. Instead of killing Zidane, he needed to find a way to use the male, not only against the Nightfury pack, but for his own purposes. No way he could down Bastian on his own. And despite having spent years trying to kill the Nightfury commander, he now needed him alive. Otherwise, he wouldn't get the information he needed—the secret to unlocking energy-fuse and initiating the bond between mates.

Tilting his wings, Ivar banked hard. Wind shear rattling his scales, he headed back across the island, toward the house and Zidane. *"Follow my lead when we get in there, Sveld."*

A nasty gleam in his eyes, Hamersveld raised a brow. *"Take it, we're pivoting?"*

"One hundred and eighty degrees."

"Thought you'd see it my way."

He usually did.

A brilliant strategist, Hamersveld never led him astray. Something to appreciate about the male. The fact his XO packed a wallop, carried around a serious amount of lethal, only added to the effect, making Ivar glad he'd befriended the male. A commander of warriors, after all, could never have enough firepower at his back. Every little bit counted. Particularly, with the Nightfuries—and now Zidane—in his sights, the Meridian realignment around the corner, and the mystery of energy-fuse to solve.

So much to do. Not a lot of wiggle room.

Time to saddle up. Yippee-ki-yay, motherfucker.

20

Winding her way along the narrow country road, Angela put the pedal down. The SUV's engine rumbled, rocketing her into the last S-curve leading up to Black Diamond. She took the corner too fast, riding the edge, needing the release, desperate to outrun the anxiety. The truck lurched. A death grip on the wheel, she powered through the bend and roared up the hill.

High beams eating through the dark, she watched bright LEDs slice across the blacktop, making the center lines glow. Splashes of light hit the thick forest on either side of the road. Tall pines stood shoulder to shoulder with huge redwoods and giant oaks. A curious mix. Beautiful in sunlight. Ominous in the black of night.

Heavy fog descended, ghosting across the road as she crested the rise. She roared along the straight stretch, looking for landmarks edging the woods. A crooked tree limb. A cracked boulder sitting along one shoulder. The broken, rusted-out mailbox sitting in front of a place that didn't exist anymore. Almost home. Less than five minutes, and she'd be turning into the hidden entrance, roaring up the gravel drive and putting the Denali to bed inside Black Diamond's garage. All while hoping her mate wasn't home to notice.

Her eyes cut to the dashboard.

The clock read 3:37 AM.

Angela bit down on a curse. She was late. So freaking late. Much later than she'd planned to be before sneaking out of the lair. Par for the course while in investigation mode. Part of the job while following a lead, or a hunch... or whatever the hell she'd been doing tonight. The thought gave her pause. The fact she didn't know what took her out of the lair—without backup, something she'd agreed never to do—didn't bode well for her.

Felt like compulsion.

Seemed like insanity.

What it was, was nothing good.

Rikar was going to lose his mind. Be so angry she'd get more than a spanking. He'd introduce her to orgasm denial (something he'd threatened the last time she broke the rules), keep her on the edge of sexual pleasure, refuse to let her come until she got the message. Until she agreed. Until she begged and pleaded and promised to follow the protocols set up to ensure her safety. Annoying, but necessary in the world she now inhabited.

One full of Dragonkind.

Angela sighed.

God.

She was so messed up. Worrying him was not her usual MO. She was smart. She was responsible. She was not the kind of person who went off half-cocked and put herself in danger... until recently.

A bad taste entered her mouth.

Angela shook her head. She needed to figure out what the hell was wrong with her. Why she couldn't settle. The reason every time Rikar kissed her good-bye, she couldn't stay put. Restlessness set in the second he left the lair, making her mind race and her spirit churn. Flexing her hands on the wheel, Angela reached for calm. She pulled in a breath, deploying the technique Mac taught her. Deep inhale. Long exhale. Catch and release.

It didn't help.

The sense of foreboding deepened. The claw and grind beneath her skin remained, making her body ache and her head hurt.

A harsh prickle clawed up her spine, hitting the base of her skull. The dull ache bloomed into true pain. More breaths in. An equal amount out as she swung around the last bend. Mist swirled over the blacktop, puffing against the front grill. Yellow paint tried to glow beneath her headlights. No such luck. Worn by the elements, faded by time, the rural road didn't see a lot of use. Maintenance crews never came out to fix potholes, never mind repaint lines on the asphalt. And the guys? Forget about them. None of the Nightfuries like riding in a cage. The warriors preferred to fly out of the lair, like each one had tonight.

Lucky for her.

If one of the boys had stayed home, the instant she slid inside the SUV, he'd have been on her ass. Standing in front of the garage doors, arms crossed, a scowl on his face, nixing her plans to escape for the night. More often than not, Sloan was the one who screwed up her plans, standing in her way, encouraging her to be patient, keeping her occupied with computer searches.

Busy work.

Annoying most of the time.

Lately, she hadn't minded. Staying busy kept her from crawling out of her skin. But with the Nightfury computer genius out of the lair, she'd slipped beneath radar. A good thing too, given her unauthorized foray into the city meant she'd met Sasha Cooper. A woman she'd liked the moment they began talking. Over a cup of tea and a box of crushed Oreos of all things. Odd in many ways. Fun in others.

Angela didn't make friends easily, but with Sasha, the conversation flowed. No need to search for things to say. No uncomfortable moments. Just ease, instant acceptance, and ready friendship. Along with a strong sense of kinship Angela only felt when she spent time with the other women mated to Nightfury warriors.

Her sisters.

Her new family.

Women who always looked out for her, and she for them.

So, yeah. Her immediate connection to Sasha counted as odd. Different. Absolutely abnormal outside the Nightfury pack. The realization made suspicion surface. Who was Sasha Cooper? What kept drawing Angela into her neighborhood? Why were her instincts screaming the woman was important, another piece in her investigation's incomplete puzzle? Excellent questions. A new angle to consider. Good information to add to the mix and see where she landed—closer to the truth, or farther from understanding.

Mind flipping through facts and her interaction with Sasha, Angela put on the brakes. Taillights flashed, painting the gloom red behind her as she turned into the hidden driveway. Tires spun off pavement and rolled onto gravel. Static electricity pricked her skin as the energy shield protecting the Nightfury lair reacted, drifting over the truck, scanning her bio-signal like a bar code, deciding whether or not to let her in. She eased off the accelerator, slowing down, creeping forward through a narrow break in the trees, giving it time to recognize her.

Resistance pushed against the SUV.

The Denali's big V8 rumbled.

Soft sound scratched over steel, rocking her inside the cab, making her imagine the magical shield was a monster. An invisible one with hands and claws drifting over the truck, learning its shape to determine its threat level. It held her less than a minute, raking the metal, examining her, welcoming her home before letting her go.

"Thanks," Angela murmured, giving the monster its due.

Three taps rapped across the hood.

She smiled, taking that as an "you're welcome" be-fore putting her foot back on the accelerator. Listening to the crunch of rock under the tires, she pointed the SUV up the hill, navigated the twists and turns and rolled into the forecourt of the aboveground lair. She turned the wheel, driving away from the sprawling complex toward a detached garage set back in a wooded area. Huge building. Two-story steel struc-ture. Three industrial-sized doors guarding its face.

Flipping the sun visor down, Angela reached for the garage door opener.

She didn't make it.

Before she pressed the button, the middle door started to open. Metal gears ground into motion. The massive panel opened an inch at a time. White-knuckling the steering wheel, Angela held her breath. Planted shoulder-width apart, black combat boots appeared in the gap between the door edge and the concrete floor. A strong pair of long legs came next. She bit her bottom lip as trim hips, a wide chest with muscled arms crossed in front of it, and Rikar's face came into view. Expression set in hard lines, his ice-blue eyes shimmered with an intensity that made her shiver.

Her gaze connected with his through the windshield.

Her breath caught.

Her skin started to tingle.

Never failed. Every single time Angela looked at her mate, she reacted the same way. With blistering heat and unquenchable need. Tall. Strong. Big, blond, and beautiful. Her mate was a masterpiece. A marvel of masculine appeal. Rikar could be gentle. He could be playful, rough and rowdy... or pissed off, like he was now... didn't matter. Her reaction to him never softened. Day by day, hour by hour, minute by minute, her love for him only grew stronger.

Eyes aglow, frost crackling above his shoulders, Rikar took a breath, no doubt to tamp down his temper. His attempt failed. She knew it when he bared his teeth and growled at her.

"Shit," she muttered.

Uncrossing his arms, he flexed his hands. A muscle ticked along his jaw as his chin tipped down, and he stared at her from beneath furrowed brows. "Angel."

Swallowing, she raised her hands. "I can explain."

A lie.

One he heard from fifty feet away. Even though

she was locked inside the steel hull of an SUV. Double extra, super *shit*. Supersonic dragon-guy hearing. Nothing like it. A skill to marvel at and envy, but... perhaps another time. She needed to focus. Fast. Without delay, 'cause Rikar was on the move, and she was neck-deep in trouble for breaking the rules.

21

Warmth flickered across his feet, nudging Gage awake. He surfaced layer by layer, in rippling waves. Awareness washed in, grogginess ebbed out. Muscles twitching, he opened his eyes. Awash with last remnants of sleep, his dragon stretched, uncoiling inside him. Slow but sure, his senses contracted, clearing the visual blur.

A beige canopy came into focus.

Gage stared at it, wondering where he'd landed. He wasn't in his room inside the loft at Black Diamond. Nor was he bedded down inside the one he usually chose at the safe house after a night of fighting. Looked like... he blinked. He didn't know. Didn't recognize the surroundings. Or remember what the hell he'd been doing last night.

Blank screen in his mind.

Nothing but a giant hole on the memory front.

Frowning at the curved canvas above his head, he shifted around a bit. Not a lot. Hardly any movement at all. Just enough to determine how concerned he should be—and do a quick threat assessment.

Nothing hurt.

No danger lurking nearby.

All his limbs were still attached. A bonus, for sure, but... fuck. He felt strange. Muscles loose. Heavy-limbed. Thick-headed. More than just relaxed—slug-gish. As though he'd been knocked off his mental and physical grid, launched into free fall and run headfirst into something hard. Which led him to now—south of his usual sharp, nowhere near the vicinity of normal.

With a grimace, Gage turned his head. Grey dots clouded his vision. He blinked the spots away, and after a moment of extreme concentration, took stock. Lying flat on his back. Thick cushions beneath him, a blanket settled low on his hips, mind hazy and body floating. No energy depletion. He was topped up; so full, power crackled through him, zipping in his veins, making him realize his fingertips tingled. And the usual bone-deep hunger he suffered from had taken a hiatus.

A trickle of wariness seeped in.

Trying to jumpstart his brain, brimming with so much energy he suspected foul play, Gage flexed his hands. Sensation fired. His brain turned over, sput-tering as comfort took up the cause, rolling over him like a steamroller. Flattened by the feeling, Gage prodded his get-up-and-go. Nothing. Not a twitch from his dragon half. The beast refused to move, too blissed-out to care what caused the contentment.

Bad fucking influence.

Gage knew it when another round of relaxation rolled in, supplanted his mind, and pulled him back under.

Lost to delight, his eyes slid closed. Gage sank deeper into the cushions, surrendering to the mo-ment, going with the flow, allowing himself to drift. A first for him. Usually, the second his eyes opened, his feet hit the floor and he got mobile. Faster was always better in his mind, but...

Not today.

Right now, he wanted to luxuriate in the fullness. To relax and be lazy, allow peace to settle in and stay awhile.

Breathing deep, he floated in the mental swirl, surfacing every once in a while. The warmth that woke him climbed, moving over his feet, past his ankles, heating his skin. Sounds filtered in—birdsong, the sound of tumbling water, leaves rustling in the breeze. Scents played in the shifting air, teasing his senses. Greenery. Fog. Fresh air and... his brows contracted... female. Hints of spice mixed with sugar and thermal springs. On him. Around him. Beautiful and intoxicating and... unbelievably arousing.

Realization rippled through him.

His brain powered back on, shoving him out of repletion, into awareness.

His eyes snapped back open. Gage glanced down. His chest tightened as his gaze landed on a cascade of honey-blond hair. He felt her next, warm, soft, snug against him. Skin to skin, naked in his arms. His heat warming her. Her beauty surrounding him.

Still asleep, lying crossways on his chest, she pinned him to the cushions, head nestled on his shoulder, face turned away, one of her thighs tucked between his own. Weighed down by his female, Gage's mouth curved. Jesus. How the hell did she sleep like that—with her chest pressed to his? Had to be hard to breathe, but no way was he complaining.

He liked her draped over him. Nothing like waking up to find his mate all over him, her hair in his face, her scent in his nose, her soft skin beneath his palms.

Another round of bliss rolled through him.

A purr left his throat as Gage got with the program and sent his hands roaming. One skimmed the length of her spine. The other moved down to cup the curve of her ass, holding her in place while he explored, relearning her shape. Such delicate bones. So much beauty contained in such a small package. Samantha. His mate. Beyond gorgeous. And so fucking greedy in bed, she'd kept him up for hours, nearly wearing him out.

Which was saying something, given his stamina.

"Fuck," he murmured, replaying the festivities, not minding her neediness, or the compulsion that drove it.

Samantha wanted him. A point of pride for any Dragonkind male. Sexual heat, blistering need, was expected between mates, but... wow. He hadn't been ready for the intensity, or her boldness. Once he started it with her, she hadn't held back, becoming so desperate for him, at one point, she fought for the top, used her month on him, then ridden him to spectacular effect, making him come harder than he ever had before. Magnificent. Phenomenal. So crazy good that by the time he called it a night and passed out, he'd built seven orgasms in her and taken three of his own.

His mouth curved.

A fantastic finish to a less than stellar night.

As the thought took root, reality crept back in. Gage clenched his teeth. What a clusterfuck. First the mess inside the diner, next Azrad, then Nian. The namby-pamby had taken a hit. A bad one, and Haider? Shit. His best friend hadn't sounded good during the last link-up. He'd been impatient, angry, about to lose his cool, which didn't bode well for anyone.

Smarter than ninety-nine point nine percent of Dragonkind population, Haider possessed an impressive array of talents. A skill set that was wide, varied, and unusual. His brilliance was the kind that kept on giving, no matter the situation, circumstance, or number of warriors involved. A gifted negotiator, he backed up his intelligence with unerring instinct, unparalleled tenacity, a scary sense of timing and... yeah, wait for it... unfailing patience.

Losing his cool wasn't part of his repertoire.

Ever.

Which made last night an anomaly.

One that worried Gage. He sensed Haider's control slip the instant it happened. From well over five miles away. Another concern. Emotion that strong never occurred in a vacuum. It couldn't be contained, always leaked, coating everything it touched, exploding without warning. When that happened, things went from bad to worse and males got hurt, so...

Yeah.

Another conversation was in order.

He needed to get a better lock on Haider's state of mind. The sooner the better, 'cause it wasn't just Prague plaguing his best friend. Something else was on the male's mind. A truth Gage knew he'd have to dig out if he wanted to help his friend and set things right, once and for all.

Bastian was right.

He was the only one qualified to do it. As Metallics with strong wills, Haider and Nian wouldn't respond well to outside influence. Not even the Nightfury commander's.

Frowning up at the canopy, Gage played with the ends of Samantha's hair, wondering how best to approach the situation. A beatdown? His pursed his lips. A bare-knuckled fight might do it—get the conversation started—but with Osgard and a new mate to look after, Gage preferred to go another route.

Hope would need to be brought in. Forge's female knew what she was doing. She'd helped Osgard. She'd guided him in his new role as sire to a teenage son. Gage recognized her value. Had learned loads from her. Now he understood the power of talking out a problem and clearing the air.

Haider and Nian wouldn't like it. Not at first. He didn't care. Both would get on board and deal. Otherwise, he'd get the kind of fight he loved, and his packmates would receive more than either could handle.

Mind on the problem, he watched his fingers work in his mate's hair. Soft strands. Thick tendrils. As glorious as the female who owned it. Shifting beneath her, he gathered the heavy mass with one hand and swept it to one side, off her back and out of his face. He hated to do it. Didn't want to move, much less wake her, but it was time to get into the house. The sun was coming up, topping the trees shading the patio, flickering over his bare feet as night bowed to the light of day.

Any other time, he would've stayed outside and indulged his dragon half. His beast enjoyed basking in the early morning sun. A part of his makeup. As a bronze dragon, the legacy of his ancestors lived in him. In centuries past, his subset of Dragonkind oversaw the care and upkeep of the Sun Temple, standing guard at its entrance, performing rituals, paying tribute to the Sun Goddess, keeping the old ways alive. Not a possibility anymore. The Goddess's curse took daylight from Dragonkind, ensuring the old ways died and bronze dragons only flew at night. Though, a few exceptions still existed.

Gage was one of them.

He caught snatches of the sun, braving the deadly UVs on a regular basis, keeping the traditional lineage of bronze dragons alive. Most males envied his ability to tolerate direct daylight. Not that he ever lasted long in the sunshine. He got thirty minutes on a good day —a narrow slice of time—before his eyes started to sting, his skin began to burn, and the sun chased him inside.

A gift to be thankful for, on another day.

Right now, he needed to rouse his mate and get inside. Ensure Haider made it home in once piece, and Nian wasn't dead.

Wrapping his arms around Samantha, he turned on his side. A gentle shift. The tender sweep of his hand along her side. A soft kiss against her temple. No reaction. She didn't move. Didn't make a sound. Didn't so much as bat an eyelash. Cradling her, he drew his nose along the side of hers and caressed the back of her thigh with his fingertips. Reveling in the feel of her, he hooked her knee over his hip and set his mouth against the sensitive spot behind her ear.

He nuzzled.

Samantha sighed, but didn't wake.

His mouth curved. Wow. She was out. As in *OUT*, dead to the world, so exhausted by energy feedings and lovemaking, she was practically comatose.

The sun rose higher in the sky.

The heat on his feet morphed into an unpleasant prickle.

"Fuck it." No time to waste, and no need to wake her.

She needed sleep to recover.

He needed to get the hell off the daybed.

Win-win with the added bonus of expediency.

Inching backwards on the cushions, he lifted the

blanket, slipped from beneath it and out of her arms. As he moved across the cushions, he drew the fleece up and over her, shielding her from the nip in the air.

His bare feet touched down on cold stone beside the lounger.

Her nose wrinkled in protest.

He smiled as she grumbled in her sleep and reached out in search of him, enjoying the fact nothing but his retreat garnered a reaction. Soothing her with his touch, he ran his hand over her shoulder and down her back. She settled. He conjured a pair of his favorite jeans. As worn denim settled on his lower half, he folded the canopy back, leaned over the wide bed, and picked her up, blanket and all. Back in his arms, she sighed and tucked in as he pivoted toward the house.

Nabbing her backpack off the patio on the fly-by, he strode toward a pair of sliding doors. Glass panes reacting to the rising sun, the modern sliders, embedded in a section of wall-to-wall windows, darkened a little at a time. A necessary feature in any Dragonkind home. The powerful shielding spell protected warriors from UV rays, blocking out sunlight, allowing males to move around during daylight hours without worry. Like Black Diamond, Magnolia House boasted a monster all its own. Designed and conjured by Haider, the spell was a nasty, unbeatable, malevolent force that took its job seriously, refusing entry to all but the Nightfury pack while hiding the safe house from enemy Dragonkind.

Gage loved the thing.

He also hated it.

The monster had a mind of its own, along with a temper. Sometimes, the spell exerted its authority, leaving marks, taking its pound of flesh before allowing him inside the house. Other times, he sailed right through. No show of temper. Zero bruises to report. Just a simple scan of his dragon DNA, then open doors. Gage hoped today was one of those days. With the sun in full bloom and Samantha in his arms, he didn't need the hassle.

Approaching the slider, he murmured his request.

Already watching him from the magical abyss, the monster's eyes narrowed.

Gage asked again... *politely*.

The spell's attention shifted to the female he carried. It snarled. He kept walking, pace steady, shoulders squared. The super conductor inside his mind powered up. Magnetic force burned through his veins. Magic painted the air, sparking around him. Supercharged ions tumbled toward the door. Debris blew across the patio. Three feet from the slider, Gage whispered a command. The lock flipped open as the doorknob rattled. The monster held on a second longer, refusing him entrance, then growled, and let go.

The glass panel slid open.

Without breaking stride, Gage crossed the threshold into the living room and—

"Shit," he muttered, stopping short.

Feet planted inside the door, he listened to the panel hiss closed behind him. Sunlight faded. Gloom descended. The prickle raking his skin disappeared as he scanned the carnage. Coffee table overturned. Armchairs shoved out of the way, one tipped over on its side. Couch askew. Picture frames hanging crooked on the walls. Condom wrappers all over the place. Nian passed out, sprawled like a starfish on the floor in the middle of the room... with two females. Both brunettes. Both pressed up against Nian, one with her head resting on his feet, the other curled into his side with her head on his shoulder. All butt naked. All fast asleep in a sated pile on an area rug Gage never wanted to step foot on again.

Curling Samantha closer, he scowled at the namby-pamby. Fucking Nian. Total pain in his ass. Though he was glad to see Haider not only got the male home, but also provided what he needed—an energy feeding to close up his wound. By the looks of the thick, pink line bisecting Nian's abdomen, a nasty one. The kind of injury that might've killed him if Haider hadn't acted fast.

Shaking his head, Gage dragged his attention from the tangled-up trio and put his feet in gear. He'd come back for Nian later, after he put his mate to bed and contacted Sloan. He needed to make arrangements for Osgard. His son wouldn't bed down and get the sleep a youngling required without reassurance from Gage. Next up—Haider. Looking in on his friend, ensuring he fed before the females keeping Nian company in the living room went home, needed to happen before he crawled in with Samantha and got more shut-eye.

Haider wouldn't like the plan.

Gage didn't blame him. He also didn't care.

For some messed-up reason, his friend flirted with energy-greed, refusing to connect to the Meridian through a female, depriving himself of the nourishment he needed to stay healthy. A dangerous state for any Dragonkind male, but especially problematic for Haider.

The male expended a lot of energy on a regular basis, maintaining the magical shields protecting Black Diamond and Magnolia House from enemy detection. Older, more mature, the spell surrounding the rural lair required less maintenance (the entire reason Haider had been able to travel to Prague for the Arch-

guard festival). Add the safe house into the equation—
a younger, more volatile enchantment—and even
Haider's considerable skills became taxed.

Which meant his friend must feed.

Now. Today. No more delays. No more coddling, or
making exceptions for the mental and emotional turmoil he and Haider suffered after returning from Europe. Gage was done. Done avoiding the truth. Done
giving Haider breathing room. Done watching his
friend hurt himself. Like it or not, the male would
feed. Even if Haider balked, and Gage ended up
having to force his friend into the arms of a female to
see it done.

EXHAUSTION WEIGHING HIM DOWN, Sloan finished
sterilizing the stainless-steel medical table, then
stepped around it, and headed across the clinic. Boots
thumping across industrial-grade linoleum, he by-
passed the neonatal bed, nudged a rolling cart out of
his way, his attention on the double doors at the back
of the room. Hammering the locking bar with his
knee, he shoved the wider one open.

Heavy steel swung wide.

Well-oiled hinges sighed.

He barely noticed as he stepped over the
threshold and entered the hallway beyond. Embedded in twelve-foot ceilings, halogen lights
hummed above his head, casting shadows on
wooden doors marching along one side of the corridor. Seven doors, seven rooms, complete with separate en suites. Large. Comfortable. Designed with
one purpose in mind—recovery after a hard night of
fighting. A place for him and his brothers-in-arms to

rest and recover after being stitched up inside the clinic.

Each suite saw a lot of use on a regular basis.

Such was life.

Never a dull moment.

He was part of a warrior pack. A lethal group of males considered elite by most Dragonkind; the rest thought he and his brothers were savages. A label he refused to dispute. The Nightfuries used brutality like a weapon, wielding it whenever the situation warranted, unwilling to back down in the face of a righteous fight. Something he enjoyed about his brothers-in-arms. A truth Sloan admitted he'd ignored... until tonight.

Thank the Goddess for Bastian.

His commander recognized what Sloan, somewhere along the line, forgot to remember. He was a warrior, born and bred. He enjoyed a good fight. Thrived on the action and needed the exercise as much (maybe more) than his packmates. He was more than a brain sitting behind a computer terminal. All right, so he wore the title of IT genius well, carrying a tool box full of specialized skills that dovetailed with modern technology.

Not unusual.

Each of the Nightfuries excelled at something specific. Bastian had recruited each of his brothers-in-arms for a reason. For their fighting abilities, sure, but also for what each male brought to the table. No matter the situation, his packmates contributed, deploying their gifts in a myriad of ways. One thing he'd noticed, though. Unlike him, the warriors he lived with never forgot who and what they were—lethal males with a mission, purpose, and the need to get blood on their claws every once in a while.

Stopping in front of the third door, Sloan looked down at his hands. He flexed his fingers, enjoying the ache in his knuckles. Fuck, he'd had fun tonight. Liked being part of a fighting triangle again. Reveled in pitting his skills against enemy dragons in full flight. Loved seeing blood on his scales and hearing his opponents squawk when his claws sank deep.

Nowhere near civilized. Savagery on steroids.

Sloan didn't care. He was a male with needs, and Bastian was right. Holding back was no longer an option. It was far past time he gave his vicious side—the beast who lived inside him—the airtime it needed.

Dropping his hands, he returned his attention to the door... and what lay beyond. He tilted his head and listened for telltale signs. His earth dragon senses fired, amplifying his ability to hear through solid rock. All quiet. No voices coming from inside the recovery room. Just the quiet beep of the heart rate monitor and the snick of a screwdriver at work.

He murmured a command. The door handle turned and—

A buzz lit off between his temples.

A second later, Gage knocked on his cerebral cortex.

Completing the link, Sloan greeted his friend. *"Yeah?"*

"You good?" Gage asked, sounding so relaxed Sloan stilled... and immediately went on high alert.

Powering down his magic, he left the door closed, and standing in the hallway, reached out with his mind to assess the situation. Something was off. Not by a little, by a lot. Gage never sounded happy, relaxed, or anything close to blissful. The male was the poster boy for abrasive, rude, and hostile. If he plugged "surly" into the search engine on his computer, Sloan was pretty sure a picture of Gage would appear on-screen.

"*Are you?*" he asked back, mining the cosmic link for information. Huh. Weird. No disturbance in Gage's life force. No apparent head injuries. Nothing mind-altering in his friend's bloodstream. Sloan's brows collided. "*You take a hit or something?*"

"*Off some primo weed, you mean?*"

"*Fucking hell, brother.*"

Gage snorted, then laughed outright. "*Claimed my mate, man. Found her in the diner. Tucking her into bed right now.*"

Sloan sucked in a sharp breath. "*Your mate?*"

"*Yeah, she's the goldsmith. Walked in, ran straight into her,*" Gage said, voice muffled by rustling fabric. Cotton sheets or a heavy comforter, maybe.

Envy curdled in his gut. Sloan shut it down, shoving jealousy aside. Nothing good came from coveting what others possessed. Fingers crossed, his time would come. Right now, he needed to be happy for his brother. "*Wicked, Gage. Happy for you, man.*"

"*Thanks, Sloan,*" Gage said, voice quiet, but full of appreciation. "*Not sure what I'm doing, but... fuck. She's something. So beautiful, she takes my breath away.*"

Par for the course for a Dragonkind male. Once he met his mate, no other female existed for him.

"*You'll get the hang of it,*" he murmured, wondering when he'd get his turn. When his mate would show up. Or if she ever would. "*The others have.*"

Gage grunted, not sounding convinced. "*B tell you we're bedding down at the safe house today?*"

"*Who's we?*"

"*Haider, Nian, and me.*"

Figured. Through thick and thin, Metallics always stuck together.

"He didn't have a chance." Putting himself in reverse, Sloan pressed his shoulders against the wall opposite the door and settled in. *"We got home and... shit, brother."*

"What happened?"

"Myst, she—"

"The baby?"

"Yeah. He came six weeks early."

"She okay?"

"B got to her before she bled out, so yeah," he said, staring at the door unseeing, reliving the past few hours. Hell for Bastian. Worse for Myst. Pure torture for him as Sloan delivered his commander's son, getting stuck in the past, imagining how alone his own female must've felt while in labor. How frightened she must've been when she realized she wasn't going to make it, and neither was his son. *"It was touch and go for a while, but all good now. She's healing. Baby's healthy. Strong. Weighed in at eight pounds, seven ounces."*

"Thank fuck," Gage murmured, echoing the sentiment of the entire Nightfury pack. Everyone who'd stopped in to see B, Myst, and the newest addition to the Nightfury pack in the aftermath. *"Good weight for a preemie."*

No question.

Bastian's son didn't look as though he'd been born nearly a month and a half early. He looked healthy and strong. Was alert and had taken to breastfeeding faster than expected. Nothing wrong with the little guy's instincts. Nothing wrong with his parents now that Myst was out of the woods.

"Name?"

"Not yet." Sloan's lips twitched, remembering Myst's reaction when Forge's son became part of the

pack, and Wick tried to name the infant *Viper*. *"B'll have his hands full during the naming ceremony."*

Gage chuckled. *"No doubt."*

Mind on the couple and new infant inside the room, Sloan pushed away from his lean against the wall. *"Anything you need?"*

"Yeah." The quiet click of a door closing spiraled through mind-speak. *"Need a favor."*

"What?"

"Osgard."

"Already got him."

A pause, then a sharp, *"What?"*

"He's with me. In the room with Bastian and Myst. Helped me deliver the baby."

"Seriously?"

"Yeah."

"He okay?"

"He's a fucking rock star. Bastian went ballistic—"

"I can imagine."

Ignoring the interruption, Sloan kept talking. *"Wouldn't allow any of the other warriors near Myst, so I improvised. Hope helped too, but when it became too intense, she got pale and Forge pulled her out. Oz stayed. Fuck, Gage... he's wicked smart. Cool under fire. He came through like a champ. Couldn't have done it without him."*

Gage grunted. *"Proud of him."*

"Me too. Told him. You do the same when you get home."

"About that. Need you to look out for him today."

"Not a problem."

"Sloan, he won't sleep without me watching his back. You're gonna have to step in... bed down in the loft."

The idea made his skin crawl. His beast recoiled. A nasty burst of energy sparked down his spine, upping the sensation. Sloan twitched. His muscles went rigid as he battled to control his reaction. He never slept aboveground. Ever. His earth dragon needed to be deep underground, surrounded by miles of granite, connected to the energy emitted from the Earth's core.

"Sloan."

"Give me a sec."

"Sorry, Sloan. I know what I'm asking," Gage said, tapping into his unease. *"I'd ask another brother, but Oz knows and trusts you."*

Swallowing the bad taste in his mouth, he cleared his throat. *"Got it."*

Gage exhaled a rough breath. *"Thanks, man. Owe you one."*

"No," he growled, pushing his discomfort away. *"Family does for one another. Oz needs this, you need it, I got your back."*

"Solid," he murmured, relief in his tone. *"You're fucking solid, Sloan."*

Uncomfortable with the praise, Sloan shrugged it off. *"Whatever."*

Reading him right, his friend huffed in amusement.

Sloan rolled his eyes. *"See you tonight. Oh, and Gage?"*

"Yeah?"

"Try not to kill Nian."

"It'll be hard, but I'll do my best," Gage said, annoyance bleeding through the link. *"Later."*

Sloan didn't bother to sign off. He cut the connection, then put his feet in gear. Twisting the knob, he pushed the door open and stepped over the threshold. As he cleared the frame, his eyes swept the room. His brain took a quick snapshot. Myst curled on her side in the middle of the king-sized bed, Bastian wrapped around her, homemade quilt tucked around them both. Baby in the basinet beside her on the mattress. Following her newborn son's lead, she was fast asleep.

B was not.

Wide awake and plugged into the Meridian, Bastian manipulated the stream, looping the current end over end, feeding his mate a steady course of healing energy. A low-grade hum shimmied in the room. Dimmed down overhead lights flickered as the buzz intensified and B's gaze landed on him.

His commander tipped his chin.

Sloan nodded back, and stopping beside the bed, checked the machine monitoring Myst's vitals. Strong heartbeat. Pink back in her cheeks. Breath even and sure. Relief struck a chord, moving through him as he glanced at the other occupant in the room.

Busy assembling the base for the basinet, Osgard frowned at the instruction manual. As he read, the screwdriver he held bobbed in his hand. Picking up a long bolt, he slotted the shaft through a hole, attaching another piece to the half-constructed contraption.

"Oz," Sloan said, getting the youngling's attention.

Gage's son looked up. Light blue eyes met his.

Sloan debated a second, then decided sharing the news fast was better than delivering it slow. "Your sire's stuck in town."

Osgard's brow furrowed. Processing the information, he straightened away from the base and stared at him. "Magnolia House?"

Sloan nodded. "Grounded by sunlight."

"He's okay?"

"Yeah, but not able to make it home."

A guarded looked entered Osgard's eyes. His expression moved from open to closed as his hand tightened on the handle of the screwdriver. His knuckles went white. Sloan's stomach clenched. Goddamn Zidane and the Archguard. The abusive bastards had done a number on the kid, traumatizing him so badly Osgard found it difficult to relax around anyone but Gage. Not even Haider with his solid presence and smooth way with words had been able to crack the youngling's guard.

Anything unexpected, and Osgard shut down.

Sloan had seen it before and understood the compulsion. Terror did that to a male, carving deep into the mind, elevating physical responses, urging retreat into safe spaces. Real or imagined. A threat was a *threat*. No negotiating with a scared kid when he spiraled, which meant...

He needed to stop Osgard from taking the tumble. Right now. Before he went somewhere inside his mind Sloan couldn't reach.

"Oz, look at me," he said, tone firm.

Seconds ticked into more. Felt like forever before Osgard leveled his chin and met his gaze.

He walked closer, stopping three feet away. In the youngling's space, but not in his face. "You're safe with me, young gun."

"I know," Osgard murmured, even though his expression said he didn't.

"Your sire asked me to look out for you today. Gage would never do that if he didn't trust me. You're safe with me, Osgard," he said, repeating himself, hoping the message slipped through the kid's defenses. Holding eye contact, he reached out. His hand landed on Osgard's shoulder. He flinched. Sloan held the line, giving him a reassuring squeeze. "You sleep in your own bed. I'm gonna bunk in Gage's. Yeah?"

Swallowing, the kid set the screwdriver on the bedside table. "Okay."

"Good. Let's go." Dropping his hand, Sloan glanced toward the bed. Voice hushed, he asked, "B— you need anything?"

Pale green eyes met his over the top of Myst's head. "No, brother. Go. Get some sleep."

He tipped his chin and, waving Osgard toward the door, followed him out into the hallway. But as he turned toward the clinic, unease set in. Tension invaded his muscles and bones, weighing him down, slowing his pace. Forcing himself to keep walking, Sloan rolled his shoulders, fighting the apprehension, hoping like hell his brother's trust wasn't misplaced. Osgard needed what his adopted sire always gave him —calm, patient, and steady.

Problem was, he didn't feel anything close to calm. It had been decades since he'd slept aboveground. So long, he wasn't sure how his dragon half would react. Dread joined the discomfort prickling across his skin. Could be bad. Could move from terrible to worse as the day progressed, which made him worry about the youngling, and how he'd react if Sloan couldn't keep it together and lost his cool inside the loft.

He drew in a deep breath, then let it go.

No help for it. A promise given was a promise kept. He'd given his word to Gage. And would keep it, even if it killed him.

22

R ed scales gleaming in the porch light, Ivar folded his wings and landed in front of the bungalow. His paws touched down without making a sound. Unease ghosted through him. He didn't like the stillness. It was too quiet. So unlike the big look-at-me entrances Zidane liked to make.

Tension rolled in on the heels of his disquiet.

Fire sparked, rising from his scales, flickering over his shoulders. The unusual color of his irises took up the cause, casting a pink glow as he scanned the low-slung structure with cedar-shingled siding.

His eyes narrowed on the offensive-looking place. Crumbling front walkway. Crooked roofline. Sagging eaves. Not much square footage. His guess—two small bedrooms, three at most. Maybe an office somewhere in the mishmash of shoddy human construction.

Gaze still glowing with pink ire, Ivar snuffed out the flames. Smoke rose like spindles from his spikes, permeating the air as his scales cooled. Giving the house a last once-over, he shifted from dragon to human form and conjured his clothes. Jeans and a long-sleeved shirt settled on his skin. He added his favorite leather jacket to the mix and a pair of combat boots as Hamersveld set down beside him. Just as silent. On guard. Shark-grey scales clicking through the hush. Black eyes rimmed with blue, alert and looking for trouble.

Sharing his XO's view of the situation, Ivar tipped his chin.

Hamersveld nodded back, then fired up mindspeak. *"Fen—head on a swivel. Take the high ground. Squawk if you see anything."*

Still airborne, the wren chirped in answer. A short burst of noise. Shrill sound waves spiraled out. Pinpricks of pain raked his temples. Ivar shuddered, watching the miniature dragon rocket over the house, contrails streaming from his wingtips, heading for the cliffs at the back of the bungalow.

Shaking off the effects, Ivar glanced at his friend. *"Jesus, he's loud."*

Busy stomping his feet into his boots, Hamersveld shrugged. *"You get used to him."*

Doubtful.

Fen's ability to wreak havoc—and down warriors—with his war cry wasn't an idea a smart male got used to, not that it mattered right now. With Zidane lurking nearby, he didn't have time to argue the point.

Returning his attention to the house, Ivar started toward the front door. Boot soles crunching over gravel and crumbling concrete, he mounted the porch stairs. Two steps up. A narrow stretch of porch to reach the main entrance. With a murmur, he unleashed his magic. Heat flickered through his veins. Pink flames webbed between his fingertips, arching like electricity. He hummed in enjoyment as the faded wooden door swung open. Hinges creaked. Warmth rushed out, fighting for supremacy with cold air.

Ignoring the heated wash, he dipped his head beneath the lintel and walked into the entryway.

Neat.

Tidy.

Everything in its place.

Fresh coat of paint. Colorful area rug just inside the door. No pictures on the walls. Wellingtons lined up next to a tribe of running shoes and a lone pair of high-heeled boots on a rubber mat. Jackets hung on pegs to the right of the door. Small sizes. All belonging to a female. Not a male size in attendance.

Footfalls softened by the runner underfoot, he moved up the hallway. The zip in the air caught his attention. High frequency with a decided magnetic tang. Intense feminine energy with a sharp edge. His dragon senses tuned in, scenting the air, reading the vibration, realizing what it meant.

A high-energy female made her home here.

A powerful one.

One that most males would give their eyeteeth to possess.

With a low growl, he tracked the energy signal left behind by the owner, passed an ancient but clean kitchen, then walked through a living room with a fireplace and furniture purchased four decades ago. A bank of large windows with striped curtains faced the cliffs, looking out on huge redwoods and the sparkling surface of Puget Sound.

Crappy house.

Spectacular view.

No wonder the female stayed.

Dragging his focus from the scenery, Ivar skirted the coffee table, and using his mind, shoved double doors open on the opposite side of the room. Remnants of strong energy wafted out, telling him whoever she was, the female spent more time inside the room he stood on the edge of than any other inside the house.

He scanned the space before he entered.

A workshop of some kind. Big tables. Lots of equipment sitting on the scarred surfaces. A small smelter with an exhaust fan in one corner. And sitting on the edge of the lone armchair facing the door—Zidane, feet flat on the floor, forearms resting on thighs, hands laced between, black eyes leveled on him.

Two warriors stood behind him.

The blond, Ivar knew, the dark-haired male, he didn't.

Keeping his attention on Zidane, Ivar raised a brow. "Needed a break? Decided this was as good a place as any to take a load off?"

Zidane huffed. "Good to see you too, Ivar. It's been too long."

Not long enough.

Thirty years between encounters was too soon. If given a fairy godmother at birth, Ivar would've wished to never lay eyes on Zidane again.

"You look good, *zi kamir*." The chair creaked as Zidane pushed to his feet. "Relaxed. Well-fed. Wonder why?"

Refusing to take the bait, Ivar walked further into the workshop, establishing dominance, allowing Zidane to read the intent in his body language, sending a clear message. One Zidane needed to heed. The bastard wasn't in Prague anymore. He stood in Razorback territory, a place Ivar controlled. The past held no sway here. What once was, was no more. He wasn't a fledgling dragon under the Archguard's thumb, but a commander of warriors, a male hardened in battle and steeped in the kind of viciousness Zidane not only recognized, but would do well to respect.

"Seattle's been good to me," he said, stopping beside one of the workbenches.

"I know," Zidane murmured, calculation in his dark eyes. "I'm aware of my sire's extra-curricular activities... and how you benefit."

Ivar sighed. Here they went. Same old, same old. Zidane excelled at the art of manipulation. He enjoyed frightening others by initiating power plays. Ones that involved invoking his sire's name. Most males would've balked. Backed down. Bowed beneath the subtle suggestion that defying Zidane meant incurring the Archguard's wrath.

At one time, Ivar might've cared.

He no longer did.

Time had matured him. Going head-to-head with Bastian night after night had sharpened his skills. Not much scared him anymore. In fact, nothing did, except, well... the thought of hurting Sasha. The mere idea messed with his chi. Threw him off balance so badly, Ivar wasn't sure he'd ever regain equilibrium. But Zidane would never know about her. Not now. Not ever, so... fuck him and the crew he brought to Seattle. Zidane and the males with him were shit out of luck. Damned to failure if their leader kept making assumptions based on the past, not where he stood now.

"You think I care what you know?"

Zidane stilled. His gaze sharpened on Ivar's face. "You should. You've taken, now it's time to give back."

"Careful, *my brother*," he said, translating Dragonese's "*zi kamir*" into English. "You've flown out from beneath your sire's wing. Rodin's protection doesn't extend this far."

Yakapov, the blond warrior standing behind Zidane, shifted in warning.

Zidane raised his hand, tamping down his first-in-command's temper. "You threatening me?"

"Not a threat. A warning. Simple courtesy. You're not in Prague anymore. We operate under a different set of rules here."

"So I've heard. Fucking uncivilized."

"You open your mouth, bullshit comes out," Hamersveld said, entering the fray. "I've seen the inside of your kill room. Know what you do to males and females there... for fun."

Unfazed by the accusation, Zidane's mouth curved. His attention strayed to Hamersveld. "A warrior needs his amusements. A pity I wasn't there when you visited, Sveld. With you, I would've had even *more* fun."

A low growl rumbled from Hamersveld's throat.

Ivar flicked his fingers.

His XO quieted, respecting his pace, allowing him to lead the conversation. A necessary strategy. One he and Hamersveld discussed before entering the house. As much as Ivar disliked the Archguard asshole, Hamersveld hated him more. No clue why. His friend refused to talk about Prague and what happened to him there. Eventually, Ivar would pry it out of him. In the meantime, he needed to keep Hamersveld on a tight leash and the interaction with Zidane short. Otherwise, his XO would lose the loose hold he had on his temper, let his freak fly, and drown the arrogant prick.

An engaging idea.

Ivar would've paid to see it, but... alas. Killing Zidane, wiping out his warriors, would bring more Archguard attention. An annoyance he wanted to avoid, if at all possible.

"You asked for the meet," he said as the aggression in the room settled. Leaning his hip against the work-bench, Ivar pretended nonchalance, sifting through the tools on the table. Metal tools bumped into iron casts flecked with silver and gold. He picked one up and, turning the mold over in his hand, returned his attention to the leader of Archguard's kill squad. "What do you want, Zidane?"

"A place to roost."

"You're a big boy. You can find your own accommo-dations."

Hamersveld grunted behind him, no doubt swal-lowing a laugh.

A nasty gleam in his dark eyes, Zidane's brows rose. "I'm not welcome in your lair?"

"No," Ivar said, holding the line, unwilling to give ground. No one but him and his personal guard en-tered 28 Walton Street. Way of his world. Dragonkind didn't play well with others, never mind invite out-siders into the space where they slept.

Ever.

No exceptions.

Zidane knew it. He lived by the same principles, which made his request the opening volley in a nego-tiation. The bastard was fishing, determined to get something Ivar possessed.

"You're not welcome in my home."

"My family's money paid for it."

"Old news. Past tense as well. Your sire and I have ended our arrangement."

"Just as you completed construction. Convenient."

Ivar shrugged. "I've always had good timing."

"True, but—"

"Move on," he said, tone soft with warning. "No more games. Tell me what you really want."

Black eyes hard on his, Zidane hesitated.

Holding his gaze, Ivar waited.

One minute moved into another before the male nodded. "You're harder than I remember. A more worthy adversary."

"I'm tickled pink you think so. I'll sleep better today knowing it," he said, sarcasm out in full force. Hamersveld made a strangled sound behind him. An unexpected curl of humor swirled through him. Jesus. His XO had a warped sense of humor. Something he could've done without while facing off with Zidane. Wanting to kick his friend, Ivar smoothed his expression, keeping the amusement at bay. "Doesn't answer my question."

"Warriors," Zidane murmured, watching him closely, looking for a chink in his armor. "Skilled fighters who know their way around Seattle and the Nightfury pack."

"*Hristos*," Hamersveld muttered. "You've got to be kidding me."

Zidane's gaze narrowed. "Not talking to you, Sveld."

Loosening the leash, Ivar stayed silent, letting his XO run with his idea.

"What did you think? That it would be easy?" Hamersveld asked, Norwegian accent thickened by the snarl in his undertone. "That you'd waltz in here and first night out, you'd kill Bastian and his warriors? Silfer's balls—only brought six warriors with you. Arrogant whelp. The Nightfury pack aren't lightweights. They don't give a shit what the Archguard thinks. Bastian's boys'll take you apart scale by fucking scale, and you've got the balls to walk in here unprepared and expect Ivar to cover your ass?"

"Watch your mouth," Yakapov growled, stepping around the chair.

"Get out of our fucking city," Hamersveld growled back. "Come back when you're prepared. Or better yet —don't. Stay. I'll enjoy watching you die."

"Ivar." One hand planted in the center of Yakapov's chest, Zidane held his warrior back. "Put a leash on your dog."

Hamersveld snarled, attempting to step around him.

He sidestepped, keeping his friend behind him. "Water dragon, Zidane. Best find some respect, otherwise..."

Ivar let the threat dangle, reminding his opponents of the destructive nature of the element Hamersveld commanded. And how much Dragonkind feared it.

Zidane flinched. Not a lot. Hardly at all. The asshole shut the reaction down fast, but Ivar saw it and pressed his advantage. "How many do you think you need to round out your contingent?"

"Eight... to start."

He huffed. Of course. Another power play. Clumsily deployed, but Ivar recognized the threat without difficulty. Zidane wanted to do more than complete his mission and eliminate the Nightfury pack. He had designs on Seattle. Planned to take it all—usurp Ivar's authority, take his warriors one by one, then his territory. He saw the play. The sadistic asshole wanted to become commander of the Razorback pack, instead of returning to Prague. Figured. A male as ambitious as Zidane needed to control his own destiny. No way he'd pass up an opportunity to slip from beneath his sire's thumb. Freedom, after all, was a powerful pull.

Ivar paused, thinking on the fly. "You may have

four. Warriors of my choosing. I'll bond each over to you for a period of three months... on one condition."

"What?"

"I want one of the Nightfuries taken alive and handed over to me," he said, initiating a play of his own. He needed to know how energy-fuse and the mating ceremony worked. Bastian and his band of bastards possessed the information. If making a deal with Zidane got him what he needed faster, all the better.

"Why do you need one alive?"

"Payback." A lie. One designed for Zidane. The male not only understood revenge, but got a sexual charge from torturing others. "Maximum pain to Bastian for years of aggravation."

"Anyone but Gage," Zidane said, flexing his fingers. "I get my claws on him, he's mine."

"Agreed."

Zidane nodded. "One other thing."

Ivar raised a brow, asking without words.

"I want one of the HEs in your stable."

The muscles bracketing his spine tensed. Fire ghosted over the nape of his neck as his temper started to shimmer.

Baring his teeth, Hamersveld reacted first. "Fuck off."

"Only fair," the bastard said, twisting the knife, enjoying the reaction his request elicited. "You've got a cellblock full of them."

Banking his fire, Ivar shook his head. "Not going to happen. You want a high energy female, go find your own."

"All right, then I claim this one."

His brows contracted. "This one?"

"The female who owns this house—Samantha

Redhook," he said, telling Ivar he'd done his home-
work. In a very short period of time. "Gage protected
her tonight. If she resurfaces, I want her. You locate
her first, you bring her to me. Firm. No negotiating.
That's the deal—four of your warriors and Redhook in
exchange for the first Nightfury I capture alive. Do we
have an accord?"

"You've got a hard-on for Gage—why?"

"Do you care?"

"Not really." Though, he found it interesting.

Zidane should want Bastian captured and killed
first. Daddy Dearest certainly would. Rodin might
play by his own rules, but he respected ancient Dragonkind ways, believing in the old adage—kill the commander, dismantle the pack. His firstborn son,
however, seemed to take a different view. One that included downing Gage alive and taking the female he
protected.

"Ivar," Zidane growled when he hesitated. "Do we
have a deal?"

"We do," he said, eying the warrior he didn't trust
and never would. "Sun's up soon. Best get a
move on."

The muscle behind Zidane shuffled, playing fol-
low-the-leader as the male headed for the door. Ivar
watched him go without moving. Heavy footfalls
thudded across wooden floors and area rugs. The
front door opened and closed. A burst of sizzling energy erupted, burning through the air. Wings flapped
and... lift off. The prickle beneath his skin downgraded, then ceased as the energy signature of each
male faded in the wake of their departure.

Silence descended.

He tossed the mold he held onto the table. Metal
clanged against metal as the mishmash hit the

wooden surface. Glancing at his XO, he raised his brow.

"I hate that prick."

Ivar's lips twitched. "Understatement of the century. You ever gonna tell me what happened with him in Prague?"

Hamersveld made a face.

He huffed, then got back on point. "What did you think?"

"I think he's after more than the Nightfury pack."

"*Da*," he said, relieved his XO thought the same thing, and he wasn't just being paranoid. "Never thought I'd say this, but—"

"I hope Bastian kills the bastard."

"Odds?"

"Sixty-forty, Bastian's way."

Pursing his lips, Ivar released a pent-up breath. "I don't know. Zidane's got more up his sleeve. No way he arrived with only six warriors. My guess? He's got more stashed away. Outside the city, maybe. He only wants Razorbacks to make inroads into our pack."

Hamersveld nodded. "Invade from the inside out."

"You got four warriors in mind to loan him?"

"Yeah."

"Good," he murmured, glancing around the room, then out the open double doors. "We need to worry about Zidane turning any of them to his cause?"

His XO shook his head.

Ivar nodded, then powered up his magic.

Heat whirled into the room, coating the ceiling, splashing along the walls, flowing over wooden floors. Closing his eyes, Ivar manipulated the spread, mapping every room, knitting together an impenetrable net inside his mind. Magic warped. The inferno-like fever twisted. Invisible threads solidified, taking shape and form. Casting the net, he spell-bound the house, setting a trap for the female who called the crappy bungalow home.

"What're you doing?" his friend asked, frowning.

"Ensuring we get our hands on another high-energy female."

Hamersveld looked around. Understanding dawned in his shark-black eyes. "She'll be able to enter the house, but once inside—"

"Won't be able to get out." His mouth curved. New plan up and running. No matter how things shook out, he'd covered all his bases. Revenge against the Nightfuries. Bait for Zidane. A new HE on the horizon to install inside his lair. "If she's stupid enough to come home, we'll have her."

"You serious about giving her to Zidane?"

Ivar shrugged.

Time would tell. Circumstance would dictate how he played the next hand with Zidane. He might be forced to hand over Samantha Redhook. He might not, but one thing for sure? Even without laying eyes on her, Ivar knew she'd be an excellent addition to cellblock A inside 28 Walton Street. HE number six for his breeding program. A brilliant replacement for Natalie, the female Hamersveld let get away.

23

The harsh vibration jarred Samantha awake. With a flinch, she rolled over inside the nest of blankets. Comfortable mattress. Soft sheets. Delicious masculine scent. Nothing like her bed at home. Blinking, she tried to figured out where she'd landed.

Lying belly-down, she reached for the lamp on the bedside table. A quick chain pull turned it on. Soft light flooded the room. She frowned at the headboard. Burnished antique mahogany. Hand-turned spindles. Beautiful design. Popping up onto her elbow, she glanced over her shoulder. Handstitched quilt thrown over the bottom of the bed, covering part of the thick comforter tucked around her. Same spindle arrangement in the footboard. A spool bed, a gorgeous one, hand-crafted in the 1930s. Not a lucky guess. She'd done the research, shown Grand picture after picture, pleading for one every year on her birthday.

Before he up and died on her.

The memory burned through her.

Grief pushed a sour taste into her mouth. Samantha swallowed, combating the—

The nasty vibration scored through the room again.

The lamp on the bedside table quivered. Samantha looked toward the door. The knob trembled. Another round of shaking. The picture frame on the wall tilted on its axis, sliding on its hanging cable, reacting to the... her brows collided... well, she didn't know what was going on outside her room.

Not exactly.

Leaning over the side of the mattress head-first, she pressed her hand to the floor, feeling for the cause of the disturbance. A hard thump came through the wooden floorboards. Alarm zipped through her as the last few hours came roaring back. Dragons fighting. The bronze ball, with her inside it, flying across the sky. Gage kissing her, giving her more pleasure than she thought possible.

Outside.

Under the stars.

While she participated... fully.

"Crap," she muttered as another series of thuds vibrated up her arm.

Chewing on her lip, she debated. Get out of bed and investigate? Or burrow under the covers and wait it out? Option two seemed like the safest way to go, except that left her too much time to think. To relive every second of making love with Gage, while trying not to regret it. Her eyes narrowed as options one and two seesawed inside her head.

Metallic tang wafted across the room, invading her airspace.

A mini-earthquake shook the bedframe.

With a curse, Samantha pushed upright, away from the floor. Rolling over, she flipped the covers off.

Chilly air washed in, making goosebumps rise on her skin. On her bare skin—her bare, very *naked* skin.

"Freakin'-frack." Where the hell were her clothes?

A quick scan provided a comprehensive snapshot. Pale peach walls. Dark furniture. Pretty artwork grouped in an attractive cluster above the dresser. A chair and ottoman complete with reading lamp tucked into one corner, under a wide window covered by backout shades. Her backpack on the floor beside it. None of her clothes, but a checkered flannel shirt (a la lumberjack) hung on the knob of the only other door in the room. The entrance to an en suite bathroom, maybe.

Samantha didn't care.

The well-appointed room didn't matter.

Finding something to cover up with before the brouhaha outside her door decided to make its way through it, however, did. A whole heck of a lot. By the feel of the thumping, the fight (or attack... God forbid. She really didn't want to deal with another of those) had escalated. In a major way.

Kicking off the sheet tangled around her feet, Samantha rolled across the mattress. Her feet touched down on an area rug. More thuds vibrated up through her bare soles. One eye on the bedroom door, she scurried toward the flannel. She grabbed it off the handle, and not wasting a second, flung it around her shoulders. Soft and worn, the shirt settled against her skin. The smell of musk and man enveloped her. Breathing deep, she drew more of him into her lungs.

Remembered sensation rolled through her.

Her thigh muscles quivered.

God. Gage. His shirt surrounding her. His scent all around her.

Like an addict, she took another hit, inhaling the

decadence of him, releasing her tension on the exhale. Ridiculous. Totally insane, given the thudding, but having him with her in some small way settled her. Her nerves stopped jangling as what he'd told her last night came sailing into her mind.

She was his.

He belonged to her, so... no need to freak out. Whatever was going on inside the house, he wouldn't allow to touch her.

Weird to be so certain. To believe he had her back, no matter what. And yet, she believed it. With every molecule that made her.

Attacking the buttons, Samantha made quick work of doing up the front placket, then tackled the too-long sleeves. She rolled the cuffs up her forearms, then stared at the tops of her bare feet and thanked God for huge flannel shirts. The one she wore provided excellent coverage. A necessity, given she planned to leave the room and wade into whatever was happening out there. Probably not the best strategy—crawling out the window might be better—but she refused to go that route.

Stupid maybe, but she'd given Gage her word, promising not to run. Not that she would've anyway. After witnessing what she witnessed last night, she had more questions than answers, which made her curious.

A fatal flaw of hers.

She'd never been a girl who ran from a problem. Wounded, unsure, even scared, she tackled issues head-on. Grand had loved that about her, cheering her on when her deafness presented challenges, encouraging her to solve problems in creative ways. She'd taken his advice to heart, refusing to back away from difficult situations, so really... Gage's warning had been unnecessary.

She wasn't going anywhere. She was sticking around, and with intuition urging her forward, now was as good a time as any to enter the fray. She sensed the frustration. Read the worry permeating the air. Tasted the anger and knew it emanated from Gage.

Standing in his room, dressed in his flannel, something primal burned through her, making her aware of the odd buzz in her veins. Samantha felt the pull, sensed the cosmic strings connecting him to her, and understood without being told. Or laying eyes on him. He lay before her like an open book, emotional resonance on display, allowing her to pick his mood, and what drove it, out of thin air.

Strange.

Not unlike the mind-link he used to talk to her. Every time she heard his voice inside her head.

She needed to ask him about that. Demand he explain. Unravel the mystery of Gage and the powers he wielded. Dragon-guy magic, or whatever Gage called it. A little spooky. A lot strange, but the truth didn't pull its punches. She might not understand yet, but Samantha trusted her instincts. And right now? Those were screaming at her to get moving.

Running on her tiptoes, she skirted the end of the bed and made a beeline for the door. She grabbed the brass knob. Metal trembled, pulsing beneath her palm. The hairs on her nape stood on end as she twisted the handle.

The locking mechanism released.

She threw the door open and, without hesitation, stepped into the hall. A mistake. Supremely bad timing. Instead of getting the lay of the land, she got elbowed in the shoulder. The blow knocked her backward. Off balance, she careened into the open doorway and slammed into the wooden jamb.

Oxygen left her lungs in a burst of air.

Pain spiraled across her shoulder blade.

A pair of large hands grabbed her.

More pissed off than hurt, Samantha flailed as tingles attacked her temples. A link bloomed inside her head. Understanding what it meant now, she reached out with her mind, connected, then barked, "What the hell?"

"Baby."

"Seriously, Gage—what the freaking hell?"

"Volamaia." Curled around her, he wrapped her up, pulling her hard against him, mashing her face into his chest. One hand fisted in her hair, the other ran down her back, finding the sore spot on her shoulder. She flinched. He growled, the angry sound scraping the insides of her head. *"Are you all right?"*

"I would be if you stopped smothering me," she said, voice muffled, throwing attitude. Where she got the nerve, Samantha couldn't say. Gage brought it out in her. Feeling safe with him allowed her to be less cautious, more herself. Seeking a bit of separation, she pushed against his ridiculously flat, intriguingly hard abdomen. "What's going on? Who are you fighting with?"

"Haider," he murmured, rubbing her back, his arms like steel bands around her.

Trying to save her nose, Samantha turned her head. Her cheek settled against the solid wall of his chest as she shoved him. Again. "Who?"

A different kind of buzz lit off between her temples.

"Me."

Samantha blinked as a new voice entered her

head. Deep baritone. Slight Eastern European accent. Smooth timbre, lacking the rough edge of Gage's full-bodied bass. She drew a steady breath, trying not to freak out. What was it with these dragon-guys? Was the mind-link thing standard operating procedure? Her brows furrowed as she thought about it, then decided to let it go. No need to get angry. She might not like a strange guy invading her mental space, but his ability allowed her to hear him. So yeah... getting pissy about it counted as counterproductive.

Wasted effort.

Something to be avoided.

She needed to pick her battles if she held any hope of keeping up with Gage and his fellows.

Hands fisted in the back of Gage's T-shirt, she tugged and leaned away. Strong arms tightened, flexing around her. Ear pressed to his chest, she listened to his heart slam against his breastbone. The heavy thud clued her in and... crap. He was upset. Worried he'd hurt her. Was holding onto her in the hopes of soothing the pain.

Taking a deep breath, Samantha changed tact. She stopped retreating, started advancing, and wrapped her arms around him. With a murmur, she caressed the rigid muscles bracketing his spine, willing him to relax, trying to reassure him, then added her voice. "Gage... I'm all right. Seriously. No harm done. A little space, please."

"You hit the doorjamb."

"Jarred me, that's it. I'm good, handsome. Doesn't hurt at all."

Chest expanding, Gage gave her a squeeze on the inhale. He relaxed on the exhale, allowing her some breathing room without letting her go. Big hands roamed over her shoulders. Setting her hands on his chest, she tipped her head back and looked up at him.

Shimmering bronze eyes met hers. *"You sure?"*

"Yup," she said, word playful, tone light. Raking long bangs out of her face, she tucked the strands behind her ear. "What's going on?"

Gage scowled. *"Haider's being an asshole."*

Her brows popped toward her hairline.

"Fuck you, Gage. I told you, I'm not—"

"Stop," she snapped, holding up her hand, not liking Haider's tone. Or the fact he'd cursed at Gage.

Her temper ticked up a notch, moving from shimmer to semi-boil.

Turning her head, Samantha shifted focus. Her gaze landed on the other guy standing in the hallway. Surprise ricocheted through her. Her lips parted. Good Lord. What the hell was in dragon-guy DNA? A whole collection of hot-guy genes, for sure, 'cause jeez, the man glaring at Gage was beautiful. Bona fide gorgeous, with his sharp cheekbones, angular jawline, and pale silver eyes. Almost as tall as Gage, just as broad, with long dark hair loose around his shoulders, and so much ink, Samantha knew he spent a crazy amount of time in the presence of a very talented tattoo artist.

No color in any of the ink.

Nothing but gradient—black, grey, and silver intersecting lines on his skin.

Dragging her eyes away from the phoenix rising on his arm, her attention jumped to his face. "Haider?"

Mercury-colored eyes sliced to her. *"Yeah?"*

"Why are you being an asshole?"

Gage huffed in amusement.

Haider frowned. *"I'm not—"*

"Seems to me you are." She arched her brow, challenging a man she'd never met, but somehow, felt she knew. Another strange phenomenon. Par for the course with dragon-guys. "You know how I know?"

Her question made his frown deepen into a scowl. *"No."*

"'Cause if you weren't being a jerk, Gage would be in bed with me, and I'd still be fast asleep. You woke me up, so now you owe me." Tucked against Gage, she leveled her gaze on Haider. "Spill. What's wrong?"

Dipping his head, Gage kissed her temple.

Haider sighed. *"I don't need to feed."*

"Feed?" she asked, not understanding.

"I'll explain the ins and outs of Dragonkind later, vola-maia... what it takes to keep us healthy." Mouth jumping to the top of her head, Gage gave her another squeeze. *"And Haider—that's bullshit. You haven't touched a female since we got back from Prague. You're on the edge of energy-greed."*

A muscle ticked along his jaw as Haider shifted his weight from one foot to the other. His fingers flexed a second before he looked away.

Samantha stared at his profile. Pissed-off expression. Clenched teeth. Temper set to explode. Hell, he was hurting. Maybe not physically, but emotionally, Haider was a mess. She saw it in the rigid line of his body, in the fact he refused to meet Gage's gaze.

Empathy stole through her, making her feel bad for him before the urge to kick his ass flew into view. She might not know what he needed (or anything about energy-greed), but Gage did. He knew what Haider required to stay healthy. Was doing his best to provide for his friend while Haider clung to stubbornness and pride, denying himself something he needed, making Gage worry.

The realization thumped through her, dragging

understanding along.

It was up to her.

In his state of mind, Haider couldn't hear Gage, but maybe, just maybe, he'd listen to her. A long shot. No clue whether it would work, but instinct told her it might, so... here went nothing.

Taking a deep breath, she whispered, "Pretty crappy."

Glancing at her from the corner of his eye, Haider met her gaze. *"What is?"*

"Worrying your friend," she said, watching him, allowing intuition to lead. "I mean, you are friends, right—best friends?"

Haider's eyes narrowed.

She kept at him. "You respect him? You love and value him?"

"Of course."

"Then why would you hurt him—on purpose?"

Haider flinched.

Samantha went in for the kill. "I may not understand what feeding means to Dragonkind yet, but whatever it entails, you obviously need it. By denying your needs, you worry him and hurt yourself. You have the power to put Gage's mind at ease. Why not bite the bullet and do it?"

"You don't understand," Haider growled.

"Enlighten me." Turning in Gage's arms, she pressed her back to his front. Tilting her head, she started to sign. Her hands moved. Her fingers formed the words, punctuating her message with ASL, challenging Haider in a different way. "Or better yet—dig in. Dig deep down, Haider, and find the strength to do what you must. If you won't do it for yourself, do it for Gage. Stop being selfish. Erase the worry. Settle his mind."

Watching her hands, Haider fisted his own. *"I know she's right. I know it, but—"*

"Haider," Gage said, a plea in his voice.

"I can't..." Rolling his shoulders, Haider shook his head. *"Since Prague, I can't connect. I don't wanna be touched."*

"Can't be avoid, zi kamir. You need me with you, I'll stay until you're finished. Send the female home afterward. Light contract. The bare minimum to get what you need. But this... fuck, man... it can't go on. What you're doing is dangerous."

"I know," he said through clenched teeth, conceding the point.

"Then let me help you."

"The female—she's still here?"

Gage nodded. *"Waiting in the living room."*

Haider took a deep breath.

"No sex, man." Rounding her with his arms, Gage set his chin on top of her head. *"Just a simple feeding."*

"Unfair to her. I plug into the Meridian and take her energy, she gets nothing in return." Cracking his knuckles, Haider glanced down the hall. *"Not an equitable exchange."*

"Nian's already pleased her and her friend," Gage said, surprising the heck out of Samantha. *"She's come so many times tonight, she won't want another orgasm."*

"Debatable," she mumbled, trying to lighten the mood. "Not sure there's a woman alive who'll say no to another orgasm."

Gage laughed.

Silver eyes started to twinkle as Haider grinned. *"You a sage?"*

"No, just deaf," she said, relief streaming through her as both men relaxed. "You learn a lot when forced to face your fears instead of running away from them."

Haider looked at Gage. *"Your mate, brother—total sage. Watch out for that, otherwise she'll walk all over you."*

"No worries, man. I'll just keep her in bed," Gage said, the devil in his voice. *"Won't have time to outsmart me when she can't say no to orgasms."*

"Hey!" she chirped, as Haider chuckled.

Spinning her to face him, Gage cupped her face. His eyes met hers a moment before he dipped his head. Holding her like she was precious, he treated her to a soft kiss, then swept the pad of his thumb over the apple of her cheek. *"Talked sense into him. Thank you, Samantha."*

"You're welcome," she whispered, overwhelmed by what he didn't say, but communicated with his touch —that she was valued, accepted, and yes... maybe even, loved. For who she was, deafness and all... without condition.

Maintaining eye contact, he kissed the tip of her nose, then drew away. *"You good for a while longer on your own?"*

Throat gone tight, she nodded.

His hands slid away, making her mourn the loss as he glanced at Haider. *"Let's get it done."*

With a grimace, Haider pivoted and strode down the long hallway. His footfalls fell, vibrating through the floorboards as he entered the wide landing at the top of the stairs. Rounding the banister, he disappeared down the steps.

Drawing her hair over her shoulder, Gage pressed his mouth to her temple, then followed his friend. She watched watch him go, hoping like hell Haider stayed the course, got what he needed, and Gage returned to her unscathed.

STANDING BEHIND HAIDER, Gage watched his friend lose the battle. Close contact wrecked his ability to resist, making his friend engage. With a growl, he lifted the female off her feet, pivoted and pressed her back to the wall. Hands roaming over her bare skin, Haider curled into her embrace.

The female moaned.

The Meridian flared.

Bright light flashed through the kitchen, washing over dark cabinetry as electrostatic bands that fed his kind surged. High-grade energy pulsed into the kitchen, hurting Gage's light-sensitive eyes as pendulum lights swayed over the long stretch of granite-topped island.

Attuned to the buzzing swell in the room, he held on, keeping Haider engaged until he heard him groan, accepting what was offered, taking what he required. Fingers drifting over Haider's nape, the brunette sank her hands into his hair and gasped in encouragement. Haider accepted the invitation, hooking her thigh over his hip, settling hard against her, his mouth jumping from her temple to pulse point.

Eyes closed, expression blissful, she raised her chin, giving his friend more room.

Haider took it.

Relief attacked Gage's tension, loosening worry one knot at a time. He released a pent-up breath as Haider entered the stream and started to feed. Backing away, he lifted his hands from his friend's shoulders, then turned on his heel, leaving him to finish on his own.

The best plan, all things considered.

After a couple of false starts, Haider had calmed

enough to welcome the female, allowing her to get close enough to touch him. And the brunette? Shit. She was good. Willing. Comfortable. Eager to be skin-to-skin with another Dragonkind male... open to the give and take. Haider needed an infusion of energy. She wanted the pleasure the feeding provided. A win-win all the way around, which meant...

His presence was no longer necessary.

Not right now.

Not for a while.

Deep in the energy stream, Haider was lost to hunger. Drinking deep. His dragon half focused on nothing but drawing nourishment from the source of all living things.

Giving his brother some privacy, Gage rounded the end of the large kitchen island. Bare feet silent against the floor tiles, he skirted the end of a stool, jogged down two steps and crossed into the living room. He had just enough time to rouse the other female, pay what Nian owed, and get them both moving. Her—toward the front door and into the sleek town car waiting curbside. Nian—toward the second floor and one of the empty bedrooms upstairs.

Knocked askew in the earlier melee, Gage straightened the armchair on the fly-by and approached the sleeping couple. Well-fed, spread out in the middle of the area rug, arms flung wide, eyes closed, Nian was practically comatose, deep in la-la land and the grips of healing sleep. His gaze jumped to the male's abdomen. Tangled up in female with a blanket thrown over his midriff—knees to lower chest—he couldn't see the injury responsible for downing the Archguard prince.

He performed a quick visual scan. Deep, easy breathing. Normal amount of color in his face.

Sleeping like the dead. All good. No serious or lasting ramifications. A day or two, and Nian would be right as rain.

Nudging the coffee table aside, Gage walked over a horde of crumpled condom wrappers, and hitting his haunches, set his hand in the middle of Nian's chest.

The male jolted.

Eyes the color of multihued opals flew open. Nian looked lost for a second, before his pupils contracted and his mind sharpened. Concern creasing his brow, he rumbled, "You good? Need anything?"

Gage's chest went tight. An involuntary reaction. One that pissed him off even as his heart defrosted, warming as he studied the namby-pamby. Fucking hell. Unfair. Every time he decided he disliked Nian, the male did something to redeem himself. Case in point? Waking from a deep sleep worried about Gage, not the least bit concerned about himself.

"Yeah, man," he murmured, thumping him on the shoulder with the side of his fist. "But need you mobile. Sun's up. The female needs to go home and you need to find a bed."

Rubbing sleep from his eyes, Nian frowned. "Not yet. Haider hasn't—"

"Past tense," he said, the male's concern for Haider making Gage like him a little bit more. "He's with the other female."

"Right now?"

He nodded.

"Thank the Goddess." Blowing out a breath, Nian scrubbed a hand over his face. "Was starting to worry."

"You and me both, but he's good. Connected. Deep in the stream. Getting what he needs."

"Good." Smoothing his bedmate's hair away from

her face, Nian cupped her jaw. He ran his thumb over her lips, nudging her. "Gorgeous, wake up."

She grumbled.

"*Talmina,* up and at it," his friend said, calling her "little one" in Dragonese. "Time to go."

Dark lashes lifted. Sleepy brown eyes landed on Nian. "Got nothing on today. I can stay... if you want."

"No." Softening the denial with a murmur, Nian sat up, taking her with him. Magic sparked in the air around him. The brunette blinked as he blurred her perception, hiding the fact he conjured a pair of sweatpants. Another soft word, and he tugged the blanket up, keeping her warm, shielding her bare breasts. "Get dressed. I'll walk you to the door."

Disappointment winged across her face.

Nian nudged her toward a pile of clothes strewn across the couch.

Gage pushed to his feet, deciding to let Nian and his golden tongue deal with payment and getting her out the door. Glancing toward the kitchen, he monitored Haider's progress. Almost finished. Wouldn't be long now. Then call girl number two would be on her way, and he'd be free to return to his mate. To show his appreciation for Samantha's quick thinking and targeted words.

Fuck. She'd been magnificent. Calm. In control. On point as she confronted Haider, presented her argument, and forced him to see reason. No judgement in her voice. None in her eyes either as she combined logic with emotion, shining a light through the darkness, allowing his friend to see through the shroud of pain surrounding him.

The way Haider reacted shouldn't have surprised him. The male was intuitive, able to manipulate any situation and bring others onside, into his way of thinking. He'd seen the male do it hundreds of times, but never—not once in over a hundred years—had the tables been turned. The fact Samantha deployed tactics Haider excelled at delivering, using them against him, made Gage's mouth curve up at the corners.

His friend hadn't liked being on the receiving end.

He'd listened anyway.

Which meant Gage owed his mate more of the orgasms she enjoyed so much. Not a hardship. He could spend hours buried inside her and never tire of her. She was a fantastic bedmate, but that wasn't it. Or at least, not the whole picture. What he felt when he looked at her—and talked to her—crossed boundaries and blurred emotion.

He'd never experienced anything like the connection he shared with Samantha. Her intellect, how she viewed the world, intrigued him. Her beauty made him want to get down on his knees and worship her. But her spirit... fuck. The sheer intensity of her gave him a buzz, charging parts of him he hadn't known needed powering up, making him feel more alive.

Without her even trying.

She didn't put on airs. Samantha was who she was, no artifice, straightforward in ways he found refreshing, all female. Dynamic. Charming. Beautifully magnetic.

Walking back up the steps, Gage reentered the kitchen just as Haider lifted his head. His friend groaned, and releasing the female, stumbled backward. The female sighed and slid down the wall, so deep in the pleasure rush, she didn't register Haider's retreat.

Eyes half closed, Haider swayed on his feet. "Gage."

"Here," he said, hustling around the end of the island.

Listing backwards, his friend started to go down.

Gage caught him before his ass hit the floor. With a grunt, he hauled him upright. Energy drunk, Haider tried to help, but...

Tightening his grip, he shook his head. Talk about a freak show. The male was loopy, completely uncoordinated, unable to ambulate on his own. Slinging his arm over his shoulder, Gage manhandled him, half walking, half dragging him out of the kitchen toward the stairs, but... man. The male weighed a ton.

Not surprising.

He should've expected the heavy load. Metallics weren't lightweights. His subset of Dragonkind topped the scales. The metal alloy in their systems went everywhere, threading through muscle and bone, making them heavyweights in a species that already packed a serious punch.

"The female," Haider muttered, voice slurred, head hanging, chin pressed to his chest.

"I got her." Limping around the island, Nian towed one brunette in his wake as he went to collect the other. "Go, Gage. Get him into bed."

"You solid?" he asked, attention on Nian... and the fact he favored his left side. The wound might be closed, but it wasn't healed yet. Visible above the waistband of his sweatpants, a curved pink line bisected his torso, telling anyone who cared to look where he'd been sliced open. Gage raised his brow. "Gonna be able to get upstairs?"

"Yeah."

Gaze pinned to the namby-pamby, he drilled him with a warning look. "You have trouble—holler."

Nian nodded.

At the foot of the stairs, he watched the male haul female number two to her feet. The movement made Nian wince. Clenching his teeth, Gage swallowed a growl and let the sight of his pain go. Proud to the point of self-annihilation, Nian might not like asking for help, but he would. His time with the Nightfury pack had softened his need for absolute independence, hammering home the fact he didn't need to go it alone.

Not anymore.

Gage had watched it happened. Slow, but sure, as Nian embraced pack principles and became one of them. Little by little. Day by day. Night after night. So yeah. The male would holler. He knew how much he could take. If he needed help, he'd let him know. In the meantime, he had bigger problems.

Haider wasn't tracking well.

The heavy SOB's knees kept buckling.

With a curse, Gage abandoned the haul-and-drag routine. Dipping his head, he bent and, tossing Haider over his shoulder, powered up the stairs. Taut muscles screamed in discomfort. Ignoring the pain, and his brother's grunt of protest, he took the steps two at a time. Cresting the last tread, he labored down the corridor, aiming for the bedroom Haider preferred.

Approaching the door, he murmured a command.

The lock snicked.

The heavy wooden panel swung open.

He turned sideways, making sure he didn't clobber Haider with the jamb, and focused on the king-size bed. Muscles screaming, he shuffled around the footboard. With a hop, he flipped Haider off his shoulder. His friend landed on the mattress with a slight bounce. The metal bedframe groaned. Haider rolled, settling belly-down, and flung his arms out.

Throw pillows went flying.

As the fat-bodied, tasseled mess hit the floor, Haider gave up the fight. Between one second and the next, he passed out. One moment semiconscious, the next fast asleep.

Amused the energy feeding had wrecked his friend, Gage huffed, then grabbed the quilt folded at the foot of the bed. With a quick jerk, he tossed fabric worn by time over the male sprawled facedown on the bed and left the room.

The door clicked closed behind him.

Bare feet planted on wooden floorboards, he focused on the identical one across the hall. He rolled his shoulders, trying to contain his eagerness. The best course of action. Otherwise, he'd cross the threshold, and without saying a word, attack his mate. Strip her down. Spread her beneath him. Fuck her so hard she'd feel echoes of his pounding for hours.

Excitement flickered through him at the thought.

Goddess. He wanted to do it. Lay her out and make a feast out of her, but...

Gage drew in a calming breath, struggling to control the impulse. She was new to Dragonkind. New to him. Something he must keep in mind. He needed to respect her pace. Bring her along slowly. Introduce her to his brand of sexual dominance little by little, not all at once. Otherwise, he might frighten her with the intensity of his desire. By his frenzied need to be with and inside her... and all the heated ways he longed to pleasure her.

Against his will, his imagination took flight.

Wild images flew into his head.

Compulsion gripped him, loosening his hold on control. Stark need picked his feet up, moved him forward, forcing him to cross the hall.

A death grip on his errant urges, Gage swung the door open and entered the room. His gaze landed on her. Perception blurred. The surroundings faded, and he saw nothing but her. His mate. In bed, waiting for him.

Standing just inside the room, he took her in, absorbing details, memorizing everything about her. The angle of her jaw. The promise of her body under the too-large flannel shirt. Thick, blond hair a riotous mess around her face. Pale skin glowing with vitality in the lamplight. Long legs bare as she sat cross-legged in the center of the bed. Mechanical pencil in her small hand. Sketch book in her lap. Attention on what she was drawing.

Muscles roping his abdomen pulled tight.

Desire morphed into desperation. His skin heated. His heart went apeshit, slamming against the inside of his chest as he hardened behind his button fly. An instantaneous reaction. Uncontrollable the second he laid eyes on her and...

Fucking hell.

He'd already had her three times, but no help for it. He needed her again. Now. Not five minutes from now, but... *now*. His hands in her hair. Her tongue in his mouth. Her lithe curves and sleek heat surrounding him as he connected in the way of his kind. Heart to heart. Skin to skin. Deep in the energy stream as she soothed his dragon half and fed him from the source.

Using his mind, he connected to hers.

He murmured her name.

Her pencil stilled against paper.

She looked up from the sketch pad resting in her lap. "Hey. How'd it go?"

Fighting the need to tackle her, Gage drew a deep breath.

An adorable pucker appeared between her brows. Eyes on him, Samantha tilted her head. "Any problems?"

Muscles locked, trying not to act like a savage, he shook his head.

"Good," she said, a pleased looked on her face as she bounced the pad against her bent knee. Full of abundant energy, she rapped the end of the pencil against the top sheet in a fast rat-a-tat-tat. "Glad it worked out, and... oh! Before I forget. Wanted to ask if you'd mind taking me home."

His brows collided as she knocked him off course. Must-have-her-now downgraded to hold-on-a-fucking-second, bringing his body back under control. *"Home?"*

"Yeah. To my house. I need some things and—"

"What things?"

She pointed to the drawing with the end of her pencil. "Been working on some new designs. There's a competition—a big one sponsored by Goldsmiths' Craft and Design Council—I plan to enter. Deadline's in six weeks, and even though my design concepts are almost locked, I need to make the jewelry, so I need my tools and also... a place to set up. Do you think—"

"Got lots of room at Black Diamond, volamaia," he said, understanding what she needed without being told. *Easy to make you a new workshop, but... forget the tools. I'll buy you new ones."*

A look of horror crossed her face. "Are you nuts?"

"No."

"You must be," she muttered, ignoring his answer, staring at him like he'd lost his mind. Without look-ing, she tossed the sketch pad toward the bedside ta-

ble. The instant it slapped down, sliding across the
high-gloss surface, the pencil in her hand followed.
Black bounced off white paper, skittered off the pad,
rolled off the edge, then hit the floor. "I don't want new
tools. I need my own. They're mine. They belonged to
Grand before me, and his father before him. No way
I'm leaving them there. I need to go back for them."

"Saman—"

"You want me with you. I get it. I really do. I feel it,
Gage—the connection, the pull, the need to be close.
But those tools, that equipment... it's all I have left of
him. The legacy he gave me. I won't lose it, dragon-guy
tantrum or not. I'll fight for it. I won't back down. Not
in this. That's how important it is to me." Rolling onto
her knees, she began talking with her hands. Impas-
sioned message. Graceful movements. Each word
punctuated with a hand flip and finger whirl. "My
memory of Grand is in the love he had for me, the
lessons he taught me, the time he spent teaching
them, but also, in the tools he used. If I leave them behind, I leave a piece of him, and myself, there too. I
can't—"

"Okay, wildcat. You win," he said, falling more in
love with her by the second. Family was sacred to her.
She understood commitment, the lengths and depths
you went to for a person you loved. Even after they
were gone. *"But you're not going yourself."*

She opened her mouth to protest.

*"It's too dangerous. By now, my enemies know who
you are and where you live. They scouted your house. You
go back, you risk capture. I'm not gonna lose you... ever. No
matter how important your tools are. I'll arrange for
someone to pack up your place. Move it to a safe location."*

"I don't want anyone else touching my things," she
said, reacting like a true artist, frowning at the thought

of strangers entering her private domain. "They might damage something."

"You want your tools, instead of new ones, that's the deal."

"Seriously, Gage. It won't take long to pack up my workshop and grab a few other things. Less than an hour. Maybe—"

"Take it or leave it, Samantha."

Irritation flashed in her eyes.

"But do it quick, 'cause in five seconds you're gonna be flat on your back and..." Pausing for effect, he prowled around the end of the bed. *"My mouth's gonna be between your legs."*

She blinked. "What?"

"Hanging on by a thread here, wildcat. Ask better questions. Or better yet, don't ask any at all, just get ready."

"But, we've already... I mean... *a lot.*"

"Need you again."

Her breath caught. "Are you always like this?"

"No. But I have a feeling I'm gonna be like this with you."

She shifted on the bed. Restless movement, her expression full of interest. "Not fair, Gage. You're using sex to distract me from the argument."

"It working?"

She pursed her lips, which meant *yes.*

His mouth curved. *"You want your next orgasm or not?"*

"Serious unfair advantage," she said, looking equal amounts pissed off and turned on.

"Get used to it."

Lunging at her, he grabbed the backs of her thighs. Knees planted on the comforter, he lifted her. The long tails of the shirt flipped up. He took advantage, cupping her ass, taking her down onto the bed.

Samantha gasped as she landed, and he settled between her thighs. Grazing the inside of her knee with his teeth, he moved up, and spreading her wide, licked into her labia.

He hummed as her scent and taste hit him. *"Already wet for me. Barely touched you, and you're ready for me. Fucking beautiful."*

"Holy crap," she rasped, hips rolling into the next stroke of his tongue.

"Gonna be a fun ride," he murmured, sucking on her clit.

She moaned. "What is?"

"Fucking the obstinate out of you. Winning arguments this way."

"Turnabout's fair play." Her spine arched, then twisted as he brought his fingers into play, making her ride while he suckled her. "You know, you can't just— fracking hell."

He upped the pace.

She lost the ability to talk.

Lashing her with pleasure, Gage smiled. *"Feel free to fuck me anytime you like... argument or not, Samantha. Something to know about me, though."*

"What?"

"I want something, I get it. And I almost never lose."

She twitched underneath him. Her core tightened around his fingers as she breathed, "You're annoying."

He chuckled. *"And you taste good. Bring your fire, wildcat. Come for me."*

Head tipped back, she grumbled something.

Without mercy, Gage took her over, dragged her under, listened to her explode into pleasure, not finding her annoying at all.

24

Ass planted in Gage's king-size bed, Sloan rubbed his shoulder blades against the padded headboard. The computer sitting in his lap tilted. He adjusted the angle of the screen, and without taking his gaze off the message board, reached for another pillow.

His fingertips brushed against a tasseled corner.

He took a moment to wonder at Gage's taste, then discarded the thought. No way would his brother go for fringe. The male was a jeans-and-T-shirt kind of guy. A minimalist in the truest sense of the word. The simpler his surroundings, the better Gage liked it. Which meant Daimler had wormed his way inside his private domain, brandished his magic wand, sprinkled fairy dust, or... whatever crazy-ass technique the Numbai employed on a regular basis inside the lair... and threw it all over the loft.

Floor to ceiling.

Wall to wall.

Evidence of his good taste lay everywhere.

A situation Gage no doubt hated, but was too respectful to fight. Or complain too much about. Nobody who wanted to eat well spoiled Daimler's fun,

and since his brother enjoyed good food—and insisted on it for his son—Gage was stuck with fancy
shit instead of what he preferred... the bare minimum
to get by.

His mouth curved at the thought. Freaking Gage.
The stubborn SOB had probably lost his mind after
arriving home to discover the devastating wave of
functional design Daimler left in his wake wherever
he went.

Sloan snorted, imagining the stand-off. Gage
stone-faced and pissed off. The Numbai one hundred
percent uncaring as he mixed, matched, fluffed pillows, threw afghans and affixed expensive artwork to
unadorned walls. Totally unnecessary. Luxurious living. The kind he and the other Nightfuries could live
without. Though he had to admit, the results were not
only stunning, but comfortable. Ruffled accent pillows
and all.

Stuffing another one behind his back, he sat up a
little straighter, then glanced at the bed shoved into
the back corner of the room. No frame. Just a box
spring and mattress pushed up against the wall with
fancy sheets, a thick duvet and another battalion of
throw pillows. Osgard slept among the horde, eyes
closed, breathing easy, the epitome of relaxed.

Finally.

Uncomfortable without Gage to watch over him,
finding sleep had taken the youngling a while. Understandable. He'd tossed and turned. Read a magazine
about fixing up vintage Mustangs. Gotten up three
times to get something (one of those *somethings*, he
was pretty sure, involved a butcher knife, which Osgard slipped under his pillow) before he closed his
eyes. Sloan didn't take it personally. He stayed quiet
instead, letting the male settle in his own time, setting

up shop in Gage's bed, hoping to find a little shut-eye of his own.

No such luck.

His earth dragon half rebelled, wanting to be deep underground, refusing to let him rest topside, being its usual persnickety.

An hour into trying to wrestle his beast into submission, Sloan gave up on getting any sleep and powered up his laptop, tapping into the dark net, scrolling through message boards, hunting for intel on the Archguard, searching for hidden communiques from other Dragonkind. From pack commanders in search of Bastian, rightful heir to the High Chancellery, looking for help, seeking advice... or to team up with the Nightfury pack in the fight against Rodin and the Archguard.

So far, no good.

He'd thought after the vote—and the Nightfury's official exile—other commanders would rally and coordinate, begin to form coalitions in support of Bastian and his pack. A reasonable assumption, given how unpopular the Archguard and Rodin's tactics had become. And yet... nothing. No one had reached out. Zero messages. Even so, Sloan refused to give up.

Monitoring the channels, maintaining open lines of communication, had become something of a hobby for him. He enjoyed scouring obscure corners of the internet. Excelled at picking up useful intel about the Archguard and what went on behind closed doors in Prague. Useful in many ways, frustrating in others. Since hammering the Nightfury pack with a ruling of *Xzinile* (exile sanctioned by the Archguard, expulsion for a warrior pack and from the Dragonkind community at large), Rodin had gone quiet, allowing things to settle.

A smart move on the bastard's part.

Something to be concerned about without question.

The bastard never went silent. Which told Sloan he was working on something. Working an angle in the shadows. One that gave him pause. One he needed to get a handle on before whatever pot Rodin stirred blew up in their faces.

With a flick of his finger, he scrolled down, trolling the dark net, looking for clues, following hunches, decoding message boards Dragonkind packs liked to use. He read through the contents and kept going, slipping behind firewalls, ghosting into private systems without detection and...

Nothing.

Not a single piece of information worth bringing to Bastian. Beyond frustrating. Days had gone by with nothing to show for all the time he spent going through—

His AI chirped.

A warning flashed on-screen.

Fingers flying over the keyboard, Sloan smiled. Fucking A. Another hacker was online, slithering like a snake behind him, tracking his movements across multiple servers. Typing in a line of code, he turned the tables, tagging his opponent, becoming the hunter instead of the hunted. Hands poised above his laptop, he waited for the reaction. Would the person panic and retreat? Would he or she go silent and still? Or use a brute force attack to back him off?

All interesting options.

His eyes narrowed as a string of code rolled across his screen. A second later, a chat box opened. The cursor blinked, waiting for him to accept the invitation to talk. Huh. Interesting. Not a tactic he expected. The hacker was good, shielding his or her IP address, employing a similar anti-infiltration security system to the one he used. Pursing his lips, Sloan hesitated, middle finger hovering over the enter button, then made his decision.

He hit accept.

The person on the other screen began typing. Two letters. Nothing else. Little to go on as the question landed the text box.

NF?

His fingers twitch above the keyboard as the meaning hit him. *NF*. Short for Nightfury. The hacker wanted to know which pack he called home. Gaze glued to the screen, he replied...

Why?

Nd 2 tlk.

Lctn? Pk?

U NF?

Sloan debated. He wanted the exchange, but taking it at face value wasn't smart. With tons of reasons to be cautious, and none not to be, he tapped his nail against the side of his laptop and stared at the prompt. His eyes narrowed. He needed to know who pulled the strings on the other end before committing. Problem was... if he didn't engage, he'd never find out.

Rechecking his system, he made sure his AI software was doing its job, shielding his system from attack, then hit a single key stroke.

Y

UK

Surprise made his lips part.

His brow furrowed, Sloan leaned away from the screen.

The UK meant Scotland. Forge's former pack and blood kin. No other pack claimed that territory. Stray males looking for a home gave the island a wide berth, refusing to cross Cyprus's borders. Rumored to be brutal and unforgiving, the commander of the Scottish pack wasn't the welcoming kind. Sloan had heard the rumors. Believed the hype. The warrior protected his own, guarding the island with a fierceness that made other Dragonkind back away. And if any decided to brave the wilds and enter Cyprus's territory? Sloan huffed. Shit. Males might fly in, but none ever flew back out.

Intrigued, he sent, *On scrn.*

Y

Using a trapdoor, he sent a secure link.

He watched the whirly-gig spin in the center of his screen. A video box opened. A female appeared on video, bright red hair in a riot of curls around her head, intent green eyes pointed at him, powerful aura glowing like a supernova around her. An HE sitting at a computer terminal a continent and ocean away.

At a loss for words, Sloan stared at her. Jesus. A high-energy female with serious hacking skills. Unreal. He admired her a moment longer, then refocused, realizing something important. She wasn't shielding her identity. No blurring effect on-screen. No mask either. Zero attempt to shield her face. Just a clear image that communicated she meant business.

Her gaze steady on him as she assessed him from thousands of miles away.

He tipped his chin. "Sloan."

"Ivy," she said, shifting in her office chair.

"You white hat?"

"Used to be... in my former life."

"And now?"

"I'm mated to Tydrin. I keep the system here secure."

"I do the same for my pack," he said, studying her.

He knew her mate. Not personally, but news traveled fast and wanting to protect Forge from any blowback from the Scotland, he'd done his research. Tydrin was blood brother to Cyprus, and first cousin to Forge. He didn't have all the intel, but given Forge refused to go anywhere near his former pack, Sloan knew the fallout must've been intense. The death of blood kin always hit a Dragonkind warrior hard. Forge was no exception. Didn't take a genius to figure out bad blood existed between the male and his cousins, and though Sloan had never asked for details, he knew Bastian and Mac (Forge's wingmate) had all the information. Still...

Despite the rift between Forge and Scottish pack, it was nice to see the Scots coming along, finding and mating females of their own. A good sign. One that worked in his favor. Mated males might be vicious, but they were also more reasonable when it came to negotiation. Warriors with females avoided risking their mates. Which made them more amenable to talking first. Only after all avenues of discussion were exhausted did they draw up battle plans.

"You're a Nightfury?"

He nodded.

Closing her eyes, Ivy released a long breath. "Thank God. I've been searching for months. Looking for a way in."

"You've found it," he said, one hundred percent focused on her. "Whatcha need?"

"Contact. A conversation with Bastian. I've got intel. Evidence smuggled out from inside Rodin's lair. Enough proof, we think, to topple the Archguard. Or at least, shift the balance of power. Put someone else at the top of the food chain."

"Jesus," he muttered, staring at her like she'd grown a second head.

"I know. It's huge, but Cyprus needs to talk to Bastian. Coordinate. Maybe bring other packs on board, 'cause—"

"Rodin won't give up without a fight."

"What I'm told," Ivy said, picking up a pen. She thumbed the top, depressing the button, letting it go to the tune of clickety-click-click. "Cy thinks it's going to be war."

"Probably."

"So..." she paused. "Secure video chat?"

"Yeah."

"When?"

"Let me talk to my commander," he said, checking the time. 11:37 AM. Too early to shake his brothers-in-arms out of bed. After the birth of B's son, and all the upheaval, everyone needed a good day's sleep. Mid-afternoon would be soon enough to rouse B and talk strategy. "Daylight hours here. I'll check with Bastian about a time and hit you up. You got a secure line you like to use?"

"I'll send it through."

"Good, and Ivy?" Finger poised above the trackpad on his computer, he tilted his head, warning her with a look. "Keep it tight. Once it begins, the Archguard will launch a brute force attack. In person and online. It'll be seek, hunt, and kill. You need to be ready."

"Got it covered. I'm buttoned up tight." Clicking the pen one more time, she tossed it to one side. "Good to meet you, Sloan. Ping me when you're ready. We'll get our packs talking."

He gave her a chin lift. "Later."

"You bet," she said, giving him the peace sign.

Sloan huffed in amusement and signed off. The

second the screen closed, excitement skittered through him. Progress. Finally. Fucking *finally*. After months of waiting, he sat on the precipice of success. No clue how the meeting between Bastian and Cyprus would go, but one thing for sure? To combat the Archguard—to affect real change inside Dragonkind—the old system needed to be dismantled and a new one set up. A coalition of Dragonkind must be built. Carefully selected warriors. Closely guarded inter-pack communications. Consistent coordination to ensure freedom for all of his kind.

Now all he needed to do was set it up.

But first...

He needed to talk with Bastian, clue in the rest of his brother-in-arms, and decide the best way forward. And after that? Sloan blew out a breath. He'd need to lock down Forge... and hope like hell the Scot didn't lose his mind when he discovered the pack he wanted no part of was poised to become a Nightfury ally in a war that hadn't yet started, but was about to ramp into apocalyptic.

25

F lat on her back in the middle of the bed, Angela floated in a sea of satisfaction. Eyes closed. Muscles relaxed. Brain turned off. Buoyant in the ebb and flow of mental drift. Mostly rag doll, completely worn out by her mate. A lovely feeling. The best kind of relief after wrestling with confusion the past few weeks. Though...

She still felt the incendiary flicker.

Banked, but burning bright beneath her skin.

No matter how relaxed she became, the strange buzz in her veins remained. The abrasive hum never quite let her go. Restless and wanting, the monster prowled just beneath her surface, battling to rise through deep relaxation, chaffing her senses, shredding her composure, dragging her closer to an abyss she refused to look into.

Taking measured breaths, Angela clung to the edge of oblivion, desperate to stay in the drift as unpleasant sensation tried to drag her out.

A big hand slid across her stomach. Cool palm. Chilly fingers. Gorgeous combination, the caress of her frost dragon, one that tugged at her senses.

She should move. Roll over. Burrowing into Rikar's

arms always helped, but... the time had come. She needed to stop hiding and tell him something was wrong. With her mind. With her body. With her ability to handle the stress that cropped up every time she braved what the awful buzz meant. For her. For them and the relationship she and her mate were building.

Rikar meant everything to her.

Everything.

She hadn't been with him long—a mere matter of months—but Angela knew she couldn't live without him now. The entire reason she stayed quiet, refusing to tell him the serum the Razorbacks injected her with had started to take effect. She'd tried to pretend the changes occurring inside her weren't real. A figment of her imagination. A trick of the mind. Fear at its most determined.

At first, she'd combated the anxiety with action. Wrote her symptoms down. Done research, reading medical journals, asking doctors online. She'd obsessed over every detail, then picked over her recollection of the night she'd been captured. A complete jumble of information driven by very few facts.

None of it made sense.

Like a ticking time bomb, the serum slithered through her veins, waiting for the right moment to strike.

"Angel," Rikar murmured against side of her throat. "Be right back."

Angela opened her mouth to tell him not to go. Her throat tightened as worry rose hard, strangling her voice, killing her plea for continued closeness as the mattress shifted.

A slight tug of fabric.

A barely-there jostle.

Cracking one eye open, she watched Rikar slide out from beneath the covers. Chilly air attacked her bare skin. She sighed in relief, loving the deep freeze as he rolled toward the edge of the bed. Miles of smooth skin. Oceans of rippling muscles. Heated ice-blue eyes as he glanced at her over his shoulder.

The stranglehold on her voice loosened.

She murmured his name.

He came back to her, kissing her breastbone, then the underside of her chin before he left her. Something he always did after he made love to her. He liked to touch. She liked the closeness. She hummed as his mouth drifted over her skin. Her mate. Crazy beautiful man. He'd been at her for hours, delivering nonstop pleasure, punishing her disobedience with bliss, making her come so many times she couldn't feel her toes—or much of anything else, for that matter.

His feet touched down on the area rug beside the bed.

Senses buzzing, the burn thickened inside her.

Her sensitivity to sound unspooled, grating against her eardrums, allowing her to hear the twist and crinkle of fibers under his bare soles. Minuit sound waves. Something she'd never heard before... and shouldn't be able to now.

Alarm streaked through her.

Feeling hot, sticky, and uncomfortable, she swallowed past her sore throat.

Big hand planted in the bed by her shoulder, Rikar leaned over her. "Don't go to sleep."

"Um-hmm," she mumbled as her stomach pitched.

"I'm serious," he said, deep voice rumbling as his mouth ghosted over her cheekbone. Arriving at her ear, he treated the lobe to a sharp nip, then pressed a light kiss against the sensitive spot behind it. She shivered. He growled. "Gonna get a washcloth, clean you up, then we're talking."

"Okay," she whispered, not feeling well, but unwilling to avoid the conversation anymore. Without his touch, the burn in her veins increased, making her twitch like a tuning fork. "Need to tell you. Gotta get it out."

"Yeah, you do," he whispered back. "Worried about you, angel. We don't hide shit from each other."

"I know."

"What I'm sensing in you doesn't make a whole lot of sense."

Tears stung the back of her eyes. "If you can sense it, imagine how it feels from my end."

Another soft kiss.

Strong hands caressing her skin. Another moment of relief, then...

He was gone. Leaving her with nothing but cold air, and a deep, abiding sense of guilt as he made his way to the bathroom. She listened to taps turn and water run. Seemed like forever instead of a minute, before he returned to sit on the side of the bed. Drawing his hand up the inside of her thigh, he hitched her knee, opening her to his touch. Warm terrycloth drifted between her legs. Echoes of pleasure rolled through her. She moaned as he washed himself from her body, then tossed the washcloth.

Wet towel slapped down on wooden floorboards.

Shoving the covers aside, Rikar slipped into bed and settled alongside her.

With Herculean effort, she forced her eyes open. "Hey."

His mouth tipped up at the corners. "Hey."

"You're so beautiful. Heart and soul, down to your core, beautiful." Managing to lift her arm, she trailed her fingertips along his jaw. Day-old stubble sent prickles of pleasure up her arm. Focused on his mouth, she tipped her chin, parting her lips. Getting the message, Rikar dipped his head and kissed her. Softly. Slowly. While she murmured, "I love you."

"Love you too, Angela."

"I'm sorry."

"What for?"

"Not telling you."

"Say what you gotta, angel. I'm all ears."

She swallowed around the lump in her throat. "There's something wrong with me. Really wrong, Rikar. I think, maybe, I'm..."

His brows furrowed. "What?"

"Sick."

He shook his head. "You're not."

"How do you know?"

"Energy-fuse, angel. You're my mate. We're connected. One and the same. The magic in my veins is in yours. You keep me strong by feeding me directly from the Meridian. I keep you healthy by returning it to you as healing energy," he said, pale eyes intense. "You're not sick."

"But—"

"Doesn't mean it isn't something else."

"The serum?"

"Could be, but..." He frowned, studying her face, no doubt trying to pinpoint what bothered him. "Feels more like—"

A spike of agony drilled her, slamming down her spine.

With a gasp, Angela arched. A blast of energy burned through her. Rikar jolted as the back of her head hit the bed. Baring her teeth, she closed her eyes and endured the pain.

Her body seized.

Sensation blurred, sucking her into a world filled with nothing but anguish.

"Fucking hell." Hands pressed to her shoulders, Rikar held her down, protecting her from the seizure as he threw a leg over her. Knees planted on either side of her hips, he straddled her, taking hold of her chin. "Eyes, angel. Look at me."

Unable to breathe, choking on pain, Angela forced her eyes open.

Nothing but blur above her, Rikar cursed. "Glowing."

"What?"

"Your eyes, Angela," he said, guttural tone rift with confusion. "We need to move."

"My eyes?" she choked out as another tremor racked her. "Rikar... what's... .h-happening?"

"Now, angel. Need more space. Taking you to the gym."

Her teeth started to chatter. "W-why?"

"You're shifting." Strong arms around her, he hauled her out of bed. "Don't know how. Don't know why, not a drop of dragon DNA in you, but... you're shifting. Moving from human to dragon form."

"Impossible," she rasped.

The soles of her feet hit the floor.

Her knees buckled.

Handling her like she weighed nothing, Rikar picked her up and, cradling her in his arms, sprinted across the room to the door. "Look at your hands, angel, then tell me it isn't possible."

Blinking to combat the visual and mental blur, she focused on her hands. The beginnings of pale scales formed on her skin. White claws with red tips grew from the ends of her fingertips. Not understanding, she shook her head. Hazel light from her glowing gaze shifted over her body, making her skin shimmer.

Panic gripped her along with the pain.

Her bones rattled. "Rikar."

"Got you, angel. You're safe."

"Rikar," she repeated as terror filled her.

"Trust me, mate. Hold on to the sound of my voice. I'll guide you through."

Angela tried.

She really did, but as anguish peaked and air exploded from her lungs, she couldn't contain her screams. Each one echoed inside her head, into the corridor and down the stairs, blocking out Rikar's voice as he ran, determined to provide what she needed. A lovely thought, but Angela already knew the truth. She felt it swell hard, crash in, then take her under, dragging comprehension in its wake.

She wasn't going to make it.

A powerful force had taken hold, refusing to let her go. Exerting brutal pressure, it tore through muscles, snapping her bones, stealing her air until her screams stopped and sorrow filled her. Sinking beneath a wave of agony, she mourned for her mate, for the life she would never live with a man she loved with mind, body, heart, and soul, knowing she'd never hold him again as the Meridian surged and magic ripped her apart.

26

Settled on Gage's back, Samantha hung on tight as he opened his wings and leapt skyward. With a powerful thrust, he spiraled upward, rising above houses and rooftops. The glow of porch lights fell away. Manicured trees and hedges in neighboring yards on Magnolia Street whipping in the blowback, he soared into open skies.

Lit up below her, the network of streets and highways flashed, streaming into one long, glowing snake as night traffic flowed down main arteries.

Gage gained altitude.

City glow faded.

Moonlight picked up where it left off, shining bright in a cloudless sky, making his metallic scales shimmer. She ran her hands over his interlocking dragon skin, learning the shape and feel of him. Lots of groves and ridges, smooth in some places, rough in others. Deep-seated pleasure settled even deeper. Goodness, he was gorgeous. A beauty to behold, in and out of dragon form.

Leaning to one side, she looked down at the ground. Nice view, one she never expected to see. Then again, why would she? Until the confrontation on the island, she never would've believed Dragonkind existed... or suspected one might live next door. Bet that tidbit of information would blow people's minds on Magnolia Street.

Samantha huffed, amused by the thought.

Angling his wings, Gage changed directions.

Cold wind blew in, swirling around her, flicking the end of her ponytail before a warm bubble formed around her.

A smile broke through as she let go of the spikes behind his horned head and lifted her arms. Eyes on the sky, she counted stars, watching the pinpoints of sparkle flash overhead and went with his flow. Warm air rushed over her hands. She tilted her outstretched arms, mimicking the movement of dragon wings in flight.

She couldn't help it.

Flying with Gage was magnificent. The absolute best. Way better than being trapped inside a metal ball while hurtling behind a dragon across the sky.

Invisible tethers tightened over her thighs and around her waist, securing her to his back as he left Seattle behind and flew away from the coast. Suburbia gave way to thick forest. Three-lane interstates became two-lane highways, then turned into rural roads. No streetlights. No headlights eating through the gloom. Just the moon, stars, and the man-dragon she'd spent all day getting to know.

Her smile turned into a grin.

Still pretending to fly, she tipped her head back and shouted, "Freaking awesome!"

Gage smiled at her over his shoulder. Huge fangs on display. Narrow contrails rippling from the tips of his jagged horns. Spiked spine undulating in waves behind her. A gorgeous gleam in his dark eyes, he engaged mind-speak. *"You like it?"*

"Wicked cool." Dropping her arms, she reestablished her handholds. "I want to fly with you every night."

He shook his head. *"As often as I'm able, volamaia."*

"Deal," she said, knowing he had responsibilities.

Along with the other guys.

The Nightfuries—seriously cool name for a pack of dragon-guys.

Her mouth curved as she glanced to her right. A gold dragon flew off Gage's wingtip. She looked to her left. A silver dragon took up the space on his other side. Haider and Nian, Metallic dragons like him. His wingmates, the ones who flew out of the lair with him on a regular basis. Right now, the trio formed a fighting triangle. Combat formation, three dragons strong. Information she hadn't possessed before meeting Gage. But after spending the day with him, Samantha had most, if not all, of the particulars.

Not surprising, given the way she peppered him with questions.

Something that made him laugh, but... hey. Curiosity had gotten the better of her, and once out of its stall, it galloped out of the barn. She hadn't held back. Of course, it helped she could talk to him without using ASL. Or, at least, not much of it. Habit made her use her hands. She signed without thought, but the sound of his voice inside her head, the freedom to be herself without worrying about being understood, was *everything*.

A gift so staggering, Samantha struggled to contain the emotion and failed. Her chest tightened. Tears stung the corners of her eyes. Inhaling deep, she fought the growing surge of gratefulness, marveling at how much her life had changed in such a short period of time. Gage was everything she'd never dreamed of in a man. Patient. Kind. Intuitive when it came to her. Fantastic in bed and... she bit her lip to keep from laughing... so freaking blunt, his forthrightness bordered on rude.

He didn't pull his punches.

Gage was an all-or-nothing kind of guy. A trait she admired. Particularly since he understood what she needed without being told, giving her the truth without hesitation. Samantha hadn't needed to pull the information out of him. She asked. He answered, telling her about Dragonkind, the curse of the Goddess, energy-fuse, the mating ceremony, and the mark all mated warriors wore. Somewhere along the way— between bouts of lovemaking and cooking for her—he also explained the dynamics inside the Nightfury pack.

Ten warriors.

Six females. Seven now, counting her.

A Dragonkind infant who belonged to Hope and Forge, and Gage's son, Osgard.

Oh, and Daimler, the Numbai who looked after them all.

Fascinating. Every bit of it. Though Samantha admitted it also made her nervous.

Meeting his family was a big deal. One she didn't know how to handle. Social situations scared her. Big groups made her want to turn around and run in the opposite direction. Every single time. The urge had become so strong over the years, she simply stopped trying. Avoiding social gatherings seemed easier, less stressful for her, less uncomfortable for others. Grand called it hiding from the world, but well...

Whatever.

The label didn't matter.

Fitting in with the Nightfuries, however, mattered a whole helluva lot.

Gage loved his pack. The way he talked about the warriors and women who lived inside Black Diamond spoke volumes. Each one meant something to him and, no dummy, she caught on quick.

He wanted her with him. From now on. No question about where she belonged. Which meant he planned to take her home with him. No negotiation on time frames. Zero period of adjustment for her. He intended to shove her right into the middle of things. Sink or swim. Fly or fall. Get with the program or be run over by it. Not a problem...

For a normal girl.

Trouble was, Samantha wasn't normal. She'd never been *normal*. Even before she got sick and lost her hearing, people treated her to sidelong looks. In high school, she heard the grumbled, "That girl, bad news just like her mom," as she walked past. Always the odd girl out, head in the clouds, imagination forever switched on, sketch pad in hand everywhere she went, safer on her own. Pick one. Considered them all. The list seemed endless. Toss in the fact her mother showed up drunk, high, or both to any and all school events and... yeah. Making friends hadn't been as easy as striking up a conversation.

Not that she was complaining.

Her life was just that—*her life*. She owned her mistakes, but also the parts that made her unique. She disavowed the nastiness others tried to foist on her after witnessing her mother's behavior. She hadn't earned it. Refused to own it or act the part. She was her own person, a grown woman who tackled things head-on and went after what she wanted. Her disability might be a difficultly others didn't share, but that didn't mean most people didn't wrestle with challenges and suffer setbacks.

Excellent attitude to adopt, and yet, the fact remained.

Her deafness made the easiest of social tasks difficult. Things most people took for granted—Zoom calls, chatting with strangers in cafes, standing around kitchen islands talking at parties, ordering in restaurants—made her anxious.

But this—meeting Gage's family? Making a good first impression? Being accepted into an already close-knit group that didn't like—or welcome—outsiders?

Samantha swallowed past the tightness in her throat. Hell. Just the thought was enough to give her a bad case of hives.

"Samantha," Gage said, breaking into her mini freak-out. "They're gonna love you."

She blinked. Her hands flexed on his scales. "Stop eavesdropping."

"No way. You let me in. I take advantage when needed."

"Doesn't seem fair."

"Never said I'd play fair, wildcat."

Her eyes narrowed on the back of his horned head. "I think we need some ground rules."

"How about this—I give you as many orgasms as you can handle, and you—"

A laugh escaped against her will. "You've got sex on the brain."

"Got my mate in my bed. Bound to happen."

"Seriously," she said, biting down on a grin. "Sex on the brain."

"You like it."

"I do. I like that you desire me the way you do.

Being wanted feels good," she said, unwilling to be dishonest in the face of his commitment to radical honesty. "Still, I think I'm entitled to some privacy."

"Even when you're stewing?"

"I'm not stewing, I'm just—"

"Stewing," he said, interrupting her. *"Worrying about something that doesn't factor. Listen to me, Samantha. I'm all for privacy when you need it, but not when you're thinking thoughts that upset you. Thoughts that have the power to hurt you. That happens, I'm gonna intervene, pull you out of the box you put yourself in, lid slammed down so tight over your head, you can't see clear. Not gonna sit by and watch you hurt, baby. Gonna yank you out, help you see clear."*

Well, that was...

Kind of awesome.

Samantha swallowed, fighting tears. Again. Like always when he told it to her straight, believing she was strong enough to handle it. "You're all kinds of awesome, you know that?"

"Been waiting a long time, Samantha."

"For what?"

"You," he said, voice soft, heavy with meaning.

She took a shaky breath. "God."

"No way I'm fucking it up now. No way I'm gonna let you either." More of his quiet baritone inside her head. More of the gentle insistence in his tone. *"My pack, volamaia... they're gonna love you, 'cause I already do."*

Shock widened her eyes. "What?"

Love?

He *loved* her?

Shoved off balance by his blunt admission, Samantha struggled to breathe. Her mouth opened. No sound came out. She closed it again, then shook her head. Holy crap. How had this happened? She knew Gage was important. She sensed the connection they shared deep down where instinct lived and logic took a backseat. She wanted to be with him. Craved him in ways that couldn't be natural. Acknowledging the truth, however, didn't stop the avalanche of uncertainty.

As she tumbled in the drift, Samantha faced a truth she'd been avoiding. She may only have just met him, but somehow, in the last few hours, he'd become vital to her. Crucial to her wellbeing in ways she couldn't explain and didn't understand, but... was that love, or just a bad case of infatuation?

"Know it's quick," he murmured, arresting the cascade inside her head. *"Things are happening fast, but energy-fuse isn't a joke, wildcat. Second I saw you, I knew how I felt about you. Spending time with you, taking you to bed, talking to you, has only strengthened the love I have for you. Bond's strong, Samantha, and only getting stronger."*

"Gage, I—"

"Don't need to hear it now. I'm a patient male. I'll wait for you to figure it out."

Her breath hitched.

"Okay," she whispered.

"Okay," he whispered back, the beauty of his voice undoing her one thread at a time.

As she came unstitched, he banked into a tight turn, circled wide, then folded his wings. He dropped like a stone out of the sky. His huge paws thumped down. She jolted on his back, her mind taking a quick snapshot before he shifted. An enormous one-story house to the left. Massive steel-sided garage with three industrial-sized doors to the right. A starburst of heat and shimmer exploding around her. Gage no longer in dragon form, wrapping very strong, very human arms around her.

Drawn to his warmth, she nestled into his chest. "Cool."

He grinned against the crown of her head. *"Good you like my dragon, volamaia. Better that you like being in my arms."*

"Sex on the brain," she mumbled, angling for his laugh.

He didn't disappoint.

Throwing his head back, Gage roared with laughter.

Arms tight around him, Samantha tipped her chin up to watch. Gage was gorgeous all the time. He was even more attractive when he laughed. As his amusement faded, he chuckled, bronze eyes shining with enjoyment, and dipped his head. His smiling mouth met hers. Hands playing in his hair, Samantha kissed him back, addicted to his taste, needing another hit, uncaring that Haider and Nian had landed and now stood watching her with Gage in the middle of the driveway.

A fizzle painted her temples as another voice linked in.

"Get a room, brother."

Gage lifted his head and looked at Haider. *"Jealous?"*

"Fucking right," Nian growled, making her brain vibrate. Throwing Gage a perturbed look, he prowled away from the garage, up the stone walkway toward the front door.

Gage blinked. *"When did he start swearing?"*

Haider snorted. *"You're a bad influence."*

"Damn straight," he said, a pleased look on his face. *"About time I rubbed off on the namby-pamby."*

Another snarl from Nian. *"Fuck off, Gage."*

"Wore him down." Grinning at his friend, Haider shook his head, then followed in Nian's pissed-off wake. *"Coming inside or—"*

"Oz first," Gage said, kissing her temple. *"Then the rest."*

Haider nodded, understanding the cryptic response. *"Later."*

"Yup." Grabbing her hand, he laced his finger through hers. A gentle tug got her feet moving. A fast pace made her walk-run next to Gage as he strode away from Haider. Toward the garage, away from the house. *"Time to meet my son and present your work, wildcat."*

"Osgard?"

"Yeah."

"I'm meeting Osgard?"

Glancing at her, Gage tipped his chin.

A messy tangle of nerves settled in the pit of her stomach. "Right now?"

"No sense putting it off."

Samantha drew a breath, then stomped on the beginnings of a panic attack. "But you haven't even seen the medallion, Gage. What if it isn't—"

He squeezed her hand. *"You make it?"*

"Uh... yes."

"Then already know it's fantastic. My son'll love it."

She hoped so, otherwise history would repeat itself and she'd do what she always did—make a terrible first impression.

Something that wouldn't ingratiate her to Gage's son, never mind the rest of his pack. Fear reared its ugly head. Insecurity joined the parade, killing her confidence, scoring marks on her soul as Samantha shifted the backpack on her shoulders, praying what lay inside it was good enough. Good enough to win Osgard over. Good enough to make Gage proud. Good enough for her to take her rightful place inside the Nightfury pack.

Following Gage through the open side door, Samantha took another calming breath, thinking... *no pressure.*

No pressure at all.

27

Reaching the top of the stairs inside the garage with Samantha in tow, Gage issued a mental command. The deadbolt flipped open. Polished metal gleaming in the low light, the bronze handle turned. He gave the door a gentle shove and, without breaking stride, walked into his loft.

Two pairs of eyes swung in his direction.

Ass planted at the kitchen island, Sloan tipped his chin in greeting.

Gage nodded back, giving a nonverbal thanks-for-staying-with-my-kid, then looked to his son. Relief etched on his features, Osgard tried to play it cool, tipping his chin like Sloan. A nice try, but Gage saw through the tough-guy act. Tension drained from his son's muscles, shoulders relaxing, the rigid line of his jaw softening as Osgard met his gaze, the message in his eyes clear—*thank fuck you're home.*

His lips twitched.

A muted reaction.

Osgard needed it that way. He was a smart kid with more than his fair share of pride. No way would he call his son out... or mention his relief. He might tease the youngling he adopted and now considered his own about other shit—unimportant things males razed each other about all the time—but not about needing him around. Gage enjoyed the role he'd stepped into for Osgard. Surprised the hell out of him. He never would've believed it before taking the youngling under his wing, but he loved being a sire. It felt good to be needed. Felt better to be trusted by a male who'd never trusted anybody. Until him.

Tugging on his hand, Samantha started to drag her feet.

Ignoring her nervousness, he tightened his grip and half walked, half towed her across the loft into the kitchen. "You sleep okay, kid?"

"Well enough," Osgard said, gaze moving from him to Samantha. Who now had a death grip on his arm. Sharp nails digging into the back of his hand, she took a shaky breath, but returned his son's regard when his intense blue eyes landed on her. "This her?"

"It is," he murmured, studying his son, looking for signs of unease.

Relaxed body language. Direct gaze. A bit guarded, but no hostility in the youngling's demeanor. Gage read the curiosity along with Osgard's usual caution. A natural inclination. One beaten into him by Zidane and his bastard sire. His son always looked before he leapt. Always made sure before he accepted anyone new inside his circle.

Understandable.

Smart even, given what he'd been through, but as Gage watched him, he took heart. Osgard wasn't closing down. Wasn't upset he brought a mate home, just curious about the kind of female his sire had chosen to call his own.

A good sign.

He'd been worried about his reaction to Samantha. He wanted Osgard to not only like her, but also accept her. She'd be in his life, from now until forever, and he didn't want his son to feel displaced. As though he'd lost his spot, or was less important now that Gage had claimed a mate. Unlike the other females in the lair, Samantha would be living in the space he shared with Osgard, making her home with them. If Osgard allowed it, his mate would be an excellent influence on his son. Bring the kind of softness into his life all males needed. Become a safe place for him to land at the end of each night. Teach him how to act when he found a mate of his own.

Reaching the end of the island, he positioned Samantha next to him, then turned his head so she could see his mouth. Her gaze dipped to his lips. Smart girl. She read him like she'd been born to it, picking up his intention. He didn't want to tell the others what she owned the right to share. He hoped she wouldn't hide it, but her deafness was Samantha's to share, not his to divulge.

One corner of her mouth quirked up. Raising her hand, she set her palm over his heart and pressed in, thanking him without words. Pleasure rose, whispering through him as the bond between him and her tightened another notch.

Foregoing mind-speak, he spoke out loud. "Oz, this is Samantha. *Volamaia*, meet Osgard, my son. The ugly one's Sloan."

Samantha huffed, taking the last comment as intended—as a joke.

Sloan chuckled. White teeth flashed against his dark skin as he shook his head, then translated Gage's nickname for Samantha into English. "Wildcat?"

He shrugged. "Suits her, brother. She's got claws."

Osgard grinned.

"Thank the Goddess," Sloan muttered, mouth curved up at the corners. "No other way to handle you."

"Tell it like it is, man," Samantha said, sliding her arm around his waist, settling against his side. "Though, might need a club with barbed wire wrapped around the end or... you know... a Taser. Eventually."

Brown eyes sparkling, Sloan laughed.

His son joined in, relaxing even more.

Enjoying her warped sense of humor, Gage shook his head and met her gaze. Gorgeous blue eyes twinkling. Full lips fighting a grin. Body pressed up against his. Fuck. He wanted to drag her down the hall, pin her to his bed, and finish what her teasing had started. He debated a second, then killed the urge in favor of accomplishing his goal.

"You wanna—"

"No," she said, picking up his train of thought. "I got it."

He tipped his chin.

She inhaled deep, exhaled long, and turned to the males standing in his kitchen. She glanced at Sloan, then looked at his son. "Something you should know about me."

A furrow between his brows, Osgard leaned forward. His forearms hit the granite countertop. His focus never left Samantha.

"I'm deaf." Slipping her arm from around him, she moved in front of him. The pack on her back brushed his chest as she raised her hands and started to sign. "If you want me to understand you, I need to see your face, so I can read your lips. Also..." she paused, then soldiered on, making him so proud the urge came back. Now all he could think about was stripping her bare and fucking her on the dining room table. "If you could—please don't sneak up behind me. I don't react well to that. You might end up with a fist to the throat or knee to the balls."

Speechless, Sloan stared at her.

Holding her gaze, Osgard signed something back.

Samantha went still, then jolted against him. "You know ASL?"

"A little," his son said, mouth and hands moving in tandem. "Useful skill to have when you need to stay quiet."

Shocked stupid, Gage studied his son.

Not shocked at all, Samantha smiled. "Who taught you?"

"A girl being kept in the same place as me. Her brother was deaf." Straightening away from the counter, Osgard frowned. Pain moved across his face. Gage gritted his teeth, wanting to wash the bad memories away, knowing he couldn't. After a second, Osgard's expression cleared. Hands movements hesitant, he looked at him, then back to the female making Gage's heart swell as she connected with his son. "Didn't teach me a lot, just enough to get by, but..."

He stopped signing.

Samantha waited for him to continue. When he didn't, she whispered, "You want to learn more?"

"Yeah."

"Then I'll teach you. You can practice with me."

"Cool," Osgard murmured, a little shy, mostly interested.

"And that's my cue," Sloan said softly, approval in his eyes as he looked at Samantha. "Need to check on B, Myst, and the infant. Got any intel you need me to share?"

"Tell him I spoke with Azrad." Rounding

Samantha with his arms, he set his chin on top of her head. Soft hair rasped against his whiskers. Her scent came to him. The need to lay her down and love her hard worsened. He cleared his throat. "Give me half an hour. I'll be down to brief everyone."

"I'll round up the boys." Leaving his coffee mug on the counter, his friend walked behind Osgard. He slapped the youngling on the shoulder, gave him a squeeze, then let him go and skirted the end of the island. Combat boots pointed toward the door, Sloan flicked out two fingers and headed for the above-ground lair. "Later."

"Yup," Gage said, listening to the thump of retreating footfalls.

He waited for the door to open and close, then hooked his fingers under the padded straps of her backpack. Samantha shrugged her shoulders. He stripped the pack off her back and set it in front of her on the countertop. "Time to shine, wildcat. Show us."

"Moment of truth," she muttered, laying the bag flat on the countertop.

Osgard threw him a questioning look.

He mouthed, "Wait," and returned his attention to his mate.

With a quick movement, she unzipped the bag, flipped the flap back and dug around inside. She came away with a leatherbound envelope first. Folded in three, the front of the supple navy-blue casing had been tooled with a crest of a dragon head. Eyes narrowed. Fangs bared. Scales defined. Fire flickering around the outer edge of the design. A piece of art, one that looked alive as it stared out of the flat face of the envelope.

Samantha set it to one side, then reached back inside the bag.

Taking a breath, she withdrew a box. Same color leather on the outside. Identical crest on the top. Intricate white-gold clasp holding it closed.

Holding the box, she glanced over her shoulder at him.

Encouraging her, he nodded.

Her eyes smiled at him a moment before she turned back to Osgard. She set the beautiful jewelry case down in front of him, then laid the envelope above the box on the granite countertop.

Dark blue leather gleamed beneath the glow of pendant lights. Straightening the case, she tapped the dragon cresting its top. "This is for you, Oz. Gage commissioned it for you. The envelope contains authentication papers with all the information. Date, time, and place of completion. Name of the artisan who crafted it. Everything you need to know."

"Your name," Osgard said, voice threadbare, a mere whisper. "You made it."

Samantha licked her bottom lip. "Yes."

Staring at his gift, Osgard swallowed hard.

"Open it, buddy," Gage murmured, chest tight as he watched his son react.

A slight tremble in his hands, Osgard reached out. Head bend to the task, he caressed the emblem with the pads of his fingertips, then moved to the clasp. A click sounded as the locking mechanism released. He cracked the top, opening it slowly. Tiny hinges whispered, revealing a gold medallion with the Nightfury emblem nestled inside a bed of dark blue satin.

Perfect proportions.

Brilliantly crafted.

A stunning replica of the ceremonial medallions worn by all Nightfury warriors during rituals inside the sacred rotunda.

A horse sound escaped Osgard.

"Happy birthday, kid."

"I hope you like it," Samantha said, back to being nervous.

"Fuck," his son rasped, cursing to express himself, taking after him, making Gage proud. Tears swimming in his eyes, Osgard lifted the medallion out of its box. Slowly. Reverently. With so much care, Gage's heart began to ache. Attached to a loop at the top of the crest, a heavy gold chain came with it. Placing the matched set in the center of his palm, his son closed his fist around it, then looked at him. "I'm one of you. Really yours. Official. I'm a Nightfury. I'm—"

"Oz." Stepping away from his mate, Gage rounded the end of the kitchen island. He raised his hand and curled it around the side of Osgard's neck. A tear tipped over his son's lashes. Letting it fall, Gage cupped the side of his head with his other hand. Holding the youngling secure in his grasp, he met his gaze. "You were mine the second I took you from that hellhole. It was official right then. The medallion is just a formality, but... yeah, kid. You're a Nightfury now. A member of the pack in every way."

A second tear fell.

Osgard's chest hitched.

Unable to stand it, Gage reeled him in, hugging him for the first time.

His son didn't resist. He allowed the closeness. Fist with the medallion pressed to his heart, Osgard wrapped his arm around him and returned the embrace. Setting his chin on top of his son's head, Gage held him tight. Small hands touched his waist a second before Samantha pressed her cheek to the middle of his back. He held Osgard. His mate held him, supporting him in the moment, the only way she knew how... with her touch.

How long it went on, Gage couldn't say.

Five minutes?

Ten?

He didn't know, nor did he care. He held Osgard until his breathing evened out and the tension left his muscles. Little by little, his son reclaimed his control and drew away. Wanting to hold on, knowing he couldn't, Gage respected the youngling's wishes, allowing the distance, but kept his hand curled around his nape.

He gave him a squeeze.

Inhaling deep, Osgard leveled his chin. Blue eyes still wet with tears met his. "Thanks, Dad."

Dad.

Delight grabbed hold. Love for the kid spread through him, exploding up and out, filling every corner of his soul. First time Osgard ever called him Dad, and... fucking hell, but it felt good.

"You're welcome, son," he murmured back, then lightened the mood. "Sixteen or seventeen? What have you decided?"

"March 13th, and I just turned eighteen. I'm eighteen."

"Bold move."

Osgard smiled. "I'm learning from the best."

Gage grinned back and gave his son a jostle. A quick push-pull before he let him go to collect his mate. Grabbing her wrist, he drew Samantha out from behind him. As she came around, he got a look at her face. Blue eyes shining with high emotion. Wet lashes. Big heart. His mate. So fucking beautiful. Dipping his head, Gage treated himself to a kiss, tucked her beneath his arm, then refocused on Osgard. "Try it on, kid. Let's see how it looks."

Uncurling his fingers, his son stared at the medallion in the center of his palm. A moment passed, moving into more before he gathered up the chain. He dipped his head. Heavy gold brushed over his dark hair, then settled around his neck. The perfect length, the round pendant settled against the youngling's chest.

Nestled under his arm, Samantha clapped while hopping up and down.

Osgard laughed, and using his hands, signed something to her.

Right hand raised, palm facing her chest, his mate touched her fingertips to her chin, then motioned toward Osgard. ASL, beauty in motion. A silent exchange Gage figured meant "you're welcome." Thankfulness rolled through him. His son. His mate. Getting along. Finding common ground. Enjoying each other's company. Something he wanted to stay and enjoy for the rest of the day, but with Bastian and the others waiting in the underground lair, Gage knew kicking back inside his loft wasn't a good idea.

Not with all the shit swirling around the Nightfury pack.

Decisions must be made. Battle plans needed to be drawn up. Zidane and his crew required killing sooner rather than later. So instead of sticking around, Gage kissed his mate goodbye, told his son to behave, and headed for the door. Not that the pair noticed. Samantha was too busy teaching Osgard swear words in sign language.

28

Taking the stairs two at a time, Sloan exited the underground passageway and entered the aboveground lair. Cinder block walls gave way to smooth plaster, white paint, and elaborate wainscoting. The gloom from the passageway faded. Light from overhead halogens reasserted control, leading him down a wide corridor with expensive artwork interspaced between honey-colored doors.

The smell of chocolate cake hung in the hallway.

His mouth curved even as he shook his head.

Freaking Daimler. The Numbai was up to old tricks, baking junk food with five times the normal amount of icing to ensure the females inside the lair made their way into the kitchen. Worked like a charm. Every time. Whenever Daimler got his groove on, females congregated, setting up around the massive kitchen island, keeping the Nightfury's go-to guy happy in good company.

Boots thudding across wide-planked floorboards, he ignored the Picassos, Rembrandts, and Degas, and turned right. He took the next left, weaving his way through the aboveground lair, moving away from the kitchen, toward the elevators. Not that he ever used either one of the stupid things. He always took the stairs. His dragon half balked every time he stepped inside a metal box, throwing a hissy fit.

In the outside world, he managed to tame his beast, navigating the interiors of buildings, using elevators when no other choice existed. But here, inside the lair, he refused to deny his nature. Underground always worked best. Stairs counted as the surest way to get there, if he came aboveground at all. No sense fighting what he couldn't change.

Dragon senses rambling, he walked past the elevators. Cranking the door to the stairwell open, he crossed the threshold. The second he hit the top of the downward spiral, footfalls heavy in the enclosed space, Sloan started the seven-story descent. Drilled deep into the ground, concrete steps took him down.

The smell of earth rose to surround him.

Pausing on one of the concrete landings, he closed his eyes and breathed in. His lungs filled. The welcome scent of concrete, minerals, water, and loam came to him. Sloan hummed as he exhaled. Taut muscles began to relax, releasing string by string and... man, that felt good. So much better than vibrations aboveground.

Enjoying the buzz in the air, he absorbed the natural energy emitted by the earth, then continued down the steps. As he neared the bottom, he reached out with his mind. His eyes narrowed as he drew on the bioenergy drifting through the underground lair. Individual signatures appeared on his mental screen. Myst napping inside a recovery room. Six warriors standing inside the gym. And one...

Sloan frowned.

Shit. He didn't know what the last string of energy meant. He couldn't read it. Never sensed anything remotely close to the unique signature streaming around his brothers-in-arms.

He jogged down the last flight of stairs and glanced at the keypad mounted to the wall. The electronic face lit with blue light. He punched the code with his mind. Buttons beeped. The heavy steel door swung wide. Turning right, he strode through the diamond-shaped vestibule in front of the elevators. Polished concrete funneled into a wide, high-ceiling corridor. Round lights embedded in the floor next to granite walls scarred by dragon claws rushed him toward the gym. Focused on the strange vibration, he jogged down a slight incline.

His feet slipped out from underneath him.

About to fall, he grabbed onto the side wall, then looked down. A thick slab of ice coated the floor. He looked further down the corridor. Snow blocking double doors into the gymnasium, a bunch of footprints breaking through the drift.

Watching his step on slick concrete, he followed the trail stamped in the snow. The deep freeze deepened into arctic blast. White puffs of air rushed from his mouth as he rounded the door frame and—

He stopped short. "Holy shit."

Six pairs of eyes snapped in his direction.

Sloan didn't notice. He was too busy staring at the dragon buried under a mound of snow in the center of the basketball court. Ice-blue, auburn-tipped scales glimmered under industrial lighting. Pure white spikes rode the length of the dragon's spine and tail, the same dark reddish-brown hue at the summit of each blade. Delicate of feature. Slight of frame. Not a huge male with heavy bones and thick claws. A frost dragon... one who shouldn't exist, sleeping like the dead inside Black Diamond.

His mouth opened.

Shock made him close it again.

Brows cranked low, he shook his head. "What the fuck?"

"Sloan."

Dragging his gaze from the miracle on ice, his attention bounced to Rikar. Shirtless, standing barefoot in the snow, dressed in nothing but jeans, the male lifted both hands and shrugged as if to say "the hell if I know." Frost swirled, cascading into a waterfall of snowflakes over the Nightfury first-in-command's shoulders.

Still reeling, he stared at his friend. "What the fuck?"

"An unexpected development."

"Unexpected?" Not understanding, he gaped at the male. Cold became colder. Fighting a shiver, Sloan conjured a parka, wondering when Rikar lost his mind. A distinct possibility, given *unexpected* didn't begin to describe what he was seeing. *Impossible* seemed like a better word to describe the... Sloan frowned... whatever the hell was going on.

Female Dragonkind no longer existed and hadn't for centuries. Not since the Goddess of All Things cursed their kind, denying males the ability to produce female offspring. And yet...

His attention moved back to the delicate-looking dragon.

He hadn't understood the excess energy earlier. Now, he picked up her signal. Murky became clear. Holy Goddess. Angela—smart, tough, an investigator of unparalleled talent and Rikar's mate—curled up in the middle of the underground lair's gymnasium, enjoying the winter wonderland created for her. A female he spent hours with each night, talking with her about Dragonkind, teaching her about computers and how to hack into human databases without being detected.

She'd become his companion while the other Nightfuries patrolled, hunting Razorbacks at night. He'd become her confidant, listening as she unearthed new facts about the case she was working and put the puzzle pieces together. But more importantly...

Somewhere along the way, Angela had also become his friend.

His chest tightened. "How?"

"I don't know," Rikar said, exhaustion in his tone. "We were... she was... then... it started. She hadn't been feeling well. Started a month ago. Ange didn't understand what she was feeling. Didn't know what it meant."

"Heightened perception? An itch in her veins, a buzz inside her head, the dreams?"

"Yeah."

"But she's all right now?"

"All good." Rolling his shoulders, Rikar glanced toward his mate. His eyes narrowed on Venom as the male walked a circle around Angela, boots slicing through snow drifts, studying her from all angles. "Difficult first shift, but she came through with flying colors. Might sleep for a while. A few days, maybe a week. Gonna keep the deep chill going until she wakes up."

Sloan nodded.

Made sense.

Frost dragons required snow and ice to survive. The more brutal the cold, the better Rikar's—and now Angela's—subset of Dragonkind liked it. But a fledging frost dragon needed the deep freeze more than most. First shifts were never fun, but for a female? Jesus. Rikar must've worked like hell all day. Expended tons of energy to keep her levels from dropping during the change. To ensure his mate didn't die as her body went into meltdown.

Making twin fists, Rikar glared at the male studying Angela's claws. "Ven—"

"Not gonna touch her, buddy," Venom said, hitting his haunches beside her head. Ruby red eyes trailed up her snout, over her horns, then down her flank. "Just lookin'."

With a low snarl, Rikar moved toward Venom. "Step back before I make you."

Blond hair in a man-bun at the back of his head, Venom didn't argue. He stood and retreated, respecting her mate's wishes, then shook his head. "What the hell's in that serum?"

"Excellent question," Sloan muttered, looking at the other males in the room. His attention landed on Bastian... and the newborn strapped to his chest. Hat on his small head. Wrapped in a thick blanket. Thumb stuck in his mouth. Fast asleep with his tiny ear pressed against his sire's heart. "Looks good on you, B."

Pale green eyes crinkled at the corners. "You here to check on him?"

"And Myst."

"Both're good, brother. My mate's tired, but pretty much healed. Sigvoid is healthy and strong."

Arms crossed over his chest, Wick grunted. "Good name."

B tipped his chin in agreement. "My sire's."

Forge raised a brow. "Myst agree yet?"

"The spoils go to the one who stays awake," Bastian said, grinning.

Mac huffed in amusement. "You're in for it, man."

"Aye, laddie." Purple eyes shimmering, Forge chuckled. He knew the drill. Before the Scot entered the Nightfury fold, Myst adopted his infant son, naming him before his sire got the chance, saddling Gregor-Mayhem with a human name. One Forge refused to use, which meant the little guy got called GM most of the time. "She's going tae rip you a new arsehole when she wakes up."

Venom's mouth curved. "She'll be tacking *Franklin* or some shit to the end of your son's name if you're not careful, B."

"Cross that bridge later. First..." Taking his hand from his son's back, Bastian pointed to Angela. "We need to figure out what the hell Ivar's doing to females."

"Or at least, high energy ones." Bare feet planted in the snowdrift around his mate, Rikar stroked his hand over her scales. She purred in her sleep, shifting to curl her barbed tail around his jean-clad leg. "Whatever it is, he's onto something."

"Gut-check time, boys," Sloan said, gaze on she-dragon in centuries, mind on the problem. "We've messed around for years, feuding with the Razor-backs, not taking Ivar and his asshole pack too seriously. Until he unleashed the virus in Grand Falls and started kidnapping HEs, it was fun toying with the idiots. Lots of action, few consequences. But now..."

He flicked his fingers toward Angela. "Don't know about you, but I'm done playing. I want Ivar. Want him off the street and out of the sky. Wanna know what he's been cooking in his laboratory and how he's doing it. I want to know what he knows, so we can protect Ange. 'Cause sure as shit, word gets out we've got a female dragon in the fold, first one to shift in centuries and—"

"Fucking hell," Rikar growled, curling his hand around one of his mate's spikes. "Warriors will come out of the woodwork to take her from me. From us. Just to have her or—"

"To study and dissect her," Wick said, finishing the horrifying thought.

"Motherfuck," Mac muttered.

Venom bared his teeth. "Goddamn it."

"So it starts now. We begin to build." Intense green eyes alight, Bastian raked his gaze through the group. "Knew it would come to this. Hoped it wouldn't. I moved half a world away to get away from that shit, but Rodin can't leave well enough alone. He was obsessed with my sire, and now with me. He won't stop, and the Archguard? Fucking useless. Nothing but puppets. A toothless counsel with no incentive to change."

"Then let's give 'em some," Sloan said, on board with his commander's plan.

Bastian's attention shifted to him. "You ready?"

Excitement skittered through him. "Been ready for years, B."

His commander nodded. "Then—"

"What the fuck?"

Everyone's attention swung toward the door.

Focus riveted to Angela, Gage stood on the threshold with Haider and Nian at his back. Standing in a triangle, Gage leading the pack, the other two flanking him, the trio of Metallics stared at the she-dragon sleeping at center court. Boots planted in snow. Mouths hanging open. Identical looks of stupefaction on their faces.

Sloan bit down on a smile.

He couldn't help it. Didn't matter that he'd reacted the same way. Didn't matter that it wasn't funny. Not really. The problem? The shock in the trio's eyes took his rusty sense of humor out for a spin, 'cause... shit. Not much knocked Gage off stride. His lips twitched. A chuckle escaped him. Good to know he wasn't the only one shoved off balance by the sight of Angela in dragon form.

Gage snapped his mouth shut, then glared at Rikar. "What the hell did you do to her?"

Startled by the accusation, Rikar blinked. "Wasn't me, man. I just got her through it."

"Ivar," Haider said, a snarl in his voice.

"Asshole," Nian added through clenched teeth.

"Serum," Gage murmured, jumping on his fellow Metallic's monosyllabic train. His gaze slid back to Angela. "Pretty girl you got there, Rikar."

Pride in his eyes, Rikar's mouth curved. "Gorgeous, isn't she?"

Bastian threw his best friend an amused look, then dragged everyone back on topic. "About time you three showed up. Got shit to plan. Need your input."

Interest sparked in Gage's eyes. "What are we doing?"

"Multiple points of attack," B said, attention on the Metallics. "Gage, Haider, Nian—work your contacts in Europe. Go global if you can. Be smart about it, but reach out to pack commanders. I wanna know which packs will stand with us when shit hits the fan. You need me to talk to any pack commanders, get me on the call. We're going to build a coalition with strong allies ready to go to war with the Archguard and all who stand with them."

Acting as a unit, the Metallics nodded.

Bastian turned to his first-in-command. "You're grounded until Ange is out of the woods."

"Yeah," Rikar said, without argument.

Shifting focus, B glanced at Mac, Forge, Wick, and Venom. "We're gonna do one of two things—bring Ivar to ground, put him in a box, and force the information out of him. Or find leverage against him, a pain point, something important that'll bring him to the table and get him talking."

Mind working, B paced toward the far end of the gym. Pivoting, he strode back, boots plowing through snow. He stopped next to a large bin full of basketballs covered in ice. "Sloan's right. No more fucking around. We need to know what was in the serum given to Ange and how it works. We know that, we'll share it with other Dragonkind. Take the pressure off Angela. We discover the location of Ivar's lair along the way, all the better. We're all... everyone one of us... on that. Each night we fly out, getting our claws on Ivar is no longer a side hustle, it's top priority."

All his brothers-in-arms murmured in agreement.

Rubbing his son's back, Bastian flexed his free hand. "Angela's gonna need a mentor when she wakes up."

Rikar opened his mouth to say something.

B stopped him with a sharp look. "Can't be you, brother. You're her mate, you'll coddle her during dragon combat training."

"I got her," Sloan said, surprising himself, shocking everyone else as nine pairs of eyes sliced his way.

And no wonder.

He never volunteered for anything that didn't involve computer systems. And honestly, that suited him fine most of the time, but not when it came to Angela. She deserved the best. A teacher who not only knew her well, but cared enough to push her hard. No coddling allowed. The mentor-fledgling relationship was a big deal. An important role rooted in time-honored tradition. Unbreakable bonds formed. Lasting friendships ensued. If a mentor did his job right, a fledgling warrior not only learned to take care of himself, but excelled in all situations. The kinship Forge and Mac shared was all the proof Sloan required to understand the truth.

By becoming Angela's mentor, he shouldered a huge responsibility. One that held the power to either make or break her emergence into Dragonkind.

Mac cleared his throat.

Forge looked down at his feet.

Venom threw a worried look at Wick.

"What?" he growled when no one spoke, but continued to stare at him. "I'm already teaching her how to hack computer systems. I spend more time with her night in and night out than any of you. She trusts me. I'll be her mentor."

"Solid, Sloan," Rikar murmured, looking relieved. "Appreciate it, man."

Throat gone tight, he nodded, accepting the male's trust for what it was—a big freaking deal. Dragonkind males were protective of their chosen females. The fact the Nightfury first-in-command agreed to Sloan mentoring his mate counted as a huge compliment. One that penetrated deep, piercing through until it reached his soul.

"Good, that's settled." Footfalls muffled by snow, Gage strode into the gym and joined the group. "I got a line on Azrad."

Gaze sharpening on Gage, B raised a brow. "What kind?"

"Mind-meld. He and I connected on the island."

"Thought he didnae want those kinds of strings,"

Forge said, sounding surprised. "Too afraid the Razorbacks would sense the link between him and us."

Gage shrugged. "Changed his mind."

"Smart. Good choice picking you." Standing shoulder to shoulder with his best friend, Haider leaned sideways. His shoulder bumped into Gage's, making the big male sway on his feet. "The magnetic force you wield is impenetrable. Acts like a force field. No way Ivar or any of the other Razorbacks will unravel it."

"Whatever." Uncomfortable with praise, Gage retaliated by reaching out and shoving Haider. Silver eyes sparked with good humor. Gage scowled at his friend. "Point is... your brother's in, B. All the fucking way. He's been chosen to breed one of the HE females in Ivar's stable. He's gonna keep in touch. Let me know when he and his wingmates need backup."

Venom hummed. "Might be the leverage we need. We take those HEs, Ivar'll come to the table."

Forge glanced at the male. "Why would he? Once we got 'em, it's not like we're going tae give 'em back tae the bastard."

"Data," Wick murmured.

"He'll want updates," Venom said, thoughts aligned with his best friend... per usual. Happened so often, Sloan sometimes wondered if the pair shared a brain. "All the health screens—blood tests, regular weigh-ins and check-ups, ultrasound results—if we don't pull the HEs out before the Meridian realigns and—"

Mac cursed. "Some of them end up pregnant."

"Exactly," Venom said, an unhappy look on his face.

Nian's upper lip curled. "Anyone else think this is messed up?"

"Me," Haider grumbled, crossing his arms over his chest.

"And me makes three," Gage said, making everyone laugh. "I'd rather kill Ivar than catch him."

"That'll come... eventually." Mouth curved, Bastian stared at his warrior a moment, then looked over the pack. "Anyone else got something to share?"

"Got news." Preparing to drop a verbal bomb into the proceedings, Sloan glanced at Mac. He met the male's gaze, a warning in his own. "Get ready."

Mac frowned. "For what?"

"To lock him down." As Mac's brow popped skyward, he launched the information into the gym. "Took a call today. The Scottish pack reached out through a third party."

"Who?" Wick asked, moving closer to Forge.

"Name's Ivy. White hat hacker," Sloan said, tensing as Forge's eyes began to glow. "Tydrin's mate."

Venom glanced at the Scot. "Who's that?"

A snarl left Forge's throat. "My blood cousin. Cyprus's younger brother. Bloody hell. The murdering bastards."

"Forge," Bastian said, gaze riveted to the Scot. "Get control of it. You don't know for certain your cousins were in league with Rodin. They may not have had anything to do with your family's murders."

"Bullshite. How much you wanna bet that—"

"Okay," Mac said, stepping into the breach, getting between his mentor and the rest of the pack. He raised his hands, palms up and out. A gesture meant to placate as he asked for the impossible—calm. For Forge to control the pain of losing his blood kin. Of watching his sire and brothers die in a vicious attack. Of being alienated from his former pack. A place that should've been safe for a fledging warrior, but turned out to be nothing short of hell for the Scot instead. "I get it, man. I do. Me, in your place, I'd feel the same, but guessing isn't good enough. You need to know for sure, and so do we."

Violence in his eyes, Forge growled through clenched teeth.

"Go." Standing firm in the face of his friend's rising fury, Mac squared off with him. "Go and find her."

Powerful magic unfurled in the room.

Overhead lights flickered.

Metal clanked as iced-up weight machines started to vibrate.

Sloan held his breath as Forge's grief bled into rage. Purple fire laced with acid flickered over the male's shoulders. Mac shook his head and motioned toward the exit. One second ticked into more before the Scot spun around and prowled out of the gym.

Snow and ice melted, leaving puddles in his wake.

Everyone exhaled in relief.

Mac glanced over his shoulder. Fierce aquamarine eyes met his. "B gives you the go ahead, Sloan, I'm there for the meeting. I wanna lay eyes on the Scottish jackoffs before Forge does."

He tipped his chin. "You got it, Mac."

"Good," he said, tone tight. "Gonna make sure he gets to Hope all right. Later, boys."

A round of "later, brother" followed him out the door.

He turned to his commander. "You want me to set up the meet?"

"Yeah, Sloan. Set it up," B said, before looking at each warrior in turn. Reacting to the nasty charge in the air, Sigvoid started to fuss. Dipping his head, Bastian kissed the top of his tiny toque, and murmuring to soothe his son, stepped out of the circle. "My son needs his mother. I need to check on my mate. Gage—looking forward to meeting Samantha."

"She's beautiful, B," Gage said, deep satisfaction in his bronze gaze.

"I don't doubt it." Patting his son's back with one hand, he slapped Gage on the shoulder with the other. Walking in the wet swathe of bare floor left by Forge, he crossed to the door and paused on the threshold. His gaze drifted over Angela, then moved over the males in the room. "No one flies out tonight. You've all got shit to do. Get it done."

His brothers-in-arms nodded.

Leaving the group, Sloan strode in his commander's wake. He needed to settle into the ugly-ass leather chair inside his computer lab, 'cause B was right. He had shit to do and not a lot of night left to get it done.

29

Night breeze jetting off his scales, Azrad circled into a holding pattern above the old cement factory. Infrared vision sparking, he scanned the terrain. Wide flat area, once active with dump trucks, now overgrown with weeds. Square concrete buildings with narrow windows in the center of the property, rusted pipes pitched at odd angles coming up through flat rooftop. A cluster of round cylindrical towers bracketing one end. Fledging trees and scrub bush growing between structures, strong roots rambling through once solid foundations, reclaiming lost territory from industrial human remains.

No fence around the decrepit facility.

No houses around for miles.

Nothing but thick forest encroaching upon a once thriving mill.

Buffeted by downdraft, Azrad angled his wings, riding unstable air. Wind shear whistled off the tip of his quadruple-bladed tail. His spiked spine rattled. Ignoring the hiss, he studied the landscape, looking for any pitfalls.

Azrad frowned.

Strange place for a meeting. Odd time too.

He didn't usually meet Hamersveld in the middle of bum-fuck nowhere just after twilight. All his face-to-faces with the Razorback XO happened an hour before sunrise, after a night spent patrolling, before he and his wingmates bedded down for the day.

Always downtown Seattle.

Always in a bar or coffee shop.

Not at abandoned cement factories south of the city.

The shift in behavior rubbed Azrad the wrong way. Hamersveld might not be predictable, but he'd never veered so far off the beaten path before. His instincts chattered, throwing out possible scenarios. What if he hadn't been as careful as he thought? What if he, Terranon, and Kilmar had been made as Nightfury spies? What if Ivar had figured out where he knew him from, 'cause yeah... he'd seen the Razorback commander giving him looks, trying to figure out why he recognized him.

Trying to relieve his unease, he blew out a sharp breath.

Spider venom rose from his nostrils.

As the lethal poison vaporized, streaming over his horns, Azrad shook his head. Damn his and Bastian's sire anyway. The male's dragon DNA ran true, giving his sons distinctive, shared characteristics along with similar gifts. Powerful magic was one. Almost identical bone structure counted as another. The difference? He was indigo-eyed. Bastian's irises were a pale, brilliant green.

The similarities he shared with his older brother didn't inspire confidence. Someone, at some point, was bound to notice.

Azrad hoped Ivar remained in the dark. At least,

for a while longer. He still had a lot of work left to do. A mission that would be compromised if one—or any —of the *what-ifs* bouncing around his head landed on Razorback radar. No mistakes could be made. Discovery equaled death. He needed to finish what he started.

The first half of his plan was already in place. He'd infiltrated Razorback ranks. Now to put the second part in motion—use Ivar as a stepping stone to his real target... Rodin and the other bastards responsible for his imprisonment inside Tanzenmed.

Baring his fangs, Azrad refocused on the ground.

He completed another sweep of the area.

Tweaking his sonar, he cast a wide net, moving the search radius from five to ten miles. Magic bloomed, eating through humid air, then boomeranged. Gathering speed, the radar pulses he sent out like harpoons blanketed the area, threads collecting information. He frowned as the intel came back. No Razorbacks hiding in the weeds. None lying in wait to ambush him when he landed. Not a single blip on his mental screen. Nothing to indicate enemy dragons were inside the three-mile marker... or patrolling outside it either.

Long-range sonar.

The gift that kept on giving.

An ability most Dragonkind warriors didn't possess.

Nine out of ten males could only detect another of his kind when he broke through the three-mile marker. Not Azrad. His sonar had more range. Much more. He picked up other Dragonkind from almost thirty miles away, providing details other males couldn't match. Why? No clue. So far, no one had been able to tell him. Older males didn't pretend to understand his ability. Everyone he met called it unnatural, making him feel like a freak of nature when he was younger. Now, though, he understood the snide comments for what they were—envy.

Plain and simple.

Jealousy at its greenest.

Despite others treating him to disapproving looks, he'd learned to embrace the magic he commanded. Power lived in the space between his differences and others' sameness, giving him distinct advantages. A bonus tonight, given the uncertainty of the situation he flew into with the Razorback XO.

Cranking the dial, he adjusted his radar to get a better reading. Sensation prickled along his horns. His eyes narrowed. Lots of static. Too much interference. Focused on the factory, he slowed from fast flight to quick glide, clicked his sonar one notch and...

Energy bled through the powerful spell surrounding the factory.

Azrad bared his fangs. There it was—the vicious hum in the air made sense now. About time he picked up the vibration, 'cause... holy fuck. The energy shield was a doozy, protecting a rundown, long-forgotten human mill.

A place of no importance.

Banking into a tight turn, he reversed course and lowered his altitude. The hooked claw at the end of his wingtip dragged over the invisible barrier. Sparks flew. A screeching sound drifted into the air. The shield rippled, betraying its shape as magic warped. Azrad growled in satisfaction. Nice attempt at deflection, but... no doubt in his mind. The nasty spell walked like a duck, quacked like a duck, and had water dragon written all over it.

Dropping a magical net over the clear dome, he mined the inside for information.

Three males inside the factory.

Hamersveld, plus two Razorback warriors with more guts than brains.

He should know. He'd beaten the shit out of both males—more than once—during the dragon combat competition while sequestered in the Cascade mountain range with Ivar's pack.

Tilting his horns, he amplified the signal, mapping each warrior's unique energy signature. Huh. Surprising. He hadn't expected the Razorback XO to pick the pair. Not for the breeding program. Rampart and Midion, two members of Ivar's personal guard, were better choices. Pairing either male with a high energy female would produce what Ivar wanted—strong offspring with powerful magic. The guards were strong fighters with keen minds, nothing like the idiots standing inside the cement factory waiting for him and his friends to arrive.

Firing up mind-speak, he opened a secure line. *"Three males inside—Sveld, plus two others."*

"And we make five. Five warriors. Five HE females on offer," Terranon said, holding steady on his right wingtip. *"You think Sveld's assigning us our females tonight?"*

"Man, I hope so." Playing sweeper, Kilmar rocketed over the treetops, beating the bushes, searching for enemy warriors in the weeds, hoping he got to kill someone. *"The sooner we meet the HEs, the quicker we get them to safety. Out from under Ivar's thumb."*

A wave of eagerness rolled through him.

He could hardly wait. Felt as though he'd been waiting forever to be accepted by the Razorback inner circle. Being undercover, waiting for the right oppor-

tunity to strike, weighed heavy on him. After weeks of
playing the game, his patience slipped a little more
each night. Now, he held on by his fingernails, praying
his mission neared its end as he waited for Ivar to give
him an opening. One that would ensure the females
being mistreated not only got out, but did so safely.

Not an easy proposition.

A delicate balance needed to be struck.

He must act the part. Pretend to be a Razorback.
Profess to beliefs he didn't hold. Become close with
enemy warriors he'd rather gut than look at day in,
day out. All the while striving to stay on an even emotional keel while he rode the razor's edge, devising
ways to rescue the HEs without jeopardizing his larger
mission—shutting down the Razorback pack and
stopping Ivar for good.

Stealing valuable females out from beneath his
nose wasn't enough.

Azrad wanted it all—the location to the SOB's private lair, the keys to the castle so he could cut the head
off the snake, blow up the entire operation, and ensure
the leader of the Razorback pack never kidnapped HE
females again.

Targeting innocent women was out of line. Uncon-
scionable. Offensive. So completely out of bounds, he
wondered why Dragonkind society at large didn't
sanction the bastard. Everyone knew what Ivar was
doing. Rodin bragged of his exploits in Prague, ap-
plauding his efforts, encouraging others of his kind to
follow the bastard's lead.

Another reason to kill the Archguard asshole.

After suffering for years inside Tanzenmed Prison,
the mistreatment of innocents was something Azrad
couldn't abide. No one—human or Dragonkind—
should have their wings clipped without cause. Major

criminals, sure. Rip those assholes apart. Inject them with poison. Sit them in an electric chair. Whatever. He didn't care what happened to people who broke the law, but... abusing a woman with the good fortune to be born high energy?

He swallowed a snarl.

No fucking way. Not on his watch.

"Azrad."

"Yeah?" Descending another fifty feet, he glanced at his friend.

"You think T-Rex is right?" Kilmar asked, calling Terranon by his nickname. *"You think we'll meet 'em tonight?"*

"Not sure, but be ready for anything. I don't trust Sveld," he said, spotting a good place to land.

Folding his wings, Azrad dropped out of the sky. Magic burned over his hide, raking his scales as he sliced through the energy shield.

His paws slammed down on a wide concrete pad.

The percussive bang echoed, ping-ponging between buildings. He curled his claws. Razor-sharp tips pierced through the nine-inch slab. Fissures opened, cracking through the quiet, stopping at the foot of a metal staircase.

"Stay on my six. Stay focused, no matter what Sveld throws at us." Glancing skyward, he watched his wingmates line up their approach. *"I know you're eager to meet the females. I am too, but... remember our objective. It's not enough to get the HEs out in one piece. We need to know where Ivar sleeps. My guess? We locate his private lair, we'll find more fucked-up shit in need of shutting down."*

Terranon growled. *"I want his link to Rodin. I want proof—"*

"My brother's working that angle," he murmured,

thinking about Bastian and the Nightfuries, a pack he hoped one day to join.

"We work it too," Kilmar said, unwilling to let go of the past. Azrad didn't blame him. Before arriving at Tanzenmed, Kilmar had been brutalized inside Rodin's pleasure pavilion. He disliked talking about it, but Azrad knew enough to know no male deserved what his friend endured before his first shift into dragon form. *"I want that fucker dead. Not dethroned —dead."*

"I hear you, KK," he said, understanding his point of view. No one deserved to be executed more than Rodin, but he needed his friend to stick to the plan. Going off script wasn't a good idea. The game he played with the Razorbacks was a dangerous one. A single misstep would tip Hamersveld off, and he and his brothers-in-arms would end up the dead ones. Nothing but piles of dragon ash in some remote corner of Washington. *"But to get there, we gotta play it smart. Keep it tight until the mission with the Razorbacks is over and Bastian reels us in."*

"Females first," Terranon said, a paragon of calm, cool, and collected—forever and always... unlike Kilmar. *"Ivar and the Archguard second."*

Kilmar grunted.

Taking that as agreement, Azrad shifted from dragon to human form and conjured his clothes. The usual settled on his body—combat boots, ripped jeans, a ratty-ass T-shirt, and a beat-up Army jacket. The black metal studs he favored pierced his nostril and eyebrow, stabilizing his mood, settling his unease, as Scandella—the red spider on his skin—crawled from her resting place over his heart while in dragon form, up his throat to settle inside the black web on the side of his neck.

"Scandal," he murmured, greeting her like he always did. With love and affection in his voice. *"Eyes open, my beautiful girl. All vantage points."*

She clicked her fangs, talking to him, returning his affection. She opened all of her eyes. Strings of power spilled from him into her. Using magical webs, she sewed her conscience into every living spider inside the factory, connecting in ways he couldn't, mapping the interior, showing him where Hamersveld set up shop.

Like cameras being turned on, multiple screens opened inside his mind.

His brothers landed at opposite ends of the parking lot.

The duo wing-flapped.

Debris blasted across the open area, pinging off concrete barriers and exposed rebar. A cloud of detritus blew toward him. Azrad raised his hand. Pebbles and dust froze mid-flurry, then fell like stones, landing in the shape of spider webs on the ground.

Terranon snorted.

Kilmar rolled his eyes. *"Show-off."*

Grinning, Azrad left his wingmates to follow and strode toward rickety-looking stairs. Rusted-out metal treads. Handrailing long gone, lying in a crumpled heap on the ground. A pair of doors hanging drunkenly on bent hinges.

Sonar scanning for trouble, Azrad took the steps two at a time.

The staircase rattled and swayed.

Ignoring the racket, he reached out with his mind. The door swung open. The smell of stale water and crumbling concrete hit him as he crossed the threshold. Spiders suspended in dark corners came out of hiding. Each one clicked a greeting. The chatter rose inside his head. He murmured back, monitoring Scandella's mental video feeds as he moved down the long hallway. Shadows closed around him. His night vision fired, allowing him to see in the dark. A couple of left turns and a doorless entryway later, he walked into a large open area.

Huge columns with chipped-off corners.

Worn, uneven floors.

A long cube van, back doors open, parked near garage doors to his right.

To his left sat a collection of obsolete construction equipment with peeling yellow paint. Boots crossed at the ankles, a redheaded Razorback stood propped against the side of one of the machines. The other male sat on the hood of a rusted-out truck with flat tires, dark hair tied back from his face, boots swinging in the breeze.

His lip curled.

A snarl rumbled up his throat.

Both males looked away, breaking eye contact.

Fine by him. He didn't have time for warriors who didn't possess enough fortitude to hold their own. His sole focus stood in the middle of the factory, arms crossed, shoulder leaning against one of the aging pillars.

Meeting Hamersveld's gaze, Azrad tipped his chin in greeting.

"About time, whelp."

He shrugged. "You wanted me here, I'm here. You gonna waste time bitching about me being late—or tell me what the hell's going on?"

The Razorback XO huffed in amusement. "Thought you'd be eager."

"For what?"

"Your female."

The muscles roping his abdomen clenched.

Azrad opened his mouth to answer.

Rolling in like a thundercloud behind him, Kilmar beat him to it. "About fucking time."

Guarding his flank, Terranon scanned the cavernous space. "Where are they?"

"Come see," Hamersveld said, crooking his index finger.

Without breaking stride, Azrad followed the Razorback XO across the factory. Hamersveld rounded a massive pillar. Floodlights came on. Illumination blazed across the open space between four columns, falling across a table. Behind it stood a flat screen TV on a tall metal stand, screen black, waiting to be powered up.

Approaching the table, Azrad focused on what sat on top of it. Five file folders. Each one a separate color —green, red, blue, yellow and orange. Centered above each one sat a square stainless-steel box. Closed lid. Precise placement. An ominous sign. One instinct insisted meant trouble.

Suspicious, he glanced at Hamersveld and raised a brow.

"You've earned first pick, Azrad." Flicking his fingers, Hamersveld pointed to the folders. "The folders contain information about the females on offer. One for each HE in Ivar's stable. Make your choice. Terranon and Kilmar choose next. Then the others."

"And the box?"

Hamersveld's mouth curved up in approval. "Sharp."

"Never been accused of being dumb."

"Pick your female, whelp," he said, eyes alight with good humor. "I'll explain the box after."

He held the male's gaze a moment longer, then relented. Arguing accomplished nothing. The idea of selecting an imprisoned female—one whose choice had been taken away—might turn his stomach, but the mission demanded it. To stop Ivar, he needed inside his lair. Accepting an HE provided the quickest path to victory, so...

Fuck it.

Better to complete the race than quit right before crossing the finish line.

Flipping the first folder open, he went down the line, studying each female's profile. All young. All accomplished. All striking, more than just pretty. One of Asian descent with shiny black hair falling in a straight sheet to her waist. One dark-skinned with beautiful almond-shaped eyes. Two looked like cheerleaders, one with a heart-shaped face and soft ginger curls, the other with gentle brown eyes, light brown hair and golden freckles.

He flipped the last file open.

His muscles contracted as his dragon half sat up and took notice. His body went haywire, firing with need. Desire flooded his senses. His fingers twitched as the yearning to touch her burned through him.

Heart beating double time, Azrad swallowed, listening to blood rush in his ears as he stared at her picture. Fierce expression full of attitude. Temper sparking in eyes the color of sapphires. A blue so pure Azrad had never seen their equal. Light blond hair tied up in a ponytail. His attention jumped to her name. Kasi Cosgrove—originally from Chicago, three years out of college, working for the Warner Institute of Science, and—

Azrad swallowed a growl.

Holy fuck.

He wanted her. The others were beautiful, but it had to be *her*.

"The blond," he murmured, battling his reaction, refusing to give away how much he desired her. Ammunition Hamersveld could use against him.

He never showed his hand before he played it. Ever. Force of habit. A lesson ingrained in him during his stint in prison. Closing the folder, Azrad tucked the orange cardstock under his arm and moved away from the table, allowing the males behind him to look at the remaining files.

He glanced at the flat screen, then back to Hamersveld. "I want to see her."

"What makes you think—"

"You brought the TV for a reason. Show me."

The Razorback XO laughed and waved his hand.

The flat screen flicked on.

Five separate squares appeared on screen, a female highlighted in each one. Azrad walked closer to the TV. The frame holding Kasi went from small to large, taking center stage, blocking out the other images. His lips parted. Goddess. Look at her. In climbing gear, she scaled a three-story wall. Bright overhead lights reflected off the surface of an Olympic-sized swimming pool at the base of the wall, throwing waves of illumination over the female freeclimbing, moving from peg to peg with complete concentration.

"Happy?"

Not even close.

He wanted Kasi out of Ivar's lair now. He wanted her safe. Not tomorrow. Not next week. *Now*. He'd start, however, by making sure he got into the same room with her.

Determination settled deep.

He drilled Hamersveld with a look. "What's in the box?"

"A tranquilizer."

"What the fuck." Pale yellow-green eyes flashing with temper, Kilmar stopped alongside him, red folder in his hands.

Carrying the yellow file, Terranon muttered, "Insurance. He's protecting the location. He doesn't want us to know where the females are being housed."

"Astute," Hamersveld murmured, walking to the table. Skirting the end, he strode between the flat screen and the edge. Flipping the boxes sitting on the plastic surface open, he revealed the capsule lying inside each one. "Two choices. You want the HE you've chosen, you take the pill and get into the back of the van. You wake up next to a high energy female and spend the next eight days in seclusion with her. You don't wanna take it, you walk away now. No hard feelings."

Razorbacks one and two moved.

Boots thumping across the concrete, each male grabbed a box, downed the pill, then headed for the cube van parked in front of the garage doors.

Not liking his options, Azrad stared at the tranquiller designated for him. His mind rebelled. Tension flickered through him. Pressing the folder against his side, his attention strayed to Kasi climbing the wall. Son of a bitch. Clever, clever water dragon. The bastard knew what he was doing.

Simple tactic.

Show a warrior something he wanted, threaten to take it away if he didn't comply. Diabolical strategy designed with two purposes in mind. One—to shield the location of Ivar's lair. Two—to test the boundaries of his trust and level of commitment to the Razorback cause.

The urge to reach out to Gage thumped through him.

Azrad wanted to do it. A simple one and done. Open mind-speak. Connect to the warrior who promised to have his back. Ask the Nightfury to link in and track the magical signature he left in his wake. A necessary step if he wanted to make it out of Razorback territory with five HEs in need of rescue.

Too bad none of that was an option.

Not with a vicious water dragon focused on him.

He was too close to the male. The second Azrad used his magic to reach out to Gage, Hamersveld would detect the connection. Which meant...

He was on his own.

Faced with a proposition he didn't like.

If he refused to cooperate, Hamersveld would learn more than Azrad wanted him to know. But... shit. The options both sucked. He didn't want to take the powerful drug. Couldn't imagine being unconscious and helpless, but now that he'd seen Kasi, his dragon half refused to leave her behind.

His eyes narrowed. "Tricky bastard."

Hamersveld smiled. "Pleasure comes at a cost, whelp. You want the blond, this is the price you pay."

Anger roared through him.

Terranon shifted beside him. "No choice."

"Seen her, want her. Gotta go, brother," Kilmar murmured, stepping toward the table.

Azrad nodded and, taking a steadying breath, did what his dragon half wanted and duty demanded. Mission trumped all. Ivar must be stopped. Kasi needed his help. No choice in the matter. So instead of fighting, he tossed the pill into his mouth and swallowed, hoping like hell he survived the night and was still breathing in the morning.

SITTING in the mobile command center parked inside one of the fire bays at 28 Walton Street, Ivar adjusted the air seat and reached out with his mind. Magic flared inside the cab. Obeying his command, the dented garage door started to roll up. Heavy chains clanged. The glow of streetlights slipped beneath the bottom edge, creeping across newly poured concrete floors.

He breathed deep as fresh air accompanied the wash of LEDs into the garage. Dust motes danced in the breeze, sparkling like jewels in front of the windshield as the solid steel panel continued to rise.

He cranked the ignition.

The big engine rumbled.

Heat blasted from open vents as the handle clicked and the passenger door swung open. Intense blue eyes met his a second before Rampart climbed inside. The cab swayed as the huge male settled into the bucket seat.

Ivar tipped his chin, asking for an update without words.

"All set," Rampart said, clicking his seatbelt into place. "Sleeping like babies. Tucked in tight."

"Midion and Syndor?"

"Already airborne."

"Good," he said, glad he'd had the foresight to leave Denzeil at the old army base in the Cascades.

He didn't have time to mess around. Not tonight when so much rested on the completion of his mission.

Years in the making, the breeding program was in the final stages. Just over a week to go until the Meridian realigned. In less than a month, he'd know if the serum he created produced the results he hoped—baby girls with Dragonkind DNA. A lofty goal. One he'd worked hard to see realized. The last thing he needed was Denzeil going postal and fucking up the plan.

At first, his warrior had balked, not wanting to be left alone in the Cascades.

Doing the dance to avoid suspicion—along with the real reason he wanted Denzeil in the mountains—he convinced the male to stay up north. As the IT and cybersecurity expert, his warrior excelled at rewiring systems. If Ivar wanted the bunker ready for the re-alignment—and he did in order to protect Sasha by locking himself down—he needed Denzeil to finish merging old technology with new. A fact to be thankful for under the circumstances. Denzeil and vulnerable females never made for a good combination.

The chains stopped clanking.

Taking his attention from Rampart, Ivar looked back toward the now open door. Twilight, the witching hour. A time when ghouls roamed the earth and his dragon half flew free, but...

Not tonight.

He had precious cargo to deliver. A mission that required he take the mobile commander center he'd converted into a hospital on wheels out for a spin... for the first time since stealing it from the SPD. Completely remodeled, the unit was a thing of beauty. High tech, on the cutting edge with satellite connectivity. Brand-new interior complete with state-of-the-art medical equipment. Eight rolling beds secured to the floor in the rear cabin. Five females fast asleep, each one settled in the bunk assigned to her.

An odd way to transport the females he kept in cellblock A, but Ivar refused to take any chances. Moving the HEs one by one presented too many challenges. The first of which began and ended with the warriors who hadn't placed top five in the Razorback dragon combat competition.

He didn't want those males anywhere near his HEs.

High energy females were a heady draw for his kind. Rare. Powerful. Coveted for their ability to feed warriors directly from the Meridian, the electrostatic bands ringing the planet. Most Dragonkind couldn't resist their allure, and never tried. Which meant Ivar needed to be on guard. A momentary lapse in judgement, a single miscue with one of his pack, and a warrior might get ideas Ivar didn't want him having. Like, oh say... attempting to steal one of the HEs out from under Ivar's control and keep her as his own.

A distinct possibility.

The entire reason he'd gone to such lengths... and taken serious precautions. Not even his personal guard had been allowed inside cellblock A. He'd done the prep work, getting each female ready for transport. No one else involved. Just him, a pair of latex gloves, a tranquilizer gun loaded with sedatives, and a hospital gurney.

Tedious work.

One hundred percent necessary to see the breeding program through to its conclusion.

Excitement mixed with trepidation, making him shift in his seat.

Gaze on the street beyond the open bay door, Ivar took a calming breath. He needed to calm the hell down. Worrying about outcomes that had yet to occur counted as a huge waste of time. He was close. So *close* to his dream becoming a reality—to having a daughter of his own.

Longing streamed through him as he pictured the promise of her. She'd be smart, and if the Goddess was good, inherit his red hair and pink irises. He'd always thought the color of his eyes was a curse, but... not anymore.

He was who he *was*. A male of purpose with the guts to chase his dreams. Hamersveld helped him understand the depth of his uniqueness. His XO always said no two warriors were alike for a reason. His race needed males of all colors, stripes, and interests to ensure Dragonkind's survival. His pink eyes were no more a curse than claws on a cat.

Flexing his fingers around the steering wheel, he hit the accelerator and eased out of the garage. The big Cummins ISL engine rumbled. Heavy-duty rubber tires squeezed on concrete as he exited the bay and rolled down the driveway fronting 28 Walton Street. Cranking the wheel, he turned left and drove past Sasha's tiny A-frame on his way out of the neighborhood.

An unnecessary detour.

Going the other way was faster, but Ivar couldn't resist checking on her. Seemed a bit compulsive, but he needed to make sure the female he wanted more than he should was safe. As he drove past, he studied the front of her house. Beat-up Jeep, mud splattered up the sides and caking the tires, sitting in the gravel drive. Porch light switched on. Lamplight glowing behind closed curtains in her front room.

Ivar exhaled in relief.

Good.

Sasha was home. Safe behind closed doors. Right where he needed her to be tonight. Most of the time, he didn't have a clue where his female might end up. Deep in the back country checking her cameras. At the institute looking after her bats. Sitting in her living room across the street, driving him to distraction as he fought the urge to visit her.

And lost.

Every damn time.

"Can't help yourself," Rampart said, amusement in his voice.

Gritting his teeth, Ivar threw the male a sharp glance.

His warrior ignored the warning. "She pretty?"

He scowled. Sasha was more than pretty. His female was extraordinary, so captivating he dreamed of her every day. Annoying in the extreme. Distracting as hell, but unbelievably beautiful too.

"Mind on the mission, Ram," he growled, looking away from the A-frame. "Not on my fucking female."

Rampart's lips twitched. "Hope to find my own one day."

Ivar scowled. "You could've had one of the HEs. I would've—"

"I know, but I'm not ready for an infant of my own. And none of the HEs appealed to me that way," he said, a furrow between his brows. "The breeding program—fuck, Ivar. I understand what you're doing is important. Even agree we need females of our own. What you're attempting could change everything. It's something our kind needs. Relying on humans isn't sustainable, so... yeah. I agree with the mission to a certain extent, but—"

"To a certain extent?"

"I don't like how it's happening. I haven't from the

beginning. Cellblock A—no fucking way. High energy or not, females should have a choice. Always."

"And you've waited to tell me this until now?"

"Couldn't talk to Lothair about it," Rampart said, throwing him a sidelong look. "Straight up, Ivar, I know you loved him, but start to finish, the male was like his blood brother. Just like Zidane. A total fucking sadist. He enjoyed hunting and hurting those females. Got a charge out of locking 'em up and watching 'em suffer."

"*Da*," Ivar said, admitting something he'd ignored a long time.

Much as he'd loved the male, his former XO hadn't been fit for the position. Lothair never challenged him. He encouraged his vicious side, feeding his anger, giving him more reasons to right the wrong done to Dragonkind by the Goddess of All Things. The more brutal the plan, the better Lothair had liked it. And seeing nothing but his objective, Ivar let himself be manipulated. Which made him one of two things—blind or an idiot.

He clenched his teeth.

Maybe it wasn't one or the other. Maybe he was both.

"So you talked to Sveld."

Rampart nodded. "Became clear quick he wasn't on board. Heard him talking to you, figured he had it covered. He's as uncomfortable with the breeding program as I am."

"I know," Ivar murmured, and he did.

Hamersveld hadn't hidden how he felt about the HEs inside the lair. Part of the reason Ivar was now one high energy female short of the six he wanted. The instant Hamersveld laid eyes on Natalie, his challenges to the methods Ivar used to produce girl offspring began. Unphased by the power he wielded as Razorback commander, his new XO never pulled his punches. Unlike his predecessor, he voiced his opinions and made his positions on a myriad of topics clear. From the moment the male learned of cellblock A, he'd been after Ivar to disband it. To get creative and find different ways to achieve the same results.

The idea intrigued Ivar.

He loved science. Enjoyed tweaking variables and hunting for smart solutions to complex problems. Toss in a good challenge, and... hell. Consider him one hundred percent on board. But then, he'd already been before Rampart shared his concerns. Hamersveld had done the legwork, bringing Ivar around to his way of thinking. No more HEs would be hunted and captured for the purposes of breeding in the future, but he must see the first test batch through. He couldn't abandon the project in the middle of it.

The females were already prepped with the serum and promised to strong warriors. And honestly? He needed the data mating the HEs to members of his pack would provide.

A Catch Twenty-two.

Please his XO (and now Rampart) and let the females go. Take the data from one breeding cycle and see where he came out. Two options. Only one real choice.

"After this round, we're done," Ivar said, merging onto the interstate. "I won't do it this way again. I'll find other ways to collect the data I need to breed baby girls of our own—*da?*"

"Yeah, man. Agreed."

Ivar nodded and, hitting the gas, brought the big truck up to speed, heading south toward the old cement factory where Hamersveld waited.

Firing up mind-speak, he pinged his XO. *"Sveld— any trouble?"*

Static washed into his head, then cleared as the warrior linked in. *"Got weird for a few minutes, but I'm good to go here. You on your way?"*

"On the road. Thirty minutes," he said, looking at the screen embedded in the dashboard. Digital GPS maps while driving—fucking brilliant. *"Azrad?"*

"Pissed off, but he's out now."

"How pissed was he?"

"On a scale of one to ten—seven million and fifty-two."

Ivar snorted.

In on the conversation, Rampart grinned outright.

"Didn't want to take the tranq, but—"

"I bet," Ivar said, imagining the warrior's reaction. It couldn't have been pretty.

"Kilmar and Terranon helped give him a nudge. The blond put him over the edge."

The blond?

His eyes narrowed. Recall flared as he took a mental stroll through the files he kept on his HEs. A picture of the blond morphed in his mind. Ah, yes. Kasi Cosgrove. A spitfire full of attitude. The female who almost escaped with Natalie before his personal guard intervened, retrieved and brought her back.

His mouth curved.

Figured Azrad would pick her. The fierceness of her personality more than matched the male's warrior frame of mind.

"Everyone settled into his unit?" he asked, referring to the apartment suites his worker bees built under the cement factory before he mind-scrubbed and released each one back into the wilds of human society. *"Locked down?"*

"Yeah, nice and tight. Just dumped Azrad in his room.

He was the last one," Hamersveld said, heavy footfalls thumping thorough the link. *"Energy shield's humming. Blakeite is charged and crackling, so the underground facility is now secure. No one's getting in or out until after the realignment."*

"Good," he murmured, thanking his lucky stars.

Stumbling onto the abandoned cement factory had been a stroke of good fortune. Located out in the middle of nowhere, there was little to no human traffic. After discovering the factory sat on top of rich deposits of *blakeite*—a tellurite mineral that blocked a male's ability to wield magic—purchasing the property became a no-brainer.

Eyes on the road, Ivar watched the center line flash in the headlights and ticked off items on his list. Warriors secured. Individual magic—and the ability to connect with others through mind-speak—shut down by the *blakeite*. Each male unconscious and put to bed. Five high energy females in transport, about to join the male assigned to her inside very comfortable apartment suites. The Meridian set to realign in... he checked the clock on the dashboard... seven days, nine hours, and thirty-seven minutes.

Check. Check. Quadruple check.

Ivar smiled at the windshield.

He loved it when a good plan came together.

30

S tanding inside her new workshop, Samantha ran her hand along the edge of one of the new-to-her workbenches, then glanced over at the other. Two surfaces instead of one for her to make her dreams come true. One flush against the wall, the other standing in the center of the room.

Both sturdy, but old.

Storied with histories told by the scrapes, grooves, and nicks left by previous owners. The stains and scars suited her. She loved the idea someone creative had come before her, toiling on the dark wooden tops, creating beautiful things that would go out into the world and help others make beautiful memories.

She hadn't known she needed the patina of time in her workshop.

Not until Gage and Osgard carried the tables into the space designated as hers in the back corner of Black Diamond's massive garage. But as the pair set the worn workstations down, asking her where she wanted them, Samantha thought "perfect." Everything about the benches felt right. Each and every nick. All the stains steeped in the beauty of artisans past.

How Gage had known what sparked her imagination and made her feel comfortable was anyone's guess. Dragon magic, maybe. A careful study of her, no doubt. Her mouth curved. He hadn't lied. Energy-fuse was serious business, an invisible force that strengthened by the day, drawing her closer to him, making her realize how much she needed him.

Samantha leaned into the emotion, instead of away.

Crazy.

Completely bonkers.

Three days inside Black Diamond, surrounded by a pack of dragon-guys and their mates. Just *seventy-two hours* after meeting Gage, and she understood. He told her she'd figure it out. She had, and now accepted the truth. As much as he loved her, Samantha thought maybe she loved him more. Not that she'd told him yet. She nibbled on the inside of her lower lip. She should jump on that—be as honest with him as he always was with her, but...

She sighed.

How did one go about telling a man-dragon she loved him, anyway? Should she plan something special—a meal, an outing, another round of fabulous sex? Or just blurt it out willy-nilly? Seemed more important than that, monumental, like an occasion, not a moment that lent itself to off-the-cuff.

Mulling it over, Samantha frowned.

Given Gage's affinity for bluntness, blurting out how she felt might be the better option. Pursing her lips, she shook her head. Easier said than done. She'd tried telling him before he left with Haider and Nian (something about pack business), but had gotten shy and clammed up.

Her fingertips found a smooth hollow on the wooden surface. A new blemish. Another warped spot. Pleasure fizzed through her. She smiled and, reaching down, stroked her hand over one of the aging leather-topped stools. Examining its imperfections, she traced a crack in the thick, brown hide, then tucked the seat under the workbench and looked around.

Almost done.

Not much more left to do.

A good thing too. If she worked steady, she'd finish the sketches of her new designs, have time to make the jewelry, and enter the Goldsmiths' Craft and Design competition. All with a few days to spare.

Turning in a circle, Samantha surveyed her new space with a critical eye. A new bench vise sat bolted to the end of the long worktable against the wall. Three separate workstations, three standing lamps with swinging arms and wide heads sitting on the desktop. Gage had given her a sharpening stone and a standing loupe for tricky detail work. All she needed now was her own tools and...

For Daimler to stop decorating.

The Numbai refused to take no for an answer—to everything. He did what he wanted when he wanted, to hell with what she thought. She'd walked into her workshop the morning after meeting him and... poof! Polished concrete floors, instead of rough, grease-stained ones. The walls went from banged-up shabby grey to smooth, shimmering white. The accessories arrived next. An expensive curtain rod with fancy silk curtains now stretched over the long bank of windows that looked out on a thick stretch of forest.

If Daimler stopped there, she would've let it go.

He hadn't.

The Nightfury's go-to guy kept adding to her work space (without consulting her), putting up wood-framed, white-washed signs with creative sayings on her walls. The biggest one said JEWELERS in big block letters, now installed over top of the longer table. Another said—*WARNING. Genius at Work.* On the outside of her door, he hung yet another—*DO NOT DISTURB. Seriously, Just Don't.*

Samantha grinned as she replayed her last exchange with him.

He'd wanted to put an antique area rug worth a fortune under her worktables. She'd balked. He argued. She told him it was a fire hazard. He backed down, but not before he bossed Gage into dragging a velvet-upholstered, deep-seated couch with a billion throw pillows into her workshop. Which—yup, you guessed it—now sat in defiance of her opinion along the only free wall, with a smaller, even more expensive rug, complete with coffee and side tables. Setting her palm flat on her table, she frowned at the setup, thinking she'd never use it. She preferred to draw and design sitting cross-legged on Gage's bed, not—

Movement flashed in the corner of her eye.

Samantha turned toward the open door.

A redhead stood on the threshold. Green eyes sparkling, her new friend looked around, then grinned. "See Daimler's been in here."

Reading her lips, Samantha smiled back. "He tried to bring in an armchair. I chased him with one of Gage's wrenches."

Hope laughed. "Do you think it's safe for you to stop standing guard for a while?"

"Don't know. I might come back to a mural on the wall. Or, God forbid, a coatrack," she said, using her hands to sign while she talked.

"Or a martini bar."

"Always good to look on the bright side."

"Absolutely. Underestimate Daimler at your own peril." Adjusting her purse on her shoulder, Hope walked farther into the workshop. "Evie and I are heading into town. She needs some important paperwork from my office so she can take over the accounting for my practice. After that, we're hitting a lingerie shop. Wondered if you wanted to come along."

Samantha blinked as she imagined Gage's reaction to sexy underwear. Explosive would be her first guess. Out-of-this-world amazing was her second. The idea set sensitive parts of her to tingling. Still...

She needed to ask, "It's safe to leave the lair?"

"Oh, sure. I mean, we're careful about it. All the girls are, so we leave around now... late morning... and are home before sunset. With lots of time to spare. Forge worries when I'm out of the lair, so I never butt up against his boundaries," Hope said, mentioning her mate, sounding like the trauma therapist she was, respecting house rules.

Samantha nodded. "The sunlight thing."

The more time she spent with Gage—and the rest of the pack—the more she learned. Dragonkind couldn't tolerate sunlight. At all. Nightfury warriors. Razorback douchebags. Good guys or bad. Didn't matter which camp a man-dragon landed in. Exposure to UVA rays had the same effect on the entire race —blindness, loss of magical abilities, followed by death. Not a quick one either, so the second the sun came out, Dragonkind males retreated inside. Which meant the women inside the lair could venture out without worrying about being captured by a rogue pack who enjoyed hunting high energy females.

As long as everyone followed the rules, no one got into trouble.

"So, what do you think?" her new friend asked, looking hopeful. "You game?"

Another round of happiness fizzled through her.

She liked Hope and Evelyn. In truth, she liked all the women who called Black Diamond home. She'd been worried about fitting in at first, wondering if she belonged. Even before she lost her hearing, she'd never been one of the cool kids. But the second she met the other Nightfury mates, she understood something important.

Her insecurities were a load of BS.

None of them mattered.

No one cared about her deafness. Everyone welcomed her with open arms. No awkwardness. No judgement or hesitation. Just straight-up acceptance into an exclusive club full of fabulous women.

Another gift given to her by Gage.

Excitement bubbled up. She grinned at Hope. "I'll grab my purse."

"Yay!" Arms straight up in the air, Evelyn hopped up and down behind Hope. "Road trip!"

Green eyes widening in surprise, Hope threw her friend a startled look. "You're a total goofball, Evie."

White teeth flashing against her umber skin, Evelyn flicked Hope's ponytail with the tips of her fingers. As the strawberry blond hair swayed, Venom's mate raised a brow. "That your professional opinion?"

Hope rolled her eyes.

Chuckling, Samantha started for the door, trailing her friends out of her workshop. The pair headed for a dark SUV parked alongside a bunch of other cars inside the garage. An army of vehicles. So many she wondered why the Nightfury pack needed so many. Gage owned his fair share. He'd shown her the canary yellow Corvette ZRI he'd just finished restoring—and a few other muscles cars he owned—promising to teach her how to drive one soon.

Her smile turned into a grin.

Driving fast in a beautiful car accompanied by a gorgeous man.

Something to look forward to, but right now, this second, she had something else to celebrate. A day trip into Seattle with two girls who were becoming her friends.

Reaching the top of the stairs, Samantha raced into the loft. Grabbing a pad and pen from the kitchen island, she made a beeline for her new handbag sitting on the dining room table. Slapping the notepad down on the smooth wooden surface, not wanting to worry Gage, she scribbled,

Handsome,
Gone to town with Hope and Evelyn.
Be back before sunset.
XO
Sam

AFTER ADDING a heart beside her name, she reached for her purse. But as the strap of the calfskin Balenciaga settled in her hand, she paused. Her gaze strayed to her backpack hanging from a dining room chair. She debated, then took the extra minute to liberate her house keys zipped in the front pocket. Cold metal settled against her palm. She stared at the collection a second, then slipped the keyring into her bag. Her place on Bainbridge Island wasn't far from downtown Seattle.

Nothing but a fast ferry ride away.

As easygoing as Hope and Evelyn were, she knew neither would mind making a quick pit stop. All she needed was twenty minutes, half an hour, tops. Hardly any time at all to pack up the tools necessary to her and say goodbye to the house that Grand had built. After that, she'd leave her old life behind and never look back.

BEHIND THE WHEEL of the Denali, Samantha swung off the gravel road into her driveway. Sunlight blinded her a second before trees blocked the brightness. Her vision cleared. Crooked brick half-columns with cracked concrete caps on either side of the entrance came into view. The crisscross of weathered wooden fence made of railway ties ran into the side of each pillar.

Old-world charm.

Bad design combined with terrible construction technique.

Grand's attempt at keeping up with the Joneses.

She smiled a little, remembering when Grand decided the entryway into the property needed *more pizzazz*. His words, not hers. Had he asked her opinion, she would've told him taking on an outdoor project equaled a bad idea. He didn't have the patience. Neither did she, but he'd done it anyway, taking a bad idea, making it worse when he ended up elbows-deep in mortar while cursing.

Not that she caught all of the swear words.

She couldn't hear, and every time he turned away to toss a brick or kick the wheelbarrow, what he said got lost in translation. Probably for the best, given Grand's colorful vocabulary.

She huffed.

Such a good day.

An even better memory.

Putting her foot down, she drove up the long, rambling drive. The tires bumped over ruts. The SUV swayed, jostling her along with her friends. She knew Hope and Evelyn were talking. Every once in a while, she saw Hope's mouth move from the corner of her eye. Turned in her seat, Hope glanced at Evelyn over the passenger seat headrest.

Her lips moved again.

Samantha didn't turn to look at her. Didn't try to decipher what she was saying either. She didn't need to read her lips. Not right now. She was too busy remembering and memorizing, knowing today would be the last time she visited the house she'd called home for ten years.

The house wasn't big. Wasn't fancy or well-kept.

Unlike the neighbors, the property didn't have an in-ground swimming pool, tennis courts, or fifteen thousand square feet of living space. Her place was humble, a simple bungalow, sitting in the shadows of giants. A modest David to the housing industries' hulking Goliaths.

Eyes on the last bend in the road, she watched the roofline peek through a break in the trees. The house that Grand built lay at the end of the lane, far from the main, tree-lined avenue, close to the cliff edge overlooking Puget Sound. Branches swayed overhead, big oaks blocking sunrays, shepherding her toward the only place she'd ever felt safe...

Until Gage.

She pictured his face.

A deep sense of peace stole through her as she brought the SUV to a stop in front of the garage door. Throwing the Denali into park, she turned to look at Evelyn sitting in the backseat. Dark eyes on the phone in her hand, her thumbs moved over the screen. Her mouth moved a second later.

Missing the message, Samantha glanced at Hope. "What?"

"She's texting Daimler, letting him know when we'll be home. Seeing if he wants us to pick up anything."

Frowning at the screen, Evelyn waved a hand. "Go, guys. He's giving me a grocery list a mile long. I'll be in in a sec."

With a shrug, Hope popped her door open and slid out.

Grabbing her purse, Samantha followed suit. Her boot soles settled on gravel. Attention on the house, she slammed her own door and, digging for her keyring, rounded the hood. Moving ahead of Hope, she shuffled through her keys, found the one for the front door, and jogged up the front steps.

She swung the screen door open.

Hands raised, poised to shove the key into the lock, Samantha paused. Something felt off. Not a lot, just enough to capture her attention. Her eyes narrowed as an odd sensation moved through her. Feet rooted to her front porch, she looked over her shoulder at Hope.

"You feel that?"

Her friend blinked. "What do you mean?"

"You don't feel it?"

"What?"

"The house is vibrating."

Hope looked around, then shook her head. "Maybe one of your neighbors is doing some work. Landscaping or something."

Could be.

Made sense.

Heavy construction equipment would explain the

tiny tremors. And honestly? Someone was always improving something on her street. Seemed to be the way of things with people who owned big houses. Always something to demolish and redo. Always a rival neighbor to out-design, out-build, and out-spend.

Her senses began to hum.

Samantha frowned.

Hope distracted her, tapping her on the shoulder. As she looked back at her, she asked, "How long you need?"

"Fifteen, twenty minutes," she said, fitting the key into the lock. "Pack up my tools, grab a few photos, and go."

"Okay."

With a nod, Samantha flipped the deadbolt and, twisting the knob, pushed the door open. She stepped inside with Hope on her heels. The weird tremor increased. Static electricity crawled over her skin, raising the fine hairs at her nape. The air grew thick, heating around her as her feet touched down on the area rug.

The buzz in her veins became a burn.

Intuition sparked, screaming for her to retreat.

Sucking in a breath, she whirled around and yelled, "No! Hope—run!"

About to cross the threshold, her friend glanced up.

Wide green eyes met hers.

Thrusting her arms out, Samantha slammed her hands into Hope's shoulders. A look of horror on her face, Hope flew backward. Arms pinwheeling, she landed on her butt and tumbled off the low lip of the front porch. As she crashed into the flowerbed, Samantha leapt forward, trying to follow her friend and—

Slammed into a barrier.

An invisible shield as solid as a concrete wall.

She stumbled back into the foyer. Disbelief shoved her straight into panic. Shit. She should've listened to instinct. Paid closer attention to the quiet voice inside her when it told her something wasn't right. She knew the hum meant something, but...

Baring her teeth, she backed up and took a running leap at the doorway. She left her feet. Her side collided with an immovable force, throwing her backward. She hit the floor in the hallway with a bang. Air left her lungs. Rasping, she rolled onto her hands and knees, then crawled back to the entrance.

She pushed to her feet, raised her hands, and beat on the clear barrier. Red shimmer undulated, washing over the shield, radiating out with each punch.

On her feet, standing on the front walkway, Hope waved her arms to get her attention. Looking as panicked as she felt, her friend pointed to Evelyn, who now stood beside the SUV with a frightened look on her face.

Hope took a step toward the house.

"Don't," she shouted, breathing hard, heart hammering, panic buzzing in her veins. The hum around her intensified. Uncurling her fists, she pressed her palms against the invisible wall and pushed. Glowing pink and red swirls pulsed around her fingertips. No give. Zero weak spots. Solid as freaking steel. "It's everywhere. I can't get out. It's a shield... magic or something."

"Shit," Hope said, chest heaving, fear in her eyes.

"Hope—get Gage." Fear tightened its grip as panic threatened to shut down her brain. "You need to go and get Gage."

Grabbing her handbag off the ground, Hope backed away. "We'll get him. I'll get him."

Already on the move, Evelyn ran to the driver's side door. Fingers moving on the phone, she put it to her ear. A second before she disappeared inside the cab, she met Samantha's gaze. "Hang tight, Sam. We'll be back. Promise, babe. We'll get you out."

Tears in her eyes, Samantha nodded as Hope hopped into the SUV.

Before her door even closed, Evelyn put the truck in reverse. Gravel spun beneath the tires, pelting the front of the house. The passenger door bounced on metal hinges, then rebounded, slamming shut as Evelyn put the Denali in drive and sped down the driveway.

The flash of taillights disappeared.

Samantha pressed her forehead to the barrier. Closing her eyes, she counted to ten, forcing her mind to work, then moved into her house. Maybe the shield wasn't everywhere. Maybe she could find a crack, a crevice, some other place to slip out—the patio door, a window, the broken vent near the roofline inside the garage.

Twenty minutes of searching.

No success at all.

No matter what she tried, the magic surrounding the house held strong, refusing to let her out.

Hitting her knees in the center of Grand's workshop, Samantha looked around, then started to pray. For a miracle to end all miracles. For Gage to find a way to free her before night fell and rogue dragons came out to hunt. For her mate to reach her before whoever cast the spell on her house showed up and dragged her away.

31

Jagged sensation sliced down his spine, jolting Ivar from a deep sleep. Slumped in a chair, his head snapped up. His neck muscles cramped. Pain spiked through his skull. With a low curse, he sat up. Springs creaked. Rubber wheels squeaked across the linoleum floor in the antechamber of his laboratory under 28 Walton Street. Another round of pain stabbed his lower back. Gripping the armrests, he pushed his leather chair away from the desktop.

Struggling to get his bearings, he blinked away the blur.

Bolted to the wall, a bank of computer monitors came into focus.

An army of cameras up and running. Five screens showcasing multiple images. Five well-appointed, one-bedroom apartment suites under the cement factory, captured in real time.

Eyeing the setup, he studied the couples in each suite. All in bed, still fast asleep, dreaming drug-induced dreams. Males sprawled across king-size beds. Females curled on their sides, breathing easy, but turned away from the warriors sharing their space.

Except for one pair.

Azrad and the blond slept together in the middle of the big bed inside the luxurious suite. Female nestled against male. Warrior holding her close, face turned into her hair, as though he knew her value... even though he'd never met the HE he held. Well, at least, officially. By the looks of it, Azrad hadn't wasted any time "introducing" himself to Kasi, getting as close as possible, acting protective even while unconscious.

His mouth curved before he clenched his teeth to keep from laughing.

Only Azrad.

Goddess love the male. He never failed to surprise, but...

Ivar frowned. The successful pairing of his warriors with the females in his breeding program hadn't been what woke him up.

Rubbing the back of his neck, he tapped into the sensation humming beneath his skin. He calibrated the vibration, searching for its source. His magic sharpened. The remnants of sleep fell away. Ivar sucked in a quick breath. The binding spell. The shield magic he wrapped around the female's house on Bainbridge Island had gone active.

He fine-tuned the signal. Absolutely no question the trap he set had worked. He recognized the bioenergy. The HE Gage protected had come home... without her warrior to protect her... and now stood alone, unprotected, easy pickings if he reached her before the Nightfury pack arrived on the scene.

His eyes cut to the clock above the monitors.

Three hours until sunset.

With a growl, Ivar popped to his feet. The chair shot backward, banging into the round table in the center of the antechamber. The bowl of fruit tipped over. Red and green apples rolled over the edge, bouncing across the floor. One cruised into the side of his boot. Kicking it away, he headed for the door.

He needed to wake Hamersveld.

Now.

No time to waste. Every second counted.

He must reach Gage's female first. If he got his hands on Samantha Redhook before the Nightfury, he'd have all he needed to force the information about energy-fuse and the mating ceremony from Bastian. The second the Nightfury commander realized he held one of his pack's females, the bastard would move heaven and earth to get her back. Which meant he had his opening.

Sooner than he expected, but Ivar didn't care.

He never looked a gift horse in the mouth.

Ready or not, he refused to blow the opportunity he and Hamersveld needed to protect their own females. All he had to do now was plan the mission and reach her first. Before Gage and the Nightfury pack rallied and stole what he needed to keep Sasha safe.

32

Sprawled in a chair inside Sloan's computer lab, Gage kicked back and watched Nian write a name on a black magnetic strip with a gold marker. With a quick flick, he tossed it toward the white board. The narrow piece hit the surface with a smack.

Frowning, Gage stared at the name. "Ezram?"

"Commander of the Belarus pack," Nian said, sharing intel, the kind only an insider possessed. A lovely bit of luck. After spending years inside the Dragonkind aristocracy—and watching his sire operate before being elevated to a member of the Archguard—the male knew a thing or two about the packs in Europe. "He's been feuding with the Russian pack for years, and has a particular dislike for Rodin and Zidane."

Boots swinging in the breeze, ass planted on the table Bastian used for pack meetings, Haider raised a brow. "Dislike?"

Nian grinned. "Just being polite. Ezram's hatred of Zidane and the Archguard is legendary."

Gage hummed. "My kind of male."

"I liked him when I met him," Nian said, conjuring

an old-school cigarette lighter. He flicked the top open and shut it, making burnished gold sing. Click-click-snap. Click-click-snap. "Remember thinking he was solid."

"Perfectly placed too. Just a hop, skip, and jump away from Prague." Focused on the board, Haider rubbed his thumb over a silver coin. Image on its face worn off from years of him toying with it, he turned his favorite plaything over in his hand. The coin flipped, dancing over the backs of his knuckles. "And hatred for the Archguard is a definite bonus."

Gage agreed. "So, we contact his pack first."

"After the Scots," Sloan said from behind him.

He looked over his shoulder.

Dragging his eyes from his computer, Sloan swiveled his way.

The high-pitch screech of rusty springs winged across the room. Gage grimaced. He always did when he got a load of Sloan's ugly-ass chair. Beat to shit, the bright purple monstrosity took up so much room he wondered how the male got it through the door. A pity he managed it. The lair would be better off without the thing. Easier on his eyes every time he walked into the computer lab.

Ignoring the offensive-ass bucket Sloan loved—and everyone else hated—he met his friend's gaze. "You reach out to Ivy yet?"

Sloan leaned back, testing the loyalty of his chair. Purple leather groaned, threatening to split wide open as he shook his head. "Not yet. I'm going to give it a couple of days. B and Rikar need time to settle their mates and—"

"Yeah," Haider muttered, tossing the coin to his other hand. "Probably a good idea."

"Better than good." With a nod, Gage settled

deeper into his chair, liking the way Sloan was thinking. "We need those two focused when we start contacting other packs."

"Exactly." Lifting his feet off the floor, Sloan crossed his ankles and set his boots on a desktop that looked as though someone attacked it with a hatchet. "Forge needs time to come to terms too."

"Hope'll see to him," he said, thinking about the ways Samantha settled him. Three days, hardly any time at all, and he recognized her for what she was—a gift that never stopped giving. He loved the way she made him feel. Relaxed. Content. Powered up and plugged in in ways he'd never been before. His mate gave him so much—effortless connection, sexual satisfaction, complete understanding. An outstanding trifecta. "If she hasn't already."

Haider murmured in agreement.

A furrow between his brows, Nian threw him a look.

Gage stilled as perception sharpened. He shifted in his chair, staring at Nian, trying to read the expression on his face. When he couldn't, he tipped his chin. "What is it?"

Looking uncomfortable, the male flicked the lighter top again. Click-click-snap. Click-click-snap.

Gage sat up straighter. "What?"

"Nothing." Scowling at his hand, he shook his head. "It's none of my—"

"You wanna ask me something, Nian, now's the time," he said, gaze riveted to the male. "What do you want to know?"

Nian cleared his throat. "How it feels."

"How what feels?"

"Your mate... when you're with Samantha, when she feeds you, does it..." A furrow between his dark brows, Nian met his gaze. "Feel different? Is it better... more intense, more satisfying? Is she everything you need, all you imagined?"

Holding his gaze, Gage hesitated a second, then told the truth. "She's a dream, man."

"Hellfire," Nian whispered, anguish in his voice.

Reacting to the undercurrent of pain, Gage tensed. He kept trying to dislike the male. Accepting the namby-pamby had never been part of the plan, but... hell. He couldn't ignore the truth anymore. Nian had grown on him. Like fucking fungus.

Which meant he needed to accept what he couldn't change.

He might've started off disliking Nian, but didn't anymore. Somewhere along the way his animosity toward the male vanished, clearing a path into acceptance. Now, he felt the connection, his dragon half embracing what his mind wanted to refuse. Nian was a Metallic. One of his kind, a male to be respected for his fortitude and skill.

He'd proven his worth.

Over and over. Again and again.

The Archguard prince might be guarded. Gage huffed. Hell, the male cornered the market on distrustful. But then, so did he—along with the other Nightfury warriors—and since like recognized like, he understood Nian and knew he wasn't weak. The question he'd tossed in Gage's direction highlighted the kind of strength Nian possessed.

A brave inquiry.

One that opened him up to ridicule with the wrong warrior.

Most males would never have asked it.

Leaning forward, Gage studied him. Dragonkind didn't have a lot of rules, but what went on between a male and his mate was—and always would be—off limits. Period. No room for negotiation. But as he stared at Nian, he realized something important.

His packmate wasn't trying to be rude... or invasive.

Uncomfortable for having asked about energy-fuse and how it felt to connect to a female, Nian braced for his reaction. Gage read the uncertainty in his frame— stiff, guarded, desperate to hide the depth of his emotion. Everything about him screamed uneasy, and Gage understood. Nian wanted to back away, shut down the line of inquiry, but for some reason, couldn't bring himself to do it. He needed to know what Gage had to say so badly his interest bordered on obsessive.

"Is this about her?" he asked, tone soft. "The female you smuggled out of Prague?"

"Fuck," Nian said, so low he almost didn't hear him. "Never mind. Forget I asked. It's not important. I'm just—"

"Tell him, Gage." Sliding off his perch, Haider's feet hit the floor.

Setting his forearms on the tops of his thighs, Gage laced his fingers between the spread of his knees and took a deep breath. Head tilted back, he drilled Nian with an intense look and started talking. "It's beautiful and intense, a brilliance so bright, it's fucking blinding. Every time I touch her, I connect, not just to the Meridian and the energy I need, but to *her*. The bond..."

Gage frowned, searching for the right words. "Man, I don't even know how to explain it. The drive to please her is there, but it's more. Physical desire blends with an emotion so deep it's bottomless. I look at Samantha, and I know she's everything. All I'll ever want or need."

"Christ." Bowing his head, Nian raised his arms and palmed the back of his neck.

"That what you felt with her?" Gage asked, gaze steady on the male.

"You fed from her," Haider murmured, leaning back against the table edge. "Now, you're fucked up. Wanting her, needing her, but living without her."

A furrow between his brows, Nian nodded.

Feeling for the male, Gage inhaled deep and exhaled slow. "What happened?"

"Saw her, couldn't leave her to another male. I paid to get her out of there." A muscle flexed in his jaw as Nian fisted his hand around the lighter. "Rodin, the bastard. He holds auctions. Once a month. Captures, drugs, and strips females down, puts them on a stage, and members of the aristocracy bid on them. Big money. Huge revenue stream for him."

"Where Ivar's getting his money," Haider said, making assumptions. "Rodin's funding the Razorbacks, breeding program and all."

Gage nodded, but kept his focus on Nian.

"Can't prove it. Not yet. I need to get my hands on his ledgers—two sets of books, I'm sure of it, but..." Making a low sound in his throat, Nian glanced his way. A brief flash of opal-colored eyes. That's all it took. A split second, and Gage saw the heavy load of guilt the male carried in the depths of his gaze. "I didn't know about any of it, Gage. Swear, I had no idea. Not about the fight clubs, not about the females, until Rodin brought me fully into the fold. My sire knew. The bastard was involved. Helped Rodin organize everything, but... me? No way. I don't hurt females."

"What's her name?"

Nian closed his eyes. "Grace."

"Sweet name, man," Gage said, encouraging the

male to go on, to spill it all and unburden himself. Part of the mission Bastian gave him—get his fellow Metallics talking, sort out Nian and Haider, make sure each one was solid—in the heart and in the head. "She as pretty as her name?"

"Prettier. Fucking gorgeous. A *zinmera*, able to camouflage her energy. The Archguard had no idea she was high energy. I didn't either until I made her feel safe, she relaxed and her aura flared."

"Never seen a *zinmera*," Haider said, surprised by the information Nian shared.

"Yeah. Super rare." Nian said, rubbing his thumb over the face of his lighter. "I know you and Haider are worried about me. I get it. What happened in Prague is messing with my head, but more than that... it's *her*. I can't stop thinking about her. I dream of her every day. I worry about her every night. She's always on my mind. I can't..."

Trailing off, Nian blew out a long breath. "I don't know how to make it stop. Now, after the way you described it, I think maybe Grace is my mate. My female. The one meant for me like Samantha's meant for you, and if she is, I... Goddess forgive me. I let her go. I put her on a plane to keep her safe, and now—"

"Brother," Gage murmured, understanding. If he held, then lost Samantha, he'd be in a bad place too. Out of his mind, going in dangerous directions.

"Makes no sense," Nian said, looking bewildered. "I barely touched her. No sex. Not even a kiss. I just... put my hands on her once, thirty seconds, that's all."

"That's all it takes. Second I laid eyes on Samantha, I knew. Hadn't touched her yet, and still, I *knew*."

The ugly-ass chair creaked again as Sloan asked, "You give her a new name? Create a new identity?"

Raking his hands through his hair, Nian leveled

his chin. "Yeah, but I didn't look at it. I was determined to let her go, give her a better life. Lapier, my Numbai, arranged the paperwork, her new identity and bank accounts. I know she landed in New York. I know the day she left Prague and the time of her departure, nothing else."

Haider raised a brow. "Where's Lapier now?"

"Don't know. Dead, I think." Pained by the admission, Nian shook his head. "Last time I saw him, he was face down on the floor. Zidane downed him before his crew tasered and took me."

"You want, I'll find her," Sloan said, flickering his fingers toward his computer. "I got a time, date, and location. Might take some looking, but I'll find her, Nian. Track her movements after she landed, figure out where she's living now."

Nian glanced at him.

Gage stared back.

"I don't want to screw up her life," Nian said, voice guttural, looking torn.

"She'll bring you peace, brother," he said, giving it to him straight.

Haider grunted. "Something to think about, Nian. If she's meant for you, you're meant for her. Her life will be better with you in it, than with you gone."

Opening his hand, Nian stared at his lighter. A second later, he looked at the Nightfury IT wizard. "Find her."

Sloan nodded. "Let you know when I do."

"Good, that's settled." Pushing out of his chair, he approached Nian. He raised his hand. The male held steady. No flinch. Zero retreat. Allowing him to cup the side of his throat. Opal-colored eyes met his. Gage gave him a squeeze. "Treated you rough, man. Gave you a hard time. Thought you needed it, but that's over now. Welcome to the fold, Nian."

Nian swallowed. "Never had a family. Not a real one."

"You do now."

Humor sparked in his eyes. "Who would've thought—the Nightfury pack."

Haider snorted, then broke up the love fest. "Got shit to plan and Rodin to kill. We getting back at it or what?"

Releasing Nian, Gage threw his friend a sidelong glance. "Dazzle me."

Haider grinned.

All business now, Nian turned back to the board.

Two more magnetic strips went up.

Nian tapped the first one. "The Turkish pack. We get Rasmus to join the alliance, the Moroccans will jump on board, too."

"What about the rest of Europe—Austria, Germany, Sweden?" Gage asked, trying to remember which packs still existed, which had been disbanded, and any that had quietly distanced themselves from Rodin and disappeared. "Anyone left there?"

"No clue." Silver gaze trained on the board, Haider crossed his arms over his chest. "Rodin went after all of 'em hard when pack commanders refused to fall in line. None were at the Archguard festival. Could be, they've gone underground. Could be, they're all dead."

With a hum, Gage rocked back on his heels. "Need to find out."

Fingers moving on his keyboard, Sloan refocused on his screens. "I'll see what I can—"

"Master Gage!"

Daimler's voice.

Panicked tone.

The hard slap of footfalls against concrete.

Gage pivoted toward the door.

Breathing hard, Daimler flew over the threshold. His dress shoes slipped on polished cement. His shoulder slammed into the steel frame. White-faced with fear, he didn't react to the collision. Breathing hard, he stumbled to a halt halfway across the room and aimed an intense look at Gage.

Adrenaline hit him like rocket fuel. "Tell me."

Chest heaving, Daimler flinched at the harshness of his voice. "Your mate's in trouble. She, Hope, and Evelyn went into town. Shopping. Lady Samantha needed her tools, so—"

"Fuck," he growled, understanding without being told.

The Numbai ignored his curse and sailed past the interruption. Mouth moving at the speed of light, he kept talking as Gage ran around him. Sprinting up the hallway with Daimler, Haider, Nian, and Sloan on his heels, he listened to the male say shit like: 'saved Hope by pushing her out of the house,' 'trapped inside,' and 'binding spell.'

Dread spread like poison, infecting him with fear.

Running flat out, Gage killed his reaction. Samantha was in danger. He didn't have time to panic. Burning bright wouldn't help. Rage never did. He needed to focus. He needed to remain calm. He needed to move to protect his mate and do it fast. Losing control accomplished nothing. Acting with precision, however, would.

Footfalls echoing in the corridor, Gage unleashed a wave of magic.

The electronic keypad activated.

The door to the stairwell swung open.

He took the treads three at a time, listening to the

thump of footfalls behind him and gave his instructions. "Daimler, I need the two Suburbans fueled and ready to roll. Meet me in the garage with black garbage bags. We're gonna tape the bags to the insides of the windows and create a barrier between the front and backseats."

"Blackout conditions," Daimler said from behind him. "I'll see to it, Master Gage."

"Haider—talk to Mac and Wick. I need two drivers who can tolerate sunlight—J.J. and Tania are up."

"Got it," Haider said, boot soles banging on concrete. "We going to lay up at the safe house, wait for nightfall?"

"First stop—Magnolia Street. Second stop—Samantha's house."

"Shit," Haider growled. "Gage—"

"Shut it," he hissed, not needing to hear his friend's opinion. Again. For the five thousandth time. If reaching Samantha in time meant enduring more sunlight than his bronze dragon could handle, he'd do it. In a heartbeat. Vaulting up the last set of stairs, Gage punched through the door into the aboveground lair. He turned left toward the garage. "Nian."

"Here."

"Get everyone into the garage. We leave in fifteen minutes."

"On it." Firing up mind-speak, Nian sent out the call. Dragonkind's equivalent of dialing 911, the emergency signal whiplashed through the lair.

Gage ignored the blast of magic.

Nothing mattered but getting the SUVs ready. Glancing at his watch, he bit down on a curse. Less than three hours until sunset. Not a lot of time to get into the city and put together a plan, but... at least, the first part was underway. Leaving from Black Diamond at sunset wasn't an option. The flight into Seattle took half an hour. Way too long to leave his mate unprotected with rogues on her trail. He needed to reach Samantha before whoever set the trap arrived at her house and tried to take her from him.

Ivar and the Razorbacks?

Or Zidane and his crew?

Gage clenched his teeth.

Didn't matter who conjured the binding spell imprisoning his mate. Both males were the stuff of nightmares for any female. But one who belonged to him— a Nightfury—meant the bastards wouldn't go gently. They would hurt Samantha in order to hurt him. A soul-destroying thought. An even more devastating outcome, so...

No time to lose.

Traveling by daylight had just become necessary.

Something his brothers-in-arms avoided at all costs, but fucked-up situations called for unpopular methods. The only way to protect Samantha was to beat Ivar and Zidane to the punch. Before his mate ended up taken, hurt, or worse—dead.

33

Double-fisting the steering wheel, Gage waited for the cars ahead of him to drive off the ferry. The ship's horn blew. Shifting in the driver's seat of the Suburban, he looked over the top of car roofs toward the exit. Humans working at the bow of the boat. More on the pier, unlocking gates, unclipping chains, readying for the mass exodus onto Bainbridge Island.

Metal grills clanked against the dock edge.

Humans started their engines.

Big V8 already running, Gage flexed his hands on the wheel.

Behind a thick partition Daimler tacked in place, Haider punched the back of his seat. "What the fuck's going on?"

"Relax," Sloan murmured, unleashing a wave of earth magic. Drawn straight from the planet, the heady vibration filled the cab. Warm. Thick. Soothing with the scent of rain and fresh-cut grass. "Gage's got it."

"Freaking nuts. I hate it when he does this shit." A growl rolled in from the back as Haider aired his grievance before directing it at him. "I *hate* it when you do this *shit*."

"Haider—we've been over this," he said, starting to get angry at his friend. No. Correction. He'd passed pissed-off an hour ago, and now raced straight toward fury. "She's my mate. No way I'm waiting at the safe house. Not when I have the power to reach her now."

"Half an hour. Just half an hour until—"

"I don't give a shit about sundown. I need to get to her before night hits and the Razorbacks fly out."

Haider grumbled something obscene.

"Ten more minutes," Nian said, jumping on the bandwagon, trying to keep Haider calm. "And we'll be at Samantha's house. Bronze dragon voodoo, Haider. Gage can handle that much sunlight."

Haider snarled. "I swear to Christ, Gage, you go blind and I'm pulling your brain out through your eye sockets."

"That'll be interesting," he said, humor cutting through his temper, attention on the progress at the bow from the shadowed interior of the ferry.

His brothers-in-arms chuckled in the backseat.

Haider growled again.

Vehicles stared to move, line by line, rolling off the boat.

Heavy cables creaked as the ferry swayed against the pier. Trying to be patient, Gage inched forward, respecting the pace, even though it almost killed him. He wanted out now. Not five minutes from now. *Now*. Too bad human lines didn't work that way. Lined up bumper to bumper, the boat carried a full load. Everyone stayed in their lanes as dock workers directed the flow.

A thirty-five-minute ferry ride.

Two hundred vehicles packed in tight.

He sat in the number ninety-seventh spot. Not at the back, but nowhere near the front either. Smack dab in the middle as he waited for humans to get the hell out of his way.

After what felt like forever, he reached the front of the line. Dock workers waved him over the wide metal gangplank onto the island. He drove out of the belly of the beast. Sunlight bled through the windshield, burning over the backs of his hands, making his eyes sting.

With a murmur, Gage conjured some protective gear. A pair of dark sunglasses materialized on his face. Frayed and faded, his favorite baseball cap settled on his head. The Suburban's oversized tires rolled off steel onto pavement. Heat hit him, bleeding into the front seat, making sweat trickle down his spine and his stomach dip as the cars in front of him cleared.

He put the pedal down.

The big V8 rumbled as he swung off Main Street onto a side avenue.

Pulling up a map of the island in his mind, he wove his way through the back streets, using the shade of big trees to shield him from the sun as he turned onto a gravel road. The wide entrance narrowed from four to one-and-a-half lanes. Tall trees tunneled into a canopy above him. The glare of UV rays downgraded from red-hot to just-kill-me-now brutal.

Pain seared his skin.

He glanced down and swallowed a curse. Sun-burned knuckles. Blisters starting on the backs of his hands. He was at his limit. In need of the great indoors before minor injuries turned into third-degree burns.

Accelerating, Gage kept his attention on the left-hand side of the road. Colorful mailboxes flashed past. He scanned each one, searching for his mate's address. Crumbling half columns with wobbly wooden fence rails came into view.

His eyes narrowed on the plaque mortared into red brick.

A string of numbers jumped out at him.

Gage cranked the wheel. The SUV's rear end swung around. Controlling the skid, he hit the gas and accelerated into the turn. Tires spun on loose gravel. Stones pinged against the steel undercarriage. Heavy truck treads bit, grinding through gravel to meet compact earth. Twin streams of dirt arching from his tires, he roared down the winding driveway.

A roofline peeked through the huge oaks.

Sunlight drilled him through the leafless branches.

Gage grunted in pain.

"Gage," Haider said, concern in his tone. "Stop. Take a break. Climb into the back."

Rounding the last bend, seeing the house, he slammed on the brakes. Thuds sounded in the rear of the cab. His friends cursed. The truck shuddered, shocks pumping as the Suburban rocked to a stop ten feet from the small bungalow. Squinting to protect his eyes from the sun, he scanned the building.

"Holy fuck," he muttered, getting a load of the setup.

Gage gritted his teeth as he picked up the magic. Powerful weave. Fortified structure. A shield made to keep someone in, and everyone else out. Flexing his sore fingers, he shook his head. Red shimmer everywhere—walls, roof, and foundation—creating an impenetrable web around the entire building. And inside...

Gage drew a shaky breath.

He could see her through the walls. Bright orange aura burning bright, she sat on the floor, curled in a ball up in the corner of a back room on the south-east corner of the house. Open space. Big windows with curtains shut. Lots of shit scattered on two tabletops. One armchair, which... his eyes narrowed... she wasn't sitting in.

Why?

Gage frowned.

Goddess only knew.

Reaching out with his mind, he pinged her. Nothing. No movement. No connection. Zero response from his mate. She stayed in her ball, knees against a bag pressed to her chest.

Sunlight grew more intense.

His stomach sloshed as he re-scanned the house. Gage bit down on a growl. The binding spell was too strong, blocking mind-meld, which meant no way in hell he'd be able to break through it in his condition.

He needed to find another way inside.

Skin burning, eyes stinging, trying not to panic, he unclipped his seatbelt. "We're here. Coming back."

Rustling sounds from the rear of the SUV.

Seatbelt latches popping and releasing.

Thick black fabric behind the front seats parted.

Contorting his 6'8" frame, Gage shoved his shoulder between the bucket seats. Big hands grabbed hold. Two pair, one pushing, one pulling. He landed on his back, half in the front, half in the back, baseball cap on the floor, sunglasses on his chin, boots propped on the middle console.

The curtain got yanked closed.

Fierce silver eyes collided with his.

"Goddamn it, Gage," Haider growled, concern in his voice.

A black pair of peepers joined the party as Sloan peered down at him. "You okay?"

Gage blinked to clear his vision. The blur faded. "All good."

"All good." Haider scoffed. "Look at your hands, man."

Glancing down, he got an eyeful of blistered skin. "May need some aloe vera."

Nian's head popped up over one of the headrests. "You'll heal. What're we dealing with out there?"

The question yanked him back on track. "Powerful weave. No way to break through the spell without—"

"No way through it, gotta go underneath it. Bet the bastard forgot to spell-bind the concrete slab," Sloan said, dark eyes beginning to glow green. Strangely mesmerizing. Oddly calming. Crazy powerful.

Jacking upright, Gage frowned at his friend. "What the fuck, Sloan?"

The green in his gaze intensified as the male kneeled behind the front passenger seat. Fingers spread wide, he pressed his hands on the floor mats. "Hold on to something."

Earth magic whiplashed, painting the air yellow, green, and gold.

A ripple rolled beneath the truck.

The ground began to tremble.

Grabbing his shoulders, Nian dragged him out of the middle aisle into the last row of the Suburban. As his ass hit leather, an earthquake shook the truck. Sloan murmured. The tremor moved from savage shake to bone-rattling brutal. The SUV's side panels crumpled. Tires popped. Window glass whined. Gage hung on tight as thick, green vines punched through the steel undercarriage. Growing like weeds, alive with movement, the vines threaded through the solid metal frame as a sinkhole opened beneath the truck.

Shocked, no one said a word.

A death grip on an armrest, Gage stared at Sloan as the Suburban sank. Jagged rocks clawed at the sides. Steel shrieked. Sharp, thorny tips pulling, the vines tightened their grip. The glimmer of sunlight through the makeshift curtain faded as he and his packmates disappeared, truck and all, beneath the surface of the earth.

34

K nees pressed to her chest, curtains drawn, with a single lamp lit, Samantha sat on the floor in the near dark. Originating from across the room, the pool of light crept across the floor, but didn't reach her. Just as well. She liked it that way. For the first time in her life, the dark felt safer. Seemed better, even though it wasn't.

Nothing changed the fact she was an idiot.

One trapped in her house by a magic spell she didn't understand and couldn't break through, waiting for the worst to happen.

Back against the wall, curled up in the corner of Grand's workshop, she set her forehead on top of her bent knees. The bulky bag in her lap shifted. The blunt end of one of her tools poked her belly through the canvas, making her uncomfortable. Par for her course today. She hadn't been comfortable for hours. The buzz in the air refused to leave her alone. No sound. All sensation. The blitzing kind that attacked in waves. She'd tried to avoid it, moving around her house, looking for dead zones, but...

Nothing.

Nowhere was safe.

No matter what she did—or where she stood—the awful hum persisted, making her senses scream and her skin prickle. Now all she wanted to do was howl in frustration. Or agony. Samantha didn't know which. All she knew was the wait was killing her.

Opening her eyes, she peered through her lashes.

The clock on the wall stared back at her, the stilted motion of the second hand interminable. Despite the electric charge in the air, the faded hands never stopped working, doing their job, rounding the once cream, now yellow face, casting bad omens.

7:35 PM.

The edge of sundown. Almost time for dragons to fly... and her to know her fate.

Blowing out a shuddered breath, Samantha looked down the barrel of reality. Not that she wanted to. She would've preferred to remain in the dark, impervious to all the bad things that might happen in the next hour. A lovely bit of oblivion—was that really too much to ask?

The answer came as a resounding *yes*.

No matter how many times she turned her mind away from the bad, her imagination dragged it back, telling tales, tossing out scenarios, scaring her with the idea the enemy might walk through the door before her mate, and she'd never see Gage again.

"No," she whispered, curling into a tighter ball.

Never holding Gage again wasn't something she wanted to contemplate. But as time slipped away and the buzz burrowed beneath her skin, infiltrating muscles, digging into bone, making her vibrate in discomfort, Samantha decided to face the facts. He might not reach her in time. She might lose him without ever really having had him at all. So little time with her dream man. Here, then gone. Her fault. All of it, from start to finish.

Her breath hitched.

She squeezed her eyes shut to keep tears from falling. Dear God, what had she been thinking? No matter how important her tools, nothing was worth losing the man she only just found, but didn't want to live without. In short order, he'd become everything. Her reason for being. Kind of corny when she thought about it. Didn't change a thing, or make how she felt about him any less real.

Shifting on the throw pillow she'd grabbed off the couch, Samantha looked at the armchair. Grand's chair, now her chair. She frowned at the Barca-Lounger, wondering why she shied away from sitting in it today. All day long, the same overwhelming sense of aversion. A weird reaction, given she'd curled up in its familiar arms so many times before, but...

Something about the seat cushions bothered her.

The cratered foam covered in worn fabric felt wrong, as though it had been contaminated somehow. Crazy to think it, but she sensed the taint, an odd residual ooze she couldn't see, but instinct warned was there.

She sensed it all over the house.

In her bedroom. In the living room. All over the kitchen. Covering every single wall, in every single room. She clenched her teeth as the reason hit her. The asshole. Whoever invaded her house had done a walk-through, creeping through her space, touching her things, sitting in her frigging chair, leaving cosmic slime everywhere he went.

A bad taste washed into her mouth.

She made a God-that's-gross face. He'd spent time. He'd waited for her to come home. He'd cast the spell, hoping to trap her. She closed her eyes, realizing she'd made it easy for him. She'd waltzed right through the front door, falling for Dragonkind wizardry, detecting the magic surrounding her home too late.

Samantha wanted to kill him for being so clever. For invading the place Grand made safe for her and leaving his taint behind. For polluting her memories of the house she'd come home to that first day ten years ago. Emotion dragged recall to the surface, and she remembered stepping off the plane and laying eyes on her grandfather for the first time. Nothing but a scared, confused, newly deaf girl, with the drug-addicted mother who abandoned her at the hospital.

"Fuck you," she whispered, channeling Gage. Opening her eyes, she glared at the chair she knew the rogue had sat in, making himself at home in Grand's favorite spot. "Fuck you, you stupid—"

The floor trembled underneath her.

The lamp wobbled, making light dance across the walls.

Her gaze snapped toward one of the worktables. Tools she hadn't packed jumped, shimmying across the wooden surface. Releasing the death grip on her tool kit, she slapped her hands flat against the floorboards. The trembling moved from small quake to strong tremor. Pictures tilted on the walls. Chair legs bumped along the floor, butting up against table edges as the clock jumped off its hook.

Popping to her feet, she watched it fall.

Glass smashed into a side table and shattered, spilling shards across the floor. Light refracted off the broken bits as cracks snaked across the floorboards. The fissures widened. Being pushed by something underneath, the ground tented up and out. Breathing hard, clutching her bag, Samantha pressed her back to the wall. The tip of something came through the wood, drilling through the concrete slab. Debris mounding around the edges, a hole opened in the middle of the workshop.

The gap grew, increasing to the size of a manhole.

The smell of wet topsoil and running water swirled into the house.

Slithering like snakes, vines rose from the darkness, crawling over the puncture in the floor. Adrenaline punched into her veins. Her heart picked up the beat, hammering hard as she slid sideways along the wall toward the double doors. She needed to be ready to run from whatever came through the hole. Friend, foe or... her hands started to shake... monster? Anything was possible, given the world Gage occupied. But one thing for sure? No way would she stand idly by and allow herself to be captured.

Not without putting up a fight.

Forcing her legs to work, she got ready to lunge toward the door. The vines swiveled in her direction, thick ends rising like cobra heads. Samantha froze mid-escape. Multiple green heads titled, almost as though the things were looking at her, then crisscrossed, running together, knitting into a structure she recognized—a ladder.

Non-threatening. A useful tool. She bit the inside of her lip. Not something bad guys would use... would they?

Hope pierced through her fear.

Stepping away from the wall, she yelled, "Gage!"

Static burned over her temples, slicing through the awful buzz in the house. One second spilled into the next. The painful hum downgraded to an annoying hiss, then cleared as fresh air rushed into the house.

She screamed again. "Gage!"

Tingles swept over her temples. A huge hand appeared on a rung near the top of the ladder. A dark head appeared next. A glowing bronze gaze sliced in her direction.

Tears pooled in her eyes.

Already on the tips of her toes, Samantha took off running. Leaping over the rubble, she hit Gage at full speed. Her chest slammed into his. Her toolkit went flying. Gage did not. He jerked at the hard contact, upper body swinging backward. Feet planted on a lower rung, big hand gripping an upper one, he made room for her between him and the ladder.

Wrapping his free arm around her, he buried his face in her hair. *"Volamaia."*

Pressed tight to him, she burrowed in, feeling his warmth, the steady beat of his heart, his scent and strong arms around her. Her throat hurt as she rasped, "Thank God. Thank God. Thank God."

His mouth moved against her temple.

His voice sounded inside her head. *"Wrap me up, wildcat. We're going back down."*

She obeyed without hesitation, locking her legs around his hips, fisting her hands in back of his jacket, burying her face in his throat. "I'm sorry. So, so sorry. I thought I was safe during the day. I thought I could come in daylight. That it would be okay, that they couldn't get to me. I never... I never..." Her throat clogged as she lost the battle. Tears rolled over her lashes, wetting his skin. "I'm so sorry. I didn't get it. I didn't understand what you were telling me. Not really and—"

"Baby."

On a roll, she kept talking. "I thought I'd never see you again and... and... I hadn't told you. I hadn't figured it out yet. You said I would and I did, but too late. I left the lair without telling you I—"

"*Samantha—*"

"Love you too. I need you too. I don't want to live without you either."

"*Fucking hell.*"

"I know it's fast. Freaks me out a little, but I love you. I do." Her voice broke on a shaky inhale. "Please forgive me for being an idiot."

Gage gave her a squeeze. "*Samantha, beautiful... thrilled to hear you say you love me, but gonna say, your timing sucks.*"

She blinked. "What?"

"*Look at me.*"

Retreating a little, she raised her head.

Amused bronze eyes met hers. "*You telling me you love me is special. Fucking sweet, wildcat. An occasion. One that calls for a marathon session in bed and me giving you more of those orgasm you like so much. Can't do that while standing on a ladder made of vines after rescuing my mate while I worry about being attacked by rogues. So maybe, you could do me a favor and save the heartfelt shit for later?*"

She opened her mouth. Closed it again, pursed her lips, then said, "Oh."

"*Yeah—oh,*" Gage murmured, no less amused as his gaze dropped to her mouth. "*You gonna do me that favor?*"

"I'll do you that favor."

"*Obliged.*" Dipping his head, he kissed her. Soft. Sweet. Brief, but with feeling before he leaned sideways and grabbed her toolkit off the mound of dirt beside the hole.

Slinging the canvas tote over her head, he secured the wide strap on her shoulder, across her chest, adjusting the kit at her hip. Making sure she had her tools. Making sure she had what she came home to get. Making sure she had what she needed of Grand's.

God.

Seriously.

Her man-dragon... unbelievably frigging awesome.

She drew a shaky breath as her heart warmed, wondering how it was possible to love him more than she already did. Cupping his jaw, she pressed a kiss to the corner of his mouth, showing him instead of telling him. Nestling his cheek against hers, he exhaled as his hands drifted down her back. Giving her another squeeze, he unlocked her legs from around his waist and swung her to his back, settling her piggyback style.

Her arms and legs tightened around him.

Muscles flexing against her, he changed hand positions on the ladder.

"Brace, Samantha," he said, head bent, looking down between his feet. His eyes went from shimmer to glow, lighting the way as he descended into the hole. *"Sun's set. Rogues'll be airborne. Could get rough. We're not out of the woods yet."*

Pressing her cheek to the back of his shoulder, Samantha closed her eyes, wanting to kick herself. For so many things. For having tunnel vision. For being unable to let go of the past. But mostly, for putting Gage—and the rest of the Nightfury pack—in harm's way. Over a bunch of tools.

So foolish.

Totally unnecessary.

Things she believed important before weren't so important anymore. Grand's tools were replaceable. Gage was not, and as light from above faded to black down below, Samantha did something she hadn't done in a long time. Not since she lost her hearing. She started to pray. Quiet whispers in her mind, opening a silent dialogue with God, listing each Nightfury by name, asking for protection and safe passage for each and every one.

CARRYING SAMANTHA ON HIS BACK, Gage climbed down the ladder into the tunnel. The scent of wet clay and scorched earth kicked up, making his nose twitch as the light from the workshop faded. His night vision sparked, making his eyes glow, allowing him to see in the dark.

Hands and feet moving in tandem, he descended the last few feet into the passageway. Out of habit, he looked both ways. Stupid thing to do. He knew no one else stood in the underground tube. No enemy males waiting to attack him, but...

He refused to take any chances. Not after being separated from Samantha all day.

Dragon senses firing, he scanned the passageway. Beat-to-shit Suburban at one end, nothing but open space and floating stone dust an empty tunnel at the other. Curved ceiling above him. Smooth tubular sidewalls around him. Grooved stone floor underfoot. Nothing but a symmetrical shaft carved with precision straight through solid bedrock.

Amazing to see.

Even better to witness.

He hadn't known Sloan possessed the ability to burrow. Not all earth dragons did, but after watching his friend dig a channel underneath his mate's house, surprise took a backseat. Now, it was all about respect.

A powerful tremor shook the bedrock around him.

Left in Sloan's wake, small rocks rolled into the side of his boot. Dust billowed in a wave up the tunnel. Raising his hand, he cupped the back of Samantha's head. A little pressure pushed her face into the top of shoulder. Watching the cloud rush toward him, he murmured his wishes. His dragon half responded, conjuring an invisible shield around her.

Made of fine powder, the cloud hit.

Samantha coughed.

The barrier sealed around her, providing clean air, protecting her from dust and flying debris. Rocks pinged off the surface. Dust slammed into the shield, then rolled over the top as he stepped off the ladder. Gripping her forearm, he pressed her arm against his chest and, hooking his elbow over a rung, waited for the cloud to sail passed.

Another earthquake rumbled through the passageway.

Stone shrieked.

The smell of burned rock hit.

Wiping dust from beneath his nose, Gage finetuned his sonar, then sent out a ping. The web expanded, racing down the corridor, scraping over the ceiling and sidewalls, twisting around a bend as he searched for his packmates' location. His eyes narrowed, he pulled the threads, drawing information back to him.

Three males, a mile and a half away.

One with magic deployed, the other two watching.

A stronger tremor jack-hammered beneath his feet, slamming through his boot soles, rattling his bones.

"Jesus, Sloan," he muttered, amazed his friend was still digging... more than an hour after he started.

The massive energy expenditure would've crippled most warriors. Not Sloan. From the sounds of it—all the shaking and banging—his friend was nowhere near ready to slow down. Adjusting his grip on the ladder, Gage shook his head. Talk about impressive. Sloan never talked about where he came from, but after witnessing him in action today, Gage knew one thing for certain—his friend carried all the markers of a male born to a high energy female.

Powerful magic.

Potent skill set.

Unstoppable energy that connected directly to the Earth's core.

A magic so substantial, Dragonkind warriors the world over would kill for the chance to claim and control it. No doubt one of the many reasons Bastian recruited Sloan eleven years ago. Still...

Seeing him burrow—and wield earth magic—shocked the hell out of him. Not so unusual, given he'd never seen it before.

More interested in computers than sparring in Black Diamond's gym, Sloan wasn't a showboat. He didn't seek out attention or broadcast his skills. The male kept to himself most of the time. Something Gage understood, given his own aversion to having others in his private space. But earth dragons?

Shit.

Sloan's subset of Dragonkind was a special breed. One hundred percent lethal, mostly antisocial, earth dragons enjoyed being alone, spending more time below ground than above.

Something he and the others worked to change on a regular basis, inviting the male out, dragging him into conversations, razzing him on the daily. Little by little, Sloan was coming around. Engaging with his fellow Nightfury warriors. Kicking back around the dining room table. Spending more time in the company of his brothers-in-arms, flying out more, instead of staying home alone in his computer lab.

Progress on a grand scale.

A good thing. The best, given what he now knew Sloan brought to the table—a serious amount of earth dragon mojo that would make rogues turn around and flee for safer skies.

Waiting until the earthquake went from major to minor, Gage let go of the ladder. The web of vines reacted, breaking formation, slithering out of the house. The hole in the concrete slab above him closed, leaving nothing but smooth cement behind. On the move, snakelike green coils slid around his feet, then retreated down the tunnel, returning to Sloan.

With a quick pivot, Gage followed, jogging in the direction of the shake-rattle-and-bang. The thump of his footfalls disappeared beneath the sound of heavy drilling. The ground shook. More dust rained down, making the protection shield he held over Samantha undulate around her. Face tucked into the back of his neck, she hung on harder as he palmed the backs of her knees and ramped into a run.

The tunnel turned, angling into a ninety-degree corner. He sprinted around the bend. His boots slipped on a wet patch. He lost his footing and stumbled sideways.

Samantha gasped.

Gripping her thigh to keep her from falling, he planted his other hand against scorched granite and pushed off. His balance righted. Gage kept running. Light pierced through the dark, making him squint against the glare as he spotted his wingmates. Holding flashlights, boots planted in the middle of the passage, Haider and Nian stood behind Sloan. Dark skin covered in silt, hands pressed to tunnel end, elbows deep in earth, Sloan walked forward, drilling through solid rock.

Gage slid to a stop behind his fellow Metallics.

Two flashlights swung in his direction.

Gage tipped his chin.

Wonder in his expression, Nian fired up mindspeak. *"Never seen a male do this before. Unbelievable."*

"Pretty cool," he said, returning the male's grin.

"More than cool." Stepping closer to Sloan, Nian peered over his shoulder. *"I think I might wanna be an earth dragon when I grow up."*

Sloan snorted, shook his head and kept drilling.

Lips twitching, Gage glanced at Haider.

Glowing mercury eyes bounced from him to Samantha. *"She okay?"*

He nodded. *"A little freaked, but yeah, man. She's good."*

"Tough as well as a sage," Haider said, tone relieved and teasing at the same time. *"Hell, Gage. Smart female with the heart of a warrior. Wasn't kidding before, brother... you really are screwed."*

"Only in the best possible way."

Haider chuckled.

Tightening his hold on Samantha, he returned his attention to Sloan. *"We got a plan?"*

"He's drilling south. Away from Puget Sound, toward the higher cliffs," Haider said, swinging the flashlight back in Sloan's direction. *"Once he punches through, we're gonna launch straight off the rock face."*

"How long?"

"Couple of minutes," Sloan murmured, punching

through an air pocket. More dust flew. The clamor quieted a second, then started up again as his hands reconnected with stone. *"Get ready. The second the tunnel end opens, shift and get airborne. We've got rogues in the area."*

"Fuck, that was fast." Gage frowned. Not great news. Ivar was getting smarter. Instead of pulling his warriors off the island, he'd left a few behind, hunkered down somewhere, waiting for Samantha to return home. A good guess, given the number of enemy dragons patrolling the island, but... was it the Razorback pack or Zidane? Rodin's son might be a sadistic bastard, but he didn't have shit for brains. *"Head count?"*

"Can sense 'em in the sky. No idea how many," Haider said, throwing him an intense look. *"We need Bastian for an accurate head count."*

Widening the connection, Gage powered up the grid and sent out a ping. *"B—you airborne?"*

"Just." The flap of wings blasted through the connection. Multiple sets. Six strong. Sensing each of his brothers-in-arms in flight, Gage closed his eyes and said a silent thank-you. Bastian wasn't messing around. The entire Nightfury pack—Rikar included—had just left the safe house. *"How close are you to open air?"*

"In a minute or two." he said, tracking his pack's progress. *"Multiple rogues in the area. Watch your six."*

"Gotcha," Bastian said, scales rattling as he sliced into the sky. *"Seventeen miles out and closing. Be there over the island in five."*

Five minutes.

Not far away. Nowhere near close enough.

A lot happened in five minutes. Sixty seconds here, an extra thirty there, was often the difference between making it out alive. Or being roasted in midair.

Dragging his sleeve across his face, he rubbed dust from his eyes, then tapped Samantha's knee. Quick on the uptake, she took his meaning and, the uncrossing her ankles, dropped her legs from around his waist. As her feet touched down, he drew her around in front of him. Cupping her cheek, he raised her chin. Smudges on her face. Dirt around her nostrils. Blue gaze on him, trust in her eyes, no fear in her scent. Settled. Steady. Waiting for him to connect and explain.

He exhaled in relief. Sliding his fingers into the messy bun at her nape, he tugged her closer. Small hands pressed to his chest, she raised her brows.

Understanding the unspoken question, he slipped past her mental guards into her mind. *"Got some trouble."*

"How much?"

"Rogues at the gate. The enemy is already tracking us."

"Crap."

"Yeah," he said, wiping a smudge off her jaw. *"Gotta ask you to hold tight, Samantha. The second Sloan breaks through the cliff wall, I'll shift and—"*

"You asked me to brace, I'm braced," she said, startling him. Again. For the... shit. He didn't know how many times she'd surprised him. Her fortitude never failed to knock him off balance. "Do what you need to, I'll be all right."

His brows collided. *"You're gonna see things that—"*

"Like I haven't already?" She threw him a you've-got-to-be-kidding look. "Jeez, Gage. You put me in a bronze ball during the last dragon confrontation."

He blinked.

Dragon confrontation.

Fuck, she was funny.

Gage clenched his teeth to keep from laughing. *"I remember."*

"Just to say..." Stepping back a bit, Samantha signed as she spoke. "I didn't like being trapped inside that thing, but if you need to in order to fight and keep me safe, well..." Palms flipped up, fingers angled out, she shrugged.

"Hate to be the bearer of bad news, wildcat, but—"

"Gage," Sloan growled. *"Move your ass."*

The drilling stopped.

The ground ceased shaking.

As decibel levels returned to normal, a huge granite slab sheared off and fell. A dragon-sized hole opened in the cliff face. Moonlight and the distant glow of city lights ate through the darkness. Ocean waves crashed against the base of the crag. The smell of salt water exploded into the tunnel.

Standing in the middle of the opening, Sloan shifted from human to dragon form. Skin becoming dark brown scales. Hands and feet turned to snow-white paws. The bulbs on the tip of his scorpion-like tail whiplashed as wings spread wide, he spiraled out into open air. The instant he cleared the tunnel edge, Haider took flight, silver scales flashing as Nian leaped out, becoming a golden blur against the night sky.

The shiny spikes of his tail glinted in the moon-light, then disappeared above the hole.

Heaving Samantha over his shoulder, Gage sprinted toward the tunnel end. His foot connected with the edge. Muscles flexing, he vaulted away from the cliff. Damp air hit his face. Wind blasted over his skin. Gravity took hold, dragging him toward the rocks below. Shifting mid-leap, he opened his wings, spun into a tight spiral, and launched his frame skyward.

Rogue dragons roared, alerting others.

With a snarl, he called on his magic.

Razor-sharp tips of his claws inches from her head, Samantha contracted into a small ball in his palm as a bronze ball formed around her. Layering the protection, he reinforced the cage, and holding her secure, rocketed over the south end of the island. Lots of forest. Few human homes. Nine dragons, three full fighting units, on his tail.

Already.

Baring his fangs, Gage banked into a tight turn, whipping toward the confrontation instead of away. Gold scales flashed in his peripheral vision. Making room for Nian, he flipped up and over. The male settled on his wingtip as Haider and Sloan flew overhead. In fighting formation, his packmates attacked the lead rogues.

Surprised by the aggressive move, the group of Razorbacks broke formation. Four slid wide right. Five went left.

Bronze gaze aglow, Gage inhaled. Liquid metal gathered at the back of his throat. Bubbling, hissing, splashing over the back of his tongue, he held onto his exhale as he lined up two males. Leveling his wings, he counted off the seconds. Three. Two. One...

He exhaled.

The toxic stream shot from his throat.

Wings angled, the rogues in his sights tried to avoid the onslaught. Too little, too late. Bubbling with blistering heat, liquid metal splattered over enemy scales. His exhale went to work, injecting poison beneath interlocking dragon skin, hardening on contact, turning rogues into flying statues.

Joints seizing, the pair's forward momentum stalled. As muscles and bones turned to bronze, both males lost the ability to fly and, listing sideways, began to fall out of the sky.

Flying in fast, Gage slashed one with his tail. Sharp barbs slammed into yellow scales. Rogue one shattered like glass. Chunks of metal dragon rained down. Falling toward the water, the pieces turned to ash as rogue two careened into the cliffside. Metal scales flew into the air. Rock exploded up and out. The tree clinging to the bluff swayed as the second rogue died. Dragon ash puffed into a cloud of debris, floating on an updraft over the end of the island.

Hooked claws clinking against the sphere shielding Samantha, Gage swung around. Scanning the sky, he searched for another target.

Chasing two green dragons toward the harbor, Sloan blasted overhead.

Engaged in claw-to-claw combat, Haider ripped apart two others.

Gold scales shining, Nian took out one rogue and went after another.

Two dead. Six others occupied by his packmates. One unaccounted for over the island.

Circling around behind Haider, Gage looked for the stray Razorback. Movement flashed to his right. His eyes narrowed on the male retreating. Angling his wings, he swung into a turn. Another full contingent of enemy warriors uncloaked less than a hundred yards away.

"Haider—right flank," he growled, connecting through mind-speak.

"I see 'em. We need to—"

A vicious snarl blasted onto the cosmic line.

Gage grinned.

Speed supersonic, black scales nothing but a blur, Wick slammed into the side of the retreating rogue.

With a sharp twist, he snapped the male's neck. The Razorback turned to ash as Wick banked hard, slicing behind Gage.

Golden eyes glowing, Wick glanced at the bronze ball in his talon. *"Get gone."*

"Wick's right, buddy—go." On Wick's six, Venom rolled in, dark green scales glimmering, ruby-red eyes locked onto two rogues flying his way. *"Know you hate to leave a fight, but time for you to make like a magician and disappear. Get your mate to safety. We'll clean up here."*

Gage bit down on a chuckle. Fucking Venom. Trust the talkative SOB to use more words than necessary to get his point across.

"More fun for us," Forge said, arriving with Mac on his wingtip.

White scales flashing, Rikar blasted past him. *"What are you still doing here?"*

Frost hit him, dusting his bronze scales with ice. Listening to enemy dragons scream, Gage opened his mouth to answer.

"What the fuck, Gage? Drop your mate at the safe house, come back if you want, but..." With a grunt, Bastian grabbed a male by the tail. He yanked. The Razorback squawked, wing-flapping as the Nightfury commander flipped him around, grabbed one of his horns, and ripped it off his skull. *"Get out of here."*

Dragon blood arched through the air.

B tossed the horn aside and went after his escaping prey.

"Won't be anyone left to kill," Gage said, enjoying the melee as his brothers-in-arms decimated the rogue pack.

Midnight blue scales gleaming, Bastian streaked overhead. *"Anyone got a lock on Ivar?"*

A round of "not yet" came through mind-speak.

"Don't sense him," Gage said, flying around the periphery of the fight. *"He can't be inside the three-mile marker."*

"Keep looking," Bastian growled. *"Any of you get a bead on him, smoke him out. Rikar and I'll bring him to ground."*

His packmates answered in the affirmative.

Scanning the sky, seeing the battle was well in hand, Gage bugged out. *"B—I'm gone."*

Haider chimed in. *"Nian and I'll cover your six. See you back home."*

"Have fun. Don't do anything I wouldn't."

Nian laughed.

Mac snorted.

Exshaw shrieked.

Sound waves exploded across the water. Perception warped. His vision blurred as pain battered his temples. Dragon scales rattled in the concussive blast. Wings wobbling, Gage grunted, fighting to stay airborne. His brothers-in-arms cursed as Razorbacks roared in agony and lost altitude.

The wren screamed again.

"Fuck," Gage growled as he got hammered again.

"Sorry, guys," Mac muttered, then yelled at Exshaw to pipe down.

A round of grumbling ensued as Nightfuries regrouped and attacked.

Suspended in midair, Gage shook his head to clear the brain fog and whirled around. Flying away from the island, he rocketed over Puget Sound and headed for home. Much as he hated to leave his brothers-in-arms in the middle of a fight, Samantha was more important than getting his claws bloody.

Always.

Forever.

No matter what.

Worried about her state of mind, Gage glanced down at the sphere and saw her curled in a tight ball with her eyes squeezed shut. His chest went tight. Goddess forgive him. She was breathing too fast, fighting panic, struggling to block out the violent reality of battle.

With a curse, he increased his wing speed. *"Samantha."*

"I'm all right. I'm all right," she rasped, teeth chattering as she tried to reassure him.

"Breathe, volamaia. We're going home."

Still compressed into a tight ball, she nodded. "Okkay."

"Okay," he whispered back as air caught in her lungs.

The hitch sounded painful, as though she fought lockdown and the onslaught of a full-blown panic attack. Gritting his teeth, Gage wanted to kick himself. He'd scared her. After the terror of being trapped in her house while she imagined the worst, witnessing a dragon battle was too much for his mate. No matter how strong—or how hard she *braced*—Samantha could only take so much. She was new to him, but more importantly, his ways were new to her.

Baptism by fire.

In less than a week, she'd gone from being a citizen in the human world to a full-fledged member of his. Not an easy shift to make, which meant...

He needed to get her home.

The faster he arrived at Black Diamond, the quicker she'd be in his arms. A necessary tactic. For her, as well as for him. His mate required soothing. He needed more reassurance she was all right. Only after he stripped her down, pressed her skin to his, and fed her a round of healing energy would he move onto other things. Important things like... giving Samantha the words she wanted to hear, all of the heartfelt shit his mate excelled at delivering.

35

A spring in her step, Samantha tucked her sketch book under her arm and shut the door to the loft behind her. Stepping onto the wide landing, she looked down from her perch, scanning the expansive space Gage called a garage. Her mouth curved. She shook her head. Her mate was a mixture of beautiful intensity and shoulder-shrugging nonchalance. The master of understatement, 'cause...

She huffed.

Garage, her ass.

Warehouse was a more apt description. One full of expensive vehicles. Vintage muscle cars sat alongside cool-looking motorcycles, tricked-out SUVs and sleek race cars. All parked with precision. Each in its designated spot. Not a one out of place.

Just the way her mate liked things.

Nice. Neat. And tidy.

Right now, though, the expansive space was empty but for the vehicles that called it home. No man-dragon huddle around the front bumper of a car. No Osgard digging through tall toolboxes looking for a wrench... or whatever part Gage needed. No sign of her mate standing at one of the metal workbenches, bent over whatever machine he happened to be ripping apart and putting back together.

Which happened a lot.

Much to her dismay.

Her workshop was full of machines Gage didn't yet understand. Milling and laser machines. An ultrasonic cleaner and magnetic polisher. A gold-melting furnace. A centrifuge casting unit. And last but not least, the *pièce de résistance*—a vacuum investment casting tabletop machine she loved... and had been forced to protect from him more than once. Every time she turned around, he was ripping something of hers apart, trying to figure out how it worked.

Annoying.

Also, adorable.

A mostly forgivable offense since he always put whatever he took apart back together. Tweaking the motor. Souping up the horsepower. Improving the wiring system, making whatever he worked on better than when it came out of the box. A skill she admired, even as she braced every time she walked into her workshop, looking for the empty spot on her worktable along with the machine she'd lost to Gage's curiosity for a few hours.

Skipping down the stairs, Samantha stuck the pencil she held behind her ear. She should enjoy the peace and quiet while she had it. No way it would last. Not with Gage hovering like a mother hen. Something else she found annoying, though, she understood what drove his concern.

Her reaction to the battle over Bainbridge Island.

Samantha sighed, wishing she could take it back, knowing she couldn't.

Gage told her to brace. She thought she had, but

after being imprisoned in her house, on edge all day while imagining the worst, watching Gage kill other dragons took an emotional toll. Much to her embarrassment, she'd become so frayed, she'd fallen apart on the flight home. Been on the verge of tears...

Until he took her to bed.

The moment his arms closed around her, the second she felt the connection grab hold, she settled down. And slept like a baby.

Gage had not.

He'd been worrying about her ever since.

Samantha nibbled on her lower lip, wanting to kick herself. Again. For the hundredth time. His concern was sweet, but she wanted Gage to understand—*really get*—what she kept telling him. She was all right. Really, truly, in a good place. Settled inside Black Diamond. Comfortable with the other girls. Enjoying the time she spent with Osgard.

Samantha smiled as she reached the bottom of the stairs. Gage's son was a scream—smart, funny, and coming out of his shell. Talking to her. Telling her things. Trusting her more and more each day. Which meant...

Gage needed to get with the program.

No matter how she acted after the battle, she wasn't a lightweight. It might take her time to process things, but once she did, it was done. Over and put to bed, so...

No need for him to watch her every move.

Or worry she'd fall apart again.

Stepping off metal treads onto the concrete floor, Samantha turned right into her workshop. Motion sensors went active. Overhead lights turned on, and the beauty of her new space hit her. High timber-beam ceilings. Pearl white walls. Wide windows blacked out by magic, keeping sunlight out. Spacious, pretty, well-appointed, with its antique worktables, silk curtains, and fancy couch sitting against one wall.

Just the way Daimler wanted it.

He'd even brought in a vintage coffee bar complete with an expensive expresso machine that put most cafes to shame. One she still didn't know how to use and was certain Gage would rip apart any day now.

Feet planted in the doorway, she took it in, then pursed her lips. She wanted to chasten the Numbai for invading her space, but, well...

She couldn't argue with the results.

Her workshop was gorgeous. Serene. Elegant. Classy. A space with great bones, fitting for the beautiful jewelry she planned to create in it.

With a sigh, she crossed to the worktable in the center of the room. Tossing her sketch book on the scarred surface, she dragged a stool from beneath the edge. Without looking, she sat down on the cracked leather seat, pulled her favorite mechanical pencil from behind her ear, and flipped the front cover of her book open.

Loose leaf papers spilled out.

Her final designs. Twelve in total. A set she needed to whittle down to six for the competition.

Shuffling through the sketches, she studied each one with a critical eye, looking for flaws, wondering which designs would garner top marks with the judges. Pencil moving over paper, she added details here and there, re-sketched a ring from different angles, writing her thoughts in the margins—type of metal to use, what precious stones might work best, playing with design composition.

Settling in, Samantha drew freehand, allowing her imagination to roam, mind on nothing but—

A tingle swept over her nape, yanking her out of the flow.

Lifting her head, she glanced toward the door. Gage standing in the door frame, looking gorgeous with his hands shoved in his front pockets, shoulder propped against the jamb, bronze gaze fixed on her.

Delight fizzled through her. Never failed. Every time she caught sight of him, she reacted the same way. With serious amounts of I'm-so-happy-to-see-you.

Unable to contain her joy, she smiled at him.

He didn't smile back.

Her smile faltered. "Everything all right?"

Chest rising on a deep breath, he shook his head.

Dropping her pencil, Samantha pushed away from her workbench. The stool bumped along the floor behind her. Focused on her mate, she skirted the table, crossed the room and invaded his space.

Her body collided with his. As her palms settled against his chest, he lifted his hand and curled it around the side of her neck. His heat ghosted through her. She leaned in, giving him more of her weight, knowing her closeness soothed him, determined to give him what he needed.

Sliding her hand over his T-shirt, she caressed his shoulders. "What's wrong?"

His dark brows contracted.

Tingles attacked her temples.

His voice slid into her head. *"Just left the meeting with B and the others."*

"Azrad."

"Yeah," he said, concern in his eyes. *"Thought maybe I'd be able to reach him with Haider and Nian boosting the signal. Got nothing. Not even static. Every time I send out a ping, I hit a wall... a barricade of some*

kind. *Can't talk to him. Can't pinpoint his location. And now—*"

"Everyone's worried."

Gage nodded. *"I think... could be... he's dead."*

"He's the one on the inside, yes?"

"Yeah."

"Then you've got to trust him, Gage," she said, using logic to reassure him. Gage felt deep and took things hard. If Azrad died, he'd blame himself. Full stop. No talking him out of it, even though the burden wasn't his to carry. "He might be lying low. You know, gone quick-quiet to keep from blowing his cover."

Surprise shoved concern off his face.

His lips twitched. *"Quick-quiet?"*

"Well, I don't know," she muttered, seeing humor spark in his eyes. "It's how people talk in military movies."

With a huff, Gage lost the battle and grinned.

She twisted her lips to one side. "Maybe not the best reference, but still... from what you said, Azrad's smart. Trust him to know what he's doing, Gage. Maybe, he can't talk right now. Maybe, he's setting up for the takedown. He'll get in touch when it's safe for him, not convenient for you."

Full of restless energy, Gage pushed away from his lean against the door frame. As he straightened, so did she, moving with him as his hand slid to the nape of her neck. His thumb stroked over her pulse point. Back and forth. Soft circles. Warm caresses. A gentle trail over her skin.

Holding his gaze, Samantha murmured his name as he flicked at the end of her ponytail. He broke eye contact to watch the blond strands sway. Playing with the ends, he threaded his fingers through her hair.

"Five days 'till the realignment, wildcat," he said,

voice quiet, tone guttural. *"He shoulda reached out by now. Given me a heads-up, so I know when and where to meet him. How best to get him out of the Razorback camp."*

"Trust him."

Wrapping his arm around her, he dipped his head. His mouth brushed the top of her head. *"Hard to do."*

"Do it anyway."

He sighed and continued to hold her.

Nestled in, she pressed her cheek to his chest, letting the silence lengthen as time spun away, and she gave him what he needed—her touch, the closeness, the steadiness of her certainty Azrad was okay. No way for her to know for sure. She'd didn't know Azrad, but if Gage or one of the other Nightfury warriors were in his position, she wouldn't be worried. Each one knew how to play the game, and intuition told her, so did Azrad.

Minutes slid into more before she broke through the quiet. "That's not all of it, Gage. Something else is bothering you."

He tensed against her. *"You reading me?"*

"Only fair since you're always in my head. Payback's a bitch, handsome."

He lifted his mouth from her hair.

Tipping her chin up, she met his gaze. Humor spiked in his eyes a second before his expression smoothed out and he went from amused to serious again. Looking a bit uncertain, he stared down at her.

Cherry-picking the topic off his brain, she dragged it into the open. "The realignment."

A muscle flexed in his jaw. *"Five days 'till it happens. We're new. So fucking new. Would be better for you, an easier adjustment if it wasn't so soon, but the hungering will happen whether I want it to or not. Nature'll take its course. Can't avoid it. We need to decide—"*

"You want more kids?"

"Yeah, but—"

"I'm game, Gage."

He blinked. *"Easy as that?"*

"Easy as that," she said, reassuring him, settling into the knowledge she wanted babies with him. Dream of a lifetime, making a family with a man who loved her, and she loved in return, inside a dragon pack that already felt and acted like one. "You've given me Osgard, and he's great. I mean, seriously, handsome—awesome kid, but I'd like to have more. Never had a sister or brother. Always thought having siblings would be fun, but..."

She paused, searching for the words she wanted—and he needed. "After losing my hearing, wasn't sure I'd get the chance to have a kids of my own. You've changed that for me, so yeah... easy as that. I'm game."

"Fuck, Samantha."

"Knew it was worrying you, so I talked to the other girls."

Unable to keep from caressing him, her hands drifted over his back. The hammering pulse of his heart beat against her palms, and hers nearly broke. He was nervous. Worried about her reaction to the re-alignment—*the hungering* and the possibility he'd get her pregnant before she was ready. Which left him unsure of his welcome...

Even after her telling him she loved him.

"Listen to me, handsome. I'll say this one more time. You need to get it." Leaning away, she sought a bit of separation. As he gave it to her, she raised her hands and began to sign, reinforcing her words with ASL. "I love you. You're mine, I'm yours. I'm settled in. One hundred percent invested. Good with all the man-dragon stuff—"

He snorted.

She ignored him. "Nothing wrong with being cautious. Seriously, Gage, I appreciate the fact you're worried about me... interested in my opinion and what I want. That's what a good partner does for the one he loves, but, handsome, please stop worrying. I'm a big girl. I've got no problem voicing my opinion, and I'm telling you... I'm ready when you are. You want to lock down this time, give Osgard more time to adjust—works for me. You want to go for it—that works for me too."

Wonder sparked in his eyes, making his bronze irises shimmer.

Attuned to him, she gave him a squeeze. "What do you want, Gage?"

"You... every way I can have you," he said, voice thick, eyes bright with emotion. *"I don't wanna sleep without you, even for one night. I wanna see you grow round with my infant. I wanna give Oz a brother. I want my mating mark on your skin and yours on mine."*

Her lips curved. "Then it's decided. No lockdown."

"No lockdown," he growled, stripping the elastic from her hair. Long strands fell in waves around her shoulders. Burying his hands in it, he dipped his head. Sharp teeth nipped her bottom lip, making her tingle in interesting places. *"And the mating ceremony. Soon as possible."*

"You asking me to marry you?"

"You love me?"

"Yeah."

"You want me to knock you up?"

Surprise pushed laughter from her chest. "Yeah."

"Need to hear you say it, wildcat," he murmured, eyes catching fire, igniting with desire so stark she felt the burn.

"I love you, Gage."

"Again."

"I love you," she whispered, lips moving against his.

"Love you too, Samantha," he whispered back, kissing her deep, delivering his taste, making her impatient for more of him. *"Fuck, but I love you. We're gonna make beautiful babies together."*

"We *so* are," she said, growing restless as desire dragged her under. Fisting her hands in his hair, she popped up onto her tiptoes and, tilting her head, kissed him harder. Her tongue stroked over his. His hands slid over her ass, pulling her tighter against him. "How about we start practicing right now?"

Holding her steady, mouth brushing hers, he walked her backward across the shop. Releasing his grip on her hair, he slid his hand down her back, around her waist, and yanked on the front of her jeans. The button popped. The zipper gave way. Not wasting a second, his fingers slipped beneath the denim, under lace and *in*, finding her on the first try.

Wet coating his fingers, he worked her with strong strokes.

A hard spike of pleasure scored through her. Prickles attacked her skin. Her spine arched. Her hips jerk. Her breath caught on a gasp.

"Gage."

On a mission, he kicked the coffee table out of his way.

The backs of her calves collided with the front of the couch.

"Gonna fuck you on the couch you didn't want."

"Good thinking," she said, shivering as his threat rolled through her. "At least the thing'll get used for something."

He grinned against her mouth.

Her core tightened around his fingers.

"Beautiful, wildcat. Fucking gorgeous."

"Gage," she rasped, so close, she felt pleasure cresting. "Need it."

"Gonna give it?"

"Yes."

Curling his fingers, he rubbed over a sensitive spot inside her. Over and over. Again and again. Driving her wild, making her hold on tight. No other option. Only thing she could do when Gage decided to give her one of the orgasms she enjoyed so much. This time, though, he was determined to do more than just make her come. He wanted to push her over the edge hard. Make her scream and do it fast.

"Deep and rough, volamaia. *That the way you want it?"*

"Please."

Gage murmured against her mouth.

She saw the door close from the corner of her eye as her spine touched down on seat cushions. Following her down, Gage landed on top of her. He reared. She lifted her hips, helped him strip off her jeans, then spread her legs, giving him more access, on board with going fast. He rewarded her, bathing her in bliss as she dragged his T-shirt up his back.

Breaking the kiss, he raised his head long enough to yank the T-shirt over his head, then came back—mouth hungry, fingers sliding through her heat, building passion into a frenzy. One Samantha welcomed as she reveled in his need, loving his intensity, thanking God fortune favored the brave, gifting her with the man she now called her own.

A dream come true.

A love made real.

Beauty resplendent. All she wanted. All she needed. A new beginning and endless future wrapped up in the promise of the man-dragon meant for her. Made for her. Hers to love from now until the end of forever.

ACKNOWLEDGMENTS

This book has been a long time coming. I'd like to say it came easy, but it didn't. Then again, sometimes the most difficult stories to tell are the most fun to write. I want to thank each and every one of you (my fabulous readers) for being patient, sticking with me and holding on tight while waiting for me to write FURY OF DESTRUCTION. I hope the wait's been worth it, and you love Gage and Samantha's story as much as I do.

While I'm at it, I'd also like to say a huge thank you to Christine Witthohn, literary agent extraordinaire. You've always believed in me. I'll forever love you. We make a great team.

Thanks as well to Tanya and the wonderful team at Oliver Heber Books. It's amazing working with all of you. I'm so grateful to be part of your crew.

To my family – you're the best. Love you to the moon and back. I couldn't do it without you.

A NOTE FROM THE AUTHOR

Thank you for taking the time to read Fury of Destruction. If you enjoyed it, please help others find my books so they can enjoy them too.

Recommend it: Please help other readers find this book by recommending it to friends, readers' groups, and discussion boards.

Review it: Let other readers know what you liked or didn't like about Fury of Destruction.

Follow me on Facebook, Instagram and Bookbub to get all the latest news.

Sign up for my Newsletter and get exclusive VIP giveaways, freebies and sales throughout the year.

Book updates can be found at www.CoreeneCallahan.com

Thanks again for taking the time to read my books! You make it all possible.

ALSO BY COREENE CALLAHAN

Dragonfury Scotland

Fury of a Highland Dragon

Fury of Shadows

Fury of Denial

Fury of Persuasion

Fury of Isolation

Dragonfury Bad Boy Shifter Series

Fury of Fate

Fury of Conviction

Dragonfury Series

Fury of Fire

Fury of Ice

Fury of Seduction

Fury of Desire

Fury of Obsession

Fury of Surrender

Fury of Destruction

Circle of Seven Series

Knight Awakened

Knight Avenged

Warriors of the Realm Series

Warrior's Revenge